TALES

OF

THE GOOD WOMAN.

BY

A DOUBTFUL GENTLEMAN:

OTHERWISE,

JAMES K. PAULDING.

EDITED BY WILLIAM I. PAULDING.

IN ONE VOLUME.

NEW YORK:
CHARLES SCRIBNER AND COMPANY.
1867.

CAMBRIDGE:

STEREOTYPED AND PRINTED BY JOHN WILSON AND SON.

INTRODUCTION.

The stories which I have included under the general title of "Tales of The Good Woman" were published in several books, between thirty and forty years ago; and some of the shorter ones, perhaps, in magazines or annuals, before finding place between the boards of a volume. All of the longer ones — that is to say, Dyspepsy, The Azure Hose, The Politician, and The Dumb Girl — as I learn from the "Advertisement of the Publishers" in 1836, were intended to have been covered by the above designation, and to have been prefaced by the "Memoir of the unknown author" which will be found herein-after. The first volume of tales was published in 1829, with the title-page designed; the second, brought out in 1830, in consequence of "it happening that a work was just at the time republished here with a similar title", was styled "Chronicles of the City of Gotham", and had a separate introduction, in the shape of a petition addressed to the municipal authorities of that mythical town.

All of these stories are full of little personal reminiscences, or touches of autobiography, modified and worked up by Mr. Paulding, to suit his purpose for the time being.

The farm, in "Dyspepsy", came to him through his wife. It was four or five miles back from the river, in the Highlands, and nobly descended from the great upper Philipse patent. Such as it is described are many in the neighborhood, now. The old tenants of "Mr. Ambler" are, no doubt, sketches from life, and, very probably, taken on the spot to which they are assigned in the landscape. "Mr. Lightly", the mountaineer who would "step over to Poughkeepsie" (say thirty miles) and back, in a summer day, is still remembered by living acquaintances, under the genuine name of "Hopper".

"The Dumb Girl" is voiceful with associations of his youth, the localities, allusions, and characters, all being connected with his early years in Westchester county. The heroine, however, was a good deal more of a crab than he makes out in the story. An autobiographical memorandum, written by Mr. Paulding in 1851, thus describes her:—"If I remember right she was a very well-looking tidy lass, but of this I am positive, that she was one of the greatest viragoes I ever had the ill-luck to consort with. Not being able to give vent to her feelings by speech, she resorted to action, and to this day my ears tingle when I think of her, for many is the time she has boxed them to enlighten my comprehension. But I forgive her — and her father, too, for the many long stories he used to tell of his exploits in the Revolution." The name and the sad story are fictitious.

"The Azure Hose" is the natural outcrop of a solid stratum of resistance to the adulation of English authorship, once prevalent in American "Society". This in general; and as to Lord Byron, it is to be said, that Mr. Paulding, having founded his taste upon Goldsmith, had a positive repugnance to what is called "fine" or "strong" writing, wherever it appeared. Of this style Byron was to him the embodied spirit. Accordingly he never missed a chance to give him a remembrancer. In "A Sketch of Old England", published in 1822, he handled his lordship in a half-jocose half-serious way which is entertaining enough: and he has a hit at him in "Koningsmarke", published in 1823. The heading of chapter II., Book VII., reads thus: —

> Accursed be the stars * * * * * * * * * *!
> The fulsome sun, that shines on all alike,
> Good, bad, indifferent, Tag, Rag, and Bobtail!
> Satan's abus'd, and so is honest Cain,
> And so am I — but * * * * * * * *!
>
> *Lord B———n.*

In the edition of 1836 an improvement occurs to him, and, for "abus'd", he writes "belied". So elsewhere. All this may seem a waste of powder, now that the reputation of that author has settled down into a place certainly not among the first-rates. But it must be remembered that it was a very bold estimate to make at the time.

"The Progress of The Age" comes under the head of those squibs which he was continually firing off in honor of what he regarded as the absurdities of the passing hour.

The little stories, "The Revenge of St. Nicholas", "Cobus Yerks", and "The Ride of St. Nicholas", are taken from "The Book of Saint Nicholas. Translated from the original Dutch of Dominie Nicholas Ægidius Oudenarde." Here follow the "dedication" and "advertisement" of the putative author.

TO

THE SOCIETIES OF SAINT NICHOLAS

IN THE

NEW NETHERLANDS,

COMMONLY CALLED

NEW YORK.

MOST DEAR AND WORTHY ASSOCIATES,

In obedience to the command of the good saint who is equally an object of affectionate reverence to us all, as well as in due deference to the feelings of brotherhood which attach us irrevocably to those who honour his name, his virtues, and his country, I dedicate this work to you all without discrimination or exception.

As descendants, in whole or in part, from that illustrious people who, after conquering nature by their industry and perseverance, achieved liberty by their determined courage, and learning and science by their intellectual vigour, I rejoice to see you instituting bonds of union, for the purpose of preserving the remembrance of such an honourable lineage and the ties of a common origin. While we recollect with honest pride the industry, the integrity, the enterprise, the love of liberty, and the heroism of old "*faderland*," let us not forget that the truest way to honour worthy ancestors is to emulate their examples.

That you may long live to cherish the memory of so excellent a saint, and such venerable forefathers, is the earnest wish of

Your associate and friend,

NICHOLAS ÆGIDIUS OUDENARDE.

Nieuw Amsterdam, July, 1837.

THE

AUTHOR'S ADVERTISEMENT,

WHICH IS EARNESTLY RECOMMENDED TO THE ATTENTIVE PERUSAL OF THE JUDICIOUS READER.

YOU will please to understand, gentle reader, that, being a true descendant of the adventurous Hollanders who first discovered the renowned island of Manhattan — which is every day becoming more and more worth its weight in paper money — I have all my life been a sincere and fervent follower of the right reverend and jolly St. Nicholas, the only tutelary of this mighty state. I have never, on any proper occasion, omitted doing honour to his memory by keeping his birthday with all due observances, and paying him my respectful devoirs on Christmas', and New-year's, eve.

From my youth upward I have been always careful to hang up my stocking in the chimney-corner, on both these memorable anniversaries; and this I hope I may say without any unbecoming ebullition of vanity, that on no occasion did I fail to receive glorious remembrances of his favour and countenance, always saving two exceptions — once when the good saint signified his displeasure at my tearing up a Dutch almanac, and again, on occasion of my going to a Presbyterian meeting-house with a certain little

Dutch damsel, by filling my stockings with snowballs, instead savoury oly koeks.

Saving these manifestations of his anger, I can safely boast of having been a special favourite of the good St. Nicholas, who hath ever evinced a singular kindness and suavity towards me in all seasons of my life. Further, seeing I was not only his namesake, but always reverently honoured his name to the best of my poor abilities, he hath, at sundry times of dire entanglement, more than once vouchsafed to appear to me in dreams and visions, giving me sage advice and goodly admonition, the which never failed of being of great service to me.

From my youth upward, moreover, I have been accustomed to call upon him in time of need; and this I will say for him, that he always came promptly whenever he was within hearing. I will not detain the expectant reader with the relation of these special instances touching the years of my juvenility, but straightway proceed to that which is material to my present purpose.

The reader will please to comprehend that after I had, with the labour and research of many years, completed the tales which I now, with an humble deference, offer to his acceptance, I was all at once struck dumb, with the unparalleled difficulty of finding a name for my work, seeing that every title appertinent to such divertisements hath been applied over and over again, long and merry agone. Now, as before intimated to the judicious reader, whenever I am in sore perplexity of mind, as not unfrequently happens to such as (as it were) cudgel their brains for the benefit of their fellow-creatures — I say, when thus beleaguered, I always shut my eyes, lean back in my chair, which is furnished with a goodly stuffed back and arms, and grope for that which I require in the profound depths of abstraction.

It was thus I comported myself on this trying occasion, when, lo! and behold! I incontinently fell asleep, as it were, in the midst of my cogitations, and while I was fervently praying to the good-hearted St. Nicholas to inspire me with a proper and significant name for this my mental offspring. I cannot with certainty say how long I had remained in this drowsy meditation, when I was favoured with the appearance of a vision, which, at first sight, I knew to be that of the excellent St. Nicholas, who scorns to follow the pestilent fashions of modern times, but ever appears in the ancient dress of the old patriarchs of Holland. And here I will describe the good saint, that peradventure all those to whom he may, in time to come, vouchsafe his presence, may know him at first sight, even as they know the father that begot them.

He is a right fat, jolly, roistering little fellow — if I may make bold to call him so familiarly — and had I not known him of old for a veritable saint, I might, of a truth, have taken him, on this occasion, for little better than a sinner. He was dressed in a snuff-coloured coat of goodly conceited dimensions, having broad skirts, cuffs mighty to behold, and buttons about the size of a moderate New-year cooky. His waistcoat and breeches, of which he had a proper number, were of the same cloth and colour; his hose of gray worsted; his shoes high-quartered, even up to the instep, ornamented with a pair of silver buckles, exceedingly bright; his hat was of a low crown and right broad brim, cocked up on one side; and in the button-holes of his coat was ensconced a long delft pipe, almost as black as ebony. His visage was the picture of good-humoured benevolence; and by these marks I knew him as well as I know the nose on my own face.

The good saint, being always in a hurry on errands of good fellowship, (and especially about the time of the holydays of Paas and Pinkster), and being withal a person of little ceremony, addressed me without delay, and with much frankness; which was all exceedingly proper, as we were such old friends. He spoke to me in Dutch, which is now a learned language, understood only by erudite scholars.

"What aileth thee, my godson Nicholas?" quoth he.

I was about to answer that I was in grievous embarrassment concerning the matter aforesaid, when he courteously interrupted me, saying,

"Be quiet, I know it, and therefore there is no special occasion for thee to tell me. Thou shalt call thy work 'The Book of St. Nicholas,' in honour of thy *patroon;* and here are the materials of my biography, which I charge thee, on pain of empty pockets from this time forward, to dilate and adorn in such a manner that, (foreseeing, as I do, that thy work will go down to the latest posterity), it may do honour to my name, and rescue it from that obscurity in which it hath been enveloped through the crying ignorance of past generations, who have been seduced into a veneration for St. George, St. Denis, St. David, and other doughty dragon-slaying saints, who were little better than swaggering bullies. Moreover, I charge thee, as thou valuest my blessing and protection, to dedicate thy work unto the worthy and respectable societies of St. Nicholas in this my stronghold in the New World. Thou mightest, perhaps, as well have left out that prank of mine at the carousing of old Baltus, but verily it matters not. Let the truth be told."

Saying this, he handed me a roll of ancient vellum, containing, as I afterwards found, the particulars which, in conformity with his solemn command, I have amplified into the only veritable biography of my patron saint which hath ever been given to the world. The one hitherto received as orthodox is, according to the declaration of the saint himself, scarcely more than a collection of legends written under the express inspection of the old lady of Babylon.

I reverently received the precious deposit, and faithfully promised obedience to his commands; whereupon the good St. Nicholas, puffing in my face a whiff of tobacco-smoke more fragrant than all the spices of the East, blessed me, and departed in haste, to be present at a wedding in Communipaw. Hereupon I awoke, and should have thought all that had passed but a dream, arising out of the distempered state of my mind, had I not held in my hand the identical roll of vellum, presented in the manner just related. On examination, it proved to contain the matter which is incorporated in the first story of this collection, under the title of "The Legend of St. Nicholas," not only in due recognition of his fiat, but in order that henceforward no one may pretend ignorance concerning this illustrious and benevolent saint, seeing they have now a biography under his own hand.

Thus much have I deemed it proper to preface to the reader, as some excuse for the freedom of having honoured my poor fictions with the title of The Book of St. Nicholas, which might otherwise have been deemed a piece of unchristian presumption.

The "Revenge" and the "Ride" are in Mr. Paulding's usual tone of mingled satire and sentiment, and call for no remark. Nor, indeed, does "Cobus Yerks", except to state that the localities mentioned therein are near Tarrytown, in Westchester County, New York, and that "Master Timothy

Canty", the motive power of the story, once played his part among men. The same may fairly be assumed of the little Dutchman. The original of Tim Mr. Paulding describes as follows, in the memorandum previously referred to: —

"I don't remember in what year it was that the simple people of Tarrytown were excited almost to phrenzy, by a strange apparition that made its appearance one morning, in the garret of a one-story house belonging to my brother-in-law. My recollection of this singular being is perfect, for we soon became inseparable companions. He was an Englishman and an artist, with the most odd, irregular, unneighborly countenance I ever saw."

He then gives an account of his acquaintance, not differing materially from that in the story; and, remarking that "he certainly was the greatest oddity I ever met with", states that, after two or three years' stay in the village, "having obtained specimens of all the insects in that quarter, he abruptly took his departure, no one knew whither, leaving me as a legacy The Four Seasons and Kitty Fisher."

Many years after, Mr. Paulding chanced upon this eccentric genius (now in comparatively flourishing estate) in Philadelphia, and has recorded that "Tim Canty" greeted him as of old, in a hearty and friendly way, with the title of "little vagabond".

I learn that "Sheriff Smith was killed in the place called Hard Scrabble", now known as "Rossell's Corner", about five miles from Tarrytown. John Ryer was hung at White Plains, the county-town, which is a little out of the range of country to which the narrative in strictness applies.

The Dutch words and phrases introduced in the three last-mentioned stories are spelled, as near as may be, according to the pronunciation in the State of New York; and not as they stand in the dictionary. I believe that the "j" was pronounced as "y" in English, and that the "v" had a sound between "f" and "v". Where it seemed necessary, I have appended the translation in a foot-note.

As I have mentioned notes, I may as well now state that I have added one here and there throughout the volume, where the allusion is already becoming obscure.

The story of "The Politician", first published in 1830, was, we may be sure, suggested by Mr. Paulding's early observations in the national capital; and, it may be added, was, in some respects, wonderfully illustrated in his later experiences as a magnate in Washington. His letters abound in strokes of caustic humor directed at the weaknesses of public life, and, (especially those to Irving, Brevoort, and Kemble, while Secretary of the Navy), would furnish a quite pertinent commentary on the tale.

The incident of the application for a foreign mission is one of those anecdotes which have ingrained themselves with the newspaper mind in such a way that they work to the surface, somewhere or other, every year or so; and it has been referred from time to time to almost every president of the United States. I believe the story is substantially true, or, at all events, helped on but a little, and that the circumstance actually occurred in connexion with Mr. Monroe. Whether this be so or not, I have, among Mr. Paulding's papers, come across a solicitation which is well-nigh as comprehensive, (barring the clothes), and otherwise not unamusing. He was, of course, while at the head of a Department, exposed to importunities from men in high position, applicants for their friends or followers, and from men in small place or no place, for themselves. The plea of one of these latter, asking for any office whatever, has been preserved, either through accident, or as a curiosity. The conclusion of it is suggestive, as indicating in a very naïve way the popular estimate of moral qualification for office. I give it, "*punctuatim et literatim*", with his italics :—

"I have now been engaged ten years in editorial life; and the thirteen years which I spent in the vocation of a pedagogue, have not been spent entirely in vain. I commenced at sixteen, and am now thirty nine, with good health, and good morals *considering my avocations*."

The independence of Mr. Paulding himself, as an office-holder, was something diverting, and yet worthy of all respect and even admiration. He had some piquant experience in the year 1832, running into 1833, when the system of taxing men in place for political purposes was first carried into effect. The circumstances are curious, as marking, with some precision, the era in which began that degradation of office, which of all causes perhaps has done most to damage and weaken republican sentiment and republican institutions. I should be inclined to put them on record here, but for the apprehension that I have already in this introduction over-drawn upon the patience of the reader.

In all of the compositions of Mr. Paulding which make up this volume, an extreme simplicity of machinery will be remarked; and it is but fair to observe that they should not be judged as stories, at all. It was his practice to set up a little frame of narrative, which he used as a vehicle, to carry a satire which he chose to exhibit, or a moral which he wished to convey: but of the fable itself he made little account.

Taken altogether, it may be said that these TALES OF THE GOOD WOMAN furnish an excellent measure of Mr. Paulding's capacity and range of composition. Whatever there was in him of fresh and artless feeling; of deep-seated admiration and lover-like enjoyment of Nature; of quaint, odd, satirical observation; of simple pathos; of droll intuition, or comically-original view; of national prejudice; of independent and unique, if sometimes one-eyed, judgment; of clear, queer, insight into men and things; of unforced wit, and unelaborated fun; of worship of what is grand or beautiful in the material, intellectual, or moral world; of hearty abhorrence of crime, and scorn of meanness and villainy; of disgust for purse-proud vulgarity, affectation, pretence; of raillery that plays fast by the well of tears, and laughter that is fierce with indignation;—all transfused and vivified w the peculiar *flavor*, so to speak, of the man—all, in a wo of the character that God had given him—is in these stor to be found exemplified. Good, bad, or indifferent, as in t verdict of Time they may be pronounced, I do not know any other author who could possibly have written them.

W. I.

CONTENTS.

MEMOIR

OF THE

UNKNOWN AUTHOR.

MEMOIR

OF THE

UNKNOWN AUTHOR.

It hath been so often remarked, by persons aiming at originality, that the pleasure of the reader is wonderfully enhanced by knowing something concerning the writer of the book he is about to devour, that the good-natured world actually begins to believe it true, notwithstanding it hath so often grievously yawned over the lives of divers great authors. It is for this reason that almost every work of any pretensions hath prefixed to it certain particulars concerning the writer, which in ordinary cases would be considered exceedingly frivolous, but inasmuch as they appertain to noted individuals, partake in the dignity of the association, and, like buttons of cheese-paring on a satin doublet, become illustrious by the company they keep. Nothing indeed is more certain and irrefragable, than that every thing connected with an important gentleman must of necessity be proportionably important. The world has nothing to do with the motions of ordinary men, on ordinary occasions; whether they have a good appetite and good digestion, or are in a good or bad humour, is a matter of indifference. But it is far otherwise with great persons, whose every trivial act is felt like a pulsation running through the universe. Should a tailor prick his finger with a needle, or a worthy citizen invite his friends to a dinner, nobody is the worse or the wiser but themselves. But such matters relating to kings and people of consequence are thought worthy of the most minute record. Hence it is, that the most trifling acts of illustrious persons are matters of profound interest to common folks, and that the literary world hath received such singular satisfaction from being credibly certified that my Lord Byron drank gin and water and tied his collar with a black ribbon, and that the Great Unknown is wonderfully addicted to Scotch herrings and whiskey punch.

It is doubtless for the same reasons, that almost every book of any pretensions to distinction is embellished with a likeness of the author, which, to those who have never had the happiness of seeing him, conveys a tolerably accurate idea of what he is not, and is wonderfully calculated to deceive the world in regard to his capacity. This we consider a serious grievance, and the more that, since the discovery of the new science of Phrenology, were the head accurately represented, every reader might form a judgment of the contents and character of a book from that alone, and thus avoid the task of reading it. Critics in particular would be benefited, since they would be entirely relieved from exercising their taste and discernment in estimating the merits of a work, by an examination of the organs of development in the skull of the author.

In addition to the supposed likeness of the author, it has become the practice to favour the public with an autograph, videlicet a fac-simile of his signature, which acts as a sort of security against counterfeits, and is equivalent to an endorsement showing the work to be genuine. The idea is probably borrowed from the vendors of quack medicines, who, in order to prevent any impositions upon the public but what are practised by themselves, are careful to caution the purchasers against nostrums not verified by their own hands. This fashion of prefixing the signature of authors to their works might prove rather dangerous, by enabling rogues to counterfeit them, were it not that such forgeries would prove of but little advantage, seeing that authors seldom have either much money or credit in the banks to incite the cupidity of rogues. Hence the practice hath hitherto proved of no detriment to authors, while it has been found highly advantageous to the reader, by enabling him to decide on the character of the former, not by the aid of a biography invented by some good-natured friend, but by the infallible criterion of his handwriting, than which nothing can be more decisive of an author's genius.

It is with great regret we apprise the public, that, after much diligent search and inquiry, we have not been able to obtain an authentic likeness of our unknown author, nor a specimen of his autograph. At one time we flattered ourselves we had detected the former upon a sign-post on the road leading from the Quarantine to Castleton on Staten Island, but it unfortunately turned out to be a portraiture of Captain Kidd, the famous corsair. With regard to his signature, we have failed equally in our researches. Mr. Abraham Acker, of Staten Island, to whose authority we shall frequently refer hereafter, is rather of opinion that he recollects having heard his father say, or else that he dreamed something of the kind, that our author always made his mark instead of signing his name at length. But this supposition we think quite inadmissible, as we never recollect to have heard of any man becoming illustrious as an author, who was unacquainted with the art of writing. We might easily have invented an autograph, in all probability as like that of our author as most things of the kind, but we scorn every species of imposition, and have preferred omitting these important concomitants of a modern book, to foisting upon the public anything spurious or doubtful. The work must take its chance, therefore, without either a portrait or an autograph.

We disclaim all pretensions to novelty when we observe that the lives of literary persons are for the most part destitute of interest and adventure. In days long past they lived in garrets, and nothing was more common than to find them starved or frozen to death of a frosty morning. Now, however, in this golden age of authors, we find them figuring in drawing-rooms, drinking toasts and making speeches at public entertainments, and performing all those great actions which cause a man to be wondered at while living and forgotten when dead. Still, it is doubtless no small satisfaction to the curious reader to know that there is nothing to be known worth knowing concerning the author whose work he is about to despatch. It is to gratify this laudable propensity that we proceed to detail the following particulars respecting the person who is shrewdly suspected of having indited the following Tales.

Concerning his family we regret to say little is known. Mr. Abraham Acker, of Staten Island, the only person living who recollects any circumstances connected with our author, thinks he remembers to have heard him say that he came of the same stock with the Grand Turk, the Great Mogul, the emperor of China, Prester John, the king of England, and divers other notabilities; but of this Mr. Acker, who we regret to say has nearly lost his memory, has great doubts. A similar uncertainty rests on the place, as well as the time, of his birth. When questioned as to the first, he usually replied, that he was born in the Republic of Elsewhere; but, as we cannot find such a place on any modern map, we are inclined to believe the worthy gentleman was partly mistaken.

So with respect to the time of his birth, which he once boasted was on the very day of the very year that the Dutch took Holland; but in what year of our Lord that happened we profess ourselves ignorant. But although neither the time nor the place of his birth can now probably be ascertained, there is only the greater elbow-room for conjecture. From his well-remembered fondness for hasty-pudding and pumpkin-pies, it might be inferred that he was a native of Connecticut. Mr. Abraham Acker has a notion that he has some idea of hearing his father say that this was the case; but cannot be certain whether it was hasty-pudding and pumpkin-pies, or plum-pudding and apple-dumplings, to which our author was so incontinently given. We will therefore content ourselves with stating the doubt, and leave the courteous reader to draw his own conclusions. All we shall say is, that seven villages, that will no doubt live to be great cities, have long hotly disputed the glory of his birth; an honour we consider quite equal to the contest of seven ruined cities for the nativity of Daniel, or, (as he hath been flippantly called), Dan, Homer.

On questioning Mr. Acker still farther and more closely, we gathered that our author was deeply read in the Dutch language and antiquities; and that he not only smoked mortally, but spoke reverently of St. Nicholas and Admiral Van Tromp. He likewise affected Dutch sermons and Dutch psalms. We ourselves are, for these reasons, rather inclined to the supposition of his having been originally derived from Holland; and in this we agree with Mr. Acker, who thinks he once heard his father hazard a speculation that he was of "Dutch distraction," as Mr. Acker is pleased to express it. But, adverse to this hypothesis, there is another fact remembered by Mr. Acker, to wit: that he had a most pestilent and arrant propensity to grumbling and finding fault upon all improper occasions, whence it might reasonably be inferred that he had some affinity with the English blood. As however we cannot learn that he ever obfuscated his intellectual faculties with small-beer, or attempted to hang himself even in the most gloomy period of his fortunes, but on the contrary did demean himself like a sober man, taking the ups and downs of life as they came, we consider the above theory as untenable, and the matter as again resolving itself into its original uncertainty.

In our early interviews with Mr. Acker, he related a fact that he was almost sure he heard from somebody, which served to settle this interesting point at once — namely, that our author's death was partly laid to his having gone twenty miles in a snow-storm to hear a Dutch sermon, and finding on his arrival that the vestry had decided upon having their preaching ever after in the English tongue. But what was our annoyance when, on a succeeding interview with Mr. Acker, we found he could recollect nothing of the matter, and was inclined to believe his memory was not so good as it was in the Old French War. It is therefore with no little regret, as well as mortification, that we are compelled to sit down under the painful conviction that the parentage of our author, as well as the time and place of his birth, are matters now for ever beyond the reach of inquiry.

Having thus proved to the satisfaction of the reader that nothing is to be gathered worth knowing about him, we shall proceed to discuss his life, character, and actions, of which, as very little is known, we shall have occasion to say a great deal. It appears, from the testimony of Mr. Acker, that the Alma Mater of our author was a log-hut, which was standing some fifty years since at the cross-roads, about half a mile from Castleton. Here he was taught by the best of all possible teachers, self; the school-master, a gallant bachelor and somewhat of a roué, for the most part spending the school-hours in social chat with a winsome, black-eyed dame, who lived just by, and whose husband, being a pedler, was frequently abroad, speculating in old iron and goose-feathers. The scholars were thus left to follow the bent of their genius; and Mr. Acker affirms that the excellence of this system was in after times demonstrated, not only in the vast genius of our author, but, in like manner, by the fact that he himself rose to the rank of a justice of the peace, while three or four of his school-mates became members of the legislature. There is little doubt that they would have become still more illustrious, had not the school been suddenly dissolved by the elopement of the master with the black-eyed pedler's wife, whom he carried off triumphantly in one of the honest man's own tin-carts. Hereupon the sprightly younkers set up a great shout, and scampered home, right glad of releasement from such durance vile.

Our author, after this, pursued the bent of his genius a year or two in doing nothing; being, according to tradition, a most determined idler, whose principal amusement was to join in those little parties so common in country villages, where you may see one man at work and half a dozen looking on. This however soon gave way to the delight of all delights to the contemplative philosopher, to wit: angling. He would sit on the rocky projection of some bold promontory jutting out into the unparalleled Hudson, the chief of all rivers, and put Job himself to shame. Morning, noon, and evening, there he sat watching the end of his pole, and plunged in that delicious vacuum, when the mind as it were resigning its bright sceptre, an interregnum succeeds and one calm nothingness pervades existence. Tradition says he sat so long, that at last he actually grew to the rock, and, in the attempt to extricate himself, was happy to escape with a whole skin by leaving an essential portion of his breeches sticking to a projection of hornblende, a monument to his immortal glory.

It was thus that, buried in reveries and abstractions, he attuned his mind to the depths of philosophy, and learned the most important of all arts, that of thinking. But his course of philosophy was too soon interrupted, by his being sent to another school in Jersey, about ten miles from his home, as he hath frequently mentioned to Mr. Acker with tears in his eyes. Here he staid with an old relative who lived by himself, about three miles from the school. The way was by a solitary "turpentine walk," as Mr. Acker expresses it, which led along the devious windings of a pretty stream, running at the foot of a hill. If any of our readers have ever in their boyish days been condemned to a solitary walk like this, in their way to and from school, they can judge how tedious, how irksome, how endless it was to a sprightly lad, full of life, health, mischief, and wantonness. Man was not born to live alone, nor, more especially, were boys. Often, as he said to Mr. Acker, has he sat down at the foot of some old tree, and played truant all day in weeping over his loneliness. His only resource, as Mr. Acker expresses it, was "to wrap himself up in himself," by which we understand that he tried to forget the past and the present, by looking to the future. His sole companion in those lonely walks was a poor dumb girl, who sometimes rambled with him, and who is believed to be the heroine of the story of Phœbe Angevine, in the following collection.

Our author, agreeably to his own account delivered at various times in desultory conversations with his friend Mr. Acker, continued this mode of life, passing and repassing to and from school, with no other associate, except his own melancholy thoughts, for upwards of three years. During this period his leisure hours were principally passed in wool-gathering, and the cultivation of the noble science of castle-building. His winter evenings he spent, for the most part, by the kitchen fireside, in listening to the traditionary lore of an old black sybil, almost blind, but wonderfully fond of frightening delighted youngsters and listening country-maids with stories of witches, goblins, Indians, and Revolutionary horrors. By listening to the frequent repetition of these rural romances he appears to have been imbued with that not uncommon species of credulity in which the mind, sometimes sinking under, at others triumphing over, the delusions of the imagination, alternately derides and trembles, laughs at and believes, according as we happen to be in sunshine and society, or alone and in darkness.

At the expiration of three years he left school, or the school left him, we cannot ascertain which; and here, as he was wont to say, ended his scholastic studies. He often hinted to his friend Mr. Acker that he was early thrown upon the world in one of our great cities, the name of which Mr. Acker does not recollect, where his skill in castle-building was held in little or no estimation when put in comparison with that of a tolerable mason or carpenter. His first vocation was that of junior clerk to a dry-goods-store-keeper, in which he distinguished himself by running his nose against lamp posts and being run over by carts, when going upon errands — in selling goods and forgetting to take pay for them — and in blowing a cracked flute behind the counter of evenings, so villanously, that he drove all persons of common sensibility to the other side of the street. His master, who despised philosophy, abstraction, and the fine arts, as desperate enemies to the first of all arts, that of making money, lectured him daily, and finally turned him out of the shop, as an incurable blockhead, because he refused to give his honour that a piece of chintz, which a lady was cheapening, was actually offered at less than the first cost.

Here we lose sight of our author for some years, until we find him, according to his friend Mr. Acker's recollection, in some business or other, the precise nature of which he does not recollect. He remembers, however, sufficient to know that our author made but a poor business of it, whatever it was. He was one of those unlucky people who, destined as they are to immortality, seem good for nothing in this world while living. He took every thing by the left hand, and his fingers were all thumbs. He believed every body, and trusted every body; and this species of implicit faith is of no great value in temporal things. Such a man is always a mark for the little rogues of this world, and never fails to allure about him a circle of petty depredators that are sure to bring him to ruin at last. This appears to have been the case with our author, who, as it would seem, lost his money, if he ever had any, his credit and his patience, and suddenly turning from the extreme of credulity to that of scepticism, became a hater and despiser of the world. Like the rest of mankind, he judged of it as he found, or rather made, it himself; and converted the little swarm of plunderers, whom his easy credulity had attracted from the general mass to fatten upon him, into the representatives of the whole hive.

It appears from circumstances that our author resented his misfortunes so seriously that he quarrelled with the world outright; and, to revenge himself the more effectually, retired into the bosom of Staten Island. Here he took lodgings at an obscure inn, on a by-road leading from the Narrows to the Blazing Star Ferry,* where he lived upon the lean, or rather picked the bones, of the land. This house, which has lately been pulled down, was at that time kept by a whimsical old bachelor, who, having in early life been jilted by a buxom little Dutch damsel, in revenge put up the sign of a woman without a head, which he called "THE GOOD WOMAN," thereby maliciously insinuating a horrible libel on the whole sex. Never man, — according to Mr. Acker, who resided about a quarter of a mile from the "Good Woman," — never man lived upon so little, or made a suit of clothes last so long, as did our author. Nobody could tell exactly how he lived, for he neither begged, borrowed, nor stole, nor did he labour with his hands, except in writing, which he did great part of the day, deducting the long intervals when he sat with pen suspended in his hand, watching as it were the smoke as it curled from the landlord's pipe, in a state of perfect "distraction," as Mr. Acker expressed it. We ourselves are of opinion he meant abstraction; but the difference is not material. It is not our business to solve the mystery how authors manage to exist in this world; we mean those who are condemned to live by their wits, without the aid of fashionable friends, fashionable reviewers, and fashionable readers. We leave the solution to Him who watches over the fall of a sparrow, and who sent the ravens to feed the prophet in the wilder-

* The "Blazing Star" was a tavern at Woodbridge, New Jersey, several miles from the ferry known by its name.

ness. There are certain invisible means, inscrutable to the fat kine, by which the lean kine, among which we emphatically reckon the class of authors alluded to, manage to live, and move, and have a being, as it were in spite of nature and fate. Far be it from us to draw the veil from over the hallowed retreats of indigent, unpatronized genius, struggling with the neglect of the world and its own worldly incapacities, and finally, perhaps, reaching the goal of immortality through the gloomy solitudes of a prison.

Here our author resided during the remainder of his days, which space of time comprises almost twenty years. During all this period he was absent but three times, and, on those occasions, (as we have taken the freedom to suppose), only for the purpose of disposing of his writings; for it is difficult to comprehend what other business he could have. He formed no intimacy except with Mr. Acker, whose countenance as a magistrate was convenient in defending him against the prying curiosity of the neighbourhood, and those evil suggestions which mystery, however innocent and unaffected, is sure to excite. The only remarkable actions he performed in the course of this long sojourn among the simple children of the fields and woods, were killing an opossum and a rattle-snake with sixteen rattles, the last that ever were seen on the island — exploits, which in the opinion of Squire Acker, call loudly for a biography. Finally he died, at the supposed age of four-score and ten years, without pain, and without fear, as a blameless old man should die; and slept, not with his fathers, but among the children of strangers, who knew not even whence he came.

The *younger* Mr. Acker — so he is styled by his neighbours though now nearly ninety years old — has unluckily forgotten our author's name: neither is there any person living who remembers it, so far as we have been able to ascertain. Though this must of necessity be a great disappointment to the curious reader, yet we know not that it is a circumstance much to be lamented. On the contrary, we are inclined to believe that the obscurity which, in spite of all our researches, still hovers in misty vagueness over his birth, his life, his family, and his name, may contribute materially to the interest and popularity of the present work. Obscurity is held to be one of the prime sources of the sublime; and it is a subject worthy of investigation, how far the sublimity of a work may depend upon its author being either entirely unknown, or only suspected by the public. However this may be, certain it is, that a detected author, like a detected criminal, does not stand the best chance of being admired by his friends. Having now told all we know of our author, we shall proceed to account for the manner in which the present work fell into the hands of the editor, who has lost no time in *giving* it (as the genteel phrase is) to the world.

In the course of last summer there died in the neighbourhood of the city a very wealthy old gentleman, whose heirs, according to a pious and long-established custom, quarrelling about the division of the estate, it was disposed of at public auction. Among his most valuable possessions was a large library containing many rare books and manuscripts, which, being of no use to the heirs, were sold for what they would bring. The manuscript from which the following tales have been selected was one of these. It was a prime favourite with the worthy old gentleman, who used to read it to his family with great effect of a long winter's evening, and it is recorded that not one of them ever fell asleep on these occasions, except when they were very tired. If the reader requires any other proof of the excellence of the manuscript, he will doubtless find it in a perusal of the following tales, which are faithfully printed from the original, with the exception of a few slight alterations in the spelling, which we have made on the authority of Mr. Webster's truly valuable dictionary. How the deceased old gentleman came by the manuscript is not exactly known: but Mr. Abraham Acker has some remote idea of hearing, or dreaming he heard, our author about a year before his death boast with no small degree of exultation, that he had sold a manuscript work, which cost him only eighteen years' labour, for fifteen silver dollars, to an old gentleman living in the vicinity of New York. There can be no hesitation in believing this must have been the identical work a selection from which is now offered to the public, especially when we assure the reader that Mr. Acker assured us, that he almost recollects crossing the ferry about this time with our author, who carried a large bundle of papers under his arm. This circumstance fastened itself on his memory, by the phenomenon which accompanied the old gentleman's return, to wit, the jingling of his pockets.

Be this as it may, the deceased gentleman placed almost as high a value upon this acquisition as if it could be traced in a direct line from a Coptic monastery in Upper Egypt. Whether this was owing to its intrinsic value, or to its being unquestionably unique, must be left to the judgment of the reader. At all events the possessor esteemed himself fortunate while living; but died somewhat more than a twelvemonth ago. His property, as we before premised, was sold, and has passed into the hands of strangers. The old house was purchased and pulled down by a lucky speculator in gas stock, who began to build a vast wooden palace for his posterity to sell; but he unluckily failed before it was finished, in consequence of dipping a little too deep in a cotton-speculation, whereby he got nearly smothered, and was fain to go back to his honest calling of a shaver.

What was most to be regretted, however, was the sale and dispersion of the old gentleman's library, consisting, among other valuables, of Souvenirs, magazines, romances, novels, tales, lying reports of societies, orations, biographies, and poems, all of the very latest production. This was done by the authority of persons whose names we forbear to drag before the world, although we cannot but regret that disposition to slight learning, so prevalent in this busy, thriving, and opulent metropolis. For our humble part, we were not so fortunate as to inherit any thing from our father but a good name; but, if we had, we would not have sold his old mansion-house, provided he had left one, so long as we could have kept it without robbing others of their due. Far less would we have disposed of those books that bore his venerated name—those "dead friends," as the Indians beautifully describe them, which were the blessing of his leisure, the fountains of his wisdom, the companions of his old age, — to purchase all the luxuries of modern frippery. But we beg pardon of all weeping heirs and melancholy legatees, for this digression.

It was truly mortifying, as showing the uncertain tenure of immortal fame, to see the treasures of fashionable literature knocked down for almost nothing, by the ignorant, unfeeling auctioneer, who, it was apparent, had no more respect for books than a Turk. Some one indeed bid off Miss Edgeworth at a high price, which seemed to astonish the man of the hammer, who observed she had been long out of date. "You are mistaken," replied the purchaser; "wit, and a keen observation of life and manners, based on good sense, can never be out of date, though they may be out of fashion." The English annuals were struck off to a picture-virtuoso, who declared his intention of cutting out the plates, and throwing the rest away. The American Souvenirs were knocked on the head by an unlucky observation from a spruce Englishman, who observed that they had not cost one tenth as much as "The Keepsake," which had been got up at an expense of eleven thousand guineas. The purchaser of The Keepsake, on hearing this, fancied he had got possession of a treasure, though he had only gained the sweepings of English literature, sanctioned by popular names, and embellished with a parcel of engravings from worn-out plates. Don Juan was bought by a young gentleman in whiskers, who was educating himself for a roué; and The Corsair, by a black-looking, weather-beaten, mysterious person, who was shrewdly suspected of being one of the gang of pirates dispersed and annihilated by the gallant

Commodore Porter. The Loves of the Angels, Little's Poems, and divers others of the same author, were purchased for almost nothing by a middle aged lady dressed in the extravagance of the mode, whom I afterwards recognized at the police-court as the mistress of a disorderly house. Another, but staid, grave female, in a plaid cloak, secured a bushel of the latest popular English poetry, for the use of her nursery, observing that such had been the rapid "development" of mind within a few years past, that the little children turned up their noses at Giles Gingerbread and Goody Two-Shoes. In short, a fashionable author, who thought himself sure of immortality, might here have received a mortifying lesson of the transitory nature of popular applause, and sighed over the anticipation of speedy oblivion. The last and most lamentable of these sacrifices was that of the London Literary Gazette and Blackwood's Magazine, which were bought for six cents a volume, by a famous grocer, who, comparatively speaking, hath destroyed more valuable works in the course of his business than were consumed in the Alexandrian Library.

It may be asked why we ourselves did not appropriate some of these ineffable varieties. Well, we had reasons for declining, which, however old-fashioned and obsolete, are not the worst in the world. We were fain to limit ourselves to the purchase of the manuscript to which we have so frequently alluded, for a sum which will be kept a profound secret. Whether it was so large as to amount to an imprudence on our part, or so small as to entitle the work to the scorn of all fashionable readers, is a mystery between ourselves and the auctioneer, who hath sworn by his hammer not to reveal it except to posterity.

Before concluding this interesting portion of our editorial labours, we will pause one moment, in order to anticipate the cavils of certain critics, who, we foresee, will be inclined to make themselves amends for not being able to find fault with the work itself (without doing violence to their consciences), by denying the claims of our author to his own labours. Doubtless they will insist that there is nothing in the history and character of our author, or in the scanty information derived from Mr. Acker, to justify the assumption of his being capable of inditing tales displaying a knowledge of life and an acquaintance with the fashionable world such as is found in the following work.

But let these gentleman-cavillers, who think they are marvellously conversant with high life, because they have read the Trip to Brighton and Almacks, and perhaps figured at the tea-parties of some rich broker — let them be quiet, as becomes them. They know no more of fashionable life than the authors of these works, or the broker himself; and may be likened to the mouse who fancied he had tasted the cream of the cheese, when he had only nibbled at the rind. Let them be told, and shut their mouths thereafter for ever, that there is no place in which a keen observer can attain to a clearer knowledge of the foibles and peculiarities of fashionable women, than in a fashionable store or tip-top milliner's. Where is it that they are so often found? and where else do they exhibit their tastes and propensities so frankly? It is there that their little caprices, their indecision, their extravagances, and all the changeable silk of their characters, are exhibited without disguise;

and it was doubtless while blowing his cracked flute behind the counter that our author attained to that intimate knowledge as well as nice perception of character, so agreeably exhibited in the following work, which, from having been written in that paradise of musketoes, Staten Island, at the sign of the "Good Woman," he hath sportively called, "TALES OF THE GOOD WOMAN."

To that class of ill-natured and prying readers which is ever finding out personal allusions and individual characters in the most innocent generalities, we will content ourselves with stating that our author certainly died at least ten years ago, according to the testimony of Mr. Acker, who has some idea of having attended his funeral. This single fact, we trust, will serve to do away all suspicion of any allusion to the fashionable society of to-day, since every body knows that a very large portion of those who figure as leaders in the *beau monde*, at present, were utterly unknown at that time.

NEW YORK, *April 1st*, 1829.

POSTSCRIPT.

Since writing the above we have had another interview with young Mr. Acker, who distinctly recollects that he either heard, or dreamed he heard, our author insinuate that he was the identical person who some few years since figured, in the old National Advocate, as "THE LAST OF THE COCKED HATS."

THE AZURE HOSE.

THE AZURE HOSE.

> "Sure he has a drum in his mouth!
> Clap an old drum-head to his feet,
> And draw the thunder downward."
>
> BEAUMONT AND FLETCHER.

CHAPTER I.,

OR

THE PROLOGUE.

THERE IS REASON IN THE BOILING OF EGGS, AS WELL AS IN ROASTING THEM.

IT was one of those hypocritical spring mornings, so peculiar to our western clime, when the light, cheering sunshine invites abroad to taste the balmy air, but when, if you chance to accept the invitation, you will be saluted by a killing, piercing, sea-monster of a breeze, which chills the genial current of the soul, and drives you shivering to the fireside to warm your fingers and complain for the hundredth time of the backwardness of the season. In short, it was a nondescript day, too hot for a great coat, and too cool to go without one; when one side of the street was broiling in the sun, the other freezing in the shade.

Mr. Lightfoot Lee was seated at the breakfast table with his only daughter, Miss Lucia Lightfoot Lee, one of the prettiest alliterations ever seen. She was

making up her opinions for the day, from the latest number of the London Literary Gazette, and marking with a gold self-sharpening pencil a list of books approved by that infallible oracle, for the circulating library. Mr. Lee was occupied with matters of more importance. He held his watch in one hand, a newspaper in the other. By the way, if I wished to identify a North-American beyond all question, I would exhibit him reading a newspaper. But at present Mr. Lee seemed employed in studying his watch, rather than the paper. He had good reasons for it.

Mr. Lightfoot Lee was exceedingly particular in boiling his eggs, which h[illegible] as accustomed to say re-[illegible]ed more discretion than any other branch of the great art of cookery. The preparations for this critical affair were always made with due solemnity. First, Mr. Lee sat with his watch in his hand, and the parlour door, as well as all the other doors down to the kitchen, wide open. At the parlour door stood Juba, his oldest, most confidential servant. At the end of the hall leading to the kitchen stood Pomp, the coachman; at the foot of the kitchen stairs stood Benjamin, the footman; and Dolly, the cook, was watching the skillet. "It boils," cried Dolly: "It boils," said Benjamin: "It boils," said Pompey the great: and, "It boils," echoed Juba, Prince of Numidia. "Put them in," said Mr. Lee: "Put them in," said Juba: "Put them in," said Pomp: and, "Put them in," cries Dolly, as she dropped the eggs into the skillet. Exactly a minute and a half afterwards, by his stop-watch, Mr. Lee called out, "Done;" and, "done", was repeated from mouth to mouth, as before. The perfection of the whole process consisted in Dolly's whipping out the eggs in half a second from the last echo of the critical, "done."

The eggs were boiled to his satisfaction; and Mr. Lee ate, and pondered over the newspaper, by turns. At length, all at once he started up in a violent commotion, and stumped about the room, exclaiming in an under tone to himself, "Too bad — too bad."

"What is the matter, father?" said Lucia; "is your egg overdone, or are you suffering the excruciating pangs of the gout, or enduring the deadly infliction of a hepatic paroxysm?"

"Hepatic fiddle-stick! I wish to heaven you would talk English, Lucia."

"My dear sir, you know English now is very different from what it was when you learned it."

"I know it, I know it," said he; "it is as different as a Quaker bonnet from a French hat. I see I must go to school again. You and Mr. Goshawk talk Greek to me."

"Mr. Goshawk is a poet, sir."

"Well, there is no particular reason why a poet should not talk like other people, at least on common subjects."

"Ah! sir, the poet's eye is always in a fine frenzy rolling. He sees differently from other people — to him the sky is peopled with airy beings."

"Ay; gnats, flies, and devil's-darning-needles," said Mr. Lee, pettishly. Lucia was half-angry, and put up a lip as red as a cherry.

"Ah! too bad, too bad," continued Mr. Lee, stumping about again with his hands behind him.

"What is too bad, sir?" said Lucia, anxiously.

"What is too bad?" cried he furiously, advancing

towards her with his fist doubled; "that puppy, Highfield, has not got the first honour after all, I see by the paper. The blockhead! I had set my heart upon it, and, see here!, he is at the tail of his class."

"Is that all? Why, father, I am glad to hear it. Mr. Goshawk assures me that genius despises the trammels of scholastic rust, and soars on wings of polished" —

"Wings of a goose," cried the old gentleman. He had a provoking way of interrupting Lucia in her flights; and, had she not been one of the best-natured of the azure tribe, she would have sometimes lost her temper.

"He'll be home to-morrow — I've a great mind to kick him out of doors."

"Whom, dear father?"

"Why, Highfield, to be sure."

"For what, sir?"

"For not getting the first honour — the puppy! I wouldn't care a stiver, if I hadn't set my heart upon it." And away the good man stumped, again ejaculating, "Too bad, too bad — I shall certainly turn him out of doors."

"Ah! but if you do, sir, I shall certainly let him in again. I shall be glad to see my dear, good-natured cousin Charles once more, though he has not got the first honour," said Lucia, smiling.

What more might have been said on this subject was cut short by the entrance, without ceremony, of Mr. Diodorus Fairweather, a neighbour and most particular friend and associate of Mr. Lee. These two gentlemen had a sincere regard for each other, kept up in all its pristine vigour by the force of contrast. One took every thing seriously; the other considered the world, and all things in it, a jest. One worshipped the ancients; the other maintained they were not worthy of tying the shoe-strings of the moderns. One insisted that the world was going backward; the other, that it was rolling onward in the path of improvement beyond all former example. One was a violent federalist; the other a raging democrat. They never opened their mouths without disagreeing, and this was the cement of their friendship. The mind of Mr. Lee was not fruitful, and that of Mr. Fairweather was somewhat sluggish in suggesting topics of conversation. Had they agreed in every thing they must have required a succession of subjects; but uniformly differing, as they did on all occasions, it was only necessary to say a single word, whether it conveyed a proposition or not, and there was matter at once, for the day.

"A glorious morning," said Mr. Fairweather, rubbing his hands.

"I differ with you," said Mr. Lee.

"It is a beautiful sunshine."

"But, my good sir, if you observe, there is a cold, wet, damp, hazy, opaque sky, through which the sun cannot penetrate; 'tis as cold as December."

"'Tis as warm as June," said Mr. Fairweather, laughing.

"Pish!" said Mr. Lee, taking up his hat mechanically, and following his friend to the door. They sallied forth without saying a word. At every corner, however, they halted, to renew the discussion; they disputed their way through a dozen different streets, and finally returned home, the best friends in the world, for they had assisted each other in getting through the morning. Mr. Lee invited Mr. Fairweather to return to dinner, and he accepted.

"Well, it does not signify," said Mr. Lee, bobbing his chin up and down, as was his custom when uttering what he considered an infallible dictum, — "It does not signify, but that Fairweather is enough to provoke a saint. I never saw such an absurd, obstinate, ill-natured, passionate" —

"O, father!" — said Lucia; "every body says Mr. Fairweather was never in a passion in his life."

"Well, but he is the cause of passion in others, and that is the worst kind of ill-nature."

CHAPTER II.

NECESSARY TO UNDERSTANDING THE FIRST.

Lightfoot Lee, Esq., was a gentleman of an honourable family; honourable, not only from its antiquity, but from the talents, worth, and services of its deceased members and its present representative. He possessed a large domain in one of the southern states, but preferred living in the city of New York during the period in which his daughter Lucia, who was his only child, was acquiring the accomplishments of a fashionable education. He was a good scholar, and had seen enough of the frippery of life to relish the beauties of an unaffected simplicity in speech and action. He could not endure to hear a person talking for effect, or disturbing the pleasant, unstudied chit-chat of a social party, by full-mouthed declamations, and inflated nothings delivered with all the pomp of an oracle. Grimace and affectation of every kind he despised; and, among the affectations of the day, that which is vulgarly called a blue-stocking made him the most impatient. Among the admirers whom the beauty and fortune of Lucia attracted around her, his most favourite aversion was a Mr. Fitzgiles Goshawk, who wrote doggerel rhymes almost equal to Lord Byron; and whose conversation perpetually reminded him, as he said, of a falling meteor, which, when handled, proves to be nothing but a jelly — a cold, dull mass, that glitters only while it is shooting.

Lucia, on the contrary, though naturally a fine, sensible girl, full of artless simplicity, and free from all pretence or affectation, admired Mr. Goshawk excessively. He had written much, thought little, and spoken a great deal. He had been admired by unquestionable judges, as the best imitator extant; and had passed the ordeal of the London Literary Gazette. He was the greatest prodigal on earth — in words; and it was impossible for him to say the simplest thing without rising into a certain lofty enthusiasm, flinging his metaphors about like sky-rockets, and serpentining around and around his subject like an enamoured cock-pigeon.

Our heroine, for such is Lucia, was, we grieve to say it, a little of the azure tint. She was not exactly blue, but she certainly inhabited that stripe of the rainbow; and, when reflected on by the bright rays of Mr. Fitzgiles Goshawk, was sometimes of the deepest shade of indigo. Then her words were mighty; her criticisms, peremptory; her tones, decisive; and her enthusiasm, though it might not be without effect, was certainly without cause. At times, however, when not excited by the immediate contact of a congenial spirit, she would become simple, natural, touching, affecting, and lovely. Instead of standing on stilts, striving at wit, and challenging admiration, she would remind one of Allworthy's description of Sophia Western. "I never," says that good man "heard any thing of pertness, or what is called repartee, out of her mouth; no pretence to wit, much less to that kind of wisdom which is the result of great learning and experience, the affectation of which, in a young woman, is as absurd as any of the affectations of an ape." Truth obliges us to say, that Lucia only realized this fine sketch of a young woman, when acting from the unstudied impulses of nature, among her familiar domestic associates, where she did not think it worth her while to glitter. Among the azure hose of the fashionable world, she strove to shine, the sun of the magic circle, until one turned away, as from the sun, not in admiration of its blurting midday splendours, but to seek relief in the more inviting twilight of an ordinary intellect. In short, our heroine was an heiress, a belle, a beauty; and, would it were not so, a blue-stocking — or, in the exalted phraseology of the day, an azure hose.

The morning after the conversation recorded in our first chapter, Highfield arrived. The old gentleman did not kick him out of doors as he threatened; and Lucia, though she did not therefore signalize herself by letting him in, received him with a smile and a hand of gentle welcome — one as bright as the sunbeam, the other as soft as a ray of the moon. The old gentleman was stiff—very stiff; Charles was his favourite nephew; he had brought him up, and intended, as he said, to make a man of him.

"Well, uncle," said Charles, "I hope I did not disappoint you. I promise you I studied night and day."

"Mischief, I suppose," said the other, gruffly.

"A little sometimes, uncle; but I minded the main chance. I hope you are satisfied."

"No, sir—I'm not satisfied, sir—dam'me, sir, if I will be satisfied, and dam'me if I ever forgive you!"—and the good gentleman stumped about according to custom.

Charles looked at Lucia, as if to inquire the meaning of this explosion; and Lucia looked most mischievously mysterious, but said nothing.

"Pray, sir," said Highfield, who on some occasions was as proud as Lucifer, "pray, sir, how have I merited this reception from my benefactor?"

"I've a great mind to turn you out of my doors."

"I can go without turning, sir." And he took up his hat.

"Answer me, sir—are you not a great blockhead?"

"If I am, uncle, nature made me so."

"I've a great mind to send you back to college, and make you go all over your studies again."

"What! the Greek alphabet—the Pons Asinorum—the plus and the minus—the labour of all labours, a composition upon nothing—and the worry of all worries, the examination? Spare me, uncle, this time."

"You deserve it, you blockhead."

"My excellent friend and benefactor," said Charles, approaching and taking his uncle's hand, "if I have offended you, I most solemnly declare it was without intention. If I have done any thing unworthy of myself, or displeasing to you; or if I have omitted any act of duty, gratitude, or affection, tell me of it frankly, and frankly will I offer excuse and make atonement. What have I done, or left undone?"

I declare, thought Lucia, that puts me in mind of Mr. Goshawk—how eloquent!

The tears came into the old gentleman's eyes at this appeal of his nephew.

"You've missed the first honour," exclaimed he, with a burst of indignation, mingled with affection; "O Charles! Charles!"

"Indeed, uncle, I have not. I gained it honestly and fairly, against one of the finest fellows in the world, though I say it."

"What! you *did* gain it?"

"Ay, uncle."

"And you spoke the valedictory?"

"I did, sir. The newspapers, I perceive, made a mistake, owing to a similarity between my name and that of the head dunce of the class. I should have written to let you know, but I wanted to have the pleasure of telling it myself."

"My dear Charles!", cried the old gentleman, "give me your hand; I ought to have known you inherited the first honour from your mother. There never was a Lee that did not carry away the first honour everywhere. But these blundering newspapers—the other day they put my name to an advertisement of a three-story house with folding doors and marble mantel-pieces. Lucia, come here, you baggage, and wish me joy."

"I can't, father; I'm jealous."

"Pooh! you shall love him as well as I do, before you are as old as I am."

Hum, thought Lucia, that is more than you know, father. When Lucia retired, she could not help thinking of this prophecy of the old gentleman. "He certainly is handsome; but then what is beauty in a man? It is intellect, genius, enthusiasm — mind, mind alone, — bear witness earth and heaven!, that constitutes the divinity of man. Certainly his eyes are as bright as —— and his person tall, straight, and elegant. But then what are these to the lofty aspirations of Genius? I wonder if he can waltz. He must be clever, for he gained the first honour. But then Mr. Goshawk says that none but dull boys make a figure at college. And then he talks just like common person. I wonder if he can write poetr for I am determined never to marry a man that is not inspired. He certainly is much handsomer than Mr. Goshawk; but then Mr. Goshawk uses such beautiful language! I declare I sometimes hardly know what he is saying. My cousin certainly is handsome, but his coat don't fit him half so well as Mr. Goshawk's."

How much longer this cogitation might have continued no one can divine; for the young lady was at this crisis called away to accompany her relative, Mrs. Coates, one of the smallest of small ladies, and for that reason sometimes called by her mischievous particular friends, in her absence, Mrs. Petticoats. Mrs. Coates was educated in England, as was the usage with the better sort of colonists before the Revolution, and is the fashion still among upstart people, who have not gotten over the colonial feeling. She had in early life married an English officer connected with the skirts of one or two titled families, with whose *names* the good lady was perfectly familiar. Her conversation, when not literary, or liquorary as she termed it, was all retrospective, and she talked wonderfully of Sir Cloudesley Shovel and Sir Richard Gammon, together with divers lords and ladies of the court-calendar. Her toryism was invincible, and if there was any body in the world she hated past all human understanding, it was "that Bonaparte," as she called him. Her favourite topics were the development — which she was pleased to call devilopement — of the infant mind; the progress of the age; the march of intellect; and the wonderful properties of the steam-engine, which she considered altogether superior to any man-machine of her acquaintance, except Mr. Fitzgiles Goshawk. Though in the main a well-principled woman, there was a cold selfishness in her character, and a minute attention to her own pleasure and accommodation, to the neglect of other people, that effectually prevented her ever being admired or beloved. It was a favourite boast with her, that no nation understood the meaning of the word comfort but the English; to which her cousin, Mr. Lee, would sometimes retort, by affirming it was no wonder, since no people ever thought more of their own comfort and less of that of others.

Mrs. Coates sent to invite Lucia to go out with her, to assist in the selection of a ribbon, which was always a matter of great delicacy and circumspection with Mrs. Petticoats. She admired Mr. Goshawk beyond all other human beings, because he wrote so like Lord Byron, and spoke like a whirlwind. "Ah, Lucy," would she say, "he will make an extinguished man, will that Mr. Goosehawk."

CHAPTER III.

AN AZURE MORNING.

After visiting three hundred and sixty-five stores, Mrs. Coates at length selected a ribbon of sixteen colours, and, finding the morning was not yet altogether wasted, proposed a visit to Miss Appleby, at whose house one was always sure of hearing all the news of the literary world. They found that lady surrounded by Mr. Goshawk and two or three azures, all talking high matters. Mr. Goshawk was not only a very "extinguished" but a very extraordinary man: he was always either trotting up and down the streets, or visiting ladies and talking at corners. He never seemed to study, nor did it appear how he got his knowledge; but, certain it is, he knew almost every thing. He could tell how many rings Miss Edgeworth wore on the forefinger of her left hand, and how many panes of glass there were in the great Gothic window of Sir Walter's study. He knew the name of the author of Pelham — the writer of every article in the Edinburgh and Quarterly — and the editor of the London Literary Gazette was not a more infallible judge of the merit of books. Indeed,

Mrs. Coates used to remark, "His knowledge seems absolutely inchewative, and I wonder how he finds time to digest it." Besides Mr. Goshawk, there was Mr. Puddingham, a solid gentleman who had so overcultivated a thin-soiled intellect that he prematurely turned it into a pine-barren, Mr. Paddleford, Mr. Prosser, Mr. Roth, a grumbling sententiarian critic, and Miss Overend, secretary to a charitable fund and member of an executive committee of Greek ladies.

I wish my dearly beloved readers could have been present at this congeries of stars; for it is impossible to do justice to the flights of fancy, the vast, incomprehensible nothings, the arrogant commonplaces, and the hard words, sported by our azure coterie. Here was a dwarfish thought dressed in gigantic words, and there a little toad of an idea swelled to the size of an ox, and ready to burst with its own importance; here a deplorable mixture of false metaphor and true nonsense, and there a little embryo of meaning, gasping for life and groaning under a heap of rubbish. No little sparks of innocent, unstudied vivacity; no easy chit-chat, such as diverts and rests the mind; no rambling interchange of sentiment; no gentle undertones, or musical, good-humoured responses. All were talking for effect, all striving for the palm of eloquent declamation, and bending their little stubborn bows, as if, like Sagittarius, they were going to bring down a constellation at the first shot.

Though I feel the impossibility of doing justice to this superfine palaver, yet will I attempt a sketch, a shadow, a mere outline, of some portion, if it be only for the benefit of the unlettered spinsters who as yet, perchance, may not know what is meant by "powerful talking." I confess the task is appalling, as it is unpleasant; for I do honestly and openly profess myself to have a holy horror of loud, contentious discussions, affected enthusiasm, and ostentatious display either of wealth or talents. It is offensive in man: but in woman, dear woman, whose office is to soothe, not irritate; whose voice should be soft as an echo of the mountain vales; whose wit should be accidental; whose enthusiasm, silent expression; and whose empire resides in her graces, her smiles, her tears, her gentleness, and her virtues, — it makes me mad. It is laying down the cestus of Venus, to brandish the club of Hercules.

"I insist upon it, Pelham is an immoral book," said Miss Appleby. "No man that cherishes the sacred principle, the vestal fire on which depended the existence of the Roman state, and all the social affinities that bind man and man together, could speak as the author does, of his mother."

"But my dear Miss Appleby," said Mr. Goshawk, "the author is not accountable for every thing in his book, any more than a father can be made to answer for the crimes of his children. The argument I would superinduce upon this predication is this," ——

"But sir-r-r," said the Johnsonian Puddingham, cutting in — "sir, the author of a bad book is guilty of a crime against society. Society, sir, is a congeries of certain people, whose various inflections, deflections, and" —

"My dear Puddingham," roared Mr. Roth, "the book is immoral in the perception, conception, execution, and catastrophe; sir" —

"Sir Cloudesley Shovel," — said Mrs. Coates; but

what more she would have said is in the womb of fate. Mr. Goshawk again took flight, and overshot her.

" Sir Francis Bacon ", said he —

" Sir Richard Gammon ", said Mrs. Coates —

" Dr. Johnson affirms " —

" The Edinburgh Review says " —

" The London Quarterly lays it down " —

" The London Literary Gazette ", screamed Lucia —

" Blackwood's Bombazine ", cried Mrs. Coates, yet louder. Here Highfield happened to be passing by, and Lucia called him in by tapping at the window; for she was anxious to have a little display before him. Highfield had known them all, having visited with Lucia, during his vacations. He held them, however, in so little respect, that he did not mind quizzing them now and then. His entrance put an end to the literary discussion about Pelham, and the torrent took another course.

" What do you think of Goldsmith ? " asked Miss Appleby, after the compliments.

" Goldsmid ? ", said he ; " why, I think he was a great fool to shoot himself." *

" Shoot himself ! " screamed Mrs. Coates ; " what, is he dead ? "

" Yes, madam — his affairs fell into confusion, and he shot himself; I thought you had seen it in the papers, by your asking my opinion."

It is my opinion Highfield did not think any such thing ; but of that no more.

" Lord ! " said Miss Appleby, " I don't mean Goldsmid, the broker, but Goldsmith, the poet and novelist; what is your opinion of him ? "

* An affair in England.

"Why, really, the question comes upon me by surprise; but I think him, upon the whole, one of the most agreeable, tender, and sprightly writers in the language."

"He wants power, sir," said Puddingham; "there is not a powerful passage in all his writings."

"He wants force, sir," thundered Mr. Goshawk:—"there is nothing forcible in his works; no effort; no struggle; no swelling of the tempest; no pelting of the pitiless storm against the indurated feelings of the heart; no fighting with the angry elements of those deep-buried passions, which waken at the magic touch of the Byrons, and the Great Unknowns, of this precocious age. For my part, I would not give a pinch of snuff for writings that did not awaken the passions. Lord Byron is all passion."

"Lord Byron was a distant connexion of a relative of my husband," said Mrs. Coates.

"Oh, all passion," cried Miss Appleby.

"All passion," cried Mrs. Overend.

"All passion," cried Paddleford.

And, "All passion," echoed Lucia, Mr. Prosser, and the rest of the party.

"Well, but," said Highfield, "I don't see why a writer should be always in a passion, any more than another man. I, for my part, should not like to be always in company with a fellow who was for ever cursing his stars, beating his breast, and talking of shooting himself; nor do I much relish books that address themselves to nothing but our most turbulent feelings. It is the best and purest office of works of imagination, to soothe and mitigate those malignant passions which the collisions of the world blow into a flame; and," added he with a smile, "it is the business of a young man, like me, to listen rather than preach. I beg pardon for my long speech."

Goshawk shrugged his shoulders, and looked at Lucia, as if to say, her cousin Charles was an everyday sort of person. Lucia thought his sentiments tolerable enough; but what superior man ever talked such plain English? Goshawk was determined to put down this new pretender at once.

"Sir," said he, pompously, "do you mean to deny that passion is the soul of eloquence; the marrow of poetry; the rainbow which connects the overarching skies of fancy, feeling, and imagination; the star that flashes conviction; sprinkles the dews of heaven on the head of the thirsty traveller; refines, delights, invigorates, and entrances; gives to the scimitar of the poet its brightness; to the dagger of the orator its point; to the ardour of love its purple blossoms; and to the fire of revenge its blushing fruits?"

"Beautiful! beautiful!" sighed Lucia; "what a flow of language! What a torrent of redundant ideas! What a congeries of metaphors!"—and she sighed again. The fact is, that Goshawk rolled out these incomprehensible nothings with such an imposing enthusiasm, such a rapidity of utterance, that it is hardly a reflection on Lucia's good sense that she admired them. It is only on paper that nonsense never escapes detection.

"Goshawk," said Highfield, "I hate argument. It is as bad as fighting before ladies."

"Hate argument!" cried they all together, and little Lucia among the loudest—"hate argument!"

"I confess it; I'd rather talk nonsense by the month, than argue by the hour."

"Hate argument!" cried Mr. Goshawk; "why, it is the hone on which the imagination is brought to its brightest edge."

"What a beautiful figure," said Lucia; "he talks like a rainbow."

"Hate argument!" cried the illustrious Puddingham;—"let me tell you, sir, the great Johnson considered argument as a cudgel, with which every man should be furnished, to defend himself and knock down his adversaries."

"What a charming metaphor!" said Lucia, with enthusiasm.

"Metaphor!" said Mrs. Coates,—"can you see it in the daytime? Do show me where it is, I should like to see its tail in the daytime."

"My dear aunt," said Lucia, excessively mortified, "my dear aunt, you mean the meteor."

"Child," said the other, "don't irrigate me. I know the difference between a metaphor and a meteor, as well as you do. The Liquorary Gazette could tell me that."

"Pray, sir," said Goshawk to Highfield, pompously, "what do they learn at college?"

"Why, a little logic, and"—

"And what is logic but argument?" said the other.

"My good sir, no two things can be more distinct. I have heard thousands of arguments in which there was no more logic than in the couplet of the primer—

'Xerxes the great did die,
And so must you and I.'"

"And do you mean to deny the conclusion?" said the other, with his usual enthusiasm.

"Not I," said Highfield, carelessly; "I have not the least doubt of it. I only deny that you and I shall die because Xerxes the great 'did die.'"

To an enthusiastic declamatory person by profession, there is nothing so difficult to parry, as a little, plain, direct, common-sense, conveyed in simple and brief words. Mr. Goshawk was actually puzzled; so he contented himself with asking, rather contemptuously,

"And is this all they teach at college?"

"By no means; I learnt exactly how many nuts and apples Tityrus had for his supper."

Mr. Goshawk, it is believed, never heard of but four poets—the Great Unknown, Lord Byron, Mr. Moore, and himself. He neither understood who Tityrus was, nor comprehended the sly rebuke of the reply. The indispensable armour of affectation is an absolute insensibility to ridicule.

"Oh! what a beautiful alliteration," exclaimed Lucia, who was dipping into Mr. Thomas Moore.

"'A *heart* that was *humble* might *hope* for it *here*.'"

"Charming! charming!" added she, repeating it to Highfield, who insisted that he could make a finer alliteration, extempore.

"If you do, I'll net you a silk purse," said Lucia.

"Done," said Highfield:—

"May mild meridian moonlight mantle me."

"Only make a rhyme to it, and I will add a watch chain," said the young lady.

"Lovely, lively, lisping, laughing Lucia Lightfoot Lee."

"Nonsense!" said Lucia, blushing a little.

"You asked for rhyme, not reason. I insist upon

it, I've won." The company was called upon to decide.

"There's no sublimity," said Goshawk.

"No powerful pathos," said Miss Overend.

"No exquisite tenderness," said Paddleford.

"No romantic feeling," said Miss Appleby.

"No meaning," said Mr. Roth, pompously.

"No connexion of sense," said Puddingham.

"It finds no *He Cow* * in my feelings," said Mrs. Coates.

Highfield was proceeding to prove that his two lines contained all the essentials of first-rate poetry, when, luckily for his fame, a young lady came in with a new hat, of the latest Paris fashion. The force of nature overcame the force of affectation; and the ladies all flocked round the new bonnet, leaving the reputation of our hero, as a bard, to its fate.

After this the conversation turned on more sublunary things.

"Do you know," said Miss Traddle, the young lady in the fashionable bonnet, "Do you know that the Briars have hired a splendid hotel, in Paris?"

"What!" said little Mrs. Coates, "do they keep tavern? Well, for my part, I never thought them as rich as some people did. I'm sorry for poor, dear Mrs. Briar."

"They have been presented at court!" said Miss Traddle. "What, tavern-keepers presented at court! O, but its only a French court," quoth Mrs. Coates, quite satisfied.

The information, however, stirred up, among the

* The intelligent reader need hardly be told that *he cow* is the fashionable pronunciation of echo, in England. — [*Author.*]

azures, a violent degree of envy, at the good fortune of the happy Briars.

"For my part," said Miss Appleby, who had been abroad, but was never presented—"for my part, I always declined going to court. Every body told me it was a stupid business;" and she sighed at the good fortune of the Briars.

"What a delightful thing it must be to get into the first society, abroad," said Miss Traddle.

"Why so?" asked Highfield.

"Why, why because it is of such high rank—so refined—so literary—so genteel—so much superior to the society here."

"Who told you so, Miss Traddle?"

"Why, Mrs. Vincent; you know she was at court."

"What, hin Hingland!" said Mrs. Coates, in astonishment.

"Yes, indeed; and at the sheep-shearing at Holkham; and the lord mayor's ball; and Almacks."

"What, Almacks!" cried Miss Appleby, and almost fainted.

"At Almanack's!" exclaimed Mrs. Coates; "I dont believe a word of it. Why I could never get there myself, though Sir Cloudesley Shovel and Sir Richard Gammon both made interest for me. Mrs. Vincent, indeed!, the daughter of a shaver, and wife of a —— I don't believe a word on't."

Poor Mrs. Vincent! how they all hated her for being at Almacks.

"And why not?" said Highfield.

"Because," said Mrs. Coates, "they wouldn't admit the goddess Dinah, if she was to rise from the dead. Were you ever abroad, Mr. Highfield?"

"No, but I intend to go one of these days. I wish

to undeceive myself, and get rid of that monstrous bugbear, the superiority of every thing foreign, which is inculcated by books and by every thing we see and hear, from our youth upwards."

"What," said they all, with one voice, "you don't believe in the superiority of foreign literature?"

"Not of the present day."

"Nor foreign manners?"

"No, nor morals either."

"Nor of French cookery?" quoth Puddingham.

"Nor of English poetry?" quoth Goshawk.

"Nor of Italian skies?" quoth Miss Overend, enthusiastically.

"Nor of London porter?" exclaimed Mrs. Coates.

"No, no, no, no," replied Highfield, good humouredly, yet earnestly;—"as to your Italian skies, a friend of mine assured me he was three months in Italy, and never saw a clear sky. The truth is, we take our ideas of Italian skies from English poets, who, not having an opportunity of seeing the sun at home, above once or twice a year, vault into raptures with the delight of sunshine on the Continent. Those of our countrymen who judge for themselves have assured me that, in no part of Europe have they ever seen such beautiful blue skies, such starry firmaments, and such a pure transparent air, as our summers and autumns present almost every day and every night. And as to their Venus de Medici, I need not go out of the room to satisfy myself that there is no necessity for a voyage to Europe to meet goddesses that shame all the beauties of antiquity;" and he bowed all round, to the ladies, who each took the compliment to herself, and pardoned his numerous heresies, on the score of his orthodoxy in one particular.

"I am exactly the height of the Venus de Medicine," said little Mrs. Coates; and forgot the slander on the English skies. "You mean to go to Europe, and visit Almanack's, of course."

"For what, madam? To see a company of well-dressed men and women, who look exactly like ourselves — only the ladies are not half so handsome, nor do they dance half so well? No, if I go abroad at all, it will be to learn properly to estimate the happiness of my own country.

The ladies, though they could not get over the silly and vulgar notion of the superiority of everything abroad, all thought Highfield a very polite, agreeable young fellow; and Lucia found herself on the very threshold of relishing a little common-sense. The party soon after separated, having spent a most improving morning.

CHAPTER IV.

SHOWING THE GREAT ADVANTAGES ARISING FROM HAVING A DISCREET FRIEND.

Though years bring with them wisdom, yet there is one lesson the aged seldom learn, namely, the management of youthful feelings. Age is all head, youth all heart; age reasons, youth feels; age acts under the influence of disappointment, youth under the dominion of hope. What wonder, then, that they so seldom agree? Mr. Lee had, for more than half a score of years, been pondering on the beautiful congruity of a match between his daughter and his nephew. He had enough for both; they were of a corresponding age; both handsome, amiable, and intelligent; and they had been brought up together, until within the last few years that Highfield remained at college. It was most reasonable, most likely, and most natural, that they should fall in love, marry, and be happy. Therefore he had long since determined in his own mind, that they should fall in love, marry, and be happy. Alas! poor gentleman — even experience had failed in teaching him, that the most likely things in the world are the least likely to come to pass. He communicated his plans to his friend, Mr. Fairweather: —

"I intend Highfield shall live with us," said he, "and thus he will have every opportunity to make himself agreeable."

"You had better forbid him the house," said the other.

"Forbid him the —— I shall do no such thing," said Mr. Lee, somewhat nettled; "but you are not serious?"

"Faith am I."

"How so?"

Mr. Fairweather was of the Socratic school, without knowing much of Socrates; for he held the ancients in little respect.

"Have you not observed, my good friend," said he, "that matrimony does not in general answer the great end of human happiness?"

"Now I tell you what, Mr. Fairweather, I know what you are after; you want to catch me in your confounded, crooked interrogations; but it wont do, I tell you it wont do, sir," said Mr. Lee, chafing.

"No, no, upon honour, I have no such intention; only answer me frankly. Have you not made the observation?"

"Well, then, I have," answered Mr. Lee, with some hesitation, and feeling exactly like a fly in the anticipation of being caught in a cobweb.

"Very well: don't you think this arises from their seeing too much of each other — becoming too intimate — and thus losing the guard which the little, salutary restraints of the constitution of society interpose before marriage, giving way, in consequence, to a display of temper and habits that weakens, if not destroys, affection?"

"Certainly — certainly I do," quoth the other.

"Very well: do not two young people, living together in the same house, associating on terms of the most perfect intimacy, also see a great deal of each other calculated to unveil the mysteries in which love delights to shroud his glorious deceptions? The young lady comes down to breakfast, with her hair in papers — an old, faded, black-silk or calico frock — a shoe out at the sides, and a holé in her stocking — she scolds the servant, and gets into a passion, (for it is impossible to be always a hypocrite), — and ten to one they become so easy together, that they will not scruple at last to contradict, quarrel with, and at length care no more for, each other, than people generally do who have had a free opportunity of seeing all their faults at full length."

"All this is very true; but then — but go on, sir."

"Very well; the case stands thus: — Marriages are

seldom very happy. Why? Because the parties are too much together. Why? Because they live in the same house, and see all each other's faults. Ergo, if you want two young persons to become attached, and marry, you should take a course directly opposite to that of matrimony. Instead of shutting your daughter and nephew up together, your best way will be, as I said before, to turn him out of doors."

"There! there! I knew you'd have me at last; I felt you were all the time drawing your infernal snares around me. Sir, you're enough to provoke a saint, with your Socratics."

"I never meddle with Socrates, or Socratics, my good friend; but Socrates, notwithstanding his ignorance of steamboats, spinning-jennies, railroads, and chemistry, is, upon the whole, good authority in cases of the kind we are discussing. He certainly saw too much of his lady."

"Then you seriously advise me to turn my nephew out of doors, to bring about a union? Why, I did threaten it the other day, and Lucia told me she would certainly let him in again."

"Then my dear friend, here you have the whole secret of the matter. Only persuade the young lady that you don't approve of the young gentleman for a son-in-law, and the business is done."

"Confound it, be serious, can't you? I want your advice as a friend."

"Well, I have given it, and you don't like it. I think it best then that you try the other extreme, and shut them up together all day in the same room. Don't you think, my good friend, that much of the misery of married life arises from young people not being sufficiently acquainted with the habits and tempers of each other beforehand?"

"Certainly, certainly."

"Very well: and don't you think the best way of obviating that evil is to let them see as much of one another as possible?"

Here Mr. Lee made his friend a most profound and reverential bow. "I remember," said he, "having read, in Monsieur Rabelais, that the great Panurge, being inclined to marry, consulted divers philosophers without success, when the thought came across him to ask the opinion of a fool, who soon satisfied his doubts on the subject." Whereupon he seized his hat and stumped out of the room, followed by his friend. But they did not separate; they stuck together like a pair of wool-cards with the teeth standing opposite ways, and finished the morning, more attached to each other than ever.

CHAPTER V.

PURE AZURE.

Mr. Lee, after troubling himself exceedingly in concocting and maturing a plan to bring about a speedy union between his daughter and nephew, at length in despair hit upon the best in the world, which was, to let matters take their own course, and leave the event to Providence. Had he persevered in this, it had been all the better; but I profess to have heard a vast many people talk of trusting to Providence, who still would be meddling and putting in their oar, and spoiling every thing. However, it is necessary to the happiness of mankind, that they should fancy themselves the spiders that weave the web, instead of the flies that are caught in it.

In the meantime, Lucia and Highfield were much together. Lucia liked him extremely; she liked his good-humour, his vivacity, his spirit, and his generous forgetfulness of himself; she even thought him rather handsome, and quite a sensible young man. But her ideas of men had been formed from the declamations of the azure club, with which she had been intimately associated for the last few years. It was here that she learned to consider words of much more consequence than actions, talents than temper, enthusiasm than common-sense, and an utter incapacity for usefulness as the best test of genius. She was often struck with the manly sense and unpretending beauty of Highfield's sentiments; but then they were expressed with such a nakedness, such a poverty of words, such a natural simplicity, that all the azures pronounced him a very common-place sort of a person, that would never set the world crying about nothing, or be himself miserable without cause.

"For my part," said Goshawk, "I like sublimity, obscurity, grandeur, mistiness — I hate a speech, or a passage, that I can comprehend at the first glance. Give me, to grope in the whirlwind; mount into the depths of the multitudinous ocean; dive into the evanescent fleecy clouds, that gallop on the midnight sunbeams which sparkle in yon star-spangled attic story; and grapple with the chaos of the mind." And he sunk on the sofa, overpowered with his emotions.

"And I," exclaimed Miss Appleby, holding a smelling-bottle to his inspired nose, "I delight to fling—" here she flourished a pinch of snuff she held between her thumb and finger right into the expanded nostrils of the great Puddingham, who began to sneeze like ten tom-cats—"I delight to toss back the curtains of night and darkness—to climb those unfathomable abysses where lurk the treasures of inspired thought, glittering like the eternal snows of the inaccessible Andes. I love to rise on the wings of the moonbeam—sink under the weight of the zephyr—and lose myself in the impenetrable brightness of transcendent genius, giving to the winds their whistle, the waves their roar, the stars their brightness, and the sun its fires."

"And I," cried little Mrs. Coates, "as Sir Richard Gammon used to say, prefer those soul-infusing alligators, that stir the mountain spirit up to the dromedary of fever heat—"

"The dromedary of fever heat!" said Roth,—"what sort of a dromedary is that?"

Lucia whispered Mrs. Coates, who replied in some agitation,

"I mean, allegory, and thermometer. How could I make such a mistake? But I was carried away by the intensity of my feelings. I like—"

Each one of the party was now so anxious to let likings be known, that there was no one but Highfield to listen. Even Lucia mingled her tuneful nonsense with the incomprehensible jargon. There was not one of these good people that would not have made a decent figure in life, in their proper sphere, (as indeed all persons do), had they only been content to keep within it, and talk common-sense on ordinary occasions, refraining from the affectation of enthusiasm when there was nothing to excite it. A pause at length ensuing, Miss Appleby turned suddenly to Highfield, and asked him,

"O, Mr. Highfield, I hope you admire those beautiful historical romances, and romantic histories, that come out every day nowadays? What a charming thing it is to read novels and study history at the same time!"

"Why, in truth, madam," said Highfield, "I don't pretend to criticism, and hardly ever read reviews, when I can find any thing else to read."

"Not read reviews!"

"Not read the Edinburgh!", cried Mr. Roth, who never uttered an opinion that he did not get from that renowned Scottish oracle.

"Not read the Quarterly!", exclaimed Puddingham, who was a believer in the infallibility of the English oracle.

"Nor the Liquorary Gazette!", quoth little Mrs. Coates.

"Well then, let us hear *your* opinion, sir," at length said Puddingham, with a supercilious air, implying that it was not worth hearing.

"Such as it is, you are welcome to it. I confess I do not agree with those who believe that a knowledge of history may be obtained by studying romances. The very name of romance presupposes fiction; and how is the reader, unless already critically versed in history, to distinguish between what is fact and what is fiction? The probability is, that he will jumble them together, and thus lose all perception of what is history, and what romance. He may come, in time, to mistake one for the other, and confound a Waverley novel with Hume, or the Tales of my Landlord with Plutarch's Lives."

"Ah! that Plutarch's Lives is a delightful romance," exclaimed Mrs. Coates.

"Romance!" said Highfield; "my dear madam, I am afraid you are already in the state of doubt I hinted at. Plutarch's Lives compose one of the best authenticated memorials of history."

"Well," cried Mrs. Coates, "did ever any body hear of such an imposition! Every thing is so perfectly natural, I took it for a historical romance. I am resolved never to read another word of it."

"Many besides yourself, madam," said Highfield, smiling, "have lost their relish for truth, by a habit of reading little else than the daily succession of half-truth half-fable productions, perpetually issuing from the press. I think I could give a receipt, which would enable any person of ordinary intellect to concoct one of these at least twice a year, without any extraordinary exertion."

"Oh, let us hear it by all means," said Puddingham, disdainfully.

"Come then," said the other. "Take a smattering of history; a little knowledge of old costumes and phraseology; a little superstition, consisting of a belief in clouds, dreams, and omens; a very little invention, just enough to disguise the truth of history; a very little vein of a story, with very little connection; a mighty hero, and a very little heroine. With these, compound a quantity of actions without motive and motives without action, adventures that have no agency in producing the cat. and a catas- trophe without any connection dventures. Put all these in a book, cement the r with plenty of high-sounding declamations, t a certificate from an English review or ne ", and you have a romance, of which more copi be sold in a fortnight than of the best history in world in a year."

"By the bye," said Miss Appleby, "have you read Moore's Life of Byron, and heard that Murray, the great London bookseller, has purchased the copy-right of his minor poems for three thousand seven hundred guineas?"

"What a proof of the prodigious superiority of his genius!" cried Miss Overend. "I have read that Milton sold his Paradise Lost for fifteen pounds."

"What a noble testimony to the wonderful development of mind!" cried Puddingham. "But I believe, Mr. Highfield, you don't believe in the vast improvement of the age?", added he, in his usual pompous vein.

"Not much," replied the other; "I think the age of Milton was quite as learned and wise as the present. If Milton were now living, an obscure author or obnoxious politician, I doubt whether Murray would give him fifteen pounds for his Paradise Lost, at a venture, unless indeed he could secure a favourable review."

"What a divine misanthrope was Lord Byron!", exclaimed Miss Appleby; "how I should glory in being loved by a man that hated all the rest of the world!"

"My dear madam," said Highfield, "wouldn't you be afraid he might kill you with kindness?"

"I would die such a glorious death."

"And .on too. You would be immortalized, if . account of its rarity."

" was a jewel of a man! Such an inspired pt for his fellow-creatures! Don't you think certain sign of his superiority over the rest of .e world?"

"And don't you think his utter disregard of the customs and prejudices of society a proof of his lofty genius?", added Miss Overend.

"Why no, I can't say I do. But I have no disposition to find fault with the dead—it is against an old maxim I learned at college."

"It is much easier to give an opinion than to support it," said the sententious Puddingham. "Pray give us your reasons, Mr. Highfield."

"I had rather not," said he; "I am somewhat tired of his lordship, and heartily wish his cruel biographers would let his memory rest in peace."

But they all insisted.

"Well then, since I can't get off with honour, I must not disgrace myself before this good company. In the first place, I don't believe his lordship despised the world whose applause and admiration he was continually seeking. His contempt was sheer affectation. But if he had really despised it, I should have a worse opinion of him."

"As how, my good sir?" said Puddingham.

"Because I consider misanthropy a proof of either weakness or wickedness. To divest mankind of all the virtues, as does the misanthrope, is to free ourselves virtually from all moral obligations towards them. One may become justly indifferent to this world, but to hate it seems to me only a proof that a man is bad himself, and wants an excuse for indulging his wicked propensities, by robbing his fellow-creatures of all claim to the exercise of justice and benevolence. He is like the pirate, who throws away his allegiance, only that he may make war on every flag."

Here the great Puddingham took an emphatic pinch of snuff; and, after sneezing violently, said, "Go on, sir; go on."

"Neither do I believe that a disregard to the common maxims of life is proof of a superior mind. Men of great genius, indeed, very often pay little attention to mere fashions and fashionable opinions, be-because these have nothing to do with the settled principles of religion or morality. But, so far as respects my own reading or experience, I never met with a man of very extraordinary powers of mind who despised or disregarded those ordinary maxims of life which are essential to the very existence of society; much less have I met one of this class who prostituted his genius to the injury of morals and religion, or devoted himself exclusively to low, grovelling, mischievous attempts to weaken their influence on mankind. I have never found such men for ever wallowing in the mire of sensuality, or indulging a malicious misanthropy by sarcasms and reasonings against social ties and duties. — Shall I go on?" said Highfield, after a pause.

"Oh, by all means," said Puddingham, condescendingly.

"The world of fashion has been pleased to place Lord Byron beside, if not on a level with, the great names of ancient and modern literature; and, whatever may be my own opinion, I am to estimate him by that standard — if I please. But I don't please to do so. He will not bear a comparison with any of these. A great genius always devotes himself to great subjects; or, if he sometimes condescends to trifle, it is only by way of a little relaxation. We do not find Homer, Virgil, Dante, Tasso, Milton, and others of the great 'heirs of immortality,' attempting to reach the summit of fame through the dirty, winding, paths of ribaldry and sensuality — converting their muse into a pander to vice, or tilting against society and morals, and, both by example and precept, inciting to the violation of the highest duties of man to man, and man to woman. Their genius was nobly exercised in celebrating the glories of their country; the triumphs of their religion; the renown of virtuous heroes; and the beauties of fortitude, disinterestedness, magnanimity, justice, and patriotism. We never find the highest gift of Heaven coupled with the lowest propensities to profligacy and vice. It is only your second or third rate men who are found pleading an exemption from the duties and obligations of morality, on the score of their superior genius. To my taste, Lord Byron is, besides all this, far below the first rank of poets, in sublimity, invention, pathos, and especially in the power of expressing his ideas and feelings with that happy force and richness combined with clearness and simplicity, for which they are so preëminently distinguished. There is, to my mind, more genius in Milton's Comus than in all his lordship's poetry put together. As a dramatic writer, he cannot compare with — I put Shakspeare, Beaumont and Fletcher,

Otway, Corneille, Racine, and Voltaire, out of the question — but with Webster, Southern, Dryden, and a dozen others. Childe Harold, though containing many passages of great beauty, is without plot or invention — the mere unpurposed wanderings of a splenetic sensual misanthrope, kindled into occasional wrath or enthusiasm by the sight of things at the roadside, and apparently incapable of any inspiration other than that derived from sensible objects. The Corsair, The Giaour, and Don Juan, are nothing more than the abstracted, contemplative Childe Harold, carrying his feelings and principles into practical application. The Childe merely thinks as a profligate — the others act the character; the first two in heroics, the last in doggerel and buffoonery. They are the same person, in different masks; and that person seems to be Lord Byron himself. As a satirist, he is far behind Dryden, Pope, and even Churchill; and, as a writer of quaint doggerel, he is inferior to Peter Pindar, in humour, waggishness, and satirical drollery. And now, after uttering this shocking blasphemy, I humbly take my leave." So saying, he seized his hat, and retreated with great precipitation.

This was the longest speech our hero ever uttered; and if he should take it into his head to make such another in the course of this history, he must get one of the reporters to Congress to write it down, for I demur to undertaking the task in future. Never man met with so little applause for attempting to enlighten people against their will as did our friend Highfield on this occasion. The whole coterie, Lucia among the rest, was scandalized at this atrocious criticism, and separated in confusion. Mr. Fitzgiles Goshawk escorted Lucia home, and discoursed as seldom man in his senses, talking to a woman in hers, ever discoursed before.

He spoke of being sick of the world; disgusted with the heartlessness of mankind; depressed and worn out with the intensity of his feelings; and devoured by a secret grief, which must never be known until he had gained a refuge from care and sorrow in the quiet grave. All this he uttered in language I confess myself inadequate to record; and with an affectation that must have been apparent to any one but an inexperienced girl. On going away he gave into Lucia's hand a paper, accompanied by a look that went straight to her heart. She retired to her chamber, and, unfolding the billet with trembling hands, found the following exquisite effusion: —

TO LUCIA.

I've seen the rose-bud glittering on its stalk,
 And morning sunbeams blushing round its head,
And many a wild flower greeting my lone walk,
 And many a withered wanderer lying dead;
And I have sighed, and yet I knew not why,
And listened to sweet nature's lulling lullaby.

And I have heard the woodman's mellow song,
 And sober herds winding their pensive way,
And echoing cow-bells, tinkling forth ding-dong,
 And ploughman whistling forth his roundelay —
And wept to think, ah! luckless, loveless I,
I could not die to live, nor live to die!

And I have dwelt on beauty's angel smile,
 And smiling beauty in its winsome glee,
And pondered on my weary way the while;
 And my heart sunk, and panted sore, ah me!
And my full breast did swell, and sorely sigh;
And shudder to its core, alas! I know not why.

Ah! lady, list thee to my pensive lays,
And give a sigh to my sad, sighing fate;
And ponder o'er life's wild mysterious maze;
And pity him who feels its stifling weight,
And sighs to think, and thinks to sigh again;
And finds pain pleasure, pleasure pining pain!

"How delightful," thought Lucia, wiping her eyes, "how delightful it must be to be unhappy, without knowing exactly why! To be able to gather the honey of sweet melancholy, from the flowers, the fruits, the smiles, and the beauties, of nature! To weep, where vulgar souls would sport and laugh! To complain without reason; and to banquet on the lonely musings of a heart overfraught with the exquisite sensibilities of genius!" And she sighed over the fate of this interesting man, who was thus pining away under some secret grief. She put the inspired morceau into her bosom; and that day, at least, the genius of Goshawk triumphed over the good sense, the manliness, and the wholesome, healthful vivacity, of Highfield.

I feel I ought, in justice, to apologize for my heroine, who had sense enough from nature to have detected the mawkish folly, incomprehensible nonsense, and silly affectation, of this poetical grief of Mr. Fitzgiles Goshawk. All I can say in her defence is, that she had been brought up in the midst of the azure coterie, all the members of which were considerably older than herself; had been every day accustomed to hear them praise Mr. Goshawk, and to hear Mr. Goshawk's poetry. She had grown up in habitual veneration for them all; and even the notorious blunders of her aunt were hallowed by coming from the sister of her mother. Those who know the spell which wrong precepts and early bad examples wind about the finest understanding, and how slowly and with what labour it emancipates itself, will, I hope, excuse my heroine. Such as she is I shall endeavour to exhibit her, hoping that time and experience will yet make her what she was intended to be by nature.

CHAPTER VI.

THE STORY HASTENS SLOWLY.

THE father of Lucia, though he had not become quite a sage, had yet derived considerable benefit from experience. Time is as much the friend, as the enemy, of man; and while he plants the wrinkles on our foreheads, makes some amends by sowing the seeds of wisdom in the mind. Mr. Lee had come to the conclusion, that the best way of bringing about a union of hearts was to keep the secret of his wishes to himself, and let Lucia and Highfield follow the guidance of Dame Nature. There is something in the stubborn heart of man and woman that revolts at becoming the dupe of a plan, even if it be one for bringing about exactly what it wishes above all things. I have seen an over-anxious mother drive a young man from her house, only by discovering a vehement desire to forward a match between him and the very daughter he would have selected if left to himself. In truth, we overdo things in this world, quite as often as we neglect what is necessary to be done. The parent who is perpetually watching the little child and cautioning it against harm, for the most part only excites a curious longing to try the experiment and judge for itself. So it is with grown-up children, who, like infants, are only to be warned by their own experience; and whom perpetual cautions, recommendations, and supervision, too often only incite to mischiefs of which they might otherwise never have dreamed. If there ever was a period of the world in which these maxims were exemplified, it is doubtless the present; when, if the truth must be told, so much pains have been taken, by well-meaning people with better hearts than heads, to improve mankind, that they have at length become, as it were, little better than good for nothing. But let us return to our story.

Both Highfield and Lucia, it is believed, remained quite unconscious of the intentions of the old gentleman towards them. The former was every day hinting, in the most delicate manner, his wish to enter upon some honourable pursuit, by which he might attain to independence if not distinction. But the old gentleman always put him off, with, "Time enough, Charles — time enough: look round a little, and consider a good deal, before you make your choice." Highfield was in a situation of peculiar delicacy for a high-spirited, honourable, man; and he refrained from further importunity. Still he did not feel satisfied. He was dependent; and if I were to mark out the dividing line that separates men, it should be here. On one side I would place those whose manhood rises above the degradation of a dependence on any thing but their own heads, hands, and hearts; and on the other, those inferior beings who are content to be a burthen upon their fathers or their friends, rather than launch into the ocean of life and buffet the billows.

Highfield belonged to the former class. He longed to make himself a useful and honourable citizen, by the exercise of his talents and industry. He had also another motive. It is quite impossible for two persons, especially of different sexes, to live together in the same house and preserve a perfect indifference towards each other. They will either take a liking, or a decided dislike. If they are very young, this will probably ripen into love, or antipathy. Lucia was a little too much of the azure; but I have seen the time, not quite half a century ago, when such a woman would have wakened in my heart a hundred sleeping Cupids. There was that about her which, for want of some other phrase, we call attractive — a charm, which, so far as I have ever analyzed it, consists in a well-made figure not tall; a face of mild gentleness mingled with vivacity; not always laughing, nor ever gloomy; always neat, yet never over-dressed, (for no woman can ever touch the heart, though she may overpower the senses, by her splendours); a graceful, quiet, motion; a soft, melting, mellow, voice; and a heart and an understanding, the one all nature, the other nature embellished, not spoiled, by culture and accomplishments. Such a woman, though she may not dazzle or mislead the imagination, carries with her the true, moral, magnetic influence, which lurks as it were unseen, emitting no gaudy splendours, but with a mysterious, inscrutable, power, attracting and fixing every kindred sympathy with which it comes in contact. Such, in her natural state, was Lucia Lightfoot Lee — a lovely maiden, but, alas! a little too much of the azure. Highfield had not been long an inmate of his uncle's house, before he began to feel the force of that magnetic influence I have just described; and, the moment he became conscious of it, his anxiety to leave his uncle, and pursue some mode of independent existence, became stronger.

His sense of honour was not only nice, but punctilious. He was poor and dependent; Lucia was an heiress. Had he believed it in his power to gain the affections of his cousin, he would have despised himself for the attempt. But he saw that her imagination, if not her heart, was captivated by the empty but showy accomplishments of Mr. Goshawk; and the hope of success was not strong enough to blind him to the meanness of the attempt. He began to be much from home, and, when at home, absent and inattentive; though his natural spirits kept him from being gloomy or unsocial. Lucia was too much occupied with Mr. Fitzgiles Goshawk and his mysterious sorrows to notice this; but the old gentleman began to be fidgety and impatient at the unpromising prospect of his favourite plan.

"What is the matter with you and Lucia?" said he, one day.

"Nothing, sir," replied Highfield; "we are very good friends."

"Friends! hum — ha — but you don't seem to like each other as well as you did — hey?"

"Like, sir — uncle — I am sure I have a great friendship for Miss Lee."

"Ah! hum — ha — friendship — but don't you think her a d——d fine girl — hey, boy?"

"I do, indeed, sir. I think her a sensible, discreet, well-behaved, promising young lady as you will see."

"Ah! yes — sixteen hands high; star in the forehead; trots well; canters easy; full blooded; and three years old last grass — hey? — One would think you were praising a horse, instead of my daughter," said the old gentleman, getting into a passion apace.

"My dear uncle, excuse me. It does not become me to speak of my cousin in such terms of admiration as I would employ under different circumstances."

"Circumstances!, sir — is there any circumstance that ought to prevent your seeing like other young men, and feeling and expressing yourself as they do?"

"Pardon me, sir; but I am just now thinking of quite a different matter."

"You don't say so, sir! Upon my word, my daughter is very much obliged to you. But what is the mighty affair?"

"My excellent friend, don't be angry. If you knew all, perhaps you would pity me. But I must leave you, and seek my fortune — indeed I must. I am wasting the best portion of my life in idleness."

"And suppose you are, what is that to you, sir, if it is my pleasure?"

"You have been a father to me, sir, and I owe you both gratitude and obedience. But there are duties to ourselves, which ought to be attended to. I am but a dependant on your bounty, after all — a beggar" ——

"A beggar! — 'tis false, sir, you're not a beggar. But I see how it is; you want to be made independent; you want me to make a settlement on you; you are not content to wait till an old man closes his eyes; you" ——

"Uncle," said Highfield, with his cheek burning

and his eye glistening, "do you really believe me such a despicable scoundrel?"

"Why — no — I believe you are only a fool, that is all. But I'll never forgive you; you have deranged all my plans; you have rejected the happiness I had in store for you; you will bring my gray hairs with sorrow to the grave. Yes, yes, yes, I see it, I see it — I am doomed to be a miserable, disappointed, heart-broken old man."

"For Heaven's sake, uncle, what is the matter?"

"Matter! why the matter is, you are a blockhead; you are dumb, deaf, blind; you haven't one of the five senses in perfection, or you might have known" —

"Known what, sir?"

"Why," roared the old gentleman, in a transport of rage, "you might have seen that I intended you for my son-in-law — you blockhead; that I meant to leave you and Lucia all my estate — you fool; that I had set my heart on it — you — you ungrateful villain. But I'll be even with — I'll disinherit you — I'll disown you — I'll send you to the d——l, sir, for your base ingratitude — I will."

Highfield stood a moment or two, overpowered by this unexpected disclosure of his uncle. He actually trembled at the prospect it opened before him. At length he exclaimed: —

"My best of friends, I never dreamed that such was your intention."

"Why, sir, I have cherished it, lived upon it, ever since Lucia was born. Not know it? What a blind fool you must be!"

"But you never communicated it, sir; and how could I know it?"

"Why, ay, that is true indeed. When I think of it, there is some excuse for you, as I never hinted my intention. But it is all over now; you want to leave us; and you think Lucia 'a sensible, discreet, well-behaved, promising young woman,'—sixteen hands high;"—mimicking poor Highfield, as he repeated these panegyrics.

"I think her," said Highfield, "for now I dare speak what I think—I think her all that a father could wish, all that a lover could desire in his moments of most glowing anticipation. I think her the loveliest, the best, the most accomplished, the most angelic, the most divine"—

"Ah! that will do, that will do, boy; you talk like a hero—tol-de-rol-lol!" And the old gentleman cut a most unprecedented caper. Give me your hand, boy; it's a bargain—we'll have the wedding next week."

"Ah, sir!" said the young man, with a sigh, "I doubt—you know there is another person to be consulted."

"Another person! Who do you mean, sir?"

"Your daughter, sir."

"Bless me! that is true, indeed. I had forgot that. But I'll soon bring the matter about. I'll tell her it is the first wish of my heart. If she refuses, I'll talk reason to her. If she won't listen to reason, I will talk to her like a father—I'll let her know who is master in this house, I warrant you. I'll go this instant, and settle the matter." And the old gentleman was proceeding to make good his words.

"For Heaven's sake, sir, don't be in such a hurry," cried Highfield eagerly; "you will ruin me and my hopes, if you proceed in such a hurry. Alas! sir, I fear it is too late now."

"What does the puppy mean?"

"I fear my cousin's affections are already engaged."

"To whom, sir? — tell me quick, quick, sir — to whom? I'll engage her, the baggage; I'll let her know who is who; I'll teach her to throw away her affections without consulting me — I'll shut the door in the scoundrel's face, and shut my daughter up in her chamber — I'll — why the d——l, sir, don't you answer me; what do you stand there for, playing dummy? Tell me, sir, — who is the villain that has stolen my daughter's affections?"

"I do not say positively, sir, and I have no right to betray the young lady's secrets; but I fear Mr. Goshawk has made a deep impression on her heart."

Mr. Lee was never in so great a passion before: not even with his man Juba, of whom I could never make up my mind to my satisfaction, whether he was his master's master, or which was the better man of the two. Juba was of the blood royal of Monomotapa, a mighty African kingdom. He had been in the family long enough to outlive three generations, and thus fairly acquired a right to be as crusty as his master, who, if the truth must be told, was terribly henpecked by the royal exile. The old gentleman once had a dispute at his own table with one of his neighbours at the South, and some words passed between them.

"Massa," said Juba, when the company had retired, — "massa, we can't put up wid dat: mus' call um out."

The good gentleman quietly submitted, and called out his neighbour, who fortunately apologized.

"Icod, massa," said Juba, "we brought um to de bull-ring, didn't we?"

But to return from this commemoration of our old friend, Juba.

Mr. Lee was in a towering passion. Of all the men he had ever seen, known, or read of, Mr. Goshawk was the one for whom he cherished the most special and particular antipathy. He considered him an empty, idle, shallow, affected coxcomb, without heart or intellect; a pretender to literary taste and acquirements; a contemner of useful knowledge and pursuits, whose sole business was to exhibit feelings to which he was a stranger, to excite sympathy for affected sorrows, and to impose upon the susceptible follies of ancient spinsters or inexperienced girls. "The fellow carries a drum in his head," would he say, "and is for ever sounding false alarms. You think he is going to play a grand march, but it is nothing but rub-a-dub, rub-a-dub, over and over again."

"Goshawk!" at length he cried,—"what! that starved epitome of a wind-dried rhymester; that shadow of a shadow of a shadow of a stringer of doggerel; that imitator of an imitator in the sixteenth degree of consanguinity to an original; that blower of the bellows to the last spark of an expiring fancy! Confound me if I had not rather have heard she had fallen in love with the trumpeter to a puppet show."

"My dear uncle, I don't say my cousin is actually in love with Mr. Goshawk; but I think she has a preference; a—a—at least, I am pretty sure, her imagination is full of his genius, eloquence, and beautiful poetry."

"Genius, eloquence, poetry—pish! I could make

a better poem out of a confectioner's mottoes, than he will ever write. But she shall either renounce him this minute, or I will renounce her."

Highfield begged his uncle to pause before he proceeded to such extremities. He reasoned with him on the bad policy of rousing into opposition a feeling which was perhaps only latent, and giving it the stimulus of anger, by assailing it too roughly. He cautioned him against the common error, of supposing that to forbid a thing was the best possible way of preventing its coming to pass; or that love was to be quelled by a puff of opposition. He conjured him to say nothing on the subject; to look on without interfering; to appear as if he neither saw, nor participated in, any thing going forward.

"If," said he, "I am not deceived in my lovely and sensible cousin, it is only necessary to leave her good sense and growing experience to operate, and before long they will of themselves indicate to her the error of her taste and imagination. But if I should be deceived in this rational anticipation," added he, proudly and firmly; "if I find that her heart is seriously and permanently attached, I give you my honour, I pledge my unalterable determination, that I will not permit myself to be either the motive or the instrument for forcing her inclinations. If I cannot win her fairly, and against the field, so help me Heaven, I will never wear her."

"You talk like a professor, and a blockhead to boot," said Mr. Lee, half pleased and half offended. "But hark ye, Mr. Highfield, if I take your advice, and it turns out badly, I'll disinherit you both."

"With all my heart, uncle, so far as respects myself.

Only say nothing; do nothing; and let matters take their course. We often make things crooked by taking too much pains to straighten them. 'Let us alone,' as the anti-tariff folks say."

"Your most humble servant, sir," quoth Mr. Lee, with a profound bow—"I am to play Mr. Nobody, then, in this trifling affair of the disposal of my only child?"

"Only for a little while, sir, when you shall resume the sceptre again."

"With which I shall certainly break your head, if your wise plan should happen to fail."

"Agreed, uncle. I shall then be broken-headed, as well as broken-hearted. For, by Heaven, I love my cousin, well enough to"——

"To resign her to an empty, heartless, brainless coxcomb. But come, I give up the reins to my wise Phæton, who, if he don't burn up the world, I dare swear will set the North river on fire. Here comes Fairweather: I will consult him, though I know the old blockhead will be of a contrary opinion, as he always is. Go, and make a bow to Lucia; play Mr. Goshawk, and talk as much like a madman as possible."

CHAPTER VII.

MORE PURE AZURE.

HIGHFIELD sought Lucia, and found her sitting at a window which looked out upon the beautiful bay, where the fair and noble Hudson basks its beauties for awhile in the sun before it loses itself for ever in the vast solitudes of the pathless sea. It was an April morning, such as sometimes appears in the disguise of sunshine and zephyrs, to cheat us into a belief that laughing jolly spring is come again. The bay was one wide waveless mirror, along whose surface lay here and there a little lazy mist lolling in the warm sunbeams, or sometimes scudding along before a frolic breeze that rose in playful vigour and then died away in a moment. In some places, the vessels appeared as if becalmed among the clouds, their proportions looming in imposing magnitude through the deceptive mists; and in others, you might see them exhaling the damps and fogs condensed on their sails and decks, in clouds of snow-white vapour. Here and there you could trace the course of a steam-boat to the Kills or the Quarantine, by a long pennant of dark smoke slowly expanding in the dampness of the circumambient air, and anon see her shoot, as if by magic, from the distant obscurity. The grass had just begun to put forth its spires of tender green, the trees to assume an almost imperceptible purple tint from the expansion of the buds; the noisy city lads were spinning tops, flying kites, or shooting marbles, in the walks; and now and then, a little feathered stranger, cheated by the genial hour into a belief that spring was come, chirped merrily among the leafless branches.

Lucia was at the open window, her rosy cheek leaning pensively on her snowy hand. She had just finished reading, for the twentieth time, the pathetic and interesting effusion of Mr. Goshawk. All that she could understand from it was, that he was very,

very miserable about something, she knew not what; and the mystery of his sorrows invested them with an indescribable, indefinable, interest. Not but what our heroine had her suspicions, and those suspicions increased her sympathy a hundred fold. "Unfortunate man!" would she say to herself, "he is consuming in the secret fires kindled in his bosom by the intense ardour of his genius, the acute sensibilities of his heart!"

Highfield was one of the most amiable of the tribe of lovers, nine in ten of whom, I must be allowed to say, deserve to be turned out of doors by the fair objects of their persecutions, once a day at least. If they are in doubt, they are either stupidly silent or perversely disagreeable; if they are jealous, they look and act just like fools; and if successful, there is an insulting security, a triumphant self-conceit, that, to a woman gifted with the becoming pride of the sex is altogether insufferable. I can tell a successful wooer as far off as I can see him. He does nothing but admire his leg, as he trips along; and you would fancy he saw his mistress in every looking-glass. But Highfield was gay, good-humoured, and sensible. He did not think it worth while to make himself hated because he was in love; nor to increase the preference of his mistress for another, by treating her with neglect or ill-manners. True, these things are considered the best evidence of sincere passion; but I would advise young women to beware of a man whom love makes unamiable: as I myself would beware of one whom the intoxication of wine made turbulent and quarrelsome. Both love and wine draw forth the inmost nature of man.

"Well, Lucia," said Highfield, with a familiar frankness which his intimacy and near relationship warranted—"Well, Lucia, have you begun my watch-chain yet?"

"No," said she, sighing.

"Well, my coz, when do you mean to begin it?"

"I don't know," replied she languidly—"one of these days, I believe."

"What ails you, Lucia—are you not well?"

"Not very—I have got a sort of oppression, a heaviness, a disposition to sigh; something here,"—pressing her hand on her bosom, from whence peeped forth a little corner of Goshawk's effusion. Highfield saw it, and the blood rushed into his cheeks; but he quelled the rising fiend of jealousy, and asked, in a tone of deep interest, if she would not take a walk with him on the Battery. She declined, in a tone of perfect indifference.

"Shall we go and call on Miss Appleby?" Lucia was all life and animation. She put on her hat, her shawl, and the thousand et-cætera that go to the constitution of a fashionable lady; and tripped away like a little fairy. She expects to meet Goshawk there, thought Highfield; but he neither pouted, nor was rude to his cousin, on the way. Nay, he exerted all his wit and pleasantry, and before they arrived Lucia thought to herself she would begin to net the watch-chain that very evening. They found all the azures, except Mr. Goshawk, assembled at one of the drawing-room windows, clamourously reading and clamourously applauding some verses written on a pane of glass with a diamond pencil. The reader shall not miss them. They ran as follows:

Cursed be the sun — 'tis but a heavenly hell!
Cursed be the moon, false woman's planet pale;
Cursed the bright stars, that man's wild fortunes tell;
And cursed the elements! Oh! I could rail
At power, and potentates, and paltry pelf,
And, most of all, at that vile wretch, myself!

What are the bonds of life, but halters tied?
What love, but luxury of bitter woe?
What man, but misery personified?
What woman, but an angel fallen below?
What hell, but heaven — what heaven, but hell above?
What love, but hate — what hate, but curdled love?

What's wedlock, but community of ill?
What single blessedness, but double pain?
What life's best sweets, but a vile doctor's pill?
What life itself, but dying o'er and o'er again?
And what this earth, the vilest, and the last,
On which the planets all their offal cast?

Oh! doubly cursed ——

Here, it would seem, the bard stopped to take breath; either overcome by his own exertions, or finding there was nothing left for him to curse.

"I never heard such delightful swearing," cried Miss Appleby.

"What charming curses!", cried Miss Overend.

"What touching misanthropy!", cried Mr. Paddleford.

"What powerful writing!", cried Puddingham.

"What glowing meteors!", cried Mrs. Coates, determined not to mistake meteors for metaphors, this time.

Lucia said nothing; but the tumult of her bosom told her nobody could write such heart-rending lines but Mr. Goshawk.

"Don't you think them equal to Lord Byron?" [M]iss Appleby to Highfield.

"Very likely, madam; Lord Byron wrote a vast deal of heartless fustian."

"Heartless fustian!", screamed Miss Appleby; and "heartless fustian!" echoed the rest of the azures, with the exception of Lucia, who determined not to commence the watch-chain that evening, if ever.

"Fustian! do you call such poetry, fustian — so full of powerful writing, and affording such delicious excitement? For my part, I can't live without excitement of some kind or other," said Miss Overend.

"What kind of excitement do you mean, madam," said Highfield, mischievously; "the Morgan excitement *, or the bank excitement?"

"Pshaw, Mr. Highfield, you are always ridiculing sentiment. I mean the excitement of powerful writing, powerful feeling, powerful passion, grief, joy, rage, despair, madness, misanthropy, pain, pleasure, anticipation, retrospection, disappointment, hope, and — and — every thing that creates excitement. By the bye, they say the author of Redwood † is coming out with a new novel. I wonder what it is about."

"I don't know," answered Highfield; "but I venture to predict it will be all that is becoming in a sensible, well-bred, well-educated, delicate woman, misled neither by a false taste nor affected sentiment."

* William Morgan, a member of the Masonic fraternity, abducted, and, it is supposed, murdered, in September 1826, by other masons, because he had intimated his intention of divulging certain secrets of the order. The incident, with subsequent investigation and discussion, caused a strong social and political agitation in the State of New York.

† Miss Sedgwick.

"Pooh!" said the great Puddingham, "there is no fire in her works."

"Nor brimstone either," said Highfield.

"Nor murder," said Miss Appleby.

"Nor powerful writing," said Miss Overend.

"Nothing to make the heart burst like a barrel of gunpowder," said little Mrs. Petticoats.

"Perhaps so," replied Highfield; "but a book may be worth something, without either fire, murder, or gunpowder, in it."

Here the discussion was cut short by the entrance of Mr. Goshawk, who bowed languidly to the company, walked languidly to a sofa, and, flinging himself listlessly down, leaned pensively upon his head, and sighed most piteously. Mr. Goshawk was one of the most extraordinary men living. He hated the world, yet could not live a day without attracting its notice in some way or other; he sighed for solitude, yet took every opportunity of being in a crowd; and, though confessedly the most miserable of mortals, was never so happy as when every body was admiring his secret sorrows. He had thrown himself accidentally by the side of Lucia.

"Ah! Mr. Goshawk," said she, "we've found you out!"

Goshawk knew as well what she meant as she did herself; but he looked at her with the most absent, vacant, ignorant wonder it was possible for any man to assume, as he answered,

"Found *me* out, Miss Lee?"

"Yes, yes; the verses — the beautiful verses, written with a diamond pencil, on the pane of glass. You need not deny it; nobody but yourself *could* have written such powerful poetry."

" No, no ; you can't deny it, Mr. Goshawk ; the . of Hercules is in it," cried Miss Appleby : and t. opinion was echoed by all present. Whereupon Mr. Goshawk acknowledged that, being that morning depressed by a dead weight of insupportable melancholy, he had walked forth into Miss Appleby's drawing-room, and, finding no one there, had relieved his overfraught heart, in those unpremeditated strains. The azures applied their cambric handkerchiefs to their eyes, and pitied poor Mr. Goshawk for labouring under such a troublesome excess of sentimental sadness.

The conversation then took a different turn, interrupted occasionally by the assurances of Mr. Goshawk, that his verses were all written under the impress of the moment ; though we, as authors knowing the secrets of all our brethren, are ready to make affidavit that he never wrote a line without cudgelling his poor brains into mummy, and spurring his Pegasus till his sides ran blood.

" So, there is a new Waverley coming out," quoth Puddingham, who was deep in booksellers' secrets ; " I am told, one of the principal characters is Charles the fifth."

" What, he that was beheaded at Whitehall-slip ? ", asked Mrs. Coates.

" No, my dear madam," said Highfield ; " he that resigned his crown before he lost his head."

" How I delight to read novels in which there is plenty of kings and queens ; 'tis so refined and genteel to be in such good society," said Miss Overend.

" I never get tired of kings and queens, let them be ever so stupid," said Miss Appleby ; " every thing they say is so clever, and every thing they do, so dignified."

"Well, for my part," said Highfield, "to me nothing is so vulgar an expedient of authorship, as that of introducing the reader into the society of great names, and making the bearers talk, not like themselves, but like the author. In this manner, Rochester becomes a dull debauchee; Bolingbroke, a prosing blockhead; and the greatest wits of the age, as stupid as the writer. I am tired of seeing this parade of regal and titled realities introduced as shadows to our acquaintance; and have it in serious contemplation, (unless I should happen to fall into a cureless, causeless melancholy), to write a novel, in which the principal actors shall be gods, and the common people, kings and queens. Queen Elizabeth shall lace Juno's corsets; Alexander the great, trim Jupiter's whiskers; Mary, queen of Scots, enact a beautiful bar-maid; and Charlemagne, a crier of Carolina potatoes."

"Then you don't mean to recognise any distinctions in mere mortal society?", asked Lucia, amused in spite of herself with this banter.

"Why, I don't know. I have some thoughts of a sort of geological, instead of genealogical, arrangement, to consist of the primitive, the secondary, and the alluvial. The fashionable primitives shall be those who carry their pedigrees back into oblivion — whose origin is entirely unknown; the secondary will consist of such as have not had time to forget their honoured ancestors; and the alluvial be composed of the rich washings of the other two, which have so lately made their appearance above water that there has been no time for them to become barren and good-for-nothing." Highfield was now called off by Miss Appleby.

Lucia appeared so much diverted with this whimsical arrangement that Goshawk, who, though the most abstracted of human beings, never for a moment forgot himself or his vanity, thought it high time to interfere.

"A clever young man that—a very clever young man," drawled he; "quite pleasant, but superficial—no energy, no pathos, no powerful passion, no enthusiasm, without which there can be no such thing as genius. Give me the man," cried he, with a fat and greasy flow of sonorous words,—"give me the man to whom the croaking of a cricket is the signal for lofty meditation, and the fall of a leaf a text for lorn and melancholy abstraction; one who is alone in the midst of a crowd, and surrounded when alone by myriads of sparkling imps of inspiration, millions of beings without being, and thoughts without thought; one to whom shadows are substances, and substances, shadows; to whom the present is always absent, the future always past; who lives, and moves, and has his being, in an airy creation of his own, and circulates in his own peculiar orb; who rejoices without joy, and is wretched without wretchedness; one, in short, who never laughs but in misery, or weeps except for very excess of joy—who lives in the world, a miserable yet splendid example of the sufferings endured by a superior being, when condemned to associate with an inferior race, and to derive his enjoyments from the same mean, miserable, five senses." Here he sunk back on the sofa, overpowered by his emotions.

"What a being!" thought Lucia, and fell into a painful doubt, whether such a being would ever condescend to think of her a moment, present or absent.

"He is above this world!" said she, and sighed a hundred times, to think of a man's being so much superior to his fellow-creatures.

CHAPTER VIII.

A GREAT FALLING OFF.

Returning home, our heroine threw herself on a sofa — be pleased to take notice she did not sit down, for that would have been unworthy a heroine — she threw herself on a sofa, and passed some time in sympathizing with the sufferings of Mr. Goshawk. She sighed for an opportunity of communing with him on the fathomless abyss of his mysterious miseries, and wished — O, how devoutly! — wished herself the privileged being destined at last to be the soother of his sorrows, the sharer of his thoughts, the companion of his reveries, and the better half of his abstract, inexplicable mystifications. "Would that I knew, that I could comprehend, what it is that makes him so wretched," thought Lucia, little suspecting that the poor gentleman himself would have been puzzled to tell her.

She was roused from this painfully-pleasing reverie by something which attracted her attention on the sofa. She looked at it, and rubbed her eyes — and rubbed her eyes and looked at it again. The thing was too plain, she could not possibly be deceived. She started up and rang the bell furiously, and, the servant not coming sooner than it was possible for him to come, she rang it again still more emphatically. At length Juba made his appearance, with his usual deliberation. An African gentleman of colour seldom indulges himself by being in a hurry.

"Who did that?" asked Lucia, pointing to the sofa.

Juba advanced, looked at the spot, and began to grin, with that redundant show of ivory peculiar to his race.

"Ah! Massa Fairwedder, Massa Fairwedder, he droll man, he."

"What! had Mr. Fairweather the impudence"—

"Ees, ees, he here dis mornin'," replied Juba, grinning more than ever.

Lucia immediately summoned the whole household, consisting of a troop of coloured ladies and gentlemen, whose principal business was to make work for each other. Ever since Lucia became azure, they had been suffered to do pretty much as they pleased, and it was their pleasure to do nothing but copy their young mistress in dress and behaviour as much as possible. They had a dancing-master in the kitchen, to teach them waltzing, and talked seriously of a masquerade, or a fancy-ball at least. The black cook was something of an azure herself, read all those useful little tracts which teach servants the duties of masters and mistresses, wore prunello shoes, and cooked dinner in an undress of black silk; the coachman was almost as sentimentally miserable as Mr. Goshawk; and Lucia's maid was a great admirer of Miss Wright.* The kitchen, as Dolly cook said, was quite a literary emporium, and there was always a greasy Waverley

* Fanny Wright, a "strong-minded woman" of the day.

lying on the window-sill, with which she occasionally regaled herself, while skinning an eel. The consequence of all this was that Mr. Lee's house was at sixes and sevens. There was neither master nor mistress; the ceilings of the parlour and drawing-room were festooned with cobwebs; the curtains got the jaundice; the rats overran the kitchen, and performed feats worthy of rational beings, if you could believe Dolly; and it was impossible to sit down on a chair or sofa, without leaving the print of the body in the dust which covered them. Poor Mr. Fairweather, who knew the value of neatness, and prided himself on his unspotted, unsullied black coat, had often carried off a tribute from the parlour, and, that morning, determined to give Lucia a broad hint. Accordingly he took his forefinger in his hand, and wrote in the dust that embellished the sofa four large letters, almost six inches long, that being put together constitute an abominable word, than which there is none more horrible and unseemly to the ear and eye of a good housewife. It was the sight of this that interrupted the deliciously-perplexing reverie of our fair heroine; that caused her to ring the bell with such emphasis; to call up the men-servants and maid-servants; to set the brooms, brushes, mops, and pope's-heads, going; and, finally, to declare war against rats, spiders, dust, and cobwebs, and to turn the whole house upside down. The servants wished Mr. Fairweather in Guinea, as soon as they traced the origin of this tremendous reform; the cook talked of the black skin and the white skin as being one in the eye of reason; the coachman sighed forth the unutterable agonies of a life of dependence; and the little jet-black waiting-maid talked elegantly about the rights of women. Juba insisted on his massa calling out Mr. Fairweather; but, on this occasion, the old gentleman demurred.

"Mr. Fairweather is my best friend, you blockhead."

"Guy, massa!, dat any reason why you should'nt blow he brain out?"

From that time forward, Mr. Lee's house became exemplary for its neatness. Such is the magic influence of a word to the wise! There was a reform in the whole establishment, the like of which hath never yet been brought about in the state, by any change of administration, since the establishment of the republic.

And here I deem it incumbent on me to offer to my azure and fashionable readers something like an apology for the falling-off in the tone of my narrative which they will not fail to observe in this chapter. I feel I ought to solicit their pardon for having thus descended abruptly to such vulgar matters as housekeeping; which ought to be for ever beneath the attention of all true lovers of literature and intellectual development. It is true that the goddess of wisdom once disputed with Arachne the management of the needle; but this was in times long past and never to return, before the preternatural development of the mind, the invention of flounces, or the supremacy of dancing-masters. I am aware, also, of the happy influence of a neat, well-arranged, and well-conducted household, in rendering home agreeable, and luring us from a too-zealous pursuit of the pleasures of the world; and I am not ignorant how important it is for the mistress of a family to know when things are well done, though it may not be necessary or becoming to do them herself. But I know, what is of far more consequence than all this, that if I prose any longer on such low subjects, the young gentlemen professors of nothing will inquire into my pedigree; and the azure angels, who preside over the decisions of all the gallant, fashionable critics, will pronounce me a horrid bore. A bore! — better were it to be convicted of robbing a church, or swindling to the amount of a few millions. I should then create a great public excitement; and rally round me, not only all the anti-masons, but an army of sympathetic pettifoggers besides.

CHAPTER IX.

AN ADVENTURE, BEING THE ONLY ONE IN ALL OUR HISTORY.

As the spring advanced, and the flowers, zephyrs, and warbling birds, invited out into the country for air and exercise, our heroine was accustomed to ride on horseback, than which there is nothing more healthful, graceful, and becoming in a woman, provided always she will only ride like a gentlewoman; that is, moderately. On the contrary, there is nothing which gives me more heart-felt discomposure, as a gallant bachelor, than to see a woman galloping through the streets, like a trooper — her feathers flying, her ribbons streaming to the wind, her riding-habit disordered, and herself bouncing up and down, as if she had a cork saddle under her. It is not only unbecoming and unfeminine, but dangerous, in our crowded streets; and nothing has preserved them from the most fatal accidents but the sagacity of their horses, which, doubtless, knowing the precious burthens they carry, are particularly careful neither to be frightened nor to make a false step. Were I to assume the office of mentor to the young fellows of the day, I would strenuously advise them to beware of a woman that always rides on a full gallop. Depend upon it, she will have her way in every thing; and, though she may not actually lose the bit, she will be apt to take it between her teeth — which is almost as bad.

On these occasions Lucia was generally accompanied by Miss Appleby, Miss Overend, or some one of her female friends, and escorted by Highfield and Goshawk, with the latter of whom our heroine generally fell into a tête-à-tête in the course of the ride. It was the third of May — I recollect it perfectly — when the little party of equestrians set forth on a morning ride, all gay and hopeful except Mr. Goshawk, to whom the smiles of nature were a disquiet, and the music of spring a discord. He was more than commonly miserable that day, having observed that Lucia began to sympathize deeply in his sorrows.

They worked their course safely through the various perils of Broadway, for some distance. They met a company of militia with more drums than privates, and commanded by three brigadier-generals; they encountered the great ox Columbus dressed in ribbons; they stood the brunt of kites, carts, bakers' wagons, omnibuses, charcoal-merchants, orange-men and ash-men, and beggar-women. In short, they escaped unhurt amid the war of sights, the eternal clatter and confusion of sounds, the unexampled concatenation of things animate and inanimate, natural and unnatural. The horses, indeed, sometimes pricked up their ears and wondered, but displayed no decided symptoms of affright, until, as ill-luck would have it, just as they came to the corner of Chambers street, a woman about four feet high issued suddenly forth from a shop, with a bonnet of such alarming dimensions and singular incongruity of shape and decoration, that Lucia's horse, who had never been at a fancy-ball, could stand it no longer. He wheeled suddenly round against Mr. Goshawk's steed, and reared. Mr. Goshawk was partly in a brown-study, and partly so miserable that he did not, as he afterwards affirmed, exactly recollect where he was, or what was the matter. At length he cried out, "Whoa!", with such a lofty and poetical fervour that he frightened the horse still more. He now reared worse than ever, and Lucia must have lost her seat in a few moments, when Highfield, who was a little in advance with the other ladies, being roused by Goshawk's exclamation, looked round, and was at the horse's head, on foot, in an instant. "Keep your seat if you can," said he, as he seized the bridle. A desperate contest now commenced between him and the horse, who continued rearing and plunging, both galling Highfield's body and limbs with his sharp hoofs and wrenching him violently about from side to side. Lucia still kept her seat, though almost insensible to what was going forward. It was a struggle between an enraged unruly beast and a cool determined man. Highfield still clung to the bridle, close to the horse's head, until, watching his opportunity, he seized the animal by the nostrils with so firm a gripe as to arrest his rearings for a moment, during which he seemed tremblingly to own a master. At the same instant a gentleman assisted Lucia to dismount, which she had scarcely done, when the animal, as if recovered from his astonishment, made one plunge, struck his hoofs into Highfield's breast, threw him on his back insensible, and dashed away full-speed. At the same moment Mr. Goshawk, who had been exceedingly active in protesting against the inhumanity of the crowd which stood looking on without being able to render any assistance, was likewise so overcome by his exertions that he lost his memory for a little while; after which he poured forth so eloquent a felicitation on Lucia's escape from a danger which, however slight, had harrowed up his very soul, that she remembered it long after, when she ought to have been remembering something else.

Highfield was brought to himself after a while, and, with the young lady, conveyed home in a hackney-coach. Goshawk did not accompany them; his senses were so shattered, and his feelings had so completely overpowered him, that he was incapable of any thing but the indulgence of high-wrought sentiment.

CHAPTER X.

THE TWO CUPIDS.

THE warm-hearted Mr. Lee, when he came to learn the particulars of the incident recorded in our last chapter, hugged Highfield in his arms, called him his son, and came very near letting out to his daughter the secret of his long-cherished intentions. He then fell upon the corporation, that unfortunate pack-horse, on whose back is saddled every abomination which petulance conjures into existence, or the itch for scribbling lays before the public.

"Confound the stupid blockheads!", exclaimed he. "They make laws against flying kites, exploding crackers, sticking up elephants over people's heads for signs, and cumbering the streets with empty boxes and barrels; and yet they allow the women to wear bonnets that frighten horses out of their discretion! For my part I don't see the distinction, not I."

"But, my good friend," said Mr. Fairweather, who had called in to make his friendly inquiries, "I differ with you — I think there is a marked distinction between a fine lady and an empty barrel."

"Oh well, if we differ, there is an end of the argument," quoth the other.

"An end of the argument! why, it is generally the beginning."

"Very well — very well — I have no time to argue the question now."

Mr. Fairweather took up his hat, and went away by himself, pondering in his mind what could have come over his old friend. It was the first time, since he knew him, that he had declined an argument.

Lucia and Highfield met the next morning; the former languid with her fright, the latter pale, and stiff with his bruises. Lucia was netting a purse. She thanked him, in simple, unaffected, heart-felt terms; for it is only affectation that deals in pompous phrases. The tears came into her eyes, as she noticed his wounded hands, and perceived, by the slight variations that passed over his countenance, that every motion was accompanied with acute pain.

"I shall never forget," said she, "that you saved my life."

"Nor I," said Highfield; and these two simple words were all he uttered on the subject.

Lucia was mortified that he should have missed so good an opportunity of being eloquent. She had been brought up with people who considered words of more consequence than actions, and a fine speech in celebration of an exploit of heroism far superior to the act itself. Lucia threw the purse carelessly into her work-basket; and just then Mr. Goshawk entered, to inquire how she did after the accident. Then it was that our heroine was lifted off her feet by a flow of inspired eloquence, which cast into the shade the manly simplicity of poor Highfield's courage and self-possession. He spoke of his horror at her danger — the overpowering feelings that absolutely bewildered his mind, and prevented his thinking of any thing but himself and his intense sufferings. He detailed his waking thoughts on coming home, and his terrible dreams, in which he saw her struggle with indescribable dangers, and performed acts in her behalf that no waking man ever imagined. In short, he made himself out the hero of the affair, and, before he had finished, actually persuaded Lucia that honest Highfield was but a secondary person in the business.

"Behold," said he, "how I employed the melancholy, soul-subduing, hours of the last night; for, you may suppose, I did not close my eyes."

"Oh, then I take it you dreamed with your eyes open," said Highfield, smiling.

"A man need not shut his eyes to dream, Mr. Highfield," quoth Goshawk, pompously, at the same time presenting Lucia with a perfumed sheet of paper. She opened it, and read, with sparkling eyes —

"The wings of my heart are far o'er the blue sea" —

"If the wings of his heart are far o'er the blue sea,
Permit me to ask where its legs ought to be,"

hummed Highfield, as he sauntered out of the room.

"He has no more sentiment, nor feeling, nor enthusiasm, nor genius, than — than" — Lucia could not hit upon a comparison expressive of her indignation.

"Alas! the more happy he!" sighed Fitzgiles Goshawk. "He knows not what it is to eat the bitter aloes of shattered hope, to dream of impossible attainments, to stand on tiptoe, catching at incomprehensible chimeras; to place his heart on what it dares not contemplate, except at an unapproachable distance that mocks even the imagination to despair; to die of disappointments, in what, from first to last, he knew was out of his reach; to pass from the sight of men, the light of the sun, and the perplexities of the world, and leave nothing behind him but an empty name. Oh! Lucia, pity me," cried he, taking her hand.

"I do, indeed I do," said Lucia, overpowered by this picture of mysterious griefs. "I pity, and would relieve you if I knew how. Only tell me — what is the matter?"

"I love — despairingly."

"Whom?" said Lucia, with a palpitating heart.

"One throned in yon galaxy of stars, brighter than Venus and purer than the milky way — one, of whom I wake only to dream, and dream only to awake in astonishment at my presumptuous visions — one so far above the sphere of my aspiring hopes, that, like the glorious sun, I only live in the consuming rays of her beauty, without daring to look in the full face of her brightness, lest I should be struck blind."

"Why, this must be a queen at least," said Lucia, blushing.

"The queen of love and beauty," replied Goshawk, delighted at his happy rejoinder. They remained silent a few moments, it being impossible to descend from the heights of sentimental twaddle to the level of ordinary matters, without stopping to take breath by the way.

"Tell me, Miss Lee, tell me what is love," said Goshawk at length, with a languishing air.

"I don't know," replied Lucia, in confusion.

"Shall I answer for you?", said Highfield, who entered at that moment. Lucia started a little, and Goshawk looked rather foolish.

"Love is a fantastic assemblage of the follies of childhood and the passions of age, — a little, scoundrel hypocrite, who, while rolling his hoop or chasing a butterfly, disguises, under the innocent sports of a boy, the most selfish and dishonourable intentions.

He is the deity of professions, disguises, affectation, and selfishness; is never satisfied unless acting in opposition to reason, propriety, and duty; and is pictured a child, because he studies only his own gratification, and never keeps his promises."

Goshawk seemed not to admire this sketch, but, for some reason or other, he was not so ready with a flight as usual. Lucia took up the defence of the little deity.

"Oh, what a monster you have made of him!", said she.

"But there is another and a nobler love," resumed Highfield, with more enthusiasm than he had ever before displayed in the presence of his cousin, — "there is another and a nobler love, the divinity of rational and virtuous man — a grown up, finished being, that knows no other wish than the happiness of its object; that neither lies, nor feigns, nor flatters, nor deceives; that is neither degraded by disappointment, nor presumptuous with success; that, while it respects itself, still pays a willing homage, and offers at the feet of its mistress, (what it never sacrificed to fear or favour, to the claims of man, the temptations of interest, or the tyranny of the passions), its own free-will and its power of independent action."

The tones of Highfield's voice were such as I have sometimes, but rarely, heard in my pilgrimage through this world of jarring discords; they were those that give to nonsense the charm of music, and to precept the magic of persuasion. He spoke with a manly simplicity, a chastened feeling, a firm and settled earnestness, which hypocrisy always overleaps and affectation only caricatures. Even childhood comprehends the difference, and the votaries of bad taste know the true from the false. The exertion of speaking, or, it may be, the glow of his smothered feelings, had banished for a moment his ashy paleness, and brought a fire into his cheek that added to his natural attractions. He stood with one arm in a sling, partly leaning against the mantel-piece, and there was in his whole appearance an evident struggle between the weakness of his body and the strength of his feelings.

Neither Mr. Goshawk nor Lucia made any reply. The former was cowed by the majesty of honest, unaffected manhood, giving utterance to its feelings with the simple energy of deep conviction; the latter felt as she had never felt while Mr. Goshawk was pouring out his sentimental flummery. She knew she was listening to one in earnest, who was either describing what he felt at the moment, or was capable of feeling. "He certainly must be in love with somebody. Some little red-cheeked, snub-nosed, country damsel, I dare say;" and she turned up her pretty Grecian nose at the poor girl. The perplexity of guessing who this somebody was occupied her some time, insomuch that she entirely forgot Mr. Goshawk's piece of poetry, and his beautiful language.

"I beg your pardon," said Highfield, "for coming here to interrupt you and make speeches. Your father requested me to say he wishes to speak with you, cousin."

Goshawk took his leave; Lucia sought her father, and Highfield his bed; for he was really much indisposed with his bruises.

CHAPTER XI.

SOUNDING WITHOUT BOTTOM.

MR. LEE was a man of great courage and little patience. He thought the heart of a woman like one of his eggs, that could be boiled in a minute and a half; and took it for granted Lucia must be deeply in love with Highfield since the adventure of the fashionable bonnet. Accordingly he determined to sound her forthwith, that no time might be lost. He might as well have plumbed the bottomless abysses of lake Superior; for the heart of a city belle in love is as unfathomable, if not as pure.

"Well, Lucia," said he, as she entered his library, "how do you feel after your fright?"

"Oh, quite well, sir."

"Hem — I wish I could say as much for Highfield. The doctor says he has some fever, and talks of bleeding — the blockhead — why didn't he do it before?"

"Bleeding!", cried Lucia, and her heart beat a little; "I hope it will not be necessary."

"Hem — yes. Ah! girl, you owe much to that excellent young man — hey?"

"I am sensible of it, sir, and feel it at the bottom of my heart."

"Do you? — do you, my dearest girl, at the bottom of your heart?"

"Indeed I do, sir; I shall never cease to be grateful, as long as I live."

"Grateful! — pish — pooh — gratitude!"

"My father has often told me gratitude was the

rarest of our feelings, and the most short-lived; but I shall carry mine to my grave."

"Ay — yes — yes; gratitude is a very good thing in its way; but — but there are so many ways of showing it. Now how will you show yours — hey?"

"Why, I haven't studied my part yet," said she, smiling; "I must trust to the honest dictates of my heart, to time, and circumstance, to show me the way."

"Pshaw! — time and circumstance! I believe the d——l is in you this morning, Lucia."

"I believe the deuse is in *you* this morning, father," said Lucia, smiling; "for I can't understand you."

"Very well, very well; but I want to know how you will go about showing your gratitude — hey?"

"Why, father," said Lucia, "if he is sad, I will play him merry tunes; if he is cheerful, I will laugh with him; if he is cross, I will bear with him. I will sympathize in his misfortunes, rejoice in his happiness, nurse him if he should be sick; if you turn him out of doors, as you once threatened, I will certainly let him in again; and if he should ever chance to want (what I trust in God he never will) your favour and protection, I will try and be to him your humble representative." If Lucia meant to say more, she was stopped by an unaccountable huskiness in her throat, that took away her breath.

"Ah! that will do — that will do!" cried the old gentleman, highly delighted; "and so you will love him — hey, girl? none of your wishy-washy gratitude — love him with all your heart — hey?"

"With all my heart, and as an only and beloved brother."

"Brother!, did you say?—a fiddle-stick; I—I don't want you to love him as a brother, I tell you."

"As a cousin then, sir."

"No; nor as a cousin, nor a second cousin, nor an uncle, nor grandfather, nor grandmother either," cried Mr. Lee, in wrath, and gradually raising his voice till he came to the climax of a roar.

"Ah! is it so?" thought our heroine, as at length she began to comprehend the drift of the impatient old gentleman; and she drew the impenetrable cloak of hypocrisy closely around her, at the same time conjuring up to her aid the guardian pride of female delicacy, which shrinks from the first avowal of love, and more than shrinks from owning it without the surety of answering love.

"May I go, sir?" said she, after a pause; "I promised to walk out this morning with my aunt and Mr. Goshawk."

"Confound Mr. Goshawk!—and may ten thousand of his bad verses fly away with him to Chaos and old Night, where they came from!"

"Well, father, then I will make an apology and stay at home."

"No; go where you please, and do what you please; I shall never be able to make any thing of you."

"Nothing, dear sir, but what I am—your dutiful and affectionate daughter;" and she bowed, and left Mr. Lee to congratulate himself on the progress he had made.

The reader will doubtless have observed that, during the whole of the foregoing dialogue, Lucia spoke in simple, natural language, without a single touch of azure. The reason is at hand. She felt what she was saying; and true feeling never declaims. What it has to say, it says with a simple, brief directness; as a man who is earnest in the race never stops to gather flowers by the way.

Our heroine retired to her chamber, to think. A new futurity was opened before her; for, until this interview with her father, she had never dreamed of his wishes or intentions in favour of her cousin. The truth is, her imagination was occupied with Goshawk. But now it was necessary to determine on some line of conduct in her future intercourse with Highfield. A very convenient, proper, family match!, thought she; I am rich, and he poor. I have no doubt he is very much in love with me; for I never heard of a young gentleman that was deficient in duty and affection on such occasions! And then her heart smote her with a pang, for such a thought. No, no; I will say that for my cousin, I do believe he would not marry, if he did not love, me, to gain my fortune or please my father. But then every-body will say he only married me for my money; and the mortification of such a suspicion would be intolerable. I dare say this plan has been in agitation ever since I was born; and what a business kind of business!—he is to open his mouth, and I am to fall plump into it, like a great over-ripe apple, without even being shaken a little. No, no, my dainty cousin, that won't do. And besides, what will Miss Appleby and all the rest say, if I throw myself away on a man of no literary reputation; who never figured in albums, or wrote verses on Passaic Falls; who does nothing common like an uncommon man; and who, though I confess he acts sometimes like a hero, talks just like every-body? "Ah!," said she, sighing, "I wish my money-bags were in the Red Sea, and then I could tell whether I was beloved for myself or them." This was a very foolish wish of our heroine; for, notwithstanding her beauty, her charming temper, and her natural good-sense, if her money-bags had been in the Red Sea, ten to one her admirers would have gone there to fish for them, instead of attending to her. After a vast many pros and cons, Lucia determined, in the true spirit of a woman with more than one suitor, to play them off against each other; to put to the test the ardour and stability of their passion, by trying what the patience of mortal man is capable of enduring. Mr. Goshawk was still paramount in her imagination; though, since the adventure of the ride, her feelings were somewhat enlisted on the side of Highfield. She was satisfied, in her own mind, that the former was deeply enamoured of her, else, why should he be so eloquent on all occasions on the subject of hopeless affection? With regard to the other, she was somewhat, indeed altogether, uncertain; for Highfield had too much pride, as well as delicacy, to be forever thrusting his feelings in the face of the world. I will try him, thought she. If he is only seeking me for my fortune, there will be no harm in making him a little miserable; and, if he really loves me for myself, I can always make him amends for his sufferings. She had an appointment with Mr. Goshawk for a walk, and was expecting him every moment, when the servant came in with an apology, that he was so unwell as not to be able to wait on her.

"Poor man," thought Lucia, "his mind is preying

on his delicate frame; the light is too intense for the lamp that contains it. What a misfortune it is to be born with too much sensibility!"

CHAPTER XII.

IN WHICH THE HISTORY IS PERFECTLY BECALMED.

Our heroine remained in a frame of mind requiring motion. She felt that sort of fidgeting impatience of repose which almost always accompanies the little perplexities and uncertainties of life. She took out the silk purse to net; but the thought struck her that Highfield might be too much elated if he saw her thus employed. She took up a book, and though it was one of the very latest fashionable works, she actually yawned over the first chapter. She then as a last resort took up a new garment, that had just been sent home by the mantua-maker; which fortunately gave a turn to her ideas. The sleeves were exactly the thing. She retired to her mysterious boudoir, and arrayed herself like King Solomon in all his glory. She put on a pink hat with a black velvet lining, and a feather that swept the ground; she put on her white satin cloak that hid her trim figure as effectually as a sack; and she incased her pretty ankles in spatterdashes. She arrayed herself with the foulard silk, the foulard damassé, the gros des Indes, the embroidered collar, cape, fichu, alavielle, and fiorelle — with the blonde gauze, and the decoupé gauze, the fancy ribbons, trimmings, &c., &c., &c. — in short she made herself one of the most beautiful fancy articles ever imported, before she had done. She then looked into a full-length mirror and saw that all was good: for her hat was mighty to behold, her shoulders broader than those of Samson with the gates of Gaza on his back, and not the African Venus herself — but hush, my muse, nor meddle too deeply with mysteries unknown to the sacred nine!

Highfield met her just as she was going forth into the Aceldama, the field of blood, the Flanders of the New World — BROADWAY — where more whiskered dandies have been slain outright by stout broad-shouldered ladies, and the empire of more hearts contested, than in all the universe besides. He stood in speechless admiration, for his cousin was really so beautiful that it was out of the power of milliner or mantua-maker to make her look ugly.

"Will you take me with you?" said he.

Lucia felt like the ox-eyed Juno, in her glorious paraphernalia.

The most unpropitious moment for approaching a belle is doubtless when she is full-dressed for Broadway. She treads on air; she sees herself reflected in the too-flattering mirror of her imagination; the rustling of silks whispers an alarum to her vanity; and the waving of feathers is the signal for conquering the world.

"Will you take me with you?", repeated Highfield.

How handsome and interesting he is, thought our heroine as she looked at herself in the glass. If he only had whiskers he would be irresistible.

"I am afraid," said she, "the weather is too keen

for you this morning; you look pale, and don't seem well;" — and nature forced her voice into a tuneful sympathy.

"Oh, I never was better in my life."

"Well, it is not my business," said she, again assuming the woman — "If you choose to risk it, 'tis nothing to me." And the father of hypocrisy himself could not have put on a more freezing indifference. "I am going to call on Miss Appleby; my aunt promised to meet me there."

"I'd rather go any where else with you."

"Oh, yes; I know you don't like literary people."

"I don't like pretenders to literature."

"Then let me go by myself," said she abruptly.

"No — I'll go, and take the mighty Goshawk by the beard, e'en though he were a metaphor, as saith our azure aunt."

This sally made Lucia smile, and restored her good-humour, which indeed was never long away. Her anger was never chronic, and so much the better. An unforgiving woman is worse than a man that forgives every body. Lucia put her arm within Highfield's, and they went away, as gay as boblincons in a clover meadow. Lucia forgot for a moment her plan of making him jealous; but there was a little imp of mischief at her elbow that soon put her in mind of it again.

CHAPTER XIII.

MORE AZURE.

HIGHFIELD and our heroine dropped in upon the whole azure coterie, at Miss Appleby's, with the exception of Mr. Fitzgiles Goshawk, whose absence afforded an excellent subject for declamation; especially when Lucia informed the company he was indisposed.

"Poor fellow, his sensibilities will be the death of him at last," cried Miss Appleby.

"Unfortunate youth," said Miss Overend, "his wretchedness is mysteriously affecting. By the bye, can any body tell what makes him so unhappy?"

"I dare say he is suffering the pangs of disappointment," said Puddingham.

"Disappointment in what?", said she, briskly.

"Oh, why, you know genius is always hoping impossible things, and chasing the rainbows of imagination — ever anticipating unreal joys, and reaping real sorrows. I knew a man of genius once, a great poet, who pined himself into a decline because he could not get his whiskers to grow."

"La!" said Miss Overend, "I dare say that is the cause of Mr. Goshawk's interesting melancholy; you know he has no whiskers."

"I dare say," quoth Paddleford — a sighing, whining, cork-hearted pretender to sentimental rouéism — "I dare say the poor fellow is in love with a married woman."

"Has he been to Italy?", said Miss Overend; "if

he has, I could almost swear he had fallen in love with a beautiful nun he saw through the grates of a convent."

"I shouldn't be surprised," said Mrs. Coates, "if he had committed murder."

"Murder!" screamed the other ladies.

"I mean an innocent, disinterested, sentimental murder, committed in a moment of irrigation, without any intention — what do you think, nephew?"

"I rather think it must be the whiskers, as my friend Puddingham suggested. I feel myself in the same predicament, and am sentimentally dead, for want of a muzzle *à la mode de bison*."

Lucia privately resolved that Master Highfield should pay for making sport of the hallowed and mysterious sorrows of Mr. Goshawk. She knew, or thought she knew, their origin. And to have the perplexities of pining, speechless, inexpressible passion, associated with a bison's whiskers — it was too bad! And her cousin should pay for it dearly, if he possessed the least spark of feeling. Highfield took his leave soon after, excusing himself on the score of business. But the truth was, he felt himself somewhat ailing.

"Well, Lucia," said Miss Appleby, "I suppose you had a delightfully affecting interview with your cousin, after the affair. What did he say?"

"Nothing," said Lucia.

"Nothing? What a stupid man! Why, Mr. Goshawk talked of his excruciating feelings on the occasion, till he brought tears into my eyes. Oh, such a beautiful flow of language, such powerful delineations of passion! I wish you had heard him."

" Mr. Highfield is a very common-place man," said Puddingham, pompously. " You might stand under a gate-way a whole day in a shower, without hearing him say any thing remarkable."

" What is a chance act of gallantry and presence of mind, compared with the genius that immortalizes it in words that burn and thoughts that freeze? For my part, give me the man that talks eloquently," said Mr. Paddleford.

" Yes," said Miss Overend; " mere physical courage and animal strength may *do* great things; but to *say* great things, requires the aid of a lofty, inaccessible genius, which nine times in ten is so immersed in its own sublime chrysalis, that it can't get out in time to do any thing in a case of emergency."

" To be sure," said Mrs. Coates; " a great action is often frustificated by a splendid chaotic congeries of intellectual vapours, that produce a deflection of the mind from the object before it."

Lucia, though a little affronted with Highfield, was too generous to suffer him to be undervalued in this manner, especially in his absence.

" And so, my good friends," said she, " you would persuade me that I am more indebted to Mr. Goshawk, for his elegant description of my danger, than to my cousin, who rescued me from it. I might have been in my grave by this time but for my cousin."

" But then what a beautiful elegy Mr. Goshawk would have written, my dear. You would have been immortalized. Only think of that!" said Miss Appleby.

" Yes," replied Mrs. Coates; " what is the trumpery pain of anneeheelation to the eternal immortality of living in immortal verse — of floating down upon th(stream of oblivion, into the regions of never-dyin; brightness!" Mrs. Coates waxed more azure ever day.

"My dear aunt," cried Lucia, interrupting the gr lady, who was losing herself in a Dismal Swamp grandiloquence — "my dear aunt, I am aware of superiority of words over deeds, in an age of de opment like the present, and that he who performs great action is but an instrument in the hands of th man of genius who celebrates it in never-dying verse I know too that it is mere selfishness on our part, to feel grateful for an action done in our own behalf, instinctively perhaps, and without one single good feeling on the part of him who performs it; still there is something in the gift of life that seems to deserve at least our gratitude." This was the most azure speech our heroine had made since her accident.

"The gift of life!" cried Paddleford; — "what is life, that we should be grateful for it? A scene of disappointment without hope, and hope without disappointment; a chapter, whose beginning is tears, whose last verse is written in blood; a mirror, which presents to us every day a new wretch in the same person; a spectral shadow, ever changing, yet still the same; a long lane, whose windings end where they began, and begin where they end; a rope twisted with our heart-strings, embalmed in our tears, and having at one end a slip-noose with which all mankind are at last tucked up!"

"Oh!" groaned the whole azure coterie, horror-stricken at this soul-harrowing picture.

"What language!"

"What sentiment!"

"What feeling!"

"What soul-subjewing retrospections!" exclaimed Mrs. Coates. "What a happy devilopement of mind!"

Lucia was overawed and silenced by the eloquence of Paddleford and the suffrages of all the company. She became doubtful, to say the least, as to the propriety of feeling gratitude for such a worthless gift as that of life, and relapsed into a decided preference of the gift of speech over the capacity for action. She looked on the great Paddleford as a most sublime mortal; for such indeed is the intrinsic dignity of that courage which defies death in a good cause, that even the affectation of contempt of life imposes a feeling of respect upon the inexperienced. Lucia never dreamed that Paddleford came near breaking his neck a few nights before, by jumping out of a second-story window on a false alarm of fire; or that, while professing scorn of death, he never met a funeral or heard a bell tolling, without a fit of the blue devils.

"What a beautiful dress you've got!" said Miss Overend to Lucia.

The sublime contempt of this life now suddenly gave place to an admiration of the things of this life. The whole party gathered round our heroine; and, "Where did you get this?", and, "La! how cheap!", and dissertations on the relative excellence of gros de Naples, gros des Indes, cotepaly, foulard damassé, and Palmerienne, gradually restored them to a proper feeling of resignation to the evils of this world.

CHAPTER XIV.

A VISIT, AND ITS CONSEQUENCES.

WHEN Lucia came home, she found Highfield had been obliged to lie down; and learned, from Mr. Lee, that the doctor was under great apprehension that he had received some serious injury internally, from the violence of his exertions or the kicks of the horse, in the adventure of the ride.

"I am sorry to hear it," said our heroine, and her heart echoed the sentiment.

The old gentleman was of that order of human beings whom sorrow always makes angry and fretful, instead of gentle and submissive. He had a most confirmed and obstinate impatience of grief. He was angry with Highfield for being ill; he was angry with the doctor for not having foreseen he would be ill; and he was enraged with Mr. Fairweather, because he at first made light of the matter, and then, to please his friend, hinted about a rapid decline. Now, he could not scold Highfield for being ill; nor the doctor, for he was absent; nor Mr. Fairweather, because he was not present: so he set to work, and scolded Lucia. Nine times out of ten we are not angry at the thing we pretend to be affronted with; we attack the substance under cover of the shadow.

"Oh yes!", said he in reply to Lucia's gentle yet sincere expression of sorrow, — "Oh yes! you are very sorry, I dare say. You take him into a cold north-east wind; you drag him about to milliners' shops, from one end of the town to the other; and then you are very sorry he is sick, when you yourself have made him so."

"Dear father, how cross you are to day! I am sure I did not take him out. I wanted him to stay at home; but he said he was perfectly well, and would go with me. I am sure I couldn't help his going."

"Not help his going!"

"No, sir; how could I?"

"Why, you might have knocked the puppy down."

Lucia made it a point never to laugh at her father; but it must be owned he sometimes put her to hard trials.

"If my father had taught me to box, instead of to play the piano, I might have made the attempt," said she, smiling.

"Very well, very well; you have made him sick, now try if you can't cure him. Go and make him some barley-broth."

"I? — why, my dear father, I don't know how to make barley-broth."

"Well then, go and make him some caudle."

Lucia had never heard of caudle, except in association with certain matters, and blushed like a rose.

"But I don't know how to make caudle, any more than barley-broth."

"Ay, yes; women know nothing worth knowing, nowadays. They can dance, and play the harp, and criticise books, and talk about what they don't understand; but if you want them to do a little thing for the comfort of a man's life, or the assuaging of his pains, oh! then it is, 'My dear sir, I don't know how to do it.' I wish I had sent you to a pastry-cook's, instead of a boarding-school. I dare say, if it was

Mr. Goshawk, you could talk him well directly. Go in then, and talk to your cousin a little."

"My dear father, you know" —— and she stopped short, in a flutter.

"What, you won't go and see the youth who is lying perhaps on his death-bed of wounds received in your service?"

"The customs of society, sir," ——

"Ah! the customs of society — there is another wooden god to bow down to! You can twine your arms in a waltz with some bewhiskered foreign puppy; you can go to a masquerade, or mix in midnight revels, with a thousand promiscuous sweepings of the universe, and yet — oh, the customs of the world! they make it a crime to visit the sick in their melancholy chambers, and pronounce it ungenteel to know how to administer relief to their sufferings!"

"Dear father, I would do any thing for the relief of my cousin; but" ——

"Oh, ay — any thing. You can't do what the customs of society permit, and you won't do what they do not sanction. And yet it was but the other day you made such a fine speech: — 'If he is sad, I will play him merry tunes; I will sympathize in his sorrows, and rejoice in his happiness; I will nurse him when he is sick; and if, as you once threatened, you should turn him out of doors, I will certainly let him in again.'" And the old gentleman caricatured her tone and manner without mercy. "You know every thing but what you ought to know," continued he, reproachfully.

"There is at least one thing I do know," replied the daughter, — "that it is my duty to obey the wishes of my father, when no positive duty forbids it. I will go with you, sir." And together they went into the sick man's room.

My friend, Mr. Lee — for there once lived such a man, and he was my friend — my friend, Mr. Lee, knew no more how to manage a love-affair than his daughter did of the manufacturing of caudle. Had the romance of Highfield and Lucia been in the best possible progress, he would have gone nigh to throw it back a hundred years. The old gentleman had yet to learn, that to make a woman do a thing against her will is like shoving a boat against a strong current; she will move a foot or two, slowly, while the impulse lasts, and come back like a race-horse, a hundred yards beyond the starting-pole. And yet he ought to have known it; for his wife had verified its truth often enough to impress it on his memory.

Lucia entered the chamber of the invalid somewhat against her will, and consequently but little disposed to sympathize with him. Indeed she felt extremely awkward; and this was another reason why she was not in the best possible humour. Not that she wanted a proper feeling of the benefit conferred by her cousin, but, the truth is, the indiscreet disclosure the old gentleman had made of his intentions caused her to shrink from an act which might be considered as amounting to a sanction of his wishes on her part. Add to this, I believe if the truth were known, she felt some little apprehension that Mr. Goshawk might not approve of the procedure.

The conduct of Highfield contributed to render her still more ungracious. He was no knight-errant, yet the sight of our heroine on this occasion threw him into something of a paroxysm, not unworthy of Amadis de Gaul. He ascribed the visit in the first place to her own free-will, and augured the most favourable results from the sympathy which a sight of his weakness would create. He was wrong in both cases; for, in love-matters, the imagination is every thing, and seeing is not believing. But his great error was in discovering so much gratitude for the visit that Lucia became alarmed at her own condescension, and determined to retrieve her error by behaving as ungraciously as her conscience would permit. In pursuance of this truly womanly resolution, she conducted herself with a most admirable indifference, insomuch that the good gentleman, her father, who had hardly patience to wait the boiling of an egg, became exceedingly restive. He gave his daughter divers significant looks; favoured her with abundance of frowns; and held up his finger from time to time so emphatically, that Highfield soon comprehended the whole affair. He perceived that Lucia had come unwillingly, and from that moment felt nothing but mortification at her having come at all. The whole affair ended in making Lucia dissatisfied with herself; Highfield worse than before; and Mr. Lightfoot Lee most intolerably angry. So much for obliging a young lady to do what she has no inclination for. Our heroine, having paid a short visit, retired, leaving the uncle and nephew together.

The old gentleman sat with his nether lip petulantly protruded over the upper one, his eyebrows raised, and his forehead wrinkled. The young man lay on his bed, supported by pillows.

"My dear uncle," said he, "why did you bring my cousin here against her will?"

"'Sblood sir," cried the other in a fury — "I suppose you mean to cut my throat for trying to do you a favour."

"I am sensible of your kindness, but, my dear sir, you don't go the right way to work to serve me."

"O no, not I, truly; I am an old blockhead; I am always in the wrong; I do nothing but mischief, and merit nothing but reproaches and ingratitude!"

"Ah! sir, if you only knew my heart!"

"Plague on your heart, I don't believe you have any, with your infernal coolness and patience. When I fell in love, I mounted my horse, and rode one night forty miles to visit your aunt; came to an understanding the very first visit; and went home irrevocably engaged. I hate suspense; I always did hate it, and always shall. But you, sir — dam'me, you sir!, you and Lucia will make a hard frost between you. She is all affectation, and you all patience. A patient lover — pooh!"

"But, my dear sir, why don't you let matters take their course, as you promised?"

"O certainly, sir, certainly — wait patiently, until I see my daughter run away with Mr. Fitzgiles Goshawk, because he has such a flow of words and uses such beautiful language; or till I sink under the weight of fourscore, and Lucia becomes a pedantic old maid. I dare say if I only have patience and live to the age of the patriarchs, I may have the particular satisfaction of seeing either the world or your love-affair come to an end."

"But, my dear uncle —"

"Yes, yes — I am an old blockhead, that's certain. 'Tis true, I was educated at the university; travelled over half Europe; have been a justice of the peace; a common-councilman; secretary to a literary society; a judge of a race-course; and chairman of a committee in Congress. I am not quite threescore, to be sure; but I have had some little experience — know a B from a bull's foot, and a hawk from a handsaw. But I am an old blockhead for all that, and must go to school to a conceited graduate from a country college, and a sage young lady just from the boarding-school; yes, yes, yes — " and the good gentleman walked about the room with his head down and hands behind him.

" Oh, sir, I entreat you to spare me."

" I wonder," continued Mr. Lee, communing with himself, " I wonder how people managed to live, sixty years ago. No steamboats, nor spinning-jennies, nor railroads, nor canals, nor anthracite coal, nor houses of refuge, nor societies for making the world perfect in every thing, nor silver forks, nor self-sharpening pencils, nor metallic corn-cutters, nor japan blacking, nor gros de Naples, nor gros des Indes, nor cotepaly, nor any of the indispensable requisites to a comfortable existence. What a set of miserable sinners they must have been! I don't wonder, for my part, that children govern their parents, and the young the old; seeing the world is so much wiser, better, and happier, than it was, sixty years ago." Thus the good gentleman ran on, as was his custom, until he finally lost sight of his subject and cooled in the pursuit.

" Well, my dear uncle, if you wont listen to me — "

" But I will listen; who told you, sir, I wouldn't listen — I suppose you want me to do nothing else — hey ? "

"I wanted to tell you, sir, that, I see plainly, myself and my concerns are destined to give you great and I fear unavailing trouble, and have come to a resolution —"

"Well, sir, and what is it?"

"I intend, as soon as I am well enough, to leave you, my dear uncle."

"Well, sir —"

"I have been too long a dependant on your kindness, and cannot but perceive my remaining here will be a source of contention between you and my cousin. I fear I shall never be able to touch her heart; and without the free, uninfluenced gift of her affections, I would not receive her as my wife, were she descended from heaven and with an angel's dower."

"Well, sir ?," said Mr. Lee, in breathless impatience and anger.

"I have little more to say, uncle. When I am well enough, I will endeavour to do justice to my feelings of gratitude for all that I owe you."

"And so — and so, sir, you mean to leave me, now that you have got out of the egg-shell, and can walk alone. If you do, by all that is sacred, I'll disinherit you."

"I have no claim to your estate, sir. I would consent to share it with my cousin, did her heart go with your bounty; but I will starve sooner than rob her of a shilling."

"Will nothing move you to stay with me till I am dead?", said Mr. Lee, overpowered by his feelings.

"One thing, and one only, sir. I will remain with you and be to you as a son, if you will promise on your honour that my cousin shall neither be worried, nor urged, nor entreated in any way against her inclinations; and that I myself may be left to the direction of my own sense of honour and propriety in this business. To make my cousin uneasy is not the way to win her heart, and, even if it were, it is not the mode to which I would descend."

"Well then, I do promise; I pledge my word that you shall do as you please in this affair, and that Lucia shall have her own way in every thing but in marrying that puppy sentimental, master Fitzgiles Goshawk."

"And I pledge myself, that, living or dying, so far as my actions are concerned, you shall never have reason to repent your kindness to me."

Here the conversation ended. Mr. Lee retired, and Highfield stretched himself on his bed, overcome with a weakness and perplexity of heart.

CHAPTER XV.

MUTUAL MISTAKES AND DECEPTIONS. — MR. LEE MEDITATES A MOST DARING EXPLOIT.

THE exertion and emotions of Highfield in the preceding conversation, concurring with his pain and weakness of body, brought on a dangerous fever, which confined him several weeks. During this period Lucia entirely intermitted her intercourse with the azure coterie, and saw Mr. Goshawk but once, when he came unshaven, with dishevelled locks, neglected costume, and various other insignia of a despairing lover. He talked of himself, his depression of mind, his distress at the danger in which he saw her at the time her horse was rearing and plunging. But Lucia just now was deeply touched with the danger of Highfield, and remembered that, while Goshawk had only felt, the other was suffering for his exertions to preserve her life. True feeling and real sorrows open our eyes to the full detection of those that are the spurious product of ennui or affectation, and enable us to see distinctly into the hypocrisy of others' hearts, by putting them to the test of a comparison with our own. What Lucia now felt satisfied her that her former feelings were rather reflected from the society to which she was accustomed, and the false colouring in which their false sentiment was enveloped, than from her own heart. The subjection of her excellent understanding to a long habit of associating with caricatures of literary taste, and mawkish imitations of genius and sensibility, was gradually undermined by an estrangement of some weeks, and a communion with those who felt as nature dictated, and expressed their feelings in the language of truth.

In addition to this, we hold it to be utterly impossible for any woman that ever claimed descent from simple, tender-hearted mother Eve, to behold a man suffering pain and sickness, without feeling that sympathy which renders woman, savage and civilized, wherever and in whatever circumstances she may be found, the assuager of sorrows — the nurse of calamity — the angel spirit that watches over the dying and the dead. If perchance it happen that this heaven-descended sympathy with suffering is coupled with a feeling of gratitude for some great benefit, and a consciousness that this suffering is in consequence of exertions made in her behalf, we confess we can hardly believe it possible that this natural tenderness of heart, and this feeling of gratitude, should not in the end combine to produce a still stronger sentiment, more especially in favour of a young, handsome, and amiable man. We should for these reasons be inclined to discard our heroine entirely and for ever from our good graces, had not the present crisis of affairs awakened her better self, and recalled her in some degree to the destiny for which nature had intended her.

It was more than four weeks before Highfield was decidedly out of danger. During this period he had endured much, and nature occasionally took refuge in that blessed delirium which, however painful to the observer, is a heaven of oblivion to the weary sufferer. It was at these times, when he knew nobody, and could interpret nothing which he saw or heard, that the pride and delicacy of Lucia would yield to the impulses of her heart, and she would watch for hours at his bedside, moisten his parched lips, smooth his pillow, dispose his aching head in easy positions—and once, only once, she kissed his damp cold forehead. There was nothing violent in his delirium; his wanderings were low and disjointed murmurs, connected, as far as they could be understood, with recollections of his cousin. Sometimes he would pause, and fix his unsteady wandering eyes upon her, as if some remote consciousness crossed his mind; but it was only a momentary effort of memory, and died away in the wild wanderings of a diseased imagination.

The crisis of the fever passed over, leaving Highfield a wreck, just without the gates of death. But youth and a good constitution at length triumphed, and he became convalescent. As he recovered possession of his reason, Lucia discontinued her watchings, and confined herself within the limits of ordinary attentions. Highfield sometimes thought of a confused dream, a vision of a distempered mind, representing an angel hanging over his couch and administering to his wants; but the impression gradually passed away, and he remained ignorant of the truth until long afterwards. Mr. Lee had been in a passion during the whole period of Highfield's danger, and the doctor had no peace, day or night. If he talked about bleeding or a warm bath, Mr. Lee called him a Sangrádo; if he suggested any of the ordinary remedies, he was an empiric; and if he thought of any experiment, he was a quack. In short, the poor man led a terrible life until his patient got better, when the old gentleman grew into vast good-humour, and nothing could equal his conviction of the doctor's skill. Juba, indeed, insisted that he himself had a principal hand in the cure, by concocting an African obeah of the most sovereign virtue; but his master only called him a blockhead, and sent him about his business; whereupon old Ebony went his way, muttering something that sounded not unlike "calling massa out."

It was now the beginning of June, when the infamous easterly winds, that spoil the genial breath of spring with chilling vapours, generally give place to the southern airs of summer. Lucia and Highfield had resumed their intercourse, but with no great appearance of cordiality. Highfield remained ignorant of the cares she had lavished and the tears she had shed while he was unconscious of every thing, and Lucia, fearful that he might possibly know it, shrunk with a timid consciousness from all appearance or indication of that deep feeling which late events had wakened in her bosom. He resolved, in the recesses of his mind, to refrain in future from every attention to his cousin, but such as their relationship demanded; and she secretly determined to hide the strong preference she now felt, under the impenetrable mask of cool indifference. I will not, said Highfield, mentally — I will not appeal to her gratitude or pity, for what her love denies. I, thought Lucia, scorn to repay with love, a debt of gratitude to one who seems to think that alone sufficient. Neither of them suspected the other's feelings, and pride stepped in to complete their blindness.

The consequence was, that, finding each other's society irksome and unsatisfactory, they avoided all intercourse but such as was indispensable. Highfield sought every opportunity of being from home; and Lucia was more than ever in the company of Mr. Goshawk, who became every day more miserable and incomprehensible. He talked of smothered feelings in a voice of thunder, and sighed with such emphasis, that he on one occasion dislodged a geranium pot from a front window, and came very near breaking the head of a little chimney-sweep who was sunning himself below. But Lucia, though she encouraged his affectations, from an indefinite desire to be revenged on Highfield for she knew not what, began to sicken a little at his superlative azure. Of late she had become too well acquainted with the substance of feeling and passion to be deluded by the shadow, and sometimes, amid the depression of her mind, felt a great inclination to laugh at the mighty Goshawk and his mighty verbosity. This heartless intimacy contributed still more to estrange Highfield from home and her society; for, unacquainted as he was with her real feelings, he believed in his heart that his cousin had a decided prepossession for the empty sentimentalist. He had never altogether recovered his strength or his colour; there was a paleness in his face, a lassitude about his frame, and a slow languor of motion, which gave to his appearance a touching interest; and Lucia, as she sometimes watched him without being seen, felt the tears on her eyelashes, as she noticed the wreck of his youth, and recalled to mind to what it was owing. Thus then matters stood: — Highfield was only waiting the return of his strength, to make a final effort to disengage himself from the family and pursue his fortune; Goshawk was daily meditating whether he should sell the old gentleman's lands and buy stock, when he married Lucia and succeeded to the estate; and Lucia was daily losing her vivacity, in the desperate attempt to be gay.

But what became of Mr. Lightfoot Lee all this while? The old gentleman was in the finest quandary imaginable. He grew so impatient there was no living with him, and quarrelled with Juba forty times a day. There was nobody else he could quarrel with. Mrs. Coates had gone to pay a visit to Hold Hingland, and renew her acquaintance with Sir Richard Gammon and Sir Cloudesley Shovel; Mr. Fairweather had gone to see the Grand Canal; and to Highfield he was bound by a solemn promise not to say any thing on the subject nearest his heart. Never was man so encumbered to the very throat with vexations, that almost choked him for want of a vent. Notwithstanding, he had a most ingenious way of letting off a little high steam now and then. If he happened to encounter a beggar-woman at his door, he sent her about her business, with a most edifying lecture on idleness, unthrift, and intemperance; if a dog came in his way, he was pretty sure of a kick; if a door interposed, it might fairly calculate upon a slam; and if the weather was any way deserving of reproof, it might not hope to escape a philippic. Unfortunately for Mr. Lee he had no wife, to become the residuary legatee of his splenetic humours; but then he made himself amends, by falling upon the corporation for suffering the swine to follow their instinct of wallowing in the mud, and for furnishing mud for them to wallow in; for not taking up the beggars, and for taking up so much time in passing laws instead of seeing to the execution of those already passed; for allowing the little boys to fly kites in the street; for spending money in monuments and canal celebrations; and for every thing that ever occurred to the imagination of a worthy old gentleman, who compounded for his mouth being shut on one subject, by declaiming upon a thousand others about which he did not care a fig.

He could not help seeing that his favourite project was in a most backsliding condition, and that every day Lucia was less with Highfield and more with Goshawk. Whereupon he gathered himself together, and uttered a tremendous libel upon literary pretenders, rhyming fops, empty declaimers, and sentimental puppies. Nay, he spared not the azures themselves, but pronounced their condemnation in words of such horrible atrocity, that I will not dare the responsibility even of putting them on record. I will not deny, however, that in the midst of his blasphemies he said some things carrying with them a remote affinity with common-sense. He affirmed that there was among the women of the present fashionable world a hollow affectation of literature — an admiration of affected sentiment and overstrained hyperbole; that they placed too little value on morals, and too much on manners; that an amiable disposition, together with all the qualities essential to honourable action, were held in little consideration, while they paid their court to the most diminutive dwarf of a genius, and listened with exclusive delight to frothy declamations, the product of empty heads and hollow hearts, alike devoid of manly firmness or the capacity to be useful in any honourable rank or situation. He reproached them, most bitterly, with being the dupes of false sentiment and affected sorrows; and finally concluded his diatribe by giving it as his settled opinion, that the present system of female education was admirably calculated to make daughters extravagant, wives ridiculous, and mothers incapable of fulfilling their duties. But I entreat my beloved female readers to recollect, that all this was soliloquized in a passion by an elderly gentleman, born long before the invention of steam-engines and spinning-jennies, and that I only place it on record for the purpose of showing what a prodigious "development of mind" has taken place in the world since Mr. Lee received his early impressions.

The good gentleman sat himself down in his library, and fell into a deep contemplation on the course proper to be pursued in this perplexing state of his domestic affairs. He pondered it, at least half an hour. At length he started up with almost youthful alacrity, and rung the bell. In due time, that is, in no very great haste, King Juba made his appearance.

"Juba," said Mr. Lee, "bring out my best blue coat, buff waistcoat, and snuff-coloured breeches. I am going to dress."

"No time yet, massa, to dress for dinner," said Juba.

"I tell you, bring out my best suit, you obstinate old snowball — I am going to pay a visit to a lady."

"A lady, sir, massa!"

"Ay, a lady — is there any thing to grin at, in my visiting a lady, you blockhead?"

"Juba," quoth Mr. Lee, while dressing himself, "Juba, how old am I?"

"Massa fifty-eight, last grass."

"No such thing, sir, I'm just fifty-five, not a day older. How should you know any thing about it?"

"Why, I only saw massa, de berry day he born — dat was — ay, let me see, was twenty-second day of —"

"Hold your peace, sir; you've lost your memory, as well as all the five senses, I believe."

"Well, well, no great matter if massa two, tree year older or younger — all de same a hundred years hence."

"But it is matter I tell you, sir. I'm going to be married."

"Married!", echoed Juba, his white eyes almost starting out of his ebony head — "married!" He saw at a glance such a resolution would be fatal to his supremacy.

"Ay, married; is there any thing so extraordinary in that?"

"But what Miss Lucy say to dat, massa?"

"I mean to disinherit her."

Juba's eyes opened wider than ever, and he thought to himself the debil was in his massa.

"What young massa Highfield say to dat?"

"I don't care what he says; I mean to disinherit him, too."

"Whew — whew!" was the reply of old Ebony. "Massa tell me what lady he hab in he eye?"

"Miss Appleby."

"Miss Applepie too young for old massa."

Juba had been long accustomed to call Mr. Lee "old massa," without giving offence, but now the phrase was taken in high dudgeon.

"Old master! — you blockhead, who gave you the liberty of calling me old? I'm only fifty-five, and Miss Appleby is twenty-four; the difference is not great."

"Yes; but when Miss Applepie fifty-five, where old massa be den?" quoth Juba.

This was a home question. Mr. Lee dismissed Juba, and sat down to calculate where he should be when Miss Appleby attained to the age of fifty-five. The result was altogether unsatisfactory. He again rung for Juba, and directed him to put up his best suit again.

"I have put off my visit till to-morrow."

"Massa better put him off till doomday," quoth Juba to himself; and so massa did.

CHAPTER XVI.

OUR HERO DETERMINES ON A VOYAGE.

There never was a man, or woman either, that found such difficulty in keeping silence on what was uppermost in the heart, as Mr. Lee, or who had more ingenious ways of giving side hits, and uttering wicked innuendoes. He never on any occasion missed an opportunity of launching out against addle-pated rhymesters, boys that thought themselves wiser than their betters, and girls who talked sentiment and forgot their duty. If Goshawk uttered a word of azure, he cried "Pish!"; if Lucia talked sentiment, he ejaculated some other epithet of mortal contempt; and if Highfield said any thing about honour or independence, he called him a puppy.

In the mean time matters were growing worse and worse every day. Goshawk ventured to hint pretty distinctly the nature and object of his mysterious sorrows; Lucia treated her cousin with increasing coolness; and Highfield looked paler and paler. Unable to bear his situation any longer, he one morning — it was the day after Lucia had given the watch-chain she had promised him, to Goshawk, before his very eyes — he one morning took the opportunity of being left alone with his uncle, to announce to him, that, being now sufficiently recovered from his indisposition. it was his intention to visit his relatives in the South, and spend some time with them. "Perhaps, indeed, I may not return at all," said he.

Mr. Lee was struck dumb for a moment; but whenever this happens to people, it is pretty certain they will make themselves ample amends for their silence, as soon after as possible.

"Not come back at all!", at length roared the old gentleman; "did you say that, boy?"

"I did, sir," said Highfield, firmly; "my situation here is becoming intolerable. I am harassed with anxieties, depressed by a sense of degrading dependence, and cut to the soul by perceiving every day new reasons to believe my cousin knows and despises my presumption."

"May I speak?" cried Mr. Lee, gasping for breath.

"Hear me out first, my dear and honoured sir," said the other. "When you first proposed this union to me, I considered the subject deeply. I reflected that though poor and dependent on your bounty, still, next to your daughter, I was your nearest relative; my cousin was rich enough to make it immaterial that I was poor; she was lovely, amiable, and intelligent—such a being as, when held up to the hopes and wishes of youth, could not but prove irresistible. I therefore consented to try my chance for this glorious prize by every means becoming a man of spirit and honour placed in such a delicate situation. You see the result, sir. Lucia not only feels indifferent to me, but there is every appearance that she prefers another. I am too poor and too proud to persecute or see her persecuted; and, let me add, too much attached to my cousin to remain and see her united to another man. It is therefore my settled determination to leave you the day after to-morrow. My passage is taken."

Mr. Lee was struck dumb again; but the fit did not last long.

"May I speak now — do you release me from my promise?" cried he, his eyes starting almost out of his head.

"As respects myself, sir, say what you will; but, for my cousin, I claim your promise that she shall suffer no persecution on my account."

"And so, sir, I must not speak to my own child?"

"I claim your promise, sir. Let her remain for ever ignorant of my motives for leaving you."

"Charles," said the old man, taking his hand with tears in his eyes, "are you determined to abandon me in my old age?"

"My dear uncle, my benefactor, any thing but this! I cannot stay to be murdered by inches, and stand in the way of my cousin's happiness. I must go. But wherever I do go, whatever my lot may be, my last breath of life will be all gratitude for your past kindness. I wish it were otherwise; but, for some time at least, we must part."

"Charles! Charles! my boy!" cried the warm-hearted old man, as he put his arms about his neck and wept on his shoulder. At this moment Lucia entered, and inquired anxiously what was the matter.

"The matter! you, you are the matter," exclaimed Mr. Lee, in a fury.

"Recollect your word of honour, sir," whispered Highfield to his uncle, as he left the room. The old gentleman cast a most terrible look at his daughter, and followed. But Lucia remained, musing for some time on the scene that had just passed; and it was not till she learned that Highfield was on the point of leaving home for a long while, that her perplexity became absorbed in another and more powerful feeling.

CHAPTER XVII.

HIGHFIELD ENTERS ON A VOYAGE.

JUBA was assisting his young master, or rather delaying him, in packing up his things, for the old man made a sad business of it; Lucia was in her chamber, netting a purse as fast as her eyes would let her; and Mr. Lee was in his library, writing with all his might.

"Ah, Massa Highfield!", said Juba at length, "what Miss Lucia say when you go away?"

"Miss Lucia say!" quoth the other, somewhat surprised, — "why, nothing."

"Ah, Massa Highfield!, if you only know what I know, icod! massa wouldn't stir a peg, I reckon."

"What are you talking about, Juba, and what are you doing? You've put my old boots up with my clean cravats."

"Ah, massa!, I know what I say, but I don't know what I do now, much; but, if Massa Highfield only know what I do — dat's all."

"Well, what do you know, Juba?" said Highfield, hardly knowing what he was saying at the moment.

"I know Miss Lucia break her heart when you gone."

"Pooh! Miss Lucia don't care whether I go or stay."

"Ah, Massa Highfield!, if you only see her set by your bedside when you light-headed, and cry so, and say prayers, and wipe your forehead, and kiss it"——

"What—what are you talking about, you old fool?" cried Highfield, almost gasping for breath. "If you say another word, I'll turn you out of the room."

"Ah, Juba always old fool—no young fools nowadays; all true dough, by jingo, I swear. I seed her wid my own eyes—dat's all." And he went on with his packing, slower than ever, while Highfield sunk into a deep reverie, the subject of which the reader must know little of his own heart if he requires me to unfold.

The next morning was the last they were to spend together, and the little party met at breakfast. Lucia at first had determined to have a headache, and stay in her room; but her conscious heart whispered her this might excite a suspicion that she could not bear the parting with her cousin. Accordingly she summoned all the allies of woman to her assistance. She called up maidenly pride, and womanly deceit, and love's hypocrisy, to her aid, and they obeyed the summons. She entered the breakfast-room with a pale face, but with a self-possession which I have never since reflected upon without wonder. Little was said, and less eaten, by the party. A summons arrived for Highfield's baggage, and a message for him to be on board in half an hour. Mr.

Lee rose, and taking from his pocket a paper, gave it to Highfield with a request not to look at it till he was outside the Hook. Highfield suspected its purport, and replied: —

" Excuse me, dear uncle, this once;" and he opened the paper, which was nothing less than the deed of a fine estate Mr. Lee held in one of the Southern states.

"I cannot accept this, sir," said the young man. "I cannot consent to rob my cousin of what is hers by nature and the laws." And his voice became choked with emotion.

"I insist," said the old man; "it is all I can give you now. Once I thought to give you all."

"And I too," said Lucia, but she could get no further.

"I declare, on my soul," said Highfield, "I will not, I cannot, accept it, uncle. You at least know my feelings and can comprehend my reasons, though others may not. I had rather starve, than rob my cousin, and her — I have nothing to give either of you in return." He pulled out his watch. "I must go now," said he; and his voice sunk into nothing. Lucia had been fumbling, with a tremulous hand, in her work-bag.

"My cousin is determined, I see," said she, rallying herself, "not to accept any favours from us; but — but I hope he will not refuse this purse, empty as it is. I have been a long while in keeping my promise; but, better late, they say, than never." And she burst into a torrent of uncontrollable emotion. Highfield took the purse, and put it in his bosom.

"And now, my dear uncle, farewell — may God bless you!"

criticise a book according to the latest Edinburgh or Quarterly; and yet — look at me, Lucia, and answer me too — did you not while your cousin was delirious visit his bedside?"

"I did, sir."

"And weep and wring your hands; and watch his slumbers; and minister to his comforts; — and did I not once, when I came into the room suddenly, detect you hovering over him and kissing his forehead? Answer me, as you hope for my forgiveness and Heaven's for playing the hypocrite at the price of others' health and hopes — is it not so?"

"It is, sir," said the daughter, faintly; and, sinking back on her chair, she again covered her face with her hands.

"What am I to understand from all that I saw?"

"For Heaven's sake, sir; for my sake; for the sake of your daughter; stop!" cried Highfield, whose feelings on this occasion we will not attempt to describe.

"Silence!" cried the old man; "too much has been risked, too much is at stake, and too much may be sacrificed by stopping short at this moment. Answer me, daughter of my soul," added he, kindly yet solemnly.

"You are to understand, sir, from all this, that — that, though I would not shut my heart to — to gratitude, I was too proud to force it on one who did not value it when himself. He could not insult me with indifference when unconscious of my presence."

"Oh Lucia, how unjust you have been to me You knew not my feelings, when I seemed most indifferent."

"There were two of us in the like error," replied she, with a heavy sigh.

" Stop! one moment," — cried Mr. Lee, earnestly, and looking at Lucia, who was weeping in her chair.

" Lucia," said he solemnly, " my nephew loves you, and is going from us that he may not see you throw yourself away on a puppy with a heart as hollow as his head."

" Uncle! " said Highfield.

" Nay, sir, I will speak; the truth shall out, though I travel barefoot to Rome for absolution. Yes, daughter, my nephew loves you, and with my entire and perfect approbation. And now, madam, I am going to ask you some questions, which I trust at this parting hour you will answer, not as a foolish, frivolous, girl, who thinks it proper to play the hypocrite with her father, but as a reasonable woman and an obedient child. Will you promise? The happiness of more than one depends on your reply."

Lucia uncovered her face, and, having mastered her emotions, firmly replied,

" I will, father."

" Have you given your affections to Mr. Goshawk? "

" I have not, sir."

" Do you mean to bestow them on him? "

" Never, sir."

" Are your affections engaged elsewhere? "

Lucia answered not; she could not speak, for her life.

" Yes, yes, I see how it is," said Mr. Lee; " you are deceiving your father again. You have given away your heart to some whiskered puppy you waltzed with at a fancy-ball, who can write a string of disjointed nonsense about nothing in jingling rhyme, or

"The pride of conscious dependence" — said Highfield.

"The pride of woman" — said Lucia.

"I loved you from the moment I felt the first impulses of manhood. Oh Lucia, my dear cousin, daughter of my benefactor, companion of my childhood, will you, — can you fulfil his wishes, and my hopes, without forfeiting your own happiness? Do you not despise my poverty and presumption? Do you not hate me for being a party, at least in appearance, in thus severely probing your feelings? Ah! had I known of your kindness and attentions when I was not myself, I should not when myself have forgot the deep, heart-piercing obligation; I should have been grateful — "

Mr. Lee could not bear the word. "Grateful! pooh, nonsense. The lady is grateful for past favours, and the gentleman is grateful for past sympathy. Look ye, most grateful lady, and most grateful gentleman, I have not quite so many years to live and make a fool of myself in as you have, perhaps. Now, Lucia, will you take your old father's word, when he tells you, solemnly, that Charles has loved you ever since he came from college?"

"Long before, sir!" cried Highfield, warmly.

"Hold your tongue, sir, if you please — Lucia, answer for yourself."

"I will believe any thing my father says, even were it ten times more improbable," replied she, with one of her long-absent smiles.

"And how think you he ought to be rewarded?"

"My gratitude will" —

"Now, Lucia, you are at your old tricks again; I

tell you I won't hear a word about that infernal gratitude."

"What shall I say, sir?"

"Say what your heart prompts, and do what never mortal woman did before — speak the truth, even though it make your old father happy."

"Lucia — ?" said Charles.

"Daughter — ?" said Mr. Lee.

"Charles" — said Lucia, and gave him her hand — "You shall know my feelings when it will be my duty to disguise nothing from you."

Highfield lost his passage; the ship sailed without him, taking with her all his wardrobe.

Goshawk called that morning as early as fashionable hours would permit, to take the first opportunity of enforcing his attractions on Lucia, in Highfield's absence.

"She no see any body," said Juba.

Mr. Goshawk said he had particular business. Juba demurred —

"She busy wid young Massa Highfield."

"What, is not Mr. Highfield gone?"

"No, sir, he going anoder voyage soon."

"Not gone! why, what prevented him?"

Juba grinned mortally. "Miss Lucia prevent him. — Icod, Massa Goosehawk bill out of joint, I reckon," quoth Ebony, half aside.

Goshawk soon got to the bottom of the matter, which he forthwith communicated to the azure coterie at Miss Appleby's, each of whom made a famous speech on the occasion, and voted Lucia a Goth.

"To fall in love with a man of no genius!", cried Miss Overend.

ıo can't write a line of poetry!", cried Miss y.

ıo hates argument!", cried the great Pudm.

"Who places actions before words!", cried Paddleford.

"Who never made a set speech in his life!", cried Prosser.

"Who hates passion — "

"Despises criticism — "

"And never reads a review — " cried they all together.

Every member of the azure tribe, to whom Goshawk's despairing passion had been long known, took it for granted that, having so excellent an apology, he would now certainly die of despair, or suddenly make away with himself, after writing his own elegy. He did neither; but he became, if possible, ten times more miserable than ever. He railed at this world, and the things of this world; he tied a black ribbon round his neck, drank gin and water, and ate fish every day. One minute he talked of joining the Greeks, and the next the Cherokees; sometimes he sighed away his very soul in wishes for speedy annihilation, and then he sighed away his soul again in pining for the delights of Italy, lamenting that he was not rich enough to go thither, occupy a palace, and hire a nobleman's wife to come and be his housekeeper, like my Lord Byron. Man delighted not him, nor woman neither; he sucked melancholy, as the bee sucks honey, out of every flower; the sunshine saddened him, the clouds made him gloomy, and the light of the moon threw him into paroxysms of despair.

Finally he announced his determination to reti this busy, noisy, heartless, naughty, good-for-n world, and spend the remainder of a life of pointment and misery in the great mammoth c Kentucky. But, what was very remarkable and shows the strange inconsistency of genius, there was no public place, no party, no exhibition of any kind, at which this unhappy gentleman did not make his appearance, notwithstanding his contempt of the world and its empty pleasures.

In process of time, there was a great dispersion from the tower of Babel at Miss Appleby's. That azure and sublime lady descended at last, as she said, "to link her fate, chain down her destiny, and trammel her genius," with an honest grocer from Coenties Slip, who, not being able to speak English himself, had a great veneration for high and lofty declamation. Miss Overend grew weary of the Executive Greek Committee, and paired off with a little broker, who had got rich by speculating in the bills of broken banks, and drank Champagne instead of small-beer at dinner. Paddleford married an heiress from somewhere near the Five Points; and the great Puddingham became a member of the city corporation, where he served on divers important committees, drew up sundry laws that puzzled wiser men than himself to expound, and became a sore persecutor of mad dogs and wallowing swine, insomuch that, if a cur in his sober senses, or a pig of ordinary discretion, saw him coming afar off, he would incontinently flee away like unto the wind. He became, moreover, a great philanthropist, and it was observed that he never, in the capacity of assistant-justice at the Quarter-Sessions, pronounced sentence on an offender, without first making him a low bow and begging his pardon for the liberty he was about to take.

Poor Mr. Goshawk, being thus as it were left alone, to play the haggard hermit azure-wise, continued to nourish his despair at all public places. He was a constant attendant at the Italian opera, where he kept himself awake by nodding and bobbing his admiration; beating time with his chin upon his little ivory-headed switch, and now and then crying "Bravo!" to the signorina. Every body said, what an enthusiast was Mr. Goshawk, and what a soul he had for music, until one night he mistook Yankee Doodle for "Di Tanti," which ruined his reputation for ever, as a connoisseur. By slow, imperceptible, yet inevitable degrees, he at length sunk to his proper level; for the most stupid at last will become tired of affectation, and the most ignorant detect their kindred ignorance. His loud, pompous nothings; his affected contempt of the world, and distaste for life; his disjointed, silly, and unpurposed poetical effusions; and his mysterious sorrows; — all combined, failed in the end to sustain his claim to genius. The admiration of his associates dwindled into indifference, and even the young ladies tittered at his approach. He tried the pretender's last stake — the society of strangers. He went to the Springs, where it was his good fortune to encounter the sentimental widow of a rich lumber-merchant, from the neighbourhood of the great Dismal Swamp. She was simplicity itself; she adored poetry, idolized genius, and the routine of her reading had prepared her to mistake high-sounding words for lofty ideas, and namby-pamby twaddle for genuine feeling. Goshawk thundered away at the innocent widow, and soon melted her heart, by declaiming about the emptiness of this world and the heartlessness of mankind. The poor lady came to think it the greatest condescension possible, for him to select her from this mighty mass of worthlessness. Finally, he declared his enthusiastic love.

"La! Mr. Goshawk," said the widow, "I thought you despised the world, and the people in it."

"Divine widow," cried the poet, "you belong to another world, and a higher order of beings."

Goshawk is now the happy husband of the widow, and lords it over a wide tract of the Great Dismal. He orders his gentlemen of colour to cut down pine trees, in the style of Cicero declaiming against Verres; reads Lord Byron under the shade of a bark-hut; and makes poetry extempore, while riding to church over a log causeway in a one-horse wagon with wooden springs. The widow has already discovered that her husband is no witch, for nothing makes people more clear-sighted than marriage; and the man of genius has found out that his lady has a will of her own.

Our heroine remains the happy, rational, lovely wife of Highfield, and talks just like other well-bred sensible people. She prefers Milton to Byron, and the Vicar of Wakefield to an entire new Waverley. She admires her husband, though he can't write poetry; and is a sincere convert to the opinion, that high moral principles, gentlemanly manners, an amiable disposition, a well-constituted intellect, and the talents to be useful in society, are ingredients in the character of a husband, a thousand times more important than affected sensibility, or the capacity to disguise empty nothings in bombastic words and jingling rhymes.

My worthy friend, Mr. Lightfoot Lee, is so happy, that he begins seriously to doubt whether the world is really going forward or backward. There is reason to apprehend that he and Mr. Fairweather will soon agree on this great question, and then there will certainly be an end to their long friendship.

"Ah massa," said King Juba one day to Mr. Lee, who was apt to boast of his excellent management in bringing about this happy state of things—"Ah massa, icod, if I no tell massa Highfield about dem dare visit to he bedside when he light-headed, he no marry Miss Lucia arter all."

"Pooh, you old blockhead, don't you know marriages are made in heaven?"

"May be so, massa, but old nigger hab something to do wid um for all dat—guy!"

"Get away, you stupid old ninny!"

"Massa wouldn't dare call me ninny, if I was a white man," quoth Juba, as he strutted away with the air of a descendant of a hundred ebony kings.

THE DUMB GIRL.

THE DUMB GIRL.

> Speak thou fair words, I'll answer with my eyes;
> Send thou sweet looks, I'll meet them with sweet looks;
> Tell me thy sorrows, I'll reply with tears;
> Thy joys, I'll sympathize with dallying smiles;
> Thy love, and still I'll answer with mine eyes,
> Using my lips only to kiss thee, love.

SOME thirty years ago, on a little corner of a farm belonging to an uncle of mine, lived an aged man of the name of Angevine, an "old continental," as he was called in the language of the times. He had left the neighbourhood to enter the army of the Revolution, and, after serving throughout the whole war, (and bravely too, if his own word might be taken for it), had returned, very poor. Accordingly, he was permitted by my uncle to occupy a small tenement with a garden, in a remote angle of his estate, rent free. Angevine was a gallant soldier, but rather an idle man. His delight was to talk of the Revolutionary war; — and who has a better right to talk, than a man who has lent a hand in giving liberty to his country? I have known Angevine stop on his way to mill, with a bushel of corn on his shoulder, and talk a full hour about his campaigns, without ever thinking of putting down his bag. What was his origin I know not; it was probably French: but I remember, whenever he got offended with my good uncle, (who in truth was of the family of Melchisidec), he used to be somewhat scurrilous on the subject of ancestry. He held it as a maxim, that a soldier was always a gentleman; and his conduct verified his maxim, for he never worked when he could help it, and passed most of his time in telling stories of skirmish, or battle, or quarters. His revenue was his good spirits, which generally made him a welcome intruder in all the neighbouring houses; and when they failed in that, served to reconcile him to his disappointment. I believe he was never serious except when he read his Bible, which he did every day. He would walk fifteen miles to a training, for fun; got his head frequently broken, in fun; was run over by a wagon, in fun; was pitched down a high bank, in wrestling, for fun; had his hip put out of joint, and once was put into jail — all in fun. In short, it was said of him that he talked more and worked less than any man in the county; his aphorism being, that all the good people worked for him and that it ran against his conscience to work for the wicked. He died, as he lived, in fun; — giving his pipe to one, his tobacco-box to another, his odd knee-buckles to a third; and bequeathing his Testament, which he knew by heart, to my uncle, in payment of his rent. He was a libel on all who possess the means of being happy, yet are wretched; for he enjoyed more pleasure, and created more mirth, than any man I ever knew, at the very time that, in the opinion of all reflecting persons, he ought to have been miserable.

In truth he had enough to make him so, besides poverty. He had but two children, a girl and a boy; the former was dumb, and the latter an idiot.

At the time of the old man's death, Ellee, as he was called — it was a contraction of some name I have forgotten — was about fourteen, his sister Phœbe, about sixteen years of age. The poor boy had a heart, though he had no head. His affections were singularly strong; his reason but a little beyond instinct. He loved his mother because she fed and clothed him; he loved his sister, for she was his companion, his guide, his protector, his solace; and he seemed to have a perception that she laboured under some privation which resembled his own, yet was not exactly the same. In all cases of danger, suffering, insult, or injury, he flew to his sister for refuge, and she in time became a young lioness in his defence. The boy was quite tractable, and could be made useful in many little things, such as bringing water, going of errands to the neighbours, (who understood his dumb show), and weeding the garden; until, one day, whether in mischief, or from not knowing better, he plucked up a bed of radishes for weeds. He had a singular, wild note, which he sometimes uttered when in violent agitation, and which was not unlike the low, distant whoop of the owl, though somewhat more plaintive. His chief delight was to go every where with his sister.

Phœbe was not born dumb, but lost her speech about the age of fourteen, as was supposed at the time by a shock of lightning, which paralyzed the organs of utterance without affecting her hearing. Before this happened she had learned to read and write, and her mind had been considerably improved at a school hard by, whither old Angevine had sent her at his own cost, as he boasted; though truth obliges me to confess he never paid a shilling for her schooling. At the same time, he scouted the offers which were made to bring up his children at the expense of the town. When Phœbe was smitten in this unaccountable and melancholy way, it was affecting to see her impatience at first, her succeeding despair, and the steps through which by degrees she regained her spirits and resumed her useful occupations. Ellee for a little while exhibited indications of a vague, indefinite wonder and anxiety; but in a few days all traces of these wore away, and he seemed unconscious that his sister had undergone any change. Her mother, an honest, careful, industrious creature, took it sadly to heart; but, after a time, the only effect it was observed to have upon the good woman was that she talked twice as much as ever, I suppose to make up for the silence of Phœbe. Angevine took to his Bible for days and weeks afterwards. Indeed I believe he never fairly regained his spirits, although the force of habit and constitution still caused him to exhibit the usual indications of hilarity. He died about two years after the accident.

At sixteen, Phœbe Angevine was the prettiest girl in all the surrounding country, as well as the most industrious. Indeed it was observed that Ellee was better dressed, the garden in finer order, and every thing about the house more tidy and comfortable, since the death of the "old continental." The overseers of the poor offered to take charge of poor Ellee; but both mother and daughter declared that, so long as they could maintain him, he should never be a burthen to others. This was before the poor were coaxed to become paupers, and lured into idleness and unthrift by the mistaken benevolence of morbid sensibility. I thought it necessary to add this, in order to render the anecdote credible. I don't remember ever to have seen exactly such a face and figure as those of Phœbe. Her hair was amazingly long, luxuriant, and silky; of a dark brown colour, to match her eyes; and, (what is very rare with our country girls out of New England), her skin was excessively white. Her face in particular was all lily; there was not the slightest tinge of the rose, except when the impulse of her heart drove the blood into her cheeks. It is impossible to give any idea of her features and expression; the former were rather sharp than oval, and the latter displayed the character and impress of most intense passion, or sensibility, or both. Never woman could better afford to lose her tongue, for every change of her countenance supplied its place. The two poles are not more distant than was the contrast between the lowly, subdued, and dewy eye, with which she courtesied to my good old uncle, and the flashing intensity of its rage when any one played tricks upon the simplicity of her brother, or laughed at his infirmity. Her eyes then did the errand of her tongue, and their language was terrible. Every-body wondered how she always kept herself so neat — for she was neatness itself. It was partly innate delicacy, and partly personal vanity. It was impossible to see Phœbe, without discovering at once that she knew she was handsome, and that this was seldom absent from her thoughts. She never passed a looking-glass without casting a glance; and, doubtless, many are the crystal mirrors of the neighbourhood that could murmur of her beauties, from the frequent opportunities she afforded them for contemplation. There was some excuse for her, since, independently of the singular charms of her face, her person was very remarkable. It had no pretensions to resembling that of a fashionable lady, for, in my opinion, she never wore corsets in her life; but it possessed that singular trimness and natural grace which the connoisseur will not fail to discover and admire in an Indian warrior fresh from the hand of nature. It was as much superior to the caricatures fabricated by fashionable milliners, as the virgin Miranda was to the monster Caliban.

Phœbe was fond of dress; it was her foible, nay, her fault; for it was the mischievous minister to a vanity already become the master-passion of her bosom. At church she was always the beauty, and the best-dressed of all the country girls: and he knows little of a country church that does not know how many hearts throb with envy, how many tongues overflow with gall, when the owners are outdressed and outshone by one they consider beneath them. These sometimes rudely assailed her with sneers and innuendoes. Phœbe could not answer, except with a look that no eye that ever I have seen but hers could give. The poor girl, indeed, was sadly envied and hated by the young females of her acquaintance, not only because she was handsomer and better-dressed than they, but on account of her triumphs over the rustic beaux, and the speaking, taunting glance of her eye, when she carried off the school-master, or heard some stranger ask who was that neat, pretty girl. Then her ear drank the delicious sounds, and almost made amends for the loss of the power of answering save with her eyes. Phœbe was indeed the belle of all the neighbourhood—a dangerous preëminence!, for her poverty, her idiot brother, and her own misfortune, were so many bars to any thing beyond the gratification of a passing hour. She had many admirers; but none that passed the usual bounds of rustic gallantry, none that sought her for a wife. All they did was to administer to her perilous self-conceit, and awaken thoughts and anticipations fatal to her future peace of mind.

I went to school with Phœbe, during a period of three or four years that I sojourned with my good uncle. The school-master was a gallant old-bachelor, whose house and barn had been burned by the enemy, during the Revolutionary war. Having petitioned Congress seventeen years in succession and cost the nation in speeches ten times the amount of his loss, he at last got out of patience and out of bread, and turned to the useful as well as honourable office of teaching the young idea how to shoot. He was a lazy, easy-tempered man, grievously inclined to gallantry, and novels, in the purchase of which he spent much of his superfluity. These he lent to the girls of the country round, and scarcely ever visited one of them without a love-tale in his pocket to make him welcome. I cannot say whether these useful works had any thing to do with the matter, but, certain it is, there were a number of odd accidents happened to the damsels of the neighbourhood about this time. The prettiest girl in the school was ever the greatest favourite, and the prettiest girl was Phœbe, who always had the first reading of his novels. I recollect perfectly that such was her appetite for these high-seasoned dishes, that she would read them in walking home from school, and often came near being run over in the road, so completely was she occupied with the dangers of some lone lover or imprisoned heroine. When she lost her speech, of course she quitted school; but the gallant teacher still continued to visit her, and bring the newest novels. Poor Ellee used to be sometimes out of all patience with his sister, for sitting thus whole hours without taking notice of him, and once threw a whole set of Pamela into the fire, to the irreparable loss of the rising generation.

At the age of eighteen, Phœbe had many admirers beside the school-master. Her beauty attracted the young men; but the misfortunes of herself and family restrained them within the bounds of idle admiration and homely gallantry: moreover, if this had not been the case, Phœbe was too well read in novels to relish the devoirs of these rustical and barbarous Corydons. Thus she grew up to the perfection of womanhood, her imagination inflated with unreal pictures, and her passions stimulated by overwrought scenes of sentiment, or sensuality — for it is difficult to draw the line now.

About this time, the only son of a neighbouring squire — whose wealth outwent the modest means of all his neighbours not excepting my worthy uncle, and was moreover enhanced by his official dignity — returned home, like the prodigal son of holy-writ, poor and penitent. He had in early youth been smitten with the romantic dangers of the seas; and, being restrained in his inclinations by his parents, especially his mother, ran away. He had been absent six years without ever being heard of, and the disconsolate parents long mourned him as dead. His return was therefore hailed with tears of joy and welcome: the father fell on his neck, and wept; the mother first scolded him for running away, and then kissed him till he was ready to run away again. All was joy, welcome, and curiosity; and for several days the prodigal had nothing to do but relate his adventures. He had been to the North-West Coast, to the West Indies, and to the East; he had harpooned whales in the Frozen Ocean, and caught seals in the South Sea; he had been shipwrecked on the coast of Patagonia, where he saw giants eight feet high, and stranded on the coast of Labrador, where he dined on raw fish with pigmies of not more than three; he had gone overboard with a broken yard, and was taken up ten days after, perfectly well, having lived all the while on rope-yarns and canvas; and he was carried down to the bottom in six fathoms, by the anchor, and could tell, better than the gentlemen who have lately taken up the biographies of dead-men-come-to-life, exactly how a man felt when he was drowned. In short, he had seen the Peak of Teneriffe, Mount Ætna in an eruption, the Bay of Biscay in a storm, and the sea-serpent off Nahant. Of all the heroes in a country circle, the greatest is he who can tell the most stories of wonders of his own creation. Accordingly, our hero, for such he is, was the lion of the day, the wonder of the men, and the admiration of the ladies, old and young. One day, after our Sindbad had been telling of the wonders he had seen and the perils he had encountered, the old squire suddenly asked,

"But have you brought home any money, Walter?"

"Not a cent, sir."

"Hum!" quoth the squire.

The first Sunday after his arrival, our hero went to church, whither the fame of his adventures had already preceded him. Every body looked at him during the whole sermon. The old people observed how much he had grown since he was a boy; the young ladies thought him very handsome; and the young fellows envied him, to a man. Walter in his turn looked about, with the air of a man unconscious of the notice he excited; and after making the circuit of the church with his eyes, at length rested them in evident admiration on Phœbe Angevine, who was that day dressed in her best style and looked as neat as a new pin. Phœbe blushed up to the brow, and her proud heart swelled in her bosom. She continued to steal occasional looks at him, and always found his eyes fixed upon her, not insolently, but with an air of entreaty to be forgiven the liberty they were taking. Poor Ellee had come that day to church with her, and, for the first time perhaps in her life, she felt ashamed of him and wished him away, although he always behaved himself better than some people who think themselves very wise.

It was the custom of the country at the time I speak of, (and I believe is so still), for the congregation to remain between the two services, most of them living too far off to go home and return in time for the second one. This interval is usually spent, by the good pastor, in making kind inquiries about the health and prosperity of the people; by the old men, in talking of their crops and their prospects; by the old gossips, in talking scandal; and by the young folks, in strolling about under the trees, or rambling through the church-yard, reading the epitaphs, and looking unutterable things. It is here, amid the records and memorials of mortality, the suggestions of religion, and the mouldering remains of the departed, that human passions, even among the best of us, still will exercise their irrepressible influence. Vanity contemplates her Sunday suit with glances of lively admiration; Love nourishes his idle dreams; Revenge studies modes of gratification; and Avarice plans schemes requiring years to realize;—ay, in the midst of a thousand breathless whispers, that remind men of the woful uncertainty of life; that say to the aged, Your time is but a span; and to the young children, There are shorter graves than yours in the church-yard, and smaller skulls in Golgotha.

During the time given up by the simple folks to this varied chat and amusement, Phœbe was strolling about among the rest, with the gallant school-master, and Ellee, of whom she felt more ashamed every moment; for she could not help observing—(that is, she could not help every now and then casting a sly glance at)—our hero, and seeing that he was always following her with his eyes. She wished poor Ellee at home, and the school-master in his school, teaching A, B, C.

"Well, what do you think of young Mr. Avery?" asked the school-master; "I don't admire him much, for my part."

Phœbe, all-suddenly the rose, nodded assent, with that instinctive spirit of deception which marks the beginning, middle, and end — no, not the end — of love in the female bosom. There is not a greater hypocrite in the world than a young and bashful girl, learning the first rudiments of affection.

"Who is that beautiful girl, in the white muslin gown?" asked our hero of a covey of rural belles, with whom he had become acquainted; "she seems very bashful, for I have not seen her open her mouth."

The damsels began to giggle, and titter, and exchange significant looks, which induced Walter to ask an explanation.

"She's dumb," at length said one, with another suppressed giggle, in which the others joined. They were by no means ill-natured girls, but I know not how it was, they did not like the curiosity of our hero. Women can't bear curiosity in others, except it relates to their own particular affairs.

"Dumb!", said Walter; "poor girl." Dumb, thought he, a few minutes afterwards; so much the better. And, sinking into a reverie, he asked no more questions.

The good Mrs. Angevine stayed from church that Sabbath, on account of a rheumatism. When Phœbe came home, she asked her, according to custom, where the text was, bidding her seek it out in the Bible. Phœbe shook her head, and looked confused.

"What! you've forgot, you naughty girl?"

Phœbe nodded.

"I dare say you were asleep," said the mother.

Phœbe shook her head.

" Then I dare say you were gaping at the young fellows," said the mother, angrily.

Phœbe shook her head more emphatically, and with a look of indignation. There was too much truth in this last supposition.

" Well, well," quoth the mother, " I'm sure something is *going* to happen, for you never forgot the text before."

Dreams, clouds, gypsies, and ghosts, are all prophetic nowadays, at least in fashionable novels; and why may not this remark of the good woman have been prophetic too? Certain it is, that something *did* happen before long.

It was too or three days after this memorable prediction, that young Walter Avery, being out shooting, and finding himself thirsty, stopped at the house of the widow Angevine for a drink of water. The good dame asked him in to rest himself, which invitation he accepted, and staid almost an hour, during which time he talked to the mother, and looked at the daughter. In going away, he shook poor Ellee by the hand, as an excuse for doing the same to Phœbe, which he did with a certain lingering, gentle, yet emphatic pressure, that made her blood come and go on errands from her heart to her face. Phœbe thought of this gentle pressure with throbbing pulses, and poor Ellee was as proud as a peacock, at shaking hands with such a smart young gentleman.

From this time forth no one ever came to the house without being obliged to shake hands with him half a dozen times. With that strange sagacity and quickness of observation which frequently accompany the absence of reason, he had marked the expression of Phœbe's face when Walter Avery looked at her and took her hand; and he made her blush often afterwards by a grotesque imitation of his manner. "Stop in again when you come this way," cried the old dame, highly pleased with Walter's particular notice of every thing she said. Walter was highly flattered, and assured her he would come that way often. At parting, he gave Phœbe a look that kept her awake half that night.

"Didn't I say something was going to happen, last Sunday, when you forgot the text?" said Mrs. Angevine. Phœbe was watching to see whether Walter would turn to look back as he wound round an angle of the road, and took no notice of what the good woman said; so she continued talking on to herself, for want of somebody else to listen.

"Something *has* happened," thought Phœbe, with a sigh, as Walter, in turning the angle, kissed his hand to her, and disappeared. The rest of the day she was so idle that her mother scolded her roundly. The inertness of new-born passion was gradually crawling over her, and she more than ever regretted the destruction of Pamela by the sacrilegious hand of Ellee.

From this time Walter was out every day, shooting, and, (what the old woman thought rather singular), he always grew thirsty about the time of passing her door. "It is worth while to go a mile out of the way to get a drink of such water," would he say, though it tasted a little of iron, and was not the coolest in the world. While the mother was attending to household affairs, Walter talked to Phœbe, and she answered him with her eyes. But as there are certain little promises and engagements, requiring more specific replies than even the brightest eyes can give, he one day made her a present of a silver pencil and a pocket-book, in which she sometimes made her responses in writing.

Many opportunities occurred for nourishing the growing passion of the poor girl, notwithstanding the perpetual intrusions of Ellee, who had taken a great fancy to Walter ever since he gave him the friendly shake of the hand. This had gone directly to his heart; for he seldom received such an attention, except from my kind-hearted old uncle. He never met Walter, without going up, making a strange, grotesque bow, and shaking him by the hand most emphatically. Walter sometimes wished him in the Red Sea, for he interfered with his designs, and, unknowingly, often proved the guardian genius of his sister. If they sometimes stole a march upon him, and wandered along the little river Byram which skirted the foot of the neighbouring hills, it was seldom but Ellee found them out, with the instinct of a pointer; when he would come running up, with a chuckling laugh at his cleverness, and extend to master Walter the customary greeting of his paw.

Yet they had their moments of solitude and silence, such as innocent lovers cherish as the brightest of their lives and deceivers seize upon for the attainment of their object. In the wicked twilight of the quiet woods, the purest heart sometimes swells with the boiling eddies of a youthful fancy; and it is there that the modest woman is won to the permission of little freedoms and progressive endearments, which, if not checked in time, are only atoned for by the tears of a whole life. Phœbe became gradually absorbed in the all-devouring passion. She could not relieve her heart and express her feelings in speech, and thus they preyed upon her almost to suffocation. There is no reason to doubt her entire conviction that Walter intended to marry her, for he had told her so a thousand times.

Rumour, like Echo, loves to abide among the rocks and dells, where she delights to blow her horn, the signal of awakening to a thousand babbling tongues. Rumours and scandals now began to circulate among the neighbours, all to the disadvantage of Phœbe. It was nonsense to suppose Walter intended to marry a dumb girl, and one so poor as she. His father was the richest man in the county, and he an only son. It was impossible.

"Nobody can believe it, in her right senses," cried Mrs. Toosy.

"The girl must be a fool!", cried Mrs. Ratsbane, "or something worse."

"I thought what would come of her fine clothes and foolish books," cried Mrs. Dolan.

"And then, the silver pencil," cried Mrs. Nolan.

"And the morocco pocket-book — people don't give these things for nothing," cried Mrs. Dollinger.

"The mother must be mad to think of such a thing," cried Mrs. Fadladdle.

"The girl is no better than she should be," cried Mrs. Doorise.

"She is certainly a good-for-nothing cretur," cried Mrs. Cackle.

"Lord have mercy upon us!, what is this world coming to?" cried Mrs. Skimpey, with upturned eyes: "it puts me in mind of — I don't know what."

"Heigho!" cried Mrs. Fubsy, taking a pinch of snuff, with a deep sigh;—"it puts me in mind of Joseph in Egypt."

"Well, after all, let us hope for the best," cried Mrs. Daisy.

"Amen!" answered they all; and thereupon the tea-party broke up, at five o'clock in the afternoon. Women are in fact ill-natured toads, especially towards each other, but they make it up in kindness to us bachelors. There is good reason why they should be intolerant to certain transgressions of the sex. Vice thrives apace where it carries with it no other penalty than that denounced by the laws. It is the inquest, the censure, the terrible verdict of the society in which we live and move and have our very being, that constitutes the severest punishment; and it behooves women to be inflexible in visiting sins, that, if they were to become common, would degrade them from divinities into slaves—from the chosen companions of man to the abject ministers of his pleasures. As yet, however, the censures of our tea-party were premature. Phœbe was innocent, though on the brink of a precipice.

At length Mrs. Ratsbane thought it her duty, as a neighbour and a Christian, to open the whole matter to the mother of our hero, who forthwith reported it to the squire. Not that she thought or meant he should take any steps in the affair;—(she was a remarkable, a very remarkable woman, such a woman as we doubt if the world ever produced before or ever will again);—for it was her maxim, that, as women could have no wills when they died, it was but fair they should have their wills during their lives. Never woman stuck closer to her favourite axiom, as the justice, were he living, could testify. The name of this puissant magistrate was Hezekiah Lord Avery, but his neighbours usually called him Lord Avery, a name which I shall adopt in order to give dignity to my story. It is very seldom an American writer gets so good an opportunity of ennobling his pages. His lordship was a silent man in the presence of his wife, but a great talker every where else, especially when sitting on the bench, at which times he would never suffer any body to speak a word but himself; for such was his astonishing sagacity that he always knew what a suitor was going to say, before he opened his mouth. The only *man* that ever got the better of him was a little pestilent lawyer of the township, who once spoke eight hours on a point of law, which, though it had nothing to do with the case, involved a great principle; whereupon the people sent him to Congress. Lord Avery was a man of great substance, partly derived from his father, and partly of his own acquisition; for he was what is called a lucky man. If there happened a drought all over the country that raised the price of wheat, Lord Avery was sure to have a redundant harvest; if apples were scarce, his orchards groaned with fruit; if he sold any thing it was sure to fall in price, and if he bought it was as certain to rise. In short, he was the Midas of modern times, and even his blunders turned to gold. He had a neighbour, his exact opposite — a sensible, calculating man, who was always giving advice to his lordship, but without effect. This worthy but unfortunate man never undertook any thing without the most mature deliberation, nor without consulting every body. One year, observing that all his neighbours were planting a more than usual quantity of corn, he sagely concluded that there would be a glut in the market, and planted great fields of potatoes. About harvest-time the news of a failure of crops in Europe came, and doubled the price of corn, while the good man's potatoes stood stock still. Lord Avery had gone on without caring a straw about what his neighbours were doing, and reaped a swingeing harvest. The calculator was obliged to buy corn of his lordship, who took occasion to crack a joke on his foresight.

"An ounce of luck is worth a pound of understanding," replied the long-headed man.

It is well it was, for his lordship had plenty of one and very little of the other.

Lord Avery loved his son Walter for two especial reasons; he was his only son, and he told the most entertaining stories in the world. Her ladyship, immediately on receiving the information from Mrs. Ratsbane, sought her lord, and poured it all into his ear, with additions.

"I will" — quoth Lord Avery in a passion.

"*You* will!" cried her ladyship, contemptuously — "your will is in the cherry-tree."

"Well, well, it is my opinion," said he, perfectly cool.

"Your opinion! — how often have I told you, you have no opinion of your own?"

"No opinion of my own — a justice have no opin- of his own!" thought he.

"Well, then, I think" —

"Think! — how often have I told you, there is no use in your thinking?"

"Not much!" thought his lordship, adding,

"Well then, my dear, I say — that is, I think — that is, I am of opinion — my dear, what is your opinion of the matter?"

"My opinion is, that you had better say nothing on the subject."

"What did you come and tell me of it for?", asked his lordship, a little nettled.

There is a pleasant story, that the secret of Midas' having asses' ears was finally discovered by his barber, who, unable to contain himself, at length communicated it to the earth, whence soon after sprung up certain reeds, that whispered it to the four winds, which blabbed it all over the world. Her ladyship had never heard this story, but told hers to his lordship for the same reason the barber whispered his to the earth. She wanted somebody to listen, not talk, to her.

"What did I tell it to you for?", at length replied her ladyship, after a puzzling pause; "are you not his father?"

"I wish I was his mother!", quoth his lordship.

"If you were, you'd be twice the man you are at present," retorted her ladyship. "But, what do you mean to do?" Her ladyship always asked his advice, which she as invariably took by the rule of contrary.

"Why, I mean to disinherit him, if" — said his lordship, pompously.

"*You* disinherit him! — you shall do no such thing."

"Why, then, I'll make him marry the girl."

"Marry her!" screamed her ladyship — "why, the creature is dumb!"

"Hum!", said Lord Avery; "I don't think that any mighty objection."

"Her brother is an idiot."

"Poor fellow, I'm sorry for him."

"Her mother is a fool."

"There are plenty to keep her in countenance."

"You're enough to provoke a saint."

"How should you know?" quoth Lord Avery, whose mind was wandering a little from the subject. Her ladyship insisted this was as much as telling her *she* was no saint, and thereupon made her exit in hysterics. And thus the consultation ended.

The next time Lord Avery saw his son, he questioned him on the subject of Phœbe, and received his solemn assurance of her innocence. The good man believed him, but the lady maintained its impossibility.

"Why, how do you know it is impossible?", said his lordship.

"By experience," answered the lady.

"Hum,"—quoth his lordship.

Her ladyship, finding herself in a dilemma, made her retreat, as usual, and fell into hysterics.

"Walter," said his lordship, who talked like an orator in the absence of his wife, "Walter, you must not think of marrying this poor dumb girl."

"I don't mean to," said Walter, with a sly look.

"Ah! you wicked dog!" quoth his lordship;—"but mind you don't make a fool of yourself."

"Never fear, I only mean to make a fool of the girl."

"Ah! Walter, you're a chip of the old block", said his lordship, complacently. "But I'm glad to find you don't mean to disgrace your family."

That worthy and gallant bachelor, the school-master,

came to caution Phœbe, and spoke like an oracle of the improbability that the only son of Lord Avery should marry, or be permitted to marry, the daughter of an "old continental," in her situation. He then took leave; but, being moved by her tears, left with her a new novel, in which the rustic heroine becomes a duchess. Phœbe wept for an hour after he went away, at the end of which she opened the book, and soon lost herself in the extravagances of sentiment and fiction.

Matters went on for some time after this in the usual way; the lovers took long walks together, and the neighbourhood held long talks. Her ladyship scolded, and his lordship very discreetly held his peace at home, consoling himself by making as much noise as possible abroad. All of a sudden, however, Phœbe became very sad; and was observed to weep bitterly whenever Walter came to see her, which was not now as often as before. She refused to accompany him any more in walks through the woods, or along the banks of the Byram; and he would go away in a passion, threatening never to see her again. Poor Ellee watched her, as a faithful dog watches the looks of his master; and it was apparent that he could see she was unhappy, though he only remotely comprehended the cause. He no longer, however, shook hands with Walter; and when he went away, leaving Phœbe in tears, would sit down by her side, take hold of her hand, kiss it, and utter his mournful music. He never shed tears; for nature, though she had given him feelings, had denied him the means of expressing them except by gestures and moanings. It was an aching sight to see these two poor bereaved beings thus suffering together, without the power of alleviating their sorrows, except by the silent sympathy of expressive actions and speaking looks. This sympathy was not shared by the mother, whom age and toil had rendered callous to all the ills of life, except poverty and sickness. If she took particular notice of Phœbe, it was to flout her for her idleness, or sneer at her grand lover; for the hints and tales of the neighbours had soured her mind towards her daughter, and infected her with strange suspicions.

One day Phœbe received a little billet, and, shortly afterwards, having contrived to evade the notice of Ellee, was seen to bend her course towards a retired spot, distant from any habitation. It was here she had often met Walter, and, while leaning on his bosom, tasted the joys of an innocent love, ripening into a consuming flame. A high rock gloomed over the bank of the river, as it whirled violently round a sharp angle, deep and turbid. Within the angle, and close under the side of the rock, was a little greensward, shadowed by lofty sycamores, and shut in on all sides, by the perpendicular cliff, the mountain in the rear, and the brawling torrent in front. It was a scene made for love, and it might easily be desecrated to a more malignant passion. Ellee followed his sister, as usual when he found she was gone; and, after an absence of perhaps two hours, came home without her, in a state of terrible agitation. He motioned with his hands; he ran to and fro; pointed towards the spot I have described, and attempted to drag his mother violently in that direction, gnashing his teeth and actually foaming at the mouth all the while. At length he sat down in a corner, and commenced that strange melancholy moaning which was the only sound he ever uttered. Labour and poverty harden the heart. The mother thought strange of this behaviour at first; but she was busy at work, and her mind became gradually drawn off from the poor boy.

My uncle and myself happened to come riding by at this moment; and no sooner did Ellee perceive us, than he darted out, seized my uncle's bridle, and, pointing with convulsive rapidity first to the house and then to the river, concluded his dumb-show by the customary moan. Assured that something uncommon had taken place, we alighted, and went into the house, where we found the old woman so busily engaged that she had not been aware of our coming. Ellee followed us in, hung upon our steps, watched every movement, and fixed so strained an eye upon the motion of our lips, that it seemed as if he expected to translate their very movements. On inquiring what was the matter, the good woman related all she knew; but did not seem to think any thing extraordinary had happened. It was otherwise with my uncle and myself, who determined to go under the guidance of Ellee, and see what had become of his sister. As soon as we mounted our horses and turned them towards the stream, the idiot-boy seemed to understand our object. He again began his furious gesticulations; gnashed his teeth, foamed at the mouth, and, sinking as usual into a low and plaintive quaver, ran with all his might riverward, stopping at times to see if we were coming, and beckoning us eagerly to follow.

It was now verging towards the sunset of a long day in the month of June. Ellee led us to the place where the river rolled rapidly around the sharp angle of the rock, and there again made the most violent motions. He pointed to the roots of an old branching sycamore, then twined his arms about my body and kissed me, then wrung his hands and imitated weeping as well as he could, and finally ran moaning to the river's bank, and, making as if he would cast himself in, howled most piteously, while he pointed to the deep current rolling past.

These significant actions naturally awakened in our minds the most fearful suspicions. We examined the spot with minute attention. On the bark of the old tree appeared the initials, P. A. and W. A., apparently but just cut; and, at the root, the grass seemed to us to exhibit traces of two persons having been sitting there very lately, side-by-side. A little blood was sprinkled on one of the projecting roots of the tree, and a piece of paper was picked up, crumpled together and stained with blood. On examining it more particularly, there were found upon it, written with a pencil, some words in the handwriting, (as it afterwards appeared), of Walter Avery, that seemed to form part of an invitation to meet him somewhere or other. While this scrutiny was going on, poor Ellee accompanied us with intense interest, and watched our looks, apparently to gather the impression made on our minds by these circumstances. By this time it was growing dark, and we quitted the place, notwithstanding the violent opposition of Ellee, with a determination to pursue the investigation next morning, if, on inquiry, it was found that Phœbe had not returned.

She did not return that night, nor did she make her

appearance the next morning. We accordingly again proceeded to the spot whither Ellee had before directed us, accompanied by several of the neighbours, and continued our examination. Nothing more was observed that could throw light on the affair, though the river was closely searched upon both banks for some miles below. The general conclusion was, that she had been made away with in some way or other, and suspicion fell strongly upon Walter Avery. The notoriety of his courtship to Phœbe, the circumstance of the fragment of the note, and the fact that he had been seen going towards the spot where it was found, all combined, seemed to bring the fact of murder, if not home to him, yet close to his door.

The conduct of Ellee corroborated these suspicions. Whenever by any chance he encountered Walter, his rage was ungovernable; he would assail him violently with stones, or, when occasion offered, lay hold of him with all the violence of infuriate madness, tearing his clothes, biting, scratching, kicking, and foaming at the mouth, with a bitterness of rage and antipathy he never exhibited towards any other person. Rumours gathered strength every day; each one compared notes, and each had some circumstance of his own to communicate, that added to the mass of presumptions. A legal inquiry was at length instituted; but the dumb testimony of Ellee was so vague and unsatisfactory, that the grand-jury, while in their hearts they believed Walter guilty, declined to find an indictment. Still, in the eyes of all the neighbourhood, Walter was a convicted murderer and seducer. He escaped the judgment of the law, but the verdict of society condemned him. He stood, a marked man, avoided by all, feared and hated by all; in the midst of society he was alone, and he sought to be alone. It seemed as if he did not like to look in the face of any human being; and the quick apprehension with which he turned his eye, when it met the glance of others, appeared to indicate that he feared they might behold the reflection of his crime in that mirror of his soul.

Time passed on, carrying, as usual, on the bosom of his mighty stream, the wrecks of men and things.

The old lord, who never since the absence of Phœbe had once called Walter "a chip of the old block," disappeared from this world in the fullness of years. His good-fortune followed him to the last, for he sent for a physician who could not come, and thereby escaped the persecutions of the seven sciences, and died of the disease instead of the doctor. His wife soon followed; for it would seem that the lives of old people, who have lived together a long while, become intertwined. Too weak, as it were, for self-support, they lean upon each other in the down-hill course, and, like Jack and Gill, when one falls, the other comes "tumbling after." About the same time, or a little later, for my memory is now grown somewhat indistinct, the mother of Phœbe likewise departed this life; and poor Ellee was taken to my uncle's house, where he remained for the rest of his days, exhibiting, in his profound devotion to his benefactor, a libel on human reason, which ought to hide its head in shame, when told that dogs and idiots transcend it in gratitude. He died of a sort of premature old age, about three years subsequently.

Walter Avery, after the lapse of several years of

gloomy retirement, married a woman who thought his wealth a counterpoise to his delinquencies. Both lived to repent this union. He was a misanthrope, and she a shrew. The days of Walter were days of bitterness, his nights were nights of horror. It seemed as if guilt had unmanned him entirely. He was afraid to be alone in the dark; the rattling of the shutters made him start; the howling of the winds, the rolling of the thunder, every shooting-star, and every ordinary phenomenon of nature, seemed to him the menacing of Heaven's wrath, the forerunner of something dreadful. He became the slave of conscience and superstition combined, and never knew a night of tranquil and unbroken rest. Awake, he lay perspiring in vague indefinite horrors; and sleeping, he rolled from side to side, muttering unintelligible words, and moans that seemed to rend his very vitals. Guilt and remorse are the parents of superstition. Walter became a believer in dreams; as if the gracious Being whose attribute is truth would condescend to convey his intimations through what, ninety-nine times in a hundred, is only the medium of irreconcilable falsehoods and contradictory absurdities. The impression uppermost in his mind was his crime. The figure of Phœbe was ever present to his waking hours;—what wonder, then, if it haunted his dreams? Some little coincidences served to frighten him into a belief that they were more than accidental; and he gradually became a victim to the most abject superstition. In the gloom and silence of night, a thousand fantastic illusions preyed upon his guilty soul; and, when he shut his eyes, perpetual phantasmagoria of shapeless monsters danced before him, grinning in horrid deformity unlike to any human form, or wearing the well-remembered visage of Phœbe, sometimes pale sad and death-like, at others distorted by the most malignant and diabolical passions.

By degrees, as his mind and body became gradually weakened by being thus constantly assailed, a firm conviction fastened itself on his imagination, that this besetting phantasy was a malignant fiend, empowered by a just Providence to assume the shape of his victim, to punish him for his crime. He never had a child by his wife, who at length died; and that night the figure of Phœbe appeared to him as usual, pointing to a leaf in the pocket-book he had given her, which bore these words:—"You shall see me once more."

Not long after this, he was sitting on his piazza in the summer twilight, drinking the very dregs of misery, when he was roused by a little boy, about six or eight years old, who stood weeping before him.

"What do you want, sir?" cried Walter, with the impatience common to his state of mind.

"I want my mother," answered the boy, weeping bitterly.

"You fool! I am not your mother. She is not here."

"I know it, sir; but she sent me to you."

"For what, boy?"

"To bring you a letter and some things, sir," said the boy, handing him at the same time a soiled note.

Walter opened the note. It contained only two words: "Your son." And it was signed, "Phœbe Angevine."

Walter was half-insensible for a moment. Then, seizing the boy's hand, he asked, eagerly, when and where he got that letter.

"My mother gave it me this morning," said the child.

"O God!" cried Walter; "I am not then a murderer." And his hard heart melted for once into gratitude to Heaven. His next impulse was to catch the boy's hand, and study his face, where he saw, as he thought, the sparkling eye and glossy ringlets of his ruined mother; and he hugged him in his arms, and wept delicious tears. The boy did not altogether decline these endearments, but seemed hardly to understand them.

"I am your father," said Walter, at length.

"What is a father?" said the boy. "Is it any thing like my mother?"

"Not much," answered the other; and hid his face with his hands.

"No," said the boy, "I might have known that; my mother never spoke to me — she only kissed me; but I knew what she meant. Oh, I had almost forgot; she told me, with her fingers, to give you these." And he handed a small package.

This Walter opened. It contained the silver pencil-case and little pocket-book he had given to Phœbe.

"Enough," said he; "come in to your father's home:" and he led him by the hand into his house.

That evening he questioned the boy closely as to where and how he had lived, and where his mother had left him in the morning; for now he was determined to seek her, bring her to his home, and make her all the amends in his power.

"You will find it all there," answered the boy, pointing to the pocket-book. On opening it, he found it almost filled with writing, some of which was nearly illegible.

"I am hungry, and sleepy," said the boy.

Walter had supper brought him, which he ate voraciously; and, being placed in Walter's bed, he fell into a sweet and balmy sleep, such as that bed had been a stranger to for years.

Walter then proceeded to make out, as well as he could, the contents of the pocket-book. It was a wretched scrawl, full of details of misery. Connected, and in my own words, it ran as follows:—

It seems, that, on the day Phœbe disappeared, she had arrived at the trysting-place some time before her seducer; and, while waiting, had carved their initials on the bark of the old sycamore. In doing this she cut her finger, and wrapped up the wound in a piece of the note he had sent her, requesting a meeting. When he came, she had in every way through which she could make herself understood, pressed him to make her amends for the shame he had brought upon her. He had replied only by lascivious toyings and attempts to obtain new favours. Indignant at this, the poor girl was running away, when he seized her, just on the borders of the rapid river. A struggle ensued. Phœbe at length, through rage and despair, threw herself into the stream, just as Ellee, who had as usual followed her, came up; while he, forgetting in his rage the situation of his sister, furiously assailed Walter, and prevented him from affording her any assistance. She floated down the stream, kept up by her clothes and the force of the current, till she became entangled in the thick boughs of a tuft of dwarf-willows, that, as is common with this kind of tree, bent down and floated on the surface of the water. Seizing upon these, she drew herself to the bank, got out of the water, and darted into the thick wood without being perceived. It was then that, smarting under the recollection of Walter's insulting behaviour and the anticipation of certain disgrace and exposure, she formed the resolution never to return home. Accordingly, she crossed the mountain which bordered the river, and became an outcast and a wanderer.

Her infirmity of speech proved her best friend among the far-off strangers with whom she sojourned. She was treated with kindness, as one on whom the hand of Providence had inflicted the sorest evils; and she made herself useful by her habits of industry. At this time news did not travel as fast as now; for there were few readers, and fewer newspapers to trumpet forth murders and accidents of flood and field. She lived, accordingly, without seeing or hearing any inquirers or inquiries after her, and without knowing what was passing at home. When her child was born, they wished to take it away, and place it at nurse in a poor-house; but she would not consent. She nursed it and brought it up, without being a burden to any living soul. Thus years wore on, till, one day, as chance would have it, a person from the old neighbourhood came that way, and knew her at once. From him she learned all I have been relating, up to the period at which Walter's wife died. She came to a resolution at once, and departed from her asylum with her child. On arriving in the vicinity of Walter's abode, she placed herself in a situation where she would not be observed, and, instructing the boy what to do, embraced him with tears, and forced him from her much against his will. She waited to see her son received into his father's arms and taken to his home, and then disappeared from the knowledge of all, completely eluding the inquiries of Walter. On the last page of the pocket-book was written, " You shall see me once more." " Strange!", thought Walter,—" the very words of my dream!" The coincidence was singular; but where is the wonder that one dream in a whole lifetime should present some resemblance to a reality?

Walter Avery had paid the full penalty of his crime, in the misery of seven long years. He now enjoyed comparative ease, although he never, to the latest period of his life, could cast off the terrors of darkness and the leaden chains of superstition. Time swept along, and the boy Walter grew up towards manhood, giving promise of becoming as handsome as his mother, and a better man than his father. At length Walter fell sick, and lay on his death-bed. It was just in the twilight of the evening, when his son was alone with him in the room. A female figure came quietly in, and sat down by the bedside.

" Who's that?" asked Walter, in a weak whisper.

" It is my mother!" cried the youth, starting up, and kissing her affectionately.

" She said she would come and see me once more," thought Walter. " It is for the last time; now I know that I shall die." And he lay for a while almost insensible. At length he requested his son to raise him.

" Phœbe," said he, " can you forgive me?"

Phœbe pointed to their child; then placed her hand

on her heart; and, raising her still-beautiful eyes towards Heaven, leaned down and kissed him.

Walter seemed endued with new life.

"Send for Doctor Townley — quick — quick!" said he.

"You mean Doctor Barley," said his son.

"No, no; I mean Parson Townley," answered he: "run, run!"

"He wishes the doctor to pray with him," thought Phœbe, and motioned her son to obey. In the course of half an hour the clergyman arrived.

"Doctor," cried Walter, "I sent for you to marry me." "He is delirious," observed the clergyman; "he will be wedded to none but the winding-sheet and the worm, poor soul."

"Come, come; there is no time to be lost."

"Where is the bride?" said the clergyman, willing to soothe him.

"There," answered Walter; "the mother of that boy."

"Indeed!", cried the good man; "then he is not mad. I am ready, Mr. Avery. Come hither, Phœbe — I did not know you — give me your hand."

Phœbe hung back, and shook her head with determined opposition.

"For the sake of your son."

Still she refused her hand.

"For the sake of the father, then. Would you refuse him the opportunity of making his peace with Heaven, by atoning his injuries to you?"

Phœbe bowed her head with reverence, and gave the clergyman her hand. He placed it within that of the sick man, and went through with the ceremony.

"May God reward you for this act of justice!", said the clergyman.

"May God forgive me!", replied Walter.

Two weeks afterwards, Phœbe was a widow.

"Well, for my part," said Mrs. Fubsy, "I sha'n't visit her."

"Nor I," said Mrs. Cluckey.

"Nor I," said Mrs. Skimpey.

"Nor I," said Mrs. Ratsbane.

Yet they all went to see Phœbe in the course of a fortnight, and all declared she was one of the most agreeable creatures in the world. The truth is, our heroine was an excellent listener; which, in this talking republic of ours, is better than having the eloquence of a Patrick Henry, a Randolph, or a Clay.

DYSPEPSY.

DYSPEPSY.

"O cookery! cookery! That kills more than weapons, guns, wars, or poisons, and would destroy all, but that physic helps to make away some." — Anthony Brewer.

Ye who flatter yourselves that indolence and luxury are compatible with the enjoyment of vigour of health and hilarity of spirits; that the acquisition of the means of happiness is to be happy; and that the habitual pampering of the senses is not forever paid for by the depression of the immortal soul; — listen to my story, and be wise.

I am the son of a reputable gentleman, who made a good figure in the Revolutionary War, and possessed a competent estate in one of the river counties of New York. His name will be found in the old *Committees of Safety*. He ranked as colonel in the Continental Army, and acted as a deputy-commissary-general in the year 1779. In this position he committed a most enormous folly; for, finding the good people his neighbours would not exchange their goods for money that was good-for-nothing — (they were wiser than the present race, notwithstanding the march of mind) — he pledged his own credit for the supplies, without which the army, at Peekskill, would have suffered greatly. He was warmly thanked in letters from distinguished persons in the Old Congress, for people are apt to be grateful in time of danger; but, at the conclusion of the struggle, when he presented his accounts, the danger being over, the accounting officers refused to allow a credit for the debts he had incurred on his own responsibility. My father returned home, a ruined and broken-hearted man. His old neighbours pitied him, but they could not lose their money. They justly considered that charity begins at home, and that there was no moral principle obliging them to starve themselves and their children for the sake of other people. I do not blame them. They divided my father's property among them, and, finding there was nothing left, forgave him the rest of his debts. The contractors and commissaries of the day, with great appearance of reason, called him a fool for ruining himself in a station where every other man managed to grow rich. The old farmers, his neighbours, some of whom are still alive, have often told me that he deserved well of his country; but his name has been smothered under the load of great, good, and patriotic people, that have since sprung up, in these times that try men's pockets.

My father might have petitioned Congress, and died, like poor Amy Dardin and her horse,* before the members had finished making their speeches. But he was a cold, proud man, who often went without his

* Amy Dardin was the widow of a contractor, on the "Cumberland road", who presented to Congress a claim for the value of a horse that perished through some forgotten accident while the work was going on. This claim led to a vast deal of discussion.

dues because he would not ask for them. He accordingly sat down, with his little family around him, steeped in poverty; consoled himself with reading books and studying the stars, and waited in gloomy inactivity for the time, when a great pocket-book full of Continental money, and a few thousand dollars in Continental certificates, should become worth something. The Continental money, as every body knows, never recovered itself; the certificates were afterwards funded at their full value. But, previous to this, my father had, under the strong pressure of necessity, sold them for almost nothing, to a worthy friend of his, who afterwards turned out one of the most eloquent advocates of the Funding System. Heavens!, how he would talk of the sufferings and privations of the patriots of the Revolution! He certainly owed them a good turn, for he got enough by them to build a palace, and purchase half the Genesee country.

At the period of our ruin I was about ten years old, I think, and, until that time, I had been brought up as the children of wealthy country-gentlemen generally are. I had some of the feelings and a portion of the manners of a gentleman's son, which I hope I still retain, although, to say the truth, the latter part of my education was deplorable enough. My father, from the period in which he felt himself dishonoured by the rejection of his accounts, retired within himself, and seemed benumbed in heart and spirits. He passed his whole time in reading the few books that he could come at; and his temper became imperturbable, except at such times as he was routed up and forced to move from his seat. He would then exhibit symptoms of internal discomposure, make for the nearest chair, set himself down, and resume his studies. Half the time he would have forgotten his dinner, had not my mother waked him from his reverie. To be sure, our dinner was hardly worth eating; but, to the best of my recollection, I never enjoyed a better appetite, or had so little of the Dyspepsy. We were often on the very verge of want, and had it not been for the exertions of my excellent mother, who, thank God, is still living, and at least ten years younger than I am — aided by the good offices of a sister, well married in the city — we had sometimes actually wanted the necessaries of life. It was not then so much the fashion for genteel people to go begging. But it is astonishing what the presiding genius of a sensible, prudent, industrious mother, can do; what miracles indeed she can achieve, in keeping herself, her husband, and her children, decent at least. My mother did all this, and more; she sent me to school; and it is not the least of my sources of honest pride, that my education, such as it was, cost the public nothing. Women, notwithstanding what cynics may say, are born for something better than wasting time and spending money; and I hereby apprise the reader that, if ever I am guilty of a sarcasm against woman, it is only when I am labouring under the horrors of Dyspepsy.

Till the age of sixteen I never saw the city. To me it was the region of distant wonders, ineffable splendours, wise men, and beautiful women. I reverenced a New-Yorker, as I now venerate a person who has been to Paris or Rome; and I shall never forget my extreme admiration of a fine lady, the daughter of a little tailor who lived near us. She was an apprentice to a milliner, and came up during the prevalence of the yellow-fever, with three bandboxes and a pocket-handkerchief full of finery. The world of romance — the region of airy nothings, of creatures that come and go at will before the youthful fancy — was now just opening before me in long perspective. I was without employment; for if my mother had a weakness, it was one which I verily believe belongs even to the female angels. She could not forget old times, nor bear the idea that her only son should learn a trade, or slave in any useful calling.

Deprived thus of the resources of active occupation, I spent my time either in reading, or roaming at random and unpurposed through the beautiful romantic scenes which surrounded our poor, yet pleasant abode. My mind was a complete contrast to my body. The latter was indolence itself; the former a perfect vagrant. I was eternally thinking, and doing nothing. The least spark awakened in my mind visions of the future — for that was all to me — and lighted my path through ever-lengthening vistas of shadowy happiness. Sometimes I was a soldier, winning my way to the culmination of military glory; sometimes a poet, the admiration of the fair; and sometimes I possessed, what then seemed to me the sure means of perfect happiness, — ten thousand a year. For days, and weeks, and months, and years, I hardly spoke an unnecessary word. I lived in a world of my own, and millions of thoughts, wishes, fears, and hopes — millions of impulses and impressions — were born in my mind, and died away, without ever making a sign through the medium of my tongue or my pen.

The first-born of the passions is love; and love is

of earlier, as well as more vigorous, growth, in solitude. I was always enamoured of some one; for the sentiment was indispensable to my visionary existence. All ended, however, as it began, in abstract dreams and amatory reveries. It is now my pride to know that no woman was ever yet the wiser for my preference. My affection never manifested itself in any other way than by increasing shyness. I never voluntarily came near a young woman at any time; but when I was in love, I always ran away. I would as soon have met a spirit, as the object of my affections. I was moreover much given to jealousy and pique; always persuading myself, against truth and reason, that the love of which I was myself so conscious, must of necessity be understood by her from whom I was at such pains to keep it a secret. The history of my amours with imaginary mistresses, and mistresses that never imagined my love, is curious; I may one day give it to the world. But my present object is different. I will therefore only say, that I grew up to the age of seventeen or eighteen, a sheer abstract man — a being of thought, rather than action; a dweller in a world of my own fantastic and ridiculous composition; living neither in the past nor the present, but in the vast space before me. My companions were shadows of my own creation; my enjoyments were the production of these shadows. Yet, for all this, I neither became mad nor an idiot. It seemed as if I was all this time preparing myself for realities; and that my sojournings in the realm of fancy imperceptibly initiated me into that of fact. I cannot otherwise account for my early success in life, nor for the miracle of escaping its shoals and quicksands.

At the age of seventeen or eighteen, I forget which, I was sent for by an uncle — (the husband of my mother's sister) — who was a merchant of some note. At one step, I passed from the ideal to the material world. *There is but one greater step*, and that is from the material world to the world of spirits. My uncle was an honest, liberal, cross, gouty old Irish gentleman, with plenty of relations in Ireland whom he would not acknowledge, though they proved that they sprung from the same family-tree. He was an inordinate tory, a member of the Belvidere Club, and a mighty fish-eater at Becky's.* When I first went to live with him, he was getting rather infirm. His hair was as white as snow; his face as rosy as the sun in a mist; his body robust to all appearance; and, had it not been for his "damned legs" as he was pleased to say, he would have been as good a man as he was twenty years before. There is certainly a great change in the world within the last half-century. People lived at least as well as they do now, and only got the gout — now they get Dyspepsy. Can any learned physician tell me the reason of this emigration of the old enemy, from the great toe to the stomach?

The old gentleman had a heart big enough to hold all the world, except the French, the Democrats, and the multiplicity of cousins and second cousins who claimed kindred there and had *not* their claims allowed. He had in truth a most intolerable contempt for poor relations. I believe he would have served

* Becky's was the older club, and devoted to fish and beefsteaks, punch and Madeira. The Belvideres were a gay set, and launched out into Champagne or any thing. Both date back into the last century. The houses of meeting were in the outskirts of the city, overlooking the East River, and not far from Corlaer's Hook.

his wife's family the same way, but, the truth is, my aunt was — but it is a great secret — she could make him do just as she pleased, for she was the best-natured creature in the world, and none but a brute can resist a kind-hearted woman. Being a relation, I was treated to a seat at the dinner-table. The old gentleman was reckoned one of the best livers in town, and here it was, I believe, that I laid the corner-stone of my miseries. At home there had been no temptation to gluttony — here there was a sad succession of allurements, such as human nature seldom can resist, even when experience has demonstrated their ill consequences, and Death sits shaking his dart over every successive delicacy.

People talk of the mischiefs of drinking; invent remedies and preventives, and institute societies; — as if eating was not ten times more pernicious. There are a hundred die of eating to one that dies of drinking. But gluttony is the vice of gentlemen, and gentlemanly vices require neither remedies, preventives, nor societies. It is not necessary to my purpose that I should make a book out of my apprenticeship, as Goethe has done; nor am I writing the history of my uncle, else I might tell some fine stories of his life, actions, and end. His latter years were spent, as usual, in paying the penalty of former indulgences; and a complication of disorders carried him off in a green old age. In three months from the time of his death, half the county of Kilkenny claimed kindred with him. There were so many different claimants, that nobody but the lawyers could settle the matter. After three or four years, a decision was given in favour of a young man, who, on taking possession, had the mortification to discover that nothing was left. The law had become my uncle's heir. It is an excellent thing to have plenty of laws and courts of law; but then one can have too much of a good thing, and pay too much for it. Tournefort, in his Travels in the East, says, "An Italian once told me, at Constantinople, that we should be very happy in Europe, if we could appeal from our courts to the divan; 'for,' added he, 'one might go to Constantinople, and all over Turkey too, if there were occasion, before one suit could be finally decided in Europe.' A Turk," continues M. Tournefort, "pleading before the parliament of Provence, against a merchant of Marseilles who had led him a dance for many years from court to court, made a very merry reply to one of his friends, who desired to know the state of his affairs. 'Why, they are wonderfully altered,' says he: 'when I first arrived here I had a roll of pistoles as long as my arm, and my pleadings were comprised in a single sheet; but at present I have a writing above six times as long as my arm, and my roll of pistoles is but half an inch.'" I wish the law-givers, the judges, and more especially the lawyers, would recollect that time is money, and that to waste both the time and the money of suitors is a double oppression. A man might better get the bastinado promptly though wrongfully sometimes, than wait seven years for his rights, as in some Christian countries.

The death of my uncle was a lucky affair for me, as by it I lost the mischievous allurements of his table, and was thrown upon my own resources for a livelihood. Hard days make soft nights; and I found that the necessity of exertion, and the occasional difficulties in procuring a dinner, soon reinstated me in the possession of the only inheritance I received from my father — a hale constitution. It was my good fortune, as the world would call it, to meet with a young man of capital, who wanted a partner skilled in the business my uncle had followed. We accordingly entered into partnership, and our business proved exceedingly profitable. In a few years I had more money than I required for my wants, and with the necessity for exertion ceased the inclination. When a man has been toiling for years to get rich, and dreaming all the while that riches will add to his enjoyments, he must try and realize his dreams, after his endeavours have been crowned with success. I had proposed to myself a life of ease and luxury, as the reward of all my labours. Accordingly, finding myself sufficiently wealthy, I retired from the firm as an active partner, continuing however my name to the connexion, and receiving a share of the profits in return for the use of my capital.

I am now my own master, said I, as I shook the dust of the counting-house from my feet. I can do as I please, and go where I please. Now a man that has but one thing to do and one place to go to can never be in the predicament of the ass between two bundles of hay; nor be puzzled to death in the midst of conflicting temptations. At first I thought of going to Europe; but before I could make up my mind the packet had sailed, and before another was ready I had altered my mind. Next I decided for the Springs; then for the Branch; then for Schooley's mountain; and then, in succession, for every other "resort of beauty and fashion," in these United States. In conclusion, I went to none of them. I made but two excursions: one to the Fireplace, to catch trout, where I caught an ague; and the other to Sing Sing, to see the new state-prison, where I missed the ague and caught a bilious fever. Thus the summer passed away, and I may say I did nothing but eat. That is an enjoyment in which both ease and luxury are combined, and my indisposition had left behind a most voracious appetite. Towards the latter end of autumn, I began to feel I can scarcely tell how. I slept all the evening, and lay awake all the night; or, if I fell asleep, always dreamed I was suffocating between two feather beds. I was plagued worse than poor Pharaoh. I had aches of all sorts; stiff necks, pains in the shoulders, sides, back, loins, head, breast: in short, there never was a man so capriciously used by certain inexplicable, unaccountable infirmities, as I was. I dare say I had often felt the same pains before without thinking of them, because I was too busy to mind trifles; for it is a truth which my experience has since verified, that the most ordinary evils of life are intolerable, without the stimulus of some active pursuit to draw us from their perpetual contemplation. What was very singular, I never lost my appetite all this time, but ate more plentifully than ever. Indeed, eating was almost the only amusement I had, ever since I became a man of pleasure; and it was only while engaged at the table that I lost the sense of those innumerable pains which tormented me at other times.

I went to a physician, who gave me directions as to the various modes of treatment in these cases. "You are dyspeptic," said he, "and you must either eat less, exercise more, take physic, or be sick." As to eating less, that was out of the question. What is the use of being rich, unless a man can eat as much as he likes? As to exercise — what is the use of being rich, if a man can't be as lazy as he pleases? The alternative lay between being sick or taking physic, and I chose the latter. The physician shook his head and smiled, but it is not the doctor's business to discourage the taking of physic; and he prescribed, accordingly. I took medicines, I ate more than ever, and, what quite discouraged me, I grew worse and worse. I sent for the doctor again. "You have tried physic in vain; suppose you try exercise on horseback," said he.

I bought a horse, cantered away every morning like a hero, and ate more than ever; — for what was the use of exercise, except to give one impunity in eating? I never worked half so hard when I was an apprentice, and not worth a groat, as I did now I was a gentleman of ease and luxury. It was necessary, the doctor said, that the horse should be a hard trotter; and accordingly I bought one that trotted so hard, that he actually broke the paving-stones in Broadway, and struck fire at every step. O, reader!, gentle reader, if thou art of Christian bowels, pity me! I was dislocated in every joint, and sometimes envied St. Laurence his gridiron. But I will confess that the remedy proved not a little efficacious, and it is my firm opinion that, had I persevered, I should have been cured in time, had I not taken up a mistaken notion, that a man who exercised a great deal might safely eat a great deal. Accordingly, I ate by the mile, and every mile I rode furnished an apology for a further indulgence of appetite. The exercise and the eating being thus balanced, I remained just where I was before.

I sent for the physician, again. "You have tried medicine and exercise, suppose you try a regimen. Continue the exercise; eat somewhat less; confine yourself to plain food, plainly dressed; abstain from rich sauces, all sorts of spices, pastes, confectioneries, and puddings, particularly plum-puddings, and, generally, every kind of luxury; and drink only a glass or two of wine."

"Zounds! doctor, I might as well be a poor man at once! What is the use of being rich, if I can't eat and drink, and do just as I like? Besides, I am particularly fond of sauces, spices, and plum-puddings."

"Why, so you may do as you like," replied he, smiling. "You have your choice between Dyspepsy and all these good things."

The doctor left me to take my choice, and, after great and manifold doubts, resolutions, and retractions, I decided on trying the effects of this most nauseating remedy. I practised the most rigid self-denial; tasted a little of this, a very little of that, a morsel of the other, and ate moderately of every thing on the table; cheating myself occasionally by tasting slyly a bit of confectionery, or a slice of plum-pudding. Now and then, indeed, when I felt better than usual, I indulged more freely, as I had a right to do; — for what is the use of starving at one time, except to enable one's self to indulge at another? The physician came one day to dine with me at my boarding-house, the most famous eating-place in the whole city, and the most capital establishment for Dyspepsy. He came, he said, on purpose to see how I followed his prescription. I was extremely abstinent that day, only eating a mouthful of every thing now and then. The doctor, I observed, played a glorious knife and fork, and seemed particularly fond of rich sauces, spices, paste, and plum-pudding.

"Well, doctor," said I, after the rest of the company had retired, "am not I a hero — a perfect anchorite?"

"My dear sir," said he, "I took the trouble to count every mouthful. You have eaten twice as much as an ordinary labourer, and tasted of every thing on the table."

"But only tasted, doctor; while you — you — gave me a most edifying example. Faith, you displayed a most bitter antipathy to pies, custards, rich sauces, and, most especially, plum-pudding."

"My dear Ambler," said the doctor, "you are to follow my prescriptions, not my example. But, by the way, that was delightful wine, that last bottle — Bingham, or Marston, hey?"

I took the hint, and sent for another bottle, which we discussed equally between us, glass for glass. I felt so well I sent for another, and we discussed that too.

"My dear fellow," said the doctor, who by this time saw double, "my dear friend, mind, don't forget my prescription; no sauces, no spices, no paste, no plum-pudding, and, above all, no wine. Adieu. I am going to a consultation."

That night I suffered martyrdom — night-mare, dreams, and visions of horror. A grinning villain came, and, seizing me by the toe, exclaimed, "I am Gout; I come to avenge the innocent calves who have suffered in forced-meat balls and mock-turtle, for your gratification." Another blear-eyed, sneering rogue, gave me a box on the ear that stung through every nerve, crying out, "I am Catarrh, come to take satisfaction for the wine you drank this day;" while a third, more hideous than the other two, a miserable, cadaverous, long-faced fiend, came up, touching me into a thousand various pains, and crying, in a hollow, despairing voice, "I am Dyspepsy, come to punish you for your gluttony." I awoke next morning in all the horrors of indigestion and acidity, which lasted several days, during which time I made divers excellent resolutions, forswearing wine, particularly old wine, most devoutly.

This time, however, I had one consolation. The doctor, and not I, was to blame. It was he that led me into excesses for which I was now paying the penalty. I felt quite indignant. "I'll let him know," said I, "that I am my own master, and not to be forced to drink against my inclination." So I discharged the doctor who set me such a bad example, and called in three more, being pretty well assured that I should now hear all sides of the question. Professional men seldom or never agree perfectly in opinion, because that would indicate a lack of individual confidence. They retired into my dressing-room, forgetting to shut the door. Doctors in consultation should always make sure to shut the door.

"He wants excitement," said Doctor Calomel, a thunderbolt of science; "there is — that is to say, the bile has got the better of the blood, and the phlegm has overpowered the atrabile — they are struggling like fury for the upper hand. We must give him a dose of calomel."

" Not at all," quoth Doctor Jalap, whose great excellence consisted in the number of capital letters he carried at the tail of his name, insomuch that he was called the Professor of A. B. C.; "not at all — the salt, sulphur, and mercury, which Paracelsus affirms constitute the matter of all animal bodies, are in a state of disorganization. We must therefore give him two doses of calomel." What a piece of work is man!, thought I — "salt, sulphur, and mercury!"

" The body being an hydraulic engine," quoth Doctor Rhubarb, who valued himself on his theory, "the body being an hydraulic engine, our remedies must be founded on the laws of magnitude and motion; we must therefore give him three doses of calomel, in succession; the first to increase the magnitude of the stomach, the others to cause motion."

" Pish," quoth Doctor Calomel; "what nonsense is this, about salt, sulphur, and mercury! Paracelsus was a fool."

"'Sdeath!," cried Doctor Jalap — (he always swore by his old friend) — "'sdeath! sir, if you come to that, what nonsense is this about bile, and phlegm, and atrabile! And you, sir," turning to Doctor Rhubarb, "with your hydraulic machine; you might as well call a man a forcing-pump at once. Hippocrates was a great blockhead, and knew nothing of chemistry; and so was Meade, and Borelli, and the rest of the hydraulic machines."

The debate was getting hot, when Dr. Jalap, who was a man of great skill and experience in his profession, interposed the olive-branch.

" Gentlemen," said the doctor, "nothing weakens the influence of the profession, and destroys the confidence of the public in medicine, so much as the opposite opinions of physicians. Where is the use of quarrelling about the disease, when we all agree in the remedy?"

So they ordered the calomel.

But it would not do, though I continued my system of abstinence, and only barely tasted a little of every thing; at the same time compromising matters with my conscience, by drinking twelve half glasses of wine instead of six whole ones. The doctors, on the whole, did me more harm than good. Their different opinions had conjured up a hundred chimeras in my fancy, and inflicted on me a host of complaints I never dreamed of before. Sometimes the conflicts of the bile and the phlegm turned every thing topsy-turvy; anon the salt, sulphur, and mercury, fell together by the ears; and lastly, the hydraulic machine got terribly out of order. It was no joke then, though now I can look back upon these horrors as on a sea of ills that I have safely passed over. My spirits began to sink; for I considered that I had now tried all remedies, and that my case was hopeless. The fear of death, swelled into a gigantic and disproportioned magnitude of evil, came upon me. I never heard of a person dying of a disease, be it what it would, that I did not make that the bugbear of my imagination, and feel all the symptoms appropriate to it. Thus I had, by turns, all the diseases under the sun; sometimes separately, sometimes all together. The sound of a church-bell conjured up the most gloomy associations, and the sight of a church-yard withered every tendril of hilarity in my bosom. In short, there were moments of my life when I could fully comprehend the paradox, that a human being may seek death as a relief from its perpetual apprehension, even as the bird flies into the maw of the serpent from the mere fascination of terror.

It is one of the most melancholy features of the disease under which I laboured, that it creates a distorted apprehension of death — a vague and horrible exaggeration, ten times worse than the reality. In most other disorders, the pain of the body supersedes that of the mind; in this, the mind predominates over the body, and the monstrous future swallows up the present entirely. This was the case with me; and often have I welcomed an acute fit of rheumatism or colic, as a cure for anticipated evils. I had another enemy to contend with, and that was the want of sympathy. People laughed at my complaints when they saw me eat my meals with so good an appetite, for the world seldom gives a man credit for ailing in any respect, when he can eat his allowance; nor is it easy to persuade the vulgar that there is such a disease as appetite. Besides, a man who is always complaining, and never seeming to grow worse, is enough to tire the patience of Job, much more of such friends as Job and most afflicted people are blessed with. My mind was in a perpetual muddle of indecision. One day I threw all my phials, and boxes, and doses, into the street, determined to take no more physic; and the next, perhaps, sent for some more, and renewed my potions. I had lost by this time all confidence in physicians, but still continued to believe in physic.

For a while, white mustard-seed was a treasure to me; and such was my firm reliance on its wonderful virtues, that I actually indulged myself in a few extra glasses, and a few extra luxuries, on the credit of its prospective operation. I read all the guides to health, and all the lectures of Doctor Abernethy. In short, I took every means (but the only proper ones) to effect a cure. I proportioned my eating and other indulgences to my faith in the workings of my favourite panacea. When I took a dose of physic, I considered myself as fairly entitled to take a small liberty the day after; and when I rode or walked farther than usual, I made the old wine, and the sauces and plum-pudding, pay for it. It was thus that I managed to keep myself in a perfect equilibrium, and, like another Penelope, undid in the afternoon the work of the morning. I found, after all, nothing did me so much good as laughing; but, alas!, what was there for me to laugh at in this world!

The summer of my second year of ease and luxury, I was advised to go to the Springs, where all the doctors send those patients who get out of patience at not being cured in a reasonable time. Here I found several companions in affliction, and was mightily comforted to learn that some of them had been in their present state almost a score of years, without ever dying at all. We talked over our infirmities, and I found there was a wonderful family resemblance in them, — for not one of us could give a tolerable account of his symptoms. One was bilious, another rheumatic; a third was nervous, and a fourth was all these put together.

"Why don't you exercise in the open air?" said I, to this last martyr, one day.

"I catch cold, and that brings on my rheumatism."

"In the house, then?"

"It makes me nervous."

"Why don't you sit still?"

"It makes me bilious."

I thank my stars, thought I, here is a man to grow happy upon; he is worse off than myself. He became my favourite companion; and no one can tell how much better I felt in his society.

We formed a select coterie, and managed to sit together at meals, where we discussed the subject of digestion. We were all blessed with excellent appetites, and particularly fond of the things that did not agree with us.

"Really, Mr. Butterfield, you are eating the very worst thing on the table."

"I know it, my dear sir, but I am so fond of it."

"My good friend Mr. Creamwell, how can you taste that hot bread?"

"My dear sir, don't you see I only eat the crust."

"Let me advise you not to try that green corn, Mr. Ambler. It is the worst thing in the world for dyspeptic people."

"Doubtless, my dear Abstract; but I always take good care to chew, before I swallow, it."

Thus we went on, discussing and eating, and I particularly noticed that every one ate what he preferred, because, the fact was, he was so particularly fond of that particular dish, he could not help indulging in it sometimes. However, we talked a great deal on the subject of diet, and not a man of us but believed himself a pattern of abstinence. I continued my custom of riding, every fair day, and occasionally met a fat lady fagging along on a little fat pony, with a fat servant behind her. One day, when it was excessively hot, I could not help asking her how she could think of riding out in the broiling sun.

"O, sir, I'm so dyspeptic."

I happened to see her at dinner that day, and did not wonder at it.

I passed my time rather pleasantly here, with my companions in misfortune. We exchanged notes, compared our infirmities, and gave a full and true history of their rise, progress, and present state, always leaving out the eating. By degrees I became versed in the history of each. One was a literary man, and a poet. He set out in life with the necessity of economy and exertion, and practiced a laborious profession for some years, when, by great good fortune, he made a lucky speculation, that enabled him to lead a life of ease and luxury. He devoted himself to the muses, and gained enough of reputation, as he said, to make him indifferent to a thing which he perceived came and went by chance or fashion. However, he did not make this discovery until after several of his works had been condemned to oblivion. Not having the stimulus of necessity, and without the habit of being busy about nothing, than which none can be more essential to a life of ease and luxury, he gradually sunk into indifference and lassitude. He finally took to eating, and, for want of some other object, came at last to consider his dinner as the most important affair of life. In due time he lost his spirits and health, and came to the Springs to recover them.

"I ought to be happy," said he, "for I have more than a sufficiency of money; and as for fame, I look to posterity for that."

The next person of our coterie was a man who in like manner had begun the world a hardy, yet honest, adventurer. By dint of unwearied perseverance and the exertion of his excellent faculties, he had risen, step by step, on the ladder of fortune, until, at the age of fifty, he was in possession of a fair estate and an unsullied name. But he was sorely disappointed to find that what he had been all his life seeking was in fact a shadow. This is the common error of sanguine tempers; they first exaggerate the object of their pursuit, and then quarrel with it because it does not realize their expectations. "I have all I ever proposed to myself in pursuing the means of happiness," mused he, "and, for aught I can remember, I was happier in what I sought than in what I found. I will retire from these vain pursuits, and pass the rest of my life in ease and luxury." Accordingly he settled himself down, and, having nothing else to think of in the morning, his time hung heavy on him till dinner. Of consequence, he began to long for dinner-time; and, of course, dinner became an object of great consequence. It was an era in the four-and-twenty hours, and you may rely on it, gentle reader, it was properly solemnized. There are no people that eat so much as the idle. The savage, basking in the sun all day with his pipe, eats thrice as much, when he can get it, as the industrious labourer. The inevitable results of luxurious feeding associated with inaction of body and mind made their appearance in good time, and my friend was pronounced dyspeptic. Having, in the course of three years, consulted twenty-five doctors; taken a half-bushel of white mustard, and fifty kegs of Jamison's Dyspepsy crackers; and swallowed six hundred doses of various kinds — all in vain, (for he still continued to have a glorious appetite,) — he at last came to the Springs, where I had the happiness to meet him.

"I am indifferent to the world," said he, after finishing the sketch, — "I am indifferent to the world and all it contains."

"Then why do you take such pains to live?"

"I don't know," said he, with a melancholy smile; "I sometimes think Providence implanted in our hearts the fear of death, in order to enable us to endure the ills of life without fleeing to the grave for a refuge."

Another of my new friends was brought up to politics, a profession rather overstocked at present. I will not enter into particulars, but merely state, that — after scuffling at meetings; declaiming at polls; clinging to the skirts of great men; fagging on their errands; doing for them what they were ashamed to do for themselves; and sacrificing all private, social, and domestic duties to his party principles; — he at length attained an honourable public station, which, being permanent, he flattered himself would secure him an independence for life. He accordingly discontinued his active exertions, and confined himself to the laborious idleness and desperate monotony of his office, which, although it did not furnish employment, enforced the necessity of constant attendance. He grew lazy, idle, and luxurious. The morning was too long for his occupations, and the usual consequence ensued; he waited for his dinner, and made his dinner pay for it. In this way he continued, increasing in riches, and complaining of his health, and passing through the various stages of Dyspepsy; from the doctor to the horse, from the horse to the white mustard, the blue pills, and Dr. Abernethy — to every thing, in short, but the one specific. A sudden somerset of party, in which all his friends turned their coats but himself, brought him in jeopardy of office. They all insisted he had deserted his party, when, the fact was, his party had deserted him, as he solemnly assured me. Be this as it may, as his appointment was for life, and they could not get rid of the incumbent, they got at him in another way; they abolished the office — a cunning invention of modern politicians. Having nothing to keep him in town, he came to the Springs, to nurse his Dyspepsy, and rail at the ingratitude of republics.

There is but one more of the party to be mentioned. He was the gentleman-of-all-work, whose diseases were so provokingly contrasted that what was good for one was bad for the other. Being one day interrogated on the subject, he began: —

"I was born in the lap of — " (here he yawned pathetically), "and I shall die in the arms of — " (here he gave another great yawn), "but really gentlemen, I feel so nervous, and bilious, and rheumatic, this morning — I am sure the wind is easterly — pray excuse me — some other time." So saying, he yawned once more, and went to see which way the wind blew.

My readers, if they are such readers as alone I address myself to, in looking back upon the growth of whatever wisdom and experience time and opportunity may have gathered for them, will have observed that a particular branch of knowledge, or a special conviction of the understanding, will often baffle our pursuit for a long while. We grope in the dark—we lose ourselves—lose sight of the object—yet are we gaining upon it, unknown and imperceptibly to ourselves. The light is hidden, though just at hand, and, finally, all at once bursts upon us, illuminates the mind, and brings with it the full, perfect perception. Thus was it with me. I had read all the most-approved books, to come at the mystery of a man's being always sick and always hungry; and I had taken all the steps, save one, which they recommended, either as cures or palliatives. I was still in the dark, but I was approaching the light. The history of my complaining friends at once put me upon the right path. I saw in them what I could not see in myself.

On comparing their autobiographies — odious, clumsy word!—I could not but perceive a family likeness in all. They had commenced the world with active, exciting occupations, and were all too busy, as well as too poor, in their youth, to become gluttons; and, again, they had, without an exception, attained at mid-age the means of assuring a life of luxury and ease. They had arrived at stations in which they could enjoy both without the necessity of exerting either body or mind, and they did enjoy them. But they wanted something, still—they wanted a hobby-horse, a stimulus of some kind or other, sufficiently piquant to urge their minds along without dragging on the ground, or rusting out with inanity. They were in the situation of a pair of pampered horses, belonging to a friend of mine, a great mathematician, who, though he kept a carriage, never rode in it. Of course they got plump, clumsy, and dyspeptic; and never were used, without either falling lame, or tumbling on their knees. My friend cast about for a remedy, and at length hit upon one worthy of a philosopher. He invented a machine, which, being fastened to the axletree of his carriage, made an excellent corn-mill; and sent his horses out every day, to take an airing, and grind their own corn. The friction of the machine created a wholesome necessity for exertion in the horses, which, in a little time, became perfectly serviceable, active, and sprightly. My companions in misery only wanted to be under the necessity of grinding their own corn, and, like the horses of my friend the mathematician, to combine the pleasure of eating with the labour of earning a meal.

Next to this necessity for exertion is a hobby, a pursuit of some kind or other, something to awake the sleeping mind, if it be only to get up and play puss-in-a-corner. I know a worthy gentleman who has kept off Ennui and her twin sister, Dyspepsy, by a habit of going every day round all the docks, counting the vessels, and reading the names on the stern. He came nigh being drowned the other day, in leaning over the edge of a wharf to find out the name of a beautiful new ship. Another distances the foul fiend, which is as lazy as an overfed house-dog, by walking up one street and down another, examining all the new houses that are being built, counting the number of rooms, closets, and pantries, and noting divers other particulars. He can describe the marble mantel-pieces of every new house in town. But, in my opinion, the wisest of all my friends was a wealthy idler, who was fast sinking into subjection to this ghoul of the age. He all at once bethought himself of altering his dinner hour, and afterwards went about telling the news to all his friends. Let not the dingy moralists, who send out their decrees for the acquisition of happiness from the depths of darkness, and know no more of the world than a ground-mole, turn up their noses at these my especial friends. Did they know what they ought to know before they set themselves up as teachers, they would comprehend that, when men have made their fortunes by industry and economy and have paid their debt to society in useful and honourable labour, there comes a time when the bow must be unstrung — when amusements, or at least light avocations, become indispensable, and trifles assume importance, because they exercise the influence of weighty circumstances on our happiness. It is then that he who can find out an innocent mode of living, and innocent sources of recreation, which interfere with no one's happiness, and contribute to his own — which keep his mind from preying on itself, and his body healthy — is better entitled to the honours of philosophy than inexperienced people are aware.

What would have been the effect of the new light which had thus broken in upon me — whether habit would have yielded to conviction, or whether (as is generally the case with old offenders) I should have continued to act against my better reason, — I know not. Happily, as I now am convinced, I was not left to decide for myself. Fortune took the affair in her own hands. One morning I received a letter, apprising me of the failure of our house, and the probable ruin it would bring upon myself. That very day I set out for the city, with a vigour and activity beyond all praise, and proceeded directly on, without stopping by the way or once thinking of my digestion.

"Adieu," said the poet, as I took leave of him; "never trust to the present age, but look to posterity for your reward."

"Farewell," said the despiser of this world; "take care of your health, and never eat sausages."

"Good-by," said the politician; "beware of the ingratitude of republics."

"Day-day, Mr. Ambler," said the nervous gentleman; "can you tell me which way the wind blows? I wish you all hap—" here he was beset by a yawn, which lasted till I was in my carriage and on the way to the city.

Arriving in town, I plunged into a sea of troubles. The younger partner of our house, being in a hurry to grow rich, had encouraged a habit of speculating, which, unfortunately for us all, produced a pernicious habit of gambling in schemes of vast magnitude. Having thrown doublets two or three times in succession, he did not, like a wise calculator, conclude that his luck must be nearly exhausted, and retire from the game with his winnings. He doubled again, and lost all. I will not fatigue my readers with the details of a bankruptcy of this kind. It will be sufficient to say that I took the business directly in hand; nearly deranged my head in arranging my affairs; and, by dint of extraordinary industry, and I will say extraordinary integrity, managed to do what only three men before me in similar circumstances had ever done in this city since the landing of Hendrik Hudson. I paid the debts of the firm to the last farthing, leaving myself nothing but a good name, a good conscience, and a large farm in the very centre of the Highlands. I worked every day in the business, like a hero, and took no care what I should eat or what I should drink. My mind was fully occupied, and I was perpetually running about, or examining into my affairs at the counting-house.

I went to pay off my last and greatest debt, to my last creditor, a hard-featured, hard-working, gigantic Scotchman, who had the reputation of being a most inflexible dealer. When all was settled, he said,

"Mr. Ambler, of course you mean to begin business again. Remember that my credit, ay sir, my purse, is at your service. You have gained my confidence."

"I thank you, Mr. Hardup," replied I, "warmly, sincerely; for I know you are sincere in your offers. But I mean to retire into the country with what I have saved from the wreck of my fortune. I am tired of business, and too poor to be idle. I have a farm in the mountains, which, I thank God, is mine; for my creditors are all paid. You, sir, are the last."

"Very well, very well," replied Mr. Hardup, stalking about according to his wont; — "but, is your farm stocked, and all that?"

I was obliged to answer in the negative. It was almost in a state of nature. Mr. Hardup said nothing more, and I bade him farewell with a feeling of indignation at his idle inquiries. The next day, I received the following note, enclosing a check for a sum which I shall not mention: —

"SIR — You must have something to stock your farm. Pay the enclosed when you are able. I shall come and see you one of these days, when you are settled. Send me neither receipt nor thanks for the money. There is more where that came from. You have gained my confidence, I repeat; and no man ever gained that, without I hope being the better for it, sooner or later.

"Your friend and servant,

"ALEXANDER HARDUP."

"P. S. Get up early in the morning; see to matters yourself; and never buy any thing dear except a good name. A. H."

A worthy man was this Mr. Hardup; and I shall never again, while I live, judge of any body by the expression of the face, or the common report of the world.

It was in the spring of the year 1818 that I bade adieu to the city, and went to take possession of my farm, where I arrived just when the sun was gilding the mountain-tops with his retreating rays, as he sunk behind the equally high hills on the opposite side of the river. The scene indeed was beautiful to look at, but by no means encouraging to a man who was going to set himself down here and labour for a livelihood. I was received by an old man and his wife, who had occupied my farm a long time, at a very moderate rent which they never paid. The aspect of the house was melancholy — broken windows, broken chairs, and a broken table. But there was plenty of fresh air, and I slept that night on a straw-bed, and studied astronomy through the holes in the roof. The dead silence too that reigned in this lonely retreat, contrasted with the ceaseless racket of the town, to which I had been so long accustomed, had a mournful effect on my spirits, and disposed my mind to gloomy thoughts of the future. The fatigue of my journey, however, at last overpowered me, and I fell asleep in the certainty of waking next morning with some terrible malady arising from my exposed situation. It is a singular fact, that I slept that night more sweetly than I had done ever since I determined upon the enjoyment of a life of luxury and ease; and, what is equally singular, I waked early in the morning, without either a sore throat, a swelled face, or a rheumatic headache. I am certain of this, for I felt my throat, shook my head to hear if it cracked, and looked in a bit of glass to see if my face retained its true proportions. I confess I was rather disappointed. "But never mind," thought I, "I shall certainly pay for it to-morrow."

The morrow came, however, and I was again disappointed. I was sure it would come the next day. But, wonderful as it may seem, I thought I felt better than when I had slept in a feather-bed and a close room warmed with anthracite coal. I began to be encouraged, and by degrees became reconciled to the enormity of sleeping on a straw-bed, in a room where the air was playing about in zephyrs, without catching cold. My reader, if he chance to be in the enjoyment of ease and luxury, will shrink with horror from my dinners, which consisted of a piece of salt pork and potatoes for the first course, and some bread and butter, or bread and milk, for the dessert. At first, I was certain the pork would produce indigestion; but, I suppose, as there was nothing particularly inviting in it, I did not eat enough to do me any harm, for I certainly felt as light as a feather after my meals, and, instead of dozing away an hour in a chair, was ready for exercise at a minute's warning.

The old couple welcomed me to my "nice place," and were exceedingly eloquent in praise of my nice, comfortable house, the nice pork, the bread and butter, and the milk, all equally "nice." By degrees I began to be infected with their artless content, and sometimes actually caught myself enjoying the scanty comforts around me. I did not cudgel myself into an unwilling submission to necessity; but I benefited by the example of the honest old couple without reasoning at all about the matter. Reason and precept are a sort of pedagogues that, at best, bring about but a grumbling acquiescence; while example comes in the shape of a gentle guide, himself pursuing the right way, and not commanding us to follow, but beckoning us on with smiles.

I confess, when I looked about on my domain, I despaired of ever bringing it into order, beauty, or productiveness. I knew not the magic of labour and perseverance; nor did I dream that the fields around me, which seemed only fruitful in rocks and stones, could ever be made to wave in golden grain or green meadows. The only spot of all my extensive estate that seemed susceptible of improvement was about twenty acres that lay directly before my door, between two shelving rocky mountains, and through which ran a little brook of clear spring-water. But even this was so sprinkled with rocks which had rolled down from the neighbouring hills, that it was sufficiently discouraging to a man who had for several years worn spatterdashes, because he shrunk from pulling on his boots. I spent a month, nearly, in pondering on what I should first undertake, and ended in despairing to undertake any thing.

One day I was leaning over the bars at the entrance to my house, when a tall, raw-boned figure, with hardly an ounce of flesh to his complement, came riding along on a horse as hardy and raw-boned as himself. He stopped at the bars, and bade me good-morning. In justice to myself I must say that, though proud enough in all conscience, I am not one of those churls who, because they have a better coat to their backs, (which, by the way, often belongs to the tailor), think themselves entitled to receive the honest salute of an honest man with coldness or contempt. Beshrew me such arrant blockheads, they call this vulgar insolence, when, in fact, it is the impulse of nature, whispering to the inmost man that there is nothing in outward circumstances, or the difference of wealth or dress, which places one being so high above another that he must not speak to him when they happen to meet or be thrown together. Even when I was enjoying a life of luxury and ease, and possessed of great wealth, it was a pleasure to me to talk with these honest fellows in linsey-woolsey; and I will here bear this testimony, that I have gained from them more practical knowledge, heard more plain good-sense, and caught more valuable hints for the government and enjoyment of life, than I ever did from all the philosophers I ever conversed with, or all the books I ever read.

"Good morning, good morning," said the tall man on the tall horse; and, "good morning, good morning," replied I, not to be outdone in courtesy.

"I believe you don't know me," said he, after a short pause, which, short as it was, proved the longest he ever made in his conversations with me. "I believe you don't know me; my name is Lightly, and I am your next neighbour over the mountain yonder."

"And my name is Ambler," said I, "and I am heartily glad to have you for a neighbour. Won't you alight?"

"Well, I don't care if I do; it was partly my business to come and have a talk with you."

Mr. Lightly accordingly dismounted, and, fastening his horse under a tree to protect him from the sun, which was waxing hot, followed me into the house. After taking something, he looked about, first at one mountain, then at another, and at length began:—

"A rough country, this you've got into, Mr. Ambler."

"Very," replied I; "so rough, that I am afraid I shall never make any part of it smooth."

"No?" said Mr. Lightly; "why not?"

"Look at the trees."

"You must cut them down."

"Look at the rocks."

"You must grub them up, they'll make excellent stone walls."

"Doubtless, if I had the people who piled Ossa on Pelion to assist me." Mr. Lightly had never read the history of the great rebellion of the giants, and rather stared at me. "But," added I, "do you really think I can make any thing out of these mountains?"

"Do I?" said he; "only come over and see me to-morrow, and I will give you proof of it; but no, now I think of it, not to-morrow, the day after. I am going to step over to Poughkeepsie to-morrow, and sha'n't be back till sundown."

"Poughkeepsie!" cried I,—"and back again in one day! Why, 'tis sixty miles: you mean, you'll be back the day after to-morrow evening."

"No I don't. I mean to-morrow evening, God willing; but my days are much longer than yours."

"I should think so: you mean to make the sun stand still, like Joshua."

"No I don't, though my name *is* Joshua. I mean to be up at the first crowing of an old cock, that never sleeps after three in the morning, in summer."

"But, you've got a horse, why don't you ride?"

"O, that would take me two days; and I can't well spare the time. I never ride when I'm in a hurry."

So saying, Mr. Lightly, after getting my promise to come over the next day but one, took his departure, leaving me to ponder on the vast improbability of a man's walking to Poughkeepsie and back again in one day. If he does, thought I, I shall begin to believe in the seven-league boots.

On the morning appointed, my old man guided me by a winding path to the summit of the mountain; and, pointing to a comfortable-looking house, flanked by a large barn and other out-buildings, which stood in the midst of green meadows and cultivated fields, told me that was the place to which I was going. As I paused awhile to contemplate the rural scene, I could not help wishing that it had pleased Providence to cast my lot where the rocks were so scarce, and the meadows so green. Lightly saw me at the top of the hill, and, making some half a dozen long strides with his long legs, met me more than half-way up the mountain side.

"Good morning, good morning," said he, for I soon

found he was very fond of talking, and often repeated the same thing to keep himself going.

I returned his salutation, adding, "I see you have got back."

"O yes; but not quite so soon as I calculated. I went about four miles out of my way, to bring home my old woman's yarn from the manufactory, and it was almost dark before I got home."

During this brief dialogue he had shot ahead of me two or three times. "You are no great walker, I see," said Mr. Lightly.

"Why, no; I don't think I could walk sixty-eight miles a day, in the month of June, without being a little tired."

"There's nothing like trying," said he.

"I don't think I shall try," thought I.

My new friend, Mr. Lightly, kept me with him all day, showing me what he had done in the course of eight or ten years, and describing his farm as it was, when he first purchased it for little or nothing. We came to a beautiful meadow, which I could not help admiring, and wishing I had such a one on my farm.

"You have a much finer one," said Lightly.

"Where? I never saw it."

"Directly before your door."

"That! — why, it is paved with rocks."

"Well, and so was this."

"What has become of them all?"

"There they are," — pointing to the wall which surrounded the meadow.

The wall seemed a work of the Cyclops, or the builders of the pyramids, for it was literally rocks piled on rocks, "as if by magic spell." I inquired how he got them one upon the other, as I did not see any machinery.

"We had no machines but such as these," holding out his hard, bony hands, and baring part of his arms, that were nothing but twisted sinews.

"But you did not dig these rocks out of the ground, and pile them up here, all by yourself, surely?"

"No, no; not quite that, either. I have six boys, who assisted me. You shall see them; they will be home from work, presently."

"Fine boys' work! Faith, I should like to see them."

"Yonder they come," said Mr. Lightly.

I followed the direction of his eye, and beheld coming down the hill, afar off, what I took for six giants, striding onward with intent to devour us at one meal. As they advanced towards me my apprehensions subsided, for I saw, in their open countenances and clear blue eyes, indubitable tokens of harmlessness and good-nature. I never saw such men before; and here in the mountains, out of the sphere of those artificial distinctions which level in some measure all physical disparities, I could not help feeling a sort of qualm of inferiority. In the crowded city, and amid the conflicts of civilized society, the mind predominates; but here my business was to cut down trees and remove rocks, and the man best qualified for these was the great man for my money. After seeing these "boys," I did not so much wonder at the miracles they had achieved. The whole farm, in fact, exhibited proofs of the wonders which may be wrought by a few strong arms, animated and impelled by as many stout hearts.

"You see what we have done," said Lightly; "why can't you do the same?"

"My good sir, I am neither a giant myself, nor have I any sons that are giants."

"Well, well," said he, "I will tell you what was partly my reason — what was partly my reason for asking you over to see me. My youngest boy — step out, Ahasuerus — my youngest boy is just married, and, as our hive is pretty full, it is necessary that he should swarm out with his wife, who is a good, hearty, industrious girl, that will be excellent help for your old woman. You can't get on, at first, without some hard work, and you will not be able to work yourself for some time, very hard; you will want such a boy as mine, to break the way a little smooth for you."

I caught at the proposal, instantly; we were not long coming to terms, and in three days the new-married couple, the boy and the girl, were established at my house.

"She don't know any thing about house-keeping," said my old woman.

"You shall teach her," said I; and she went about her work, perfectly content.

"He is a mere boy," quoth my old man; — "what can he know of farming!"

"He will learn it of you," said I; and the old man felt as proud as a peacock.

My Polyphemus with two eyes, set to work without delay, under the direction of my old man, who talked a great deal and did nothing; and who, after having given his opinion, was content to follow that of the other. I was busy, too, looking on; running about, doing little or nothing; but taking an interest, and sympathizing with the lusty labours of the young giant Ahasuerus to such a degree, that I have often actually fallen into a violent perspiration, at seeing him prying up a large stone. Thus I got a great deal of the benefit of hard work, without actually fatiguing myself. By degrees, I came to work a little myself; and when I did not work, I gave my advice, and saw the others work. One day — it was the crisis of my life — one day, Ahasuerus and the old man were attempting to raise a rock out of the ground by means of a lever, but their weight was not sufficient. They tried several times, but in vain; whereat the spirit came upon me, and, seizing the far end of the lever, I hung upon it with all my might, kicking most manfully the while. The rock yielded to our united exertions, and rolled out of the ground. It was my victory.

"We should not have got it out without you," said Ahasuerus.

"It was all your doing," quoth the old man.

But, to tell the honest truth, I quaked in the midst of my triumph, lest this unheard-of exertion might have injured a blood-vessel, or strained some of the vital parts. That night, I thought, some how or other, I felt rather faintish and languid. But it may be I was only a little sleepy; for I fell asleep in five minutes, and did not wake till sunrise. It was some time before I could persuade myself I was quite well; but, being unable fairly to detect any thing to the contrary, I arose and walked forth into the freshness of the morning, and my spirit laughed in concert with the sprightly insects and chirping birds.

After this I became bolder and bolder, until, finally,

animated by the example of the great Ahasuerus, I one day laid hold of a rock, and rolled it fairly out of its bed. I was astonished at this feat; I had no idea that I could make the least exertion, without suffering for it severely in some way or other. I never could do it before, — and what is the reason I can do it now, thought I; I certainly used to feel very faint, sometimes, on occasion of drawing a hard cork out of a bottle. My new monitor, experience, whispered me that this was nothing but apprehension, which, when it becomes a habit and gains a certain mastery over the mind, produces a sensation allied to faintness. It embarrasses the pulsation, and that occasions a feeling of swooning. The mental impression causes the physical. I was never so happy in my whole life as when I received this lesson of experience. I was no longer afraid of dying off-hand, of the exertion of drawing a cork.

Thus we went on during the summer. The salt pork relished wonderfully; the bread and milk became a delicious dessert; and the rocks daily vanished from the meadow, as if by magic. The autumn now approached, and I bethought myself how I should get through the winter, with so many broken panes, and so many skylights in the roof of my house. There was neither carpenter nor glazier in ten miles, and I was at a loss what to do. I spoke to Ahasuerus the Great about it. "If you will get me a few shingles and nails, and some glass and putty, I will do it myself," said he. "If you can do it, so can I," said I; for I began to be a little jealous of Ahasuerus. Accordingly, I procured the materials, and, mounting on the roof, went to work zealously. It was a devil of a business; but I got through at last. It did not look very well, to be sure; but it kept out the rain, the snow, and the keen air. Encouraged at my unaccountable ingenuity as a carpenter, I turned glazier, and broke six panes of glass in no time. With the seventh, however, I succeeded; and well it was that I did so, for I had determined this attempt should be the last, and its failure would have forever satisfied me that none but a man who had learned the trade of a glazier could put in a pane of glass. As it was, I passed from the extreme of depression and vexation to that of exaltation and vanity.

"How easy it is to get on in this world, and with what small means we may attain to all the necessary comforts of life!" cried I: "men make themselves slaves, to ward off evils that are imaginary; and sweat through a life of toil, to become at last dependent on others for what they can do just as well themselves. What is the use of plaguing myself with these eternal labours; I will be idle and happy."

"Remember the poet at Saratoga."

"Remember the philosopher."

"Remember the politician."

"Remember the man of nerves," whispered memory in my ear, "and remember thyself—remember DYSPEPSY." I fled from my conclusion as fast as I could run, and worked that day harder than ever.

Winter came, and having a vast forest of wood, some of which was decaying and the remainder in full maturity, I determined to have it cut down and sold, to pay my debt to my old Scotchman. With the assistance of one or two others, Ahasuerus performed wonders in the woods, as he had done among the rocks. I forget how many cords they sent to market, but it produced enough to pay my old friend, and then I stood upon the proudest eminence an unambitious man can attain; I owed no man a penny, and I could live without running in debt. This is a great and solid happiness, not sufficiently appreciated in this age.

People that know no better are apt to think that winter in the country is one long level of dead uniformity; and that there is no enjoyment away from the fireside. But they are widely mistaken. Nature everywhere forever presents a succession of varieties, and those of winter are not the least beautiful. The short days of December and January are perhaps the most gloomy; but have this advantage, that they *are* short, and are followed by good long nights, in which it is a luxury to nestle in a warm bed and hear the wind whistle or the light fleeces of snow patting against the windows, and fall asleep thinking how much better-off we are than millions of our fellow-creatures. When the earth lies barren, with its herbage destroyed; when the forests, stripped of their leafy honours, stand bare to the winds; even then nature is not altogether desolate in these lonely mountains. The homely brown of the woods is dotted here and there by clusters of evergreens, that appear only the more beautiful from the leanness that surrounds them; and even the gravity of the old gray-beard rocks is often enlivened with spots of green moss that relieve their sober aspect. There is music too in the wintry solitudes: for, in the pure clear air, every sound is musical. The lowing of cattle — the barking of the dog and chattering of the squirrel

— the drumming of the partridge — the echoes of the fowler's gun, and of the woodman's axe whose strokes are by and by followed by the loud crash of the falling tree — all breaking in succession, and sometimes mingling in chorus, on the beautiful and buoyant air, bear with them a lonely yet touching charm, which, to a contented mind in a healthy frame, affords the means of real substantial enjoyment.

Anon, Nature puts on her robe of spotless white, the true livery of youth, beauty, and innocence; — and then, what an intense, ineffable lustre invests her all around, and everywhere! The impurities, the blemishes, and the deformities of the earth, are all hidden under the snowy veil; the roughness becomes smooth and glassy; the stagnant pools, exhaling in summer disease and death, are robbed of their poisons; the bogs are invisible, and the very swamps salubrious. All is clear, unsullied, and still; the pale image of innocent beauty, clothed for a while in the trappings of the tomb. All is soothing, but nothing lively: all grave and solemn, yet nothing melancholy. But the night is, if possible, still more holy and beautiful, when the brightness of the moon-beams sporting on the glittering surface of the snow creates a sort of female day, softer, and more tranquillizing, yet almost equally bright. Not an insect chirps or buzzes in the ear; there is no life stirring in nature's veins: her pulses stop. But a thousand glittering stars, invisible at other times, come forth, as if to view the scene stretched out below them, or watch with sparkling eyes the course of their bright queen athwart the heavens.

Then come the lengthening days, which at first

steal on imperceptibly, with steps noiseless and slow, silently unlocking the chains of winter, and setting nature free so easily that we do not hear the turning of the key. At first, the trickling of the waters from the roof, and the falling of the icicles, apprise us of the advance of the sun, to resume his glowing sceptre. Anon, the southern exposures begin to spot the vast white winding-sheet with brown; and, here and there, though very rarely, along the margin of some living spring, the tender grass begins to peep forth. Every day the empire of the sun extends by slow progression. The brooks begin again to murmur and glisten, marking their courses by the increased verdure of the grass and willows on their margins; and, by inappreciable degrees, the few sere leaves that clung all winter to the sapless branches are pushed from their hold by the swelling buds, and fall whispering to the earth, to mingle with her crumbling atoms. It is thus with all the works of nature, and with man. The young buds push off the old dry leaves; the very rocks are mutable; all feel the universal law of change, and man the most of all.

I did not spend my winter idly, but went out every day to see my wood-cutters. In order to give some interest to my walks, I purchased a gun, procured a brace of fox-hounds, and in time became a mighty hunter before the Lord. No man of sentiment has ever heard the "deep-mouthed hound," as the poet, with singular felicity, calls him, saluting the clear frosty morning with sonorous and far-sounding challenges, without feeling its inspiration in the silence of the mountains. I found their society, and that of my gun, delightful, though truth obliges me to confess that I seldom got any thing in my sporting rambles but exercise and a keen appetite. Almost the first extensive excursion I made, being intent on following the hounds, I unluckily fell through the ice into a small pond, which the melting of the first snows had formed in a little valley. I got completely wet from head to foot; and I was some miles from home. The whole way, I suffered the horrible anticipation of diseases without number; rheumatism, consumption, catarrh, sore throat, inflammation of the chest, and a hundred others. In short, I gave myself up for gone; and was in such a hurry to get home and settle my affairs, that I arrived there in a perfect glow. I lost no time in changing my dress, and, it being now evening, went directly to bed, expecting next morning to find myself as stiff as a poker. At first I fell into a profuse perspiration, and then into a sound sleep which lasted till morning. I can hardly believe it myself, at this moment; I awoke as well as ever I was in my life, and never felt any ill effects from my accident. After this, I defied the whole college of physicians, nay, all the colleges put together. I considered myself another Achilles, invulnerable even at the heel, and now cared no more for the weather than a grizzly-bear, or a seeker of the North-West passage.

Thus passed my first winter. In the spring, I paid my debt to Hardup with the product of my wood. In the summer, he came to see me. "I did not come before, for fear you would think it was to dun you," said he. He has repeated his visit every summer, for the last seven years, and he assures me every time, that, were he not Hardup, he would be Ambler. It would be tedious, neither is it necessary to the moral of my story, to detail the progress I made, and the wonders achieved by Ahasuerus, from the period at which I first took possession of my estate, to that in which I am now writing. Great as are the changes, they bear no comparison with those *I* have undergone.

My farm is now a little Eden among the high hills, whose rugged aspects only add richness and beauty to the cultivated fields. I have saved enough to add two wings to my old house, and to put it in good repair, besides building a barn and other out-houses. Every year I execute some little improvements, just to keep up the excitement of novelty, and prevent me from thinking too much about myself. Every fair day in spring, summer, and autumn, it is my custom to climb a part of the mountain which overlooks my little domain and affords a full view of its green or golden enclosures.

It lies at the head of a long narrow vale, skirted on either side by rough, rocky, steep mountains, clothed with vast forests of every growth. My house is on a little round knoll, just on the edge of the meadow, so rough at my first arrival here, but which now has not a single stone above its surface. The clear spring-brook which meanders through it, and is full of trout, forms the head of a fine stream, which, (gathering the tribute of the hills as it proceeds onward), waxes larger as it goes, and appears at different points far down the valley, coursing its bright way to the Hudson. On either side of the valley, among rocks and woods, is sometimes seen a cultivated field or two, with a house, and a few cattle; but, with this exception, there is a perfect and beautiful contrast between the bosom and the sides of the valley. The former is all softness, verdure, and fertility; the latter are stately with forests, or severe in naked sublimity. In a day made brilliant by a north-west wind I can see the junction of the little river, (of which, as being the proprietor of its parent spring, I consider myself the father), with the majestic Hudson. I wish the reader, that is, *if he is a clever man, or,* what is still better, a clever and pretty lady, would come and see my farm next summer.

I have paid but one visit to the city, and that was to my old friend Hardup, who is become very fond of me ever since he conferred a benefit. While I was one day strolling along the Battery, I exchanged one of those glances which bespeak a doubtful recognition, with a portly, rosy-cheeked man I was sure I had once known. On these occasions I generally make the advance.

" I think I have seen you before, sir," said I, " but really I can't tell exactly where."

" I am in the same predicament," replied he, smiling; " your face is familiar, though I can't recall your name."

" My name is Ambler."

" Good heavens! is it possible — " and, though glad to see me, he seemed quite astonished; — " my name is Abstract." I almost fell backwards over one of the benches. It was my friend, the man of nerves, as hale and hearty as if he had never had any nerves in his life.

" I'll not believe it," said I; " why, what has happened to you? "

"O, I'm married," he replied, "and have enough to do besides attending to my nerves; but you — you are metamorphosed too — what has come over you? Are *you*, too, married?"

"No; I'm a bachelor still," said I: "so you see there are two opposite ways to the same thing."

Having exchanged our addresses, we parted, the best friends in the world.

"You had better get a wife," cried he.

"I mean to," I replied, "as soon as I can afford the revenues of a city, to keep her in pin-money."

"Pooh!, if you can't keep her in pin-money, you can keep her in order," answered he of the nerves, and strutted away, with the air of a man who was either master at home, or so dexterously led captive as not to suspect it.

I begin to grow weary of talking about myself; and, as I have observed that listeners and readers generally get tired before speakers and authors, will here conclude my story. Its moral, I hope, cannot be mistaken. I committed to paper the result of my experience, not for the purpose of laughing at the miseries of human life, or of ridiculing the infirmities of my fellow-creatures. I wished, if possible, to persuade them that a large portion of the cares of this world, from which we are so anxious to escape, are nothing more than blessings in disguise, and thus to diminish that inordinate love of riches which is founded on the silly presumption that they are the sources of all happiness. It is under the dominion of this mistaken idea that money becomes indeed the root of all evil, by being sought with an insatiable appetite, that swallows up all our feelings of brotherhood, and causes men to prey upon each other like the wild beasts of the forest; nay, more savagely—for their instinct teaches them to spare their own species. Were mankind aware of the total inability of wealth to confer content or to make leisure delightful, they would perchance seek it with less avidity, and with fewer sacrifices of that integrity which is a far more essential ingredient in human happiness than the gold for which it is so often bartered. My history may also afford a useful example to those whose situations entail on them the necessity of labour and economy, by teaching them the impossibility of reconciling a life of luxury and ease with the enjoyment of jocund spirits, lusty health, and rational happiness.

"But what has become of your DYSPEPSY all this time?" the reader will ask.

Faith!, I had forgot that entirely!

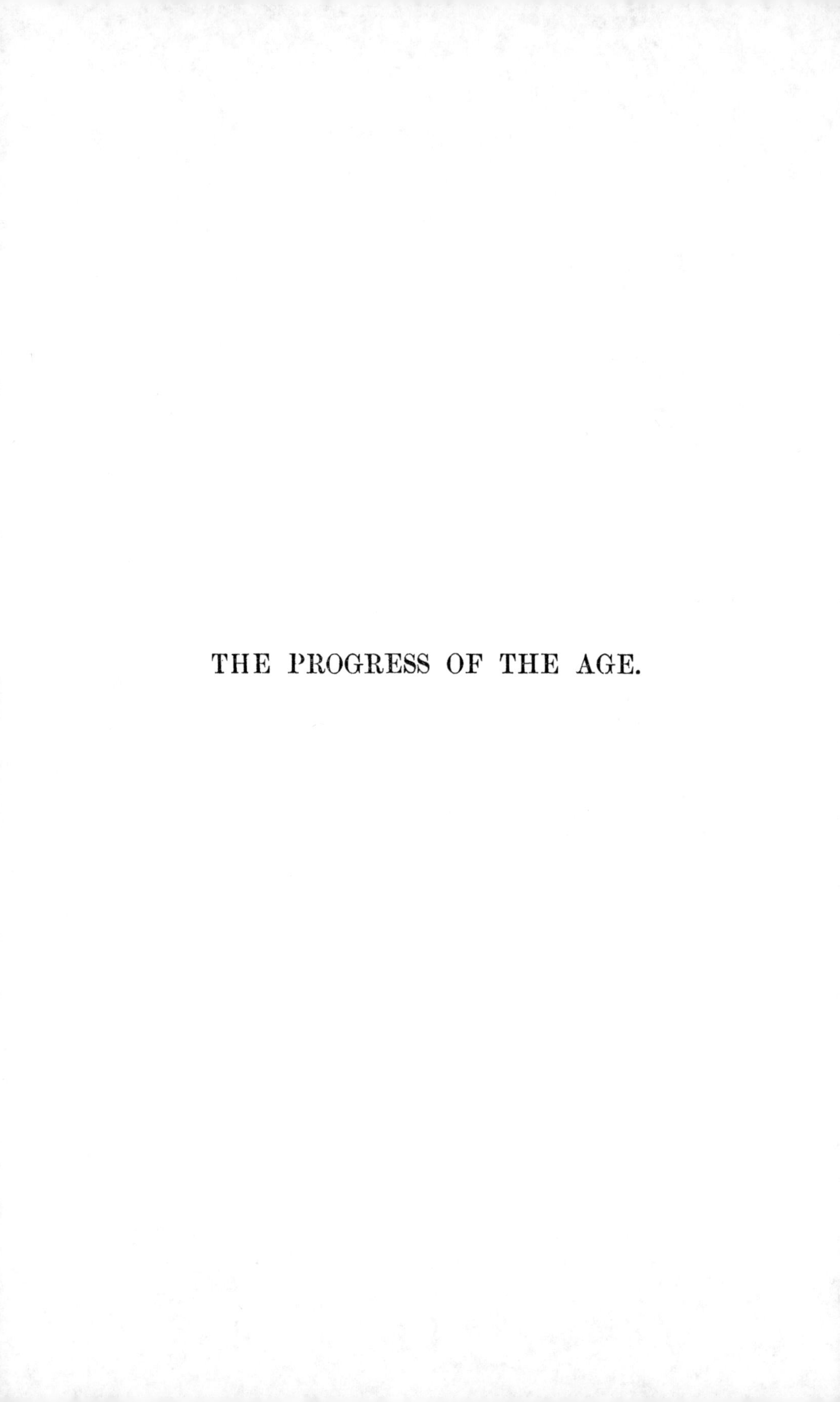

THE PROGRESS OF THE AGE.

THE PROGRESS OF THE AGE.

Squire Van Gaasbeeck (which means Goosebill in English) was for fifty good years snugly settled on the spot of his birth, happy in himself, happy in his family, and happy in the possession of three hundred acres of the best land in Greene county. His family consisted of a wife, a son, and two daughters — the latter of a ripe, marriageable age — Catharine and Rachel, called, in the familiar Dutch vernacular, *Teenie* and *Lockie.* The name of the boy, as they called him, for he was but thirty, was *Yaup*, which signifies Jacob in English.

The daughters spun and wove the linsey-woolsey and linen; the mother, with their help, made them up into garments for the squire and Yaup, who worked in the fields sometimes a whole day, with Primus the black boy, without exchanging a single word. Every year Squire Van Gaasbeeck added a few hundreds to his store; every year the governor sent him a commission as justice of the peace; and every year the daughters added to their reserve of linen and petticoats, deposited in the great oaken chest with a spring-lock, for the happy period to which every good honest girl looks forward, with gentle trepidation, mixed with inspiring hopes. There seemed to be no end to these accumulations, insomuch that, it is said, at one time, *Teenie* and *Lockie* could each muster six dozen pairs of sheets, threescore towels, a hundred petticoats, besides other articles which shall be nameless — that *Yaup* counted shirts innumerable — and the squire himself actually owned seventy-six pairs of breeches, good, bad, and indifferent, a number which he declared he never would exceed, he being an old *seventy-sixer* to the backbone.

Thus the old squire's bark floated swimmingly towards the dark gulf that finally swallows up man, his motives, his actions, and his memory, when, in an evil hour, a manufactory of woollens was established in his neighbourhood for the encouragement of "domestic industry."

There carding, and spinning, and weaving, were all carried on by that arch fiend, "productive labour." Hereupon all the women in twenty miles round threw down the distaff, the wool-cards, and the shuttle, maintaining that it was much better to leave these matters to "domestic industry" and "productive labour," than to be working and slaving from morning till night at home.

"Hum," quoth Squire Van Gaasbeeck, "this same domestic industry and productive labour is what I can't understand; it bids fair to put an end to the domestic industry and productive labour of my family, I think."

A great political economist gave him copies of all the speeches made in Congress on the subject, amounting to a hundred thousand pages, which he assured him would explain the manner in which domestic industry and domestic idleness could be proved to be twin-sisters. The squire put on his spectacles, and began to read like any egregious owl; but before he got half through he fell asleep, and dreamed of the tower of Babel and confusion of tongues. He returned the books, and the economist as good as told him he was a great blockhead. "It may be," quoth the squire; "but not all the speeches in the world will persuade me that the way to encourage domestic industry is to have all the work done abroad."

Some say, money is the root of all evil. Of this I profess myself ignorant, having never yet had enough to do me much harm. Others affirm that idleness is the genuine root, and I believe they are right. From the moment the squire's wife and daughters began to be idle at home, they began to hanker after a hundred out-door amusements which they never thought of before. They must go down to Catskill, forsooth, to buy ribbons, and calicoes, and cotton stockings, and what not. In short, they never wanted an excuse for gadding, and at last reached the climax of enormity in actually beginning to talk seriously of a voyage to New York. The squire's hair stood on end; for, at that happy period, a voyage to New York was never contemplated except on occasions of life and death. The city was talked of as a place afar off, accessible only to a chosen few; and the fortunate being who had visited it acquired an importance equal to that of a Mussulman who has made the pilgrimage to Mecca. He might lawfully assume the traveller's privilege of telling as many lies as he pleases.

"This comes of domestic industry and productive

labour," quoth the squire, who was still the better horse at home, and put a flat negative on the project, for which he got a good many sour looks. But his misfortunes were not to end here. About this time, one of those diabolical inventions which set all the world gadding appeared in the shape of a steamboat, smoking and puffing her way up to Albany. In a little while she was followed by others, so that at length it came to pass that people could go from Catskill to New York and back again in less than no time, for nothing. About three score and ten of the squire's cousins to the sixth degree, taking advantage of these facilities, came up from New York to see him, and some half a dozen staid all summer. Now the least they could do was to ask the squire's wife and daughters to visit them in the autumn in return. The squire was assailed so resolutely for his permission to accept this polite offer, that at last his obstinacy gave way, like a mill-dam in a great freshet, and carried everything before it. Madam Van Gaasbeeck and *Teenie* and *Lockie* packed up all their petticoats, and getting on board of the steamboat at the risk of their necks, under the protection of the young Squire *Yaup*, paddled down to New York as merry as fiddlers.

At the same time the squire, in imitation I believe of Marc Antony, or somebody else that he never heard of, almost loaded one of the Catskill sloops with pigs, potatoes, and other market-stuff, the whole product of which was to be turned over to the ladies for pin-money. To the young squire he confided a more important business. He had just closed a bargain with a merchant in New York, who had inherited some land in his neighborhood, for a fine farm, on which he intended to settle *Yaup* when he got married; and now intrusted him with three thousand dollars to pay for it, agreeably to contract. Squire Van Gaasbeeck was not a man to owe a shilling longer than he could help it.

The party arrived in New York without any accident, the steamboat not blowing up, that trip, and were received by the cousins and second-cousins as if they were quite welcome. But, terrible was the work the city kindred made with the costume of Madam Van Gaasbeeck and the young ladies. It was all condemned, like a parcel of slops eaten up by cockroaches, and the produce of the pigs, potatoes, and pumpkins, melted irretrievably in one single excursion into Cheapside. For the town cousins would by no means be seen in Broadway with the country cousins, and accordingly took them up to Cheapside in the dusk of the evening, where the shopkeeper, making advantage of the obscurity, cheated them finely.

Being equipped in grand costume, they were taken to the play — it was Peter Wilkins — where the old lady declared that "it was all one as a puppet show," and came very near fainting under the infliction of a pair of corsets, with which the cruel relatives had invested her.

The young squire, feeling the importance of having money in his pocket, had delayed to pay over the three thousand dollars, and carried it with him to the play, in a leather pocket-book. Impressed with the weight of his charge, he was continually putting his hand behind him to feel that all was safe, insomuch that he caught the attention of a worthy gentleman who was prowling about seeking whom he might devour. He attached himself to Master *Yaup* for the rest of the evening, and, in the crowd of the lobby, going out, took occasion to ease him of the black leather pocket-book, without his being the wiser for it till he got home. It was never recovered, notwithstanding all the exertions of that terror of evil-doers, High-Constable Hays.*

This is one of the great conveniences of paper money — a man may put a fortune in his pocket. Had the three thousand dollars been in specie, *Yaup* could not have carried them to the play.

Here was a farm gone at one blow. But this was not the worst. The good wife and daughters came home with loads of finery, and loads of wants they never knew before. There was the deuse to pay on the first Sunday morning after their return from town. The church would hardly hold their bonnets, and the parson was struck dumb, insomuch that he gave out the wrong psalm, which the clerk set to a wrong tune. Mercy upon us, what heart-burnings were here! Not one of the congregation could tell where the text was when arrived at home.

Squire Van Gaasbeeck had now a farm to pay for, and wanted every penny he could scrape together, to make both ends meet. But the shopping to Catskill went on worse than ever; and, besides this, almost every week the sloop brought up some article of finery from New York, which the city cousins assured them had just come into fashion. In short, the squire now, for the first time, felt his spirit bowed down to

* Jacob, familiarly known in New York for many years as "Old, Hays."

the earth, under the consciousness that he owed money which he could not pay.

In the progress of the spirit of the age and the march of mind, it came to pass that certain public-spirited people procured a charter, and set up a bank at Catskill for the good of mankind. The squire, in due time, was set upon by one of the directors, who smelled out that he wanted money, and persuaded him to take up a couple of thousands of the bank, with the aid of which he could make such improvements on his new purchase as would enable him to sell it for twice as much as it cost. The squire was not the man he once was. His sturdy, independent spirit, that scorned the idea of a debt, was broken down. He borrowed the money, improved the farm, and finally sold it to this very honest director, at a great profit. The director paid him in notes of the new bank, and that same morning conveyed the farm to somebody else. Squire Van Gaasbeeck was now rich again. He determined to go the next day and pay all his debts, and be a man once more.

But, unluckily, that very night the bank, and all things therein, evaporated. The house was found shut up next morning. All the books, papers, notes, and directors, had gone no one knew whither; although it was the general opinion the devil had possession of the directors. This loss half ruined Squire Van Gaasbeeck, and *Yaup* gave the finishing blow, by striking work, and swearing he would no longer battle with "the spirit of the age and the march of public improvement," which decreed he should be a gentleman. Finally, to make an end of my story, the squire was turned out of his farm by his creditors — his wife died of her corsets — the young ladies were fain to tend the spinning-jenny at the neighbouring manufactory — and Master *Yaup* became a gentleman at large, left the home of his ancestors, and was never heard of more.

An old acquaintance one day came to see the squire, now living on the charity of his brother-in-law, and inquired how he came to be in such a state. "Ah!" replied he, with a sigh, "I was half-ruined by domestic industry and productive labour; but the progress of the age and the march of public improvement finished me at last."

THE

REVENGE OF SAINT NICHOLAS.

A TALE FOR THE HOLIDAYS.

THE

REVENGE OF SAINT NICHOLAS.

A TALE FOR THE HOLIDAYS.

EVERYBODY knows that, in the famous city of New York, whose proper name is Nieuw Amsterdam, the excellent St. Nicholas — (who is worth a dozen St. Georges, with dragons to boot, and who, if every tub stood on its right bottom, would be at the head of the Seven Champions of Christendom) — I say, everybody knows that the excellent St. Nicholas, in holiday times, goes about among the people in the middle of the night, distributing all sorts of toothsome and becoming gifts to the good boys and girls in this his favourite city. Some say that he comes down the chimneys in a little Jersey wagon; others, that he wears a pair of Holland skates, with which he travels like the wind; and others, who pretend to have seen him, maintain that he has lately adopted a locomotive, and was once actually detected on the *Albany* railroad. But this last assertion is looked upon to be entirely fabulous, because St. Nicholas has too much discretion to trust himself in such a newfangled jarvie; and so I leave this matter to be settled by whomsoever will take the trouble. My own opinion is, that his favourite mode of travelling is on a canal, the motion and speed of which aptly comport with the philosophic dignity of his character. But this is not material, and I will no longer detain my readers with extraneous and irrelevant matters, as is too much the fashion with our statesmen, orators, biographers, and story-tellers.

It was in the year one thousand seven hundred and sixty, or sixty-one, for the most orthodox chronicles differ in this respect; but it was a very remarkable year, and it was called *annus mirabilis* on that account. It was said that several people were detected in speaking the truth, about that time; that nine staid, sober, and discreet widows, who had sworn on an anti-masonic almanac never to enter a second time into the holy state, were snapped up by young husbands before they knew what they were about; that six venerable bachelors wedded as many buxom young belles, and, it is reported, were afterward sorry for what they had done; that many people actually went to church from motives of piety; and that a great scholar, who had written a book in support of certain opinions, was not only convinced of his error, but acknowledged it publicly afterwards. No wonder the year one thousand seven hundred and sixty, if that was the year, was called *annus mirabilis!*

What contributed to render this year still more remarkable was the building of six new three-story brick houses in the city, and the fact of three persons' setting up equipages, who, I cannot find, ever failed in business afterwards, or compounded with their creditors at a pistareen in the pound. It is, moreover, recorded in the annals of the horticultural society of that day, (which it is said were written on a cabbage leaf), that a member produced a forked radish, of such vast dimensions, that, being dressed up in fashionable male attire at the exhibition, it was actually mistaken for a travelled beau by several inexperienced young ladies, who pined away for love of its beautiful complexion, and were changed into daffadowndillies. Some maintained it was a mandrake, but it was finally detected by an inquest of experienced matrons. No wonder the year seventeen hundred and sixty was called *annus mirabilis!*

But the most extraordinary thing of all was the confident assertion that there was but one *gray mare* within the bills of mortality; and, incredible as it may appear, she was the wife of a responsible citizen, who, it was affirmed, had grown rich by weaving velvet purses out of sows' ears. But this we look upon as being somewhat of the character of the predictions of almanac-makers. Certain it is, however, that Amos Shuttle possessed the treasure of a wife who was shrewdly suspected of having established within doors a system of government not laid down in Aristotle or the Abbé Sièyes, who made a constitution for every day in the year, and two for the first of April.

Amos Shuttle, though a mighty pompous little man out of doors, was the humblest of human creatures within. He belonged to that class of people who pass for great among the little, and little among the great; and he would certainly have been master in his own house, had it not been for a woman. We have read somewhere that no wise woman ever thinks her husband a demi-god. If so, it is a blessing that there are so few wise women in the world.

Amos had grown rich, Heaven knows how — he did not know himself; but, what was somewhat extraordinary, he considered his wealth a signal proof of his talents and sagacity, and valued himself according to the infallible standard of pounds, shillings, and pence. But, though he lorded it without, he was, as we have just said, the most gentle of men within doors. The moment he stepped inside of his own house, his spirit cowered down, like that of a pious man entering a church; he felt as if he was in the presence of a superior being — to wit, Mrs. Abigail Shuttle. He was, indeed, the meekest of mortals at home, except Moses; and Sir Andrew Aguecheek's song, which Sir Toby Belch declared "would draw nine souls out of one weaver," would have failed in drawing half a one out of Amos. The truth is, his wife, who ought to have known, affirmed he had no more soul than a monkey; but he was the only man in the city thus circumstanced at the time we speak of. No wonder, therefore, the year one thousand seven hundred and sixty was called *annus mirabilis!*

Such as he was, Mr. Amos Shuttle waxed richer and richer every day, insomuch that those who envied his prosperity were wont to say, "that he had certainly been born with a dozen silver spoons in his mouth, or such a great blockhead would never have got together such a heap of money." When he had become worth ten thousand pounds, he launched his shuttle magnanimously out of the window, ordered his weaver's beam to be split up for oven-wood, and Mrs. Amos turned his weaver's shop into a *boudoir*. Fortune followed him faster than he ran away from her. In a few years the ten thousand doubled, and in a few more trebled, quadrupled — in short, Amos could hardly count his money.

"What shall we do now, my dear?" asked Mrs. Shuttle, who never sought his opinion, that I can learn, except for the pleasure of contradicting him.

"Let us go and live in the country, and enjoy ourselves," quoth Amos.

"Go into the country! go to —" I could never satisfy myself what Mrs. Shuttle meant; but she stopped short, and concluded the sentence with a withering look of scorn, that would have cowed the spirits of nineteen weavers.

Amos named all sorts of places, enumerated all sorts of modes of life he could think of, and every pleasure that might enter into the imagination of a man without a soul. His wife despised them all; she would not hear of them.

"Well, my dear, suppose you suggest something; do now, Abby," at length said Amos, in a coaxing whisper; "will you, my onydoney?"

"Ony fiddlestick! I wonder you repeat such vulgarisms. But if I must say what I should like, I should like to travel."

"Well, let us go and make a tour as far as Jamaica, or Hackensack, or Spiking-devil. There is excellent fishing for striped-bass there."

"Spiking-devil!", screamed Mrs. Shuttle; "a'n't you ashamed to swear so, you wicked mortal! I won't go to Jamaica, nor to Hackensack among the Dutch Hottentots, nor to Spiking-devil to catch striped-bass. I'll go to Europe!"

If Amos had possessed a soul, it would have jumped out of its skin at the idea of going beyond seas. He had once been on the sea-bass banks, and got a seasoning there; the very thought of which made him sick. But, as he had no soul, there was no great harm done.

When Mrs. Shuttle said a thing, it was settled. They went to Europe, taking their only son with them. The lady ransacked all the milliners' shops in Paris, and the gentleman visited all the restaurateurs. He became such a desperate connoisseur and gourmand, that he could almost tell an *omelette au jambon* from a gammon of bacon. After consummating the polish, they came home, the lady with the newest old fashions, and the weaver with a confirmed preference of *potage à la Turque* over pepperpot. It is said the city trembled, as with an earthquake, when they landed; but the notion was probably superstitious.

They arrived near the close of the year, the memorable year, the *annus mirabilis*, one thousand seven hundred and sixty. Everybody that had ever known the Shuttles flocked to see them, or rather to see what they had brought with them; and such was the magic of a voyage to Europe, that Mr. and Mrs. Amos Shuttle, who had been nobodies when they departed, became somebodies when they returned, and mounted at once to the summit of *ton*.

"You have come in good time to enjoy the festivities of the holidays," said Mrs. Hubblebubble, an old friend of Amos the weaver and his wife.

"We shall have a merry Christmas and a happy New-year," exclaimed Mrs. Doubletrouble, another old acquaintance of old times.

"The holidays?" drawled Mrs. Shuttle; "the holidays? Christmas and New-year? Pray, what are they?"

It is astonishing to see how people lose their memories abroad, sometimes. They often forget their old friends and old customs; and, occasionally, themselves.

"Why, la! now, who'd have thought it?" cried Mrs. Doubletrouble; "why, sure you haven't forgot the oly koeks and the mince-pies, the merry meetings of friends, the sleigh-rides, the Kissing-Bridge, and the family parties?"

"Family parties!" shrieked Mrs. Shuttle, and held her salts to her nose; "family parties! I never heard of anything so Gothic in Paris or Rome; and oly koeks — oh shocking! and mince-pies — detestable! and throwing open one's doors to all one's old friends, whom one wishes to forget as soon as possible — Oh! the idea is insupportable!" And again she held the salts to her nose.

Mrs. Hubblebubble and Mrs. Doubletrouble found they had exposed themselves sadly, and were quite ashamed. A real, genteel, well-bred, enlightened lady of fashion ought to have no rule of conduct, no conscience, but Paris — whatever is fashionable there is genteel — whatever is not fashionable is vulgar. There is no other standard of right, and no other eternal fitness of things. At least so thought Mrs. Hubblebubble and Mrs. Doubletrouble.

"But is it possible that all these things are out of fashion, abroad?", asked the latter, beseechingly.

"They never were in," said Mrs. Amos Shuttle. "For my part, I mean to close my doors and windows on New-year's day — I'm determined."

"And so am I," said Mrs. Hubblebubble.

"And so am I," said Mrs. Doubletrouble.

And it was settled that they should make a combination among themselves and their friends, to put down the ancient and good customs of the city, and abolish the sports and enjoyments of the jolly New-year. The conspirators then separated, each to pursue her diabolical designs against oly koeks, mince-pies, sleigh-ridings, sociable visitings, and family parties.

Now the excellent St. Nicholas, who knows well what is going on in every house in the city, though, like a good and honourable saint, he never betrays any family secrets, overheard these wicked women plotting against his favourite anniversary, and he said to himself,

"*Vuur en Vlammen!** but I'll be even with you, *mein vrouwen*." So he determined he would play these conceited and misled women a trick or two before he had done with them.

It was now the first day of the new year, and Mrs. Amos Shuttle, and Mrs. Doubletrouble, and Mrs. Hubblebubble, and all their wicked accomplices, had shut up their doors and windows, so that when their old friends called they could not get into their houses. Moreover, they had prepared neither mince-pies, nor oly koeks, nor krullers, nor any of the good things consecrated to St. Nicholas by his pious and well-intentioned votaries; and they were mightily pleased at having been as dull and stupid as owls, while all the rest of the folks were as merry as crickets, chirping and frisking in the warm chimney-corner. Little did they think what horrible judgments were impending over them, prepared by the wrath of the excellent St. Nicholas, who was resolved to make an example of them for attempting to introduce their newfangled

* Fire and flames.

corruptions in place of the ancient customs of his favourite city. These wicked women never had another comfortable sleep in their lives!

The night was still, clear, and frosty—the earth was everywhere one carpet of snow, and looked just like the ghost of a dead world, wrapped in a white winding sheet; the moon was full, round, and of a silvery brightness, and by her discreet silence afforded an example to the rising generation of young damsels, while the myriads of stars, that multiplied as you gazed at them, seemed as though they were frozen into icicles, they looked so cold, and sparkled with such a glorious lustre. The streets and roads leading from the city were all alive with sleighs, filled with jovial souls, whose echoing laughter and cheerful songs mingled with a thousand merry bells, that jingled in harmonious dissonance, giving spirit to the horses and animation to the scene. In the license of the season, warranted by long custom, each of the sleighs saluted the others in passing with a, "Happy New-year," a merry jest, or a mischievous gibe, exchanged from one gay party to another. All was life, motion, and merriment; and as old frost-bitten Winter, aroused from his trance by the rout and revelry around, raised his weather-beaten head to see what was passing, he felt his icy blood warming and coursing through his veins, and wished he could only overtake the laughing buxom Spring, that he might dance a jig with her, and be as frisky as the best of them. But, as the old rogue could not bring this desirable matter about, he contented himself with calling for a jolly bumper of cocktail, and drinking a swingeing draught to the health of the blessed St. Nicholas, and those who honour the memory of the president of good fellows.

All this time the wicked women and their accomplices lay under the malediction of the good saint, who caused them to be bewitched by an old lady from Salem. Mrs. Amos Shuttle could not sleep, because something had whispered in her apprehensive ear, that her son, her only son, whom she had engaged to the daughter of Count Grenouille, in Paris, then about three years old, was actually at that moment crossing Kissing-Bridge, in company with little Susan Varian, and some others. Now Susan was the fairest little lady of all the land. She had a face and an eye just like the Widow Wadman in Leslie's charming picture, a face and an eye which no reasonable man under Heaven could resist, except my Uncle Toby — beshrew him and his fortifications, I say! She was, moreover, a good little girl, and an accomplished little girl — but, alas!, she had not mounted to that step in the Jacob's ladder of fashion which qualifies a person for the heaven of high ton, and Mrs. Shuttle had not been to Europe for nothing. She would rather have seen her son wedded to dissipation and profligacy than to Susan Varian; and the thought of his being out sleigh-riding with her was worse than the toothache. It kept her awake all the livelong night; and the only consolation she had was scolding poor Amos, because the sleigh-bells made such a noise.

As for Mrs. Hubblebubble and Mrs. Doubletrouble, neither of the wretches got a wink of sleep during a whole week, for thinking of the beautiful French chairs and damask curtains Mrs. Shuttle had brought from Europe. They forthwith besieged their good men, leaving them no rest until they sent out orders to Paris for just such rich chairs and curtains as those of the thrice-happy Mrs. Shuttle, from whom they kept the affair a profound secret, each meaning to treat her to an agreeable surprise. In the mean while they could not rest, for fear the vessel which was to bring these treasures might be lost on her passage. Such was the dreadful judgment inflicted on them by the good St. Nicholas.

The perplexities of Mrs. Shuttle increased daily. In the first place, do all she could, she could not make Amos a fine gentleman. This was a metamorphosis which Ovid would never have dreamed of. He would be telling the price of everything in his house, his furniture, his wines, and his dinners, insomuch that those who envied his prosperity, or, perhaps, only despised his pretensions, were wont to say, after eating his venison and drinking his old Madeira, "that he ought to have been a tavern-keeper, he knew so well how to make out a bill." Mrs. Shuttle once overheard a speech of this kind, and the good St. Nicholas himself, who had brought it about, almost felt sorry for the mortification she endured on the occasion.

Scarcely had she got over this, when she was invited to a ball by Mrs. Hubblebubble, and the first thing she saw on entering the drawing-room was a suit of damask curtains and chairs, as much like her own as two peas, only the curtains had far handsomer fringe. Mrs. Shuttle came very near fainting away, but escaped for that time, determining to mortify this impudent creature, by taking not the least notice of her finery. But St. Nicholas ordered it otherwise, so that she was at last obliged to acknowledge they were very elegant indeed. Nay, this was not the worst, for she overheard one lady whisper to another, that Mrs. Hubblebubble's curtains were much richer than Mrs. Shuttle's.

"Oh, I dare say," replied the other — "I dare say Mrs. Shuttle bought them second-hand, for her husband is as mean as pursley."

This was too much. The unfortunate woman was taken suddenly ill — called her carriage, and went home, where it is supposed she would have died that evening, had she not wrought upon Amos to promise her an entire new suit of French furniture for her drawing-room and parlour to boot, besides a new carriage. But for all this she could not close her eyes that night, for thinking of the "second-hand curtains."

Nor was the wicked Mrs. Doubletrouble a whit better off, when her friend Mrs. Hubblebubble treated her to the agreeable surprise of the French window-curtains and chairs. "It is too bad — too bad, I declare," said she to herself; "but I'll pay her off soon." Accordingly she issued invitations for a grand ball and supper, at which both Mrs. Shuttle and Mrs. Hubblebubble were struck dumb, at beholding a suit of curtains and a set of chairs exactly of the same pattern with theirs. The shock was terrible, and it is impossible to say what might have been the consequences, had not the two ladies all at once thought of uniting in abusing Mrs. Doubletrouble for her extravagance.

"I pity poor Mr. Doubletrouble," said Mrs. Shuttle, shrugging her shoulders significantly, and glancing at the room.

"And so do I," said Mrs. Hubblebubble, doing the same.

Mrs. Doubletrouble had her eye upon them, and enjoyed their mortification, until her pride was brought to the ground by a dead shot from Mrs. Shuttle, who was heard to exclaim, in reply to a lady who observed that the chairs and curtains were very handsome,

"Why, yes; but they have been out of fashion in Paris a long time; and, besides, really they are getting so common, that I intend to have mine removed to the nursery."

Heavens!, what a blow! Poor Mrs. Doubletrouble hardly survived it. Such a night of misery as the wicked woman endured almost made the good St. Nicholas regret the judgment he had passed upon these mischievous and conceited females. But he thought to himself he would persevere, until he had made them a sad example to all innovators upon the ancient customs of our forefathers.

Thus were these wicked and miserable women spurred on by witchcraft from one piece of prodigality to another, and a deadly rivalship grew up between them, which destroyed their own happiness and that of their husbands. Mrs. Shuttle's new carriage and drawing-room furniture in due time were followed by similar extravagances on the part of the two other wicked women who had conspired against the hallowed institutions of St. Nicholas; and soon their rivalry came to such a height that not one of them had a moment's rest or comfort from that time forward. But they still shut their doors on the jolly anniversary of St. Nicholas, though the old respectable burghers and their wives, who had held up their heads time out of mind, continued the good custom, and laughed at the presumption of these upstart interlopers, who were followed only by a few people of silly pretensions, who had no more soul than Amos Shuttle himself. The three wicked women grew to be almost perfect skeletons, on account of the vehemence with which they strove to outdo each other, and the terrible exertions necessary to keep up the appearance of being the best friends in the world. In short, they became the laughing-stock of the town; and sensible, well-bred folks cut their acquaintance, except when they sometimes accepted an invitation to a party, just to make merry with their folly and conceitedness.

The excellent St. Nicholas, finding they still persisted in their opposition to his rites and ceremonies, determined to inflict on them the last and worst punishment that can befall the sex. He decreed that they should be deprived of all the delights springing from the domestic affections, and all taste for the innocent and virtuous enjoyments of a happy fireside. Accordingly, they lost all relish for home; were continually gadding about from one place to another in search of pleasure; and worried themselves to death to find happiness where it is never to be found. Their whole lives became one long series of disappointed hopes, galled pride, and gnawing envy. They lost their health, they lost their time, and their days became days of harassing impatience, their nights nights of sleepless, feverish excitement, ending in weariness and disappointment. The good saint sometimes felt sorry for them, but their continued obstinacy determined him to persist in his scheme for punishing the upstart pride of these rebellious females.

Young Shuttle, who had a soul, which I suppose he inherited from his mother, all this while continued his attentions to little Susan Varian, and so added to the miseries inflicted on the wicked old woman. Mrs. Shuttle insisted that Amos should threaten to disinherit his son, unless he gave up this attachment.

"Lord bless your soul, Abby," said Amos, "what's the use of my threatening? The boy knows, as well as I do, that I've no will of my own. Why, bless my soul, Abby —"

"Bless your soul!" interrupted Mrs. Shuttle; "I wonder who'd take the trouble to bless it, but yourself! — However, if you don't, I will."

Accordingly she threatened the young man with being disinherited, unless he turned his back on little Susan Varian, which no man ever did without getting a heartache.

"If my father goes on as he has done lately," sighed the youth, "he won't have anything left to disinherit me of but his affection, I fear. But if he had millions I would not abandon Susan."

"Are you not ashamed of such a plebeian attachment? You, that have been to Europe! But, once for all, remember this, renounce this lowborn upstart, or quit your father's home for ever."

"Upstart!" thought young Shuttle; — "one of the oldest families in the city." He made his mother a respectful bow, bade Heaven bless her, and left the house. He was, however, met at the door by his father, who said to him,

"Johnny, I give my consent; but mind, don't tell

your mother a word of the matter. I'll let her know I've a soul, as well as other people;" and he tossed his head like a war-horse.

The night after this, Johnny was married to little Susan, and the blessing of affection and beauty lighted upon his pillow. Her old father, who was in a respectable business, took his son-in-law into partnership, and they prospered so well, that in a few years Johnny was independent of all the world, with the prettiest wife and children in the land. But Mrs. Shuttle was inexorable, while the knowledge of his prosperity and happiness only worked her up to a higher pitch of anger, and added to the pangs of jealousy perpetually inflicted on her by the rivalry of Mrs. Hubblebubble and Mrs. Doubletrouble, who suffered under the like infliction from the wrathful St. Nicholas, who was resolved to make them an example to all posterity.

No fortune, be it ever so great, can stand the eternal sapping of wasteful extravagance, engendered and stimulated by the baleful passion of envy. In less than ten years from the hatching of the diabolical conspiracy of these three wicked women against the supremacy of the excellent St. Nicholas, their spendthrift rivalship had ruined the fortunes of their husbands, and entailed upon themselves misery and remorse. Rich Amos Shuttle became at last as poor as a church-mouse, and would have been obliged to take to the loom again in his old age, had not Johnny, now rich, and a worshipful magistrate of the city, afforded him and his better half a generous shelter under his own happy roof. Mrs. Hubblebubble and Mrs. Doubletrouble had scarcely time to condole with

Mrs. Shuttle, and congratulate each other, when their husbands went the way of all flesh, that is to say, failed for a few tens of thousands, and called their creditors together to hear the good news. The two wicked women lived long enough after this to repent of their offence against St. Nicholas; but they never imported any more French curtains, and at last perished miserably in an attempt to set the fashions in Pennypot alley.

Mrs. Abigail Shuttle might have lived happily the rest of her life with her children and grandchildren, (who all treated her with reverent courtesy and affection), now that the wrath of the mighty St. Nicholas was appeased by her exemplary punishment. But she could not get over her bad habits and feelings, or forgive her lovely little daughter-in-law for treating her so kindly when she so little deserved it. She gradually pined away; and though she revived on hearing of the catastrophe of Mrs. Hubblebubble and Mrs. Doubletrouble, it was only for a moment. The remainder of the life of this nefarious woman was a series of disappointments and heart-burnings. When she died, Amos tried to shed a few tears, but he found it impossible; I suppose because, as his wife always said, "he had no soul."

Such was the terrible revenge of St. Nicholas, which ought to be a warning to all who attempt to set themselves up against the venerable customs of their ancestors, and backslide from the hallowed institutions of the blessed saint, to whose good offices, without doubt, it is owing, that this his favourite city has transcended all others of the universe in beautiful damsels, valorous young men, mince-pies, and New-year cookies. The catastrophe of these three iniquitous wives had a wonderful influence in the city, insomuch that, from this time forward, no *gray mares* were ever known, no French furniture was ever used, and no woman was hardy enough to set herself up in opposition to the good customs of St. Nicholas. And so, wishing many happy New-years to all my dear countrywomen and countrymen, saving those who shut their doors to old friends, high or low, rich or poor, on that blessed anniversary which makes more glad hearts than all others put together — I say, wishing a thousand happy New-years to all with this single exception, I lay down my pen, with a caution to all wicked women to beware of the revenge of St. Nicholas.

COBUS YERKS.

COBUS YERKS.

Little Cobus Yerks — his name was Jacob, but, being a Dutchman, if not a double Dutchman, it was rendered in English, Cobus — little Cobus, I say, lived on the banks of Sawmill River, where it winds close under the brow of the Raven Rock, an enormous precipice jutting out of the side of the famous Buttermilk Hill, of which the reader has doubtless often heard. It was a rude, romantic spot, distant from the high-road, which, however, could be seen winding up the hill about three miles off. His nearest neighbours were at the same distance, and he seldom saw company except at night, when the fox and the weasel sometimes beat up his quarters, and caused a horrible cackling among the poultry.

One Tuesday, in the month of November, 1793, Cobus had gone in his wagon to the market-town on the river, whence the boats plied weekly to New York, with the produce of the neighbouring farmers. It was then a pestilent little place for running races, pitching quoits, and wrestling for gin-slings; but I must do it the credit to say, that it is now a very orderly town, sober and quiet, save when Parson Mathias, who calls himself a son of thunder, is praying in secret, so as to be heard across the river. It so happened, that, of all the days in the year, this was the very day a rumour had got into town, that I myself — the veritable writer of this true story — had been poisoned by a dish of Souchong tea, which was bought, a great bargain, of a pedler. There was not a stroke of work done in the village that day. The shoemaker abandoned his awl; the tailor, his goose; the hatter, his bow; and the forge of the blacksmith was cool from dawn till nightfall. Silent was the sonorous harmony of the big spinning-wheel; silent the village song; and silent the fiddle of Master Timothy Canty, who passed his livelong time in playing tuneful measures, and catching bugs and butterflies. I must say something of Tim before I go on with my tale.

Master Timothy was first seen in the village, one foggy morning, after a warm, showery night, when he was detected in a garret, at the extremity of the suburbs; and it was the general supposition that he had rained down in company with a store of little toads that were seen hopping about, as is usual after a shower. Around his garret were disposed a number of unframed pictures, painted on glass, representing the Four Seasons, the old King of Prussia and Prince Ferdinand of Brunswick, in their sharp-pointed cocked-hats, the fat, baldpated, Marquis of Granby, the beautiful Constantia Phillips, and divers others, not forgetting the renowned Kitty Fisher, who, I honestly confess, was my favourite among them all. The whole village poured into his quarters to gaze at these chefs-d'œuvre; and it is my confirmed opinion, which I shall carry to the grave, that neither the gallery of

Florence, nor Dresden, nor the Louvre, was ever visited by so many real amateurs. Beside the works of art, there were a great many other curiosities, at least such to the simple villagers, who were always sure of being welcomed by the owner with a jest and a tune.

Master Tim, as they came to call him when they got to be a little acquainted, was a rare fellow, such as seldom rains down anywhere, much less on a country village. He was of "merry England," as they call it — at least so he said and I believe, although he belied his nativity, by being the most light-hearted rogue in the world, even when the fog was at the thickest. In truth, he was ever in a good-humour, unless it might be when a rare bug or gorgeous butterfly, that he had followed through thick and thin, escaped his net at last. Then, to be sure, he was apt to call the recreant all the "vagabonds" he could think of. He was a middle-sized man, whose person decreased regularly, from the crown of his head to the — I was going to say, sole of his foot — but it was only to the commencement of that extremity, to speak by the card. The top of his head was broad and flat, and so was his forehead, which took up at least two thirds of his face, that tapered off suddenly to a chin, as sharp as the point of a triangle. His forehead was indeed a large tract, diversified, like the country in which he had taken up his abode, with odd varieties of hill and dale, meadow and ploughland, hedge and ditch, ravine and watercourse. It had as many points as a periwinkle. The brow projected exuberantly, though not heavily, over a pair of rascally little cross-firing, twinkling eyes, that, as the country people said, looked at least nine ways from Sunday. His teeth were white enough, but no two of them were fellows. But his skull would have turned the brains of a phrenologist, in exploring the mysteries of its development. It was shaped somewhat like Stony Point — which everybody knows as the scene of a gallant exploit of Pennsylvanian Wayne — and had quite as many abruptnesses and quizzical protuberances to brag about. In the upper region of his forehead, as he assured us, he carried his money, in the shape of a piece of silver, three inches long and two wide, inserted there in consequence of a fracture he got by falling down a precipice while in hot chase of what figured in the anecdote as "a vagabond of a beetle." Descending towards *terra firma*, to wit, his feet, we find his body gradually diminishing to his legs, which were so thin, that everybody wondered how they could carry the great head. But, like Captain Wattle, each had a foot at the end of it, full as large as the Black Dwarf's. It is so long ago that I almost forget his costume. All I recollect is, that he never wore boots or pantaloons, but exhibited his spindles in all weathers in worsted stockings, and his feet in shoes, gorgeously caparisoned in a pair of square silver buckles, the only pieces of finery he ever displayed.

In the genial months of spring and summer, and early in autumn, Master Timothy was, most of his time, chasing bugs and butterflies about the fields, to the utter confusion of the people, who wondered what he could want with such trumpery. Being a genius and an idler by profession, I used to accompany him frequently in these excursions, for he was fond of me, and called me vagabond oftener than he did anybody else. He had a little net of green gauze, (so constructed as to open and shut as occasion required, to entrap the small fry), and a box with a cork bottom, upon which he impaled his prisoners with true scientific barbarity, by sticking a pin in them. Thus equipped, this Don Quixote of butterfly-catchers, with myself his faithful esquire, would sally forth of a morning into the clovered meadows and flower-dotted fields, over brook, through tangled copse and briery dell, in chase of these gentlemen-commoners of the air. Ever and anon, as he came upon some little retired nook, where nature, like a modest virgin, shrouded her beauties from the common view — a rocky glen, romantic cottage, rustic bridge, or brawling stream — he would take out his portfolio, and pointing me to some conspicuous station to animate his little scene, sketch it and me together, with a mingled taste and skill I have never since seen surpassed. I figure in all his landscapes, although he often called me a vagabond, because he could not drill me into picturesque attitudes. But the finest sport for me was to watch him creeping slily after a humming-bird, the object of his most intense desires, half-buried in the bliss of the dewy honeysuckle, and, just as he was on the point of covering it with his net, to see the little vagrant flit away with a swiftness that made it invisible. It was an invaluable sight to behold Master Timothy stand wiping his continent of a forehead, and blessing the bird for a "little vagabond." These were happy times, and at this moment I recall them, I hardly know why, with a melancholy yet pleasing delight.

During the winter season, Master Timothy was

usually employed in the daytime painting pleasure sleighs, which, at that period, it was the fashion among the farmers to have as fine as fiddles. Timothy was a desperate hand at a true-lover's-knot, a cipher, or a wreath of flowers; and, as for a blazing sun! — he executed one for the squire, that was seriously suspected of melting all the snow in ten leagues round. He would go a dozen miles on such a business, and always carried his materials on a board upon the top of his head — it being before the invention of high-crowned hats. Destiny had decreed he should follow this trade, and nature had provided him a head on purpose. In the long winter evenings, it was his pleasure to sit by the fireside, and tell enormous stories to groups of horror-stricken listeners. I never knew a man that had been so often robbed on Hounslow Heath or had seen so many ghosts in his day as Master Tim Canty. Peace to his ashes! — he is dead; and, if report is to be credited, is sometimes seen on moonlight nights in the church-yard, with his little green gauze net, chasing the ghosts of moths and beetles, as he was wont in past times.

But it is high time to return to my story; for I candidly confess I never think of honest Tim, that I don't grow as garrulous as an old lady talking about the Revolution and the Yagers. In all country villages I ever saw or heard of, whenever anything strange, new, horrible, or delightful happens, or is supposed to have happened, all the male inhabitants, not to say female, make for the tavern as fast as possible, to hear the news, or tell the news, and get at the bottom of the affair. I don't deny that truth is sometimes to be found at the bottom of a well; but in these cases she is generally found at the bottom of the glass. Be this as it may, when Cobus Yerks looked into the village inn, just to say How d'ye do to the landlady, he lit upon a party of some ten or a dozen people, discussing the affair of my being poisoned with Souchong tea. The calamity, by the way, had by this time been extended to the whole family, not one of whom had been left alive by the bloody-minded damsel, Rumour.

Cobus could not resist the fascination of these murders. He edged himself into the jury, and after a little while they were joined by Master Timothy, who, on hearing of the catastrophe of his old fellow-labourer in butterfly-catching, had stridden over, (a distance of two miles), to our house, to ascertain the truth of the report. He of course found it was a mistake, and had now returned with a nefarious design of frightening them all out of their wits with a tale of more than modern horrors. By this time it was the dusk of the evening, and Cobus had a long way to travel before he could reach home. He had been so captivated with the story, and the additions every moment furnished by various new-comers, that he forgot the time till it began to grow quite dark; and then he was so much appalled at what he had heard, that he grew fast to his chair in the chimney-corner, where he had intrenched himself. It was at this moment Master Timothy came in with the design aforesaid.

The whole party gathered round him, to know if the story of the poisoning was true. Tim shook his head; and the shaking of such a head was awful. "What! all the family?", cried they, with one voice. "Every soul of them," cried Tim, in a hollow tone —

"every soul of them, poor creatures; and not only they, but all the cattle, horses, pigs, ducks, chickens, cats, dogs, and guinea-hens, are poisoned." "What! with Souchong tea?" "No — with coloquintida." Coloquintida! the very name was enough to poison a whole generation of Christian people. "But the black bull-dog!" continued Timothy, in a sepulchral voice that curdled the very marrow of their innermost bones. "What of the black bull-dog?", quoth little Cobus. "Why, they do say that he came to life again after lying six hours stone-dead, and ran away howling like a devil incarnate." "A devil incarnate!" repeated Cobus, who knew no more about the meaning of that fell word than if it had been Greek. He only knew it was something very terrible. "Yes," replied Timothy; "and what's more, I saw where he jumped over the barn-yard gate, and there was the print of a cloven foot, as plain as the daylight this blessed minute." It was as dark as pitch, but the comparison was considered proof positive. "A cloven foot!" groaned Cobus, and squeezed himself almost into the oven, while the thought of going home all alone in the dark, past the church-yard, the old grave at the cross-roads, and, above all, the spot where John Ryer was hanged for shooting the sheriff, smote upon his heart, and beat it into a jelly — at least, it shook like one. What if he should meet the big black dog, with his cloven foot, who howled like a devil incarnate! The thought was enough to wither the heart of a stone.

Cobus was a little, knock-kneed, broad-faced, and broad-shouldered Dutchman, who believed all things, past, present, and to come, concerning spooks, goblins, and fiends of all sorts and sizes, from a fairy to a giant. Tim Canty knew him of old, for he had once painted a sleigh for him, and frightened Cobus out of six nights' sleep, by the story of a man that he once saw murdered by a highwayman on Hounslow Heath. Tim followed up the fiction of the black dog with several others, each more dread than the preceding, till he fairly lifted Cobus's wits off the hinges, aided as he was by certain huge draughts upon a pewter mug, with which the little man reinforced his courage at short intervals. He was a true disciple of the doctrine that spirit and courage, that is to say, whiskey and valour, are synonymous.

It now began to wax late in the evening, and the company departed, not one by one, but in pairs, to their respective homes. The landlady, a bitter root of a woman, and more than a match for half the men in the village, began to grow sleepy, as it was now no longer worth her while to keep awake. Gradually all became quiet within and without the house, except now and then the howling of a wandering cur, and the still more doleful moaning of the winds, accompanied by the hollow thumpings of the waves, as they dashed on the rocky shores of the river that ran hard by. Once, and once only, the cat mewed in the garret, and almost caused Cobus to jump out of his skin. The landlady began to complain that it grew late, and she was very sleepy; but Cobus would take no hints, manfully keeping his post in the chimney-corner, till at last the good woman threatened to call up her two negroes, and have him turned neck and heels out of doors. For a moment, the fear of the big black dog with the cloven foot was mastered by the fear of the two stout black men, and the spirit moved Cobus towards the door, lovingly hugging the stone jug, which he had taken care to have plentifully replenished with the creature. He sallied forth in those graceful curves which are affirmed to constitute the true lines of beauty; and report says that he made a copious libation of the contents of the stone jug outside the door, ere the landlady, after assisting to untie his patient team, had tumbled him into his wagon. This was the last that was seen of Cobus Yerks.

That night his faithful though not very obedient little wife, whom he had wedded at Tappan, on the famous sea of that name, and who wore a cap trimmed with pink ribbons when she went to church on Sundays, fell asleep in her chair, as she sat anxiously watching for his return. About midnight she waked, but she saw not her beloved Cobus, nor heard his voice calling her to open the door. But she heard the raven, or something very like it, screaming from the Raven Rock, the foxes barking about the house, the wind whistling and moaning among the rocks and trees of the mountain-side, and a terrible commotion among the poultry — Cobus having taken the great house-dog with him that day. Again she fell asleep, and waked not until the day was dawning. She opened the window, and looked forth upon as beautiful an autumnal morning as ever blessed this blessèd country. The yellow sun threw a golden lustre over the many-tinted woods, painted by the cunning hand of Nature with a thousand varied dyes; the smoke of the neighbouring farm-houses rose straight upward to heaven in the pure atmosphere, and the breath of the cattle mingled its warm vapour with the invisible clearness of the morning air. But what were all these beauties of delicious nature to the eye and the heart of the anxious wife, who saw that Cobus was not there!

She went forth to the neighbours, to know if they had seen him, and they good-naturedly sallied out to seek him on the road that led from the village to his home. But no traces of him could be found, and they were returning with bad news for his troubled mate, when they bethought themselves of turning into a by-road that led to a tavern which used whilom to attract the affections of honest Cobus, and where he was sometimes wont to stop and wet his whistle.

They had not gone far, when they began to perceive traces of the lost traveller. First, his broad-brimmed hat, which he had inherited through divers generations, and which he always wore when he went to the village, lay grovelling in the dirt, crushed out of all goodly shape by the wheel of his wagon, which had passed over it. Next, they encountered the back-board of the wagon, ornamented with C. Y. in a true-lover's-knot, painted by Tim Canty, in his best style — and anon, a little farther, a shoe, that was indentified as having belonged to our hero, by having upward of three hundred hobnails in the sole, for he was a saving little fellow, though he *would* wet his whistle sometimes, in spite of all his wife and the minister could say. Proceeding about a hundred rods farther, to a sudden turn of the road, they encountered the wagon, or rather the fragments of it, scattered about and along in the highway, and the horses standing quietly against a fence, into which they had run the pole.

But what was become of the unfortunate driver no one could discover. At length, after searching some time, they found him lying in a tuft of blackberry briars, amid pieces of the stone jug, lifeless and motionless. His face was turned upward, and streaked with seams of blood; his clothes were torn, bloody, and disfigured with dirt; and his pipe, that he carried in the buttonholes of his waistcoat, was shivered all to nought. They made their way to the body, full of sad forebodings, and shook it, to see if any life remained. But it was all in vain — there seemed neither sense nor motion there. "Maybe, after all," said one, "he is only in a swound — here is a drop of the spirits left in the bottom of the jug — let us hold it to his nose; it may bring him to life."

The experiment was tried, and, wonderful to tell, in a moment or two, Cobus, opening his eyes, and smacking his lips with peculiar satisfaction, exclaimed, "Some o' that, boys!" A little shaking brought him to himself, when, being asked to give an account of the disaster of his wagon and his stone jug, he at first shook his head mysteriously, and demurred. Being, however, taken to the neighbouring tavern, and comforted a little with divers refreshments, he was again pressed for his story, when, assuming a face of awful mystification, he began as follows: —

"You must know," said Cobus, "I started rather late from town, for I had been kept there by — by business; and because, you see, I was waiting for the moon to rise, that I might find my way home in the dark night. But it grew darker and darker, until you could not see your hand before your face, and at last I concluded to set out, considering I was as sober as a deacon, and my horses could see their way blindfold. I had not gone quite round the corner where John Ryer was hung for shooting Sheriff Smith, when I heard somebody coming, pat, pat, pat, close behind my wagon. I looked back, but I could see nothing, it was so dark. By and by, I heard it again, louder and louder, and then I confess I began to be a little afeard. So I whipped up my horses a quarter of a mile or so, and then let them walk on. I listened, and pat, pat, pat, went the noise again. I began to be a good deal frightened, but, considering it could be nothing at all, I thought I might as well take a small dram, as the night was rather chilly, and I began to tremble a little with the cold. I took but a drop, as I am a living sinner, and then went on quite gayly; but pat, pat, pat, went the footsteps, ten times louder and faster than ever. And then!, then I looked back, and saw a pair of saucer-eyes just at the tail of my wagon, as big and as bright as the mouths of a fiery furnace, dancing up and down in the air like two stage-lamps in a rutty road.

"By gosh, boys, but you may depend I was scared now! I took another little dram, and then made the whip fly about the ears of old Pepper and Billy, who cantered away at a wonderful rate, considering. Presently, bang! something heavy jumped into the wagon, as if heaven and earth were coming together. I looked over my shoulder, and the great burning eyes were within half a yard of my back. The creature was so close that I felt its breath blowing upon me, and it smelled for all one exactly like brimstone. I should have jumped out of the wagon, but, somehow or other, I could not stir, for I was bewitched as sure as you live. All I could do was to thrash away at Pepper and Billy, who rattled along at a great rate up hill and down, over the rough roads, so that if I had not been bewitched I must have tumbled out to a certainty. When I came to the bridge, at old Mangham's, the black dog, (for I could see something black and shaggy under the goggle eyes), all at once jumped up, and, seating himself close by me on the bench, snatched the whip and reins out of my hands like lightning. Then, looking me in the face and nodding, he whispered something in my ear, and put it into Pepper and Billy, till they seemed to fly through the air. From that time I began to lose my wits by degrees, till at last the smell of brimstone overpowered me, and I remember nothing till you found me this morning in the briars."

Here little Cobus concluded his story, which he repeated, with several variations and additions, to his wife, when he got home. That good woman, who, on most occasions, took the liberty of lecturing her good man whenever he used to be belated in his excursions to the village, was so struck with this adventure, that she omitted her usual exhortation, and ever afterwards viewed him as one ennobled by supernatural communication, submitting to him as her veritable lord and master. Some people, who pretend to be so wise that they won't believe the evidence of their senses when it contradicts their reason, affected to be incredulous, and hinted that the goggle-eyes and the brimstone breath appertained to Cobus Yerks's great house-dog, which had certainly followed him that day to the village, and was found quietly reposing by his master, in the tuft of briars. But Cobus was ever exceedingly wroth at this suggestion, and, being a sturdy little bruiser, had knocked down one or two of these unbelieving sinners, for venturing to assert that the contents of the stone jug were at the bottom of the whole business. After that, everybody believed it, and it is now for ever incorporated with the marvellous legends of the renowed Buttermilk Hill.

THE
RIDE OF SAINT NICHOLAS
ON
NEW-YEAR'S EVE.

THE

RIDE OF SAINT NICHOLAS

ON

NEW-YEAR'S EVE.

Of all the cities in this New World, that which once bore the name of Fort Orange * but bears it no more is the favourite of the good St. Nicholas. It is there that he hears the sound of his native language, and sees the honest Dutch pipe in the mouths of a few portly burghers, who, disdaining the pestilent innovations of modern times, still cling with honest obstinacy to the dress, the manners, and customs, of old *faderland*. It is there, too, that they have instituted a society in honour of the excellent saint, whose birthday they celebrate in a manner worthy of all commendation.

True it is, that the city of his affections has from time to time committed divers great offences, which sorely wounded the feelings of St. Nicholas, and almost caused him to withdraw his patronage from its backsliding citizens. First, by adopting the new-

* Albany.

fangled style of beginning the year, at the bidding of the old lady of Babylon, whereby the jolly New-year was so jostled out of place that the good saint scarcely knew where to look for it. Next, they essayed themselves to learn outlandish tongues, whereby they gradually sophisticated their own, insomuch that he could hardly understand them. Thirdly, they did, from time to time, admit into their churches preachings and singings in the upstart English language, until by degrees the ancient worship became adulterated in such a manner that the indignant St. Nicholas, when he first witnessed it, did, for the only time in his life, come near to uttering a great oath, by exclaiming, "*Wat donderdag is dat* * *?*" Now be it known that had he said, "*Wat donder is dat* †," it would have been downright swearing; so you see what a narrow escape he had.

Not content with these backslidings, the burghers of Fort Orange — a pestilence on all new names! — suffered themselves by degrees to be corrupted by various modern innovations, under the mischievous disguise of improvements. Forgetting the reverence due to their ancestors, who eschewed all internal improvement except that of the mind and heart, they departed from the venerable customs of the *faderland;* and, pulling down the old houses that, scorning all appearance of ostentation, modestly presented the little end to the street, began to erect in their places certain indescribable buildings, with the broadsides as it

* *Donder en Bliksem!* — Thunder and lightning! — was a favorite Dutch oath. The use of *Donderdag* — Thursday — corresponds to "darn" for "damn."

† "What the thunder does that mean?"

were turned frontwise, by which strange contortion the comeliness of Fort Orange was utterly destroyed. It is on record that a heavy judgment fell upon the head of the first man who adventured on this daring innovation. His money gave out before this monstrous novelty was completed, and he invented the pernicious system of borrowing and mortgaging, before happily unknown among these worthy citizens, who were utterly confounded, not long afterwards, at seeing the house change its owner — a thing that had never happened before in that goodly community, save when the son entered on the inheritance of his father.

Becoming gradually more incorrigible in their apostasy, they were seduced into opening, widening, and regulating the streets; making the crooked straight and the narrow wide, thereby causing sad inroads into the strong boxes of divers of the honest burghers, who became all at once very rich, saving that they had no money to go to market. To cap the climax of their enormities, they at last committed the egregious sacrilege of pulling down the ancient and honourable Dutch church, which stood right in the middle of State street, or Staats street, being so called after the family of that name, from which I am lineally descended.

At this the good St. Nicholas was exceedingly grieved; and when, by degrees, his favourite burghers left off eating sturgeon, being thereto instigated by divers scurvy jests of certain silly strangers that knew not the excellence of that savoury fish, he cried out in the anguish of his spirit, "*Onbegrypelyk!*" — "Incredible!", meaning thereby that he could scarcely believe his eyes. In the bitterness of his soul he had resolved to return to *faderland*, and leave his beloved city to be swallowed up in the vortex of improvement. He was making his progress through the streets in melancholy mood, to take his last farewell, when he came to the outlet of the Grand Canal, just then completed.* "*Is het mogelyk?*" — which means, Is it possible? — exclaimed St. Nicholas; and thereupon he was so delighted with this proof that his beloved people had not altogether degenerated from their ancestors, that he determined not to leave them to strange saints, outlandish tongues, and modern innovations. He took a sail on the canal, and returned in such measureless content, that he blessed the good city of Fort Orange as he evermore called it, and resolved to distribute a more than usual store of his New-year cookies, at the Christmas holydays. That jovial season was now fast approaching. The autumn frosts had already invested the forests with a mantle of glory; the farmers were in their fields and orchards, gathering in the corn and apples, or making cider, the wholesome beverage of virtuous simplicity; the robins, blackbirds, and all the annual emigrants to southern climes, had passed away in flocks, like the adventurers to the far West, the bluebird alone lingering to sing his parting song; and sometimes, of a morning, the river showed a little fretted border of ice, looking like a fringe of lace on the garment of some decayed dowager. At length the liquid glass of the river cooled into a wide, immovable mirror, glistening in the sun; the trees, all save the evergreens, stood bare to the

* The first boat passed though the Erie Canal to the Hudson river on the 4th of November, 1825.

keen winds; the fields were covered with snow, affording no lures to tempt to rural wanderings; the pleasures of men gradually centred themselves in the chimney-corner: — it was winter, and New-year's eve was come again.

The night was clear, calm, and cold, and the bright stars glittered in the heavens, in such multitudes that every man might have had a star to himself. The worthy patriarchs of Fort Orange, having gathered around them their children, and children's children, even unto the third and fourth generation, were disporting themselves in innocent revelry at the cheerful fireside. All the enjoyments of life had contracted themselves into the domestic circle; the streets were as quiet as a church-yard, and not even the stroke of the watchman was heard on the curb-stone. Gradually it waxed late, and the city clocks rang, in the silence of night, the hour which not one of the orderly citizens had heard, except at mid-day, since the last anniversary of the happy New-year, unless peradventure troubled with a toothache, or some such unseemly irritation.

The doleful warning, which broke upon the frosty air like the tolling of a funeral bell, roused the sober devotees of St. Nicholas to a sense of their trespasses on the waning night; and, after one good, smoking draught of spiced Jamaica to the patron saint, they, one and all, young and old, hied them to bed, that he might have a fair opportunity to bestow his favours without being seen by mortal eye. For be it known, that St. Nicholas, like all really heart-whole generous fellows, loves to do good in secret, and eschews those pompous benefactions which are duly recorded in the newspapers, being of opinion they only prove that the vanity of man is sometimes an overmatch for his avarice.

Having allowed them fifteen minutes, (which is as much as a sober burgher of good morals and habits requires), to get as fast asleep as a church, St. Nicholas, having harnessed his pony, and loaded his little wagon with a store of good things for well-behaved, diligent children, together with whips and other mementos for undutiful varlets, did set forth gayly on his errand of benevolence.

Vuur en vlammen! how the good saint did hurry through the streets, up one chimney and down another; for, as I do live, they are not such miserable narrow things as those of other cities, where the claims of ostentation are so voracious that people can't afford to keep up good fires, and the chimneys are so narrow that the little sweeps of seven years old often get themselves stuck fast, to the imminent peril of their lives. You may think he had a good deal of business on hand, being obliged to visit every house in Fort Orange, between twelve o'clock and daylight, save indeed those of some few would-be fashionable upstarts, who had mortally offended him, by turning up their noses at the simple jollifications and friendly greetings of the merry New-year. Accordingly, he rides like the wind, scarcely touching the ground; and this is the reason that he is never seen, except by a rare chance, which is the cause why certain unbelieving sinners, who scoff at old customs and notions, either really do, or pretend to, doubt, whether the good things found on Christmas and New-year mornings in the stockings of the little varlets of Fort

Orange and Nieuw Amsterdam, are put there by the jolly St. Nicholas or not. Beshrew them, say I—and may they never taste the blessing of his bounty! *Goeden Hemel** !, as if I myself, being a kinsman of the saint, don't know him as well as a debtor does his creditor! But people are grown so wise nowadays, that they believe in nothing but the increased value of property.

Be this as it may, St. Nicholas went forth blithely on his kindly errand, without minding the intense cold, for he was kept right warm by the benevolence of his heart; and, when that failed, he ever and anon addressed himself to a snug little pottle, the contents of which did smoke lustily when he pulled out the stopper, a piece of snow-white corn-cob.

It is impossible for me to specify one by one the visits paid that night by the good saint, or the various adventures which he encountered. I therefore content myself, and, I trust, my worthy and excellent readers, with dwelling briefly on those which appear to me most worthy of descending to posterity, and that withal convey excellent moral lessons, without which history is naught, whether it be true or false.

After visiting various honest little Dutch houses with notched roofs and the gable ends to the street, leaving his benedictions, St. Nicholas at length came to a goodly mansion bearing strong marks of being sophisticated by modern fantastic caprices. He would have passed it by in scorn, had he not remembered that it belonged to a descendant of one of his favoured votaries, who had passed away to his long home without having once backslided from the customs of his

* Good Heavens!

ancestors. Respect for the memory of this worthy man wrought upon his feelings, and he forthwith dashed down the chimney, where he stuck fast in the middle, and came nigh being suffocated with the fumes of anthracite coal, which this degenerate descendant of a pious ancestor, who spent thousands in useless and unbecoming ostentation, burned by way of economy.

If the excellent saint had not been enveloped, as it were, in the odour of sanctity, which in some measure protected him from the poison of this pestilent vapour, it might have gone hard with him; as it was, he was sadly bewildered, when his little pony, which liked the predicament no better than his master, made a violent plunge, drew the wagon through the narrow passage, and down they came plump into a magnificent bedchamber, filled with all sorts of finery — such as wardrobes, bedizened with tawdry ornaments; satin chairs too good to be looked at or sat upon, and therefore covered with brown linen; a bedstead of varnished mahogany, with a canopy over it somewhat like a cocked-hat, with a plume of ostrich feathers instead of orthodox valances, and the like; and a looking-glass large enough to reflect a Dutch city.

St. Nicholas contemplated the pair who slept in this newfangled abomination, with a mingled feeling of pity and indignation, though I must say the wife looked very pretty in her lace nightcap, with one arm as white as snow partly uncovered. But he soon turned away, being a devout and self-denying saint, to seek for the stockings of the little children, who were innocent of these unseemly innovations. But what was his horror at finding that, instead of being hung up in the chimney-corner, they were thrown carelessly on the floor, and that the little souls, who lay asleep in each other's arms in another room, lest they should disturb their parents, were thus deprived of all the pleasant anticipations accompanying the approaching jolly New-year.

"*Een vervlocte jonge!*",* said he to himself, (for he never uttered his maledictions aloud); "to rob his little ones of such wholesome and innocent delights! But they shall not be disappointed." So he sought the cold and distant chamber of the children, who were virtuous and dutiful, and, when they waked in the morning, they found the bed covered with good things, and were as happy as the day is long. St. Nicholas returned to the splendid chamber, which, be it known, was furnished with the spoils of industrious unfortunate people, to whom the owner lent money, charging them so much the more in proportion to their necessities. It is true that he gave some of the wealth he thus got over the duyvel's back, as it were, to public charities, and sometimes churches, when he knew it would get into the newspapers, by which he obtained the credit of being very pious and charitable. But St. Nicholas was too sensible and judicious not to know that the only charitable and pious donations agreeable to the Giver of all are those which are honestly come by. The alms which are got by ill means can never come to good, and it is better to give back to those from whom we have taken it dishonestly, even one fourth, yea, one tenth, than to bestow ten times as much on those who have no such claim. The true atonement for injuries is that made to the injured.

* An accursed boy!

All other is a cheat in the eye of Heaven. You cannot settle the account, by giving to Peter what you have filched from Paul.

So thought the good St. Nicholas, as he revolved in his mind a plan for punishing this degenerate caitiff, who despised his ordinances and customs, and was moreover one who, in dealing with borrowers, not only shaved but skinned them. Remembering not the perils of the chimney, he was about departing the way he came, but the little pony obstinately refused; and the good saint, having first taken off the lace night-cap, and put a fool's-cap in its place, and given the money-lender a tweak of the nose that made him roar, whipped instantly through the key-hole, to pursue his benevolent tour through the ancient city of Fort Orange.

Gliding through the streets unheard and unseen, he at length came to a winding lane, from which his quick ear caught the sound of obstreperous revelry. Stopping his pony, and listening more attentively, he distinguished the words, "*Ich ben liederich*,"* roared out in a chorus of mingled voices seemingly issuing from a little low house of the true orthodox construction, standing on the right-hand side, at a distance of a hundred yards, or thereabout.

"*Wat donderdag!*" exclaimed St. Nicholas; "is mine old friend, Baltus Van Loon, keeping it up at this time of the morning? The old rogue! — but I'll punish him for this breach of the good customs of Fort Orange." So he halted on the top of Baltus's chimney, to consider the best way of bringing it about, and was, all at once, saluted in the nostrils by

* This seems to be corrupted German. *Ich ben* — I am — *liederlich*, a careless dog — or, *liederreich*, say, a jolly singer.

such a delectable perfume, arising from a certain spiced beverage with which the substantial burghers were wont to recreate themselves at this season of the year, that he was sorely tempted to join a little in the revelry below, and punish the merry caitiffs afterwards. Presently he heard honest Baltus propose—"The jolly St. Nicholas!," as a toast, which was drunk in a full bumper, with great rejoicing and acclamation.

St. Nicholas could stand it no longer, but descended forthwith into the little parlour of old Baltus, thinking, by the way, that, just to preserve appearances, he would lecture the roistering rogues a little for keeping such late hours; and then, provided Baltus could give a good reason, or indeed any reason at all, for such an indecorous transgression, he would sit down with them, and take some of the savoury tipple that had regaled his nostrils while waiting at the top of the chimney.

The vapouring varlets were so busy roaring out, "*Ich ben liederich*," that they did not take note of the presence of the saint, until he cried with a loud and angry voice, "*Wat blikslager is dat?*" * — (he did not say *blixem* †, because that would have been little better than swearing) — "*Ben je be dondered*,‡ to be carousing here at this time of night, ye ancient, and not venerable sinners!"

Old Baltus was not a little startled at the intrusion of the strangers — for, if the truth must out, he was a little in for it, and saw double, as is usual at such times. This caused such a confusion in his head that

* "What the tinman does this mean?" † Lightning.

‡ "Are you be-thundered?" or, "What the Old Scratch have you got in you?"

he forgot to rise from his seat and pay due honour to his visitor, as did the rest of the company.

"Are you not ashamed of yourselves," continued the saint, "to set such a bad example to the neighbourhood, by carousing at this time of the morning, contrary to good old customs, known and accepted by all, except such noisy splutterkins as yourselves?"

"This time of the morning," — replied old Baltus, who had his full portion of Dutch courage — "this time of the morning, did you say? Look yonder, and see with your own eyes whether it is morning or not."

The cunning rogue, in order to have a good excuse for transgressing the canons of St. Nicholas, had so managed it, that the old clock in the corner had run down, and now pointed to the hour of eleven, where it remained stationary, like a rusty weathercock. St. Nicholas knew this as well as old Baltus himself, and could not help being mightily tickled at this device. He told Baltus that, this being the case, with permission of his host he would sit down by the fire and warm himself, till it was time to set forth again, seeing he had mistaken the hour.

Baltus, who by this time began to perceive that there was but one visitor instead of two, now rose from the table with much ado, and, approaching the stranger, besought him to take a seat among the jolly revellers, seeing they were there assembled in honour of St. Nicholas, and not out of any regard to the lusts of the flesh. In this he was joined by the rest of the company, so that St. Nicholas, being a good-natured fellow, at length suffered himself to be persuaded, whereto he was mightily incited by the savoury fumes issuing from a huge pitcher standing smoking in the chimney-corner. So he sat down with old Baltus, and, being called on for a toast, gave them "Old *Faderland*" in a bumper.

Then they had a high time of it, you may be sure. Old Baltus sung a famous song celebrating the valour of our Dutch ancestors, and their triumph over the mighty power of Spain after a struggle of more than a generation, in which the meads of Holland smoked, and her canals were red, with blood. *Goeden Hemel!* but I should like to have been there, for I hope it would have been nothing discreditable for one of my cloth to have joined in chorus with the excellent St. Nicholas. Then they talked about the good old times, when the son who departed from the customs of his ancestors was considered little better than misbegotten; lamented over the interloping of such multitudes of idle flaunting men and women in their way to and from the Springs; the increase of taverns, the high price of everything, and the manifold transgressions of the rising generation. Ever and anon, old Baltus would observe that sorrow was as dry as a corn-cob, and pour out a full bumper of the smoking beverage, until at last it came to pass that the honest man and his worthy companions, being unused to such late hours, fell fast asleep in their goodly armchairs, and snored lustily in concert. Whereupon St. Nicholas, feeling a little waggish, after putting their wigs the hinder part before, and placing a great China bowl upsidedown on the head of old Baltus, who sat nodding like a mandarin, departed, laughing ready to split his sides. In the morning, when Baltus and his companions awoke, and saw what a figure they cut, they all laid the trick to the door of the stranger, and never knew to the last day of their lives who it was that caroused with them so lustily on New-year's morning.

Pursuing his way in high good-humour, being somewhat exhilarated by the set-to with old Baltus and his roistering companions, St. Nicholas in good time came into the ancient *Colonie*, which, being as it were at the outskirts of Fort Orange, was inhabited by many people not well-to-do in the world. He descended the chimney of an old weather-worn house that bore evident marks of poverty, for he is not one of those saints that hanker after palaces and turn their backs on their friends. It is his pleasure to seek out and administer to the innocent gratifications of those who are obliged to labour all the year round, and who can only spare time to be merry at Christmas and New-year. He is indeed the poor man's saint.

On entering the room, he was struck with the appearance of poverty and desolation that reigned all around. A number of little children of different ages, but none more than ten years old, lay huddled close together on a straw-bed, which was on the floor, their limbs intertwined to keep themselves warm, for their covering was scant and miserable. Yet they slept in peace, and had quiet countenances; for hunger seeks refuge in the oblivion of repose. In a corner of the room stood a forlorn bed, on which lay a female, whose face, as the moonbeams fell upon it through a window without shutters, many panes of which were stuffed with old rags to keep out the nipping air of the winter night, bore evidence of long and painful suffering. It looked like death rather than sleep. A small pine table, a few broken chairs, and a dresser, whose shelves were ill supplied, made up the furniture of this mansion of poverty.

As he stood contemplating the scene, his honest old heart swelled with sorrowful compassion, saying to himself, " *God bewaar ous !*,* but this is pitiful." At that moment, a little child on the straw-bed cried out in a weak voice that went to the heart of the saint, " Mother, mother, give me to eat — I am hungry." St. Nicholas went to the child, but she was fast asleep, and hunger had infected her very dreams. The mother did not hear, for long-continued sorrow and suffering sleep sounder than happiness, as the waters lie stillest when the tempest is past.

Again the little child cried out, " Mother, mother, I am freezing — give me some more covering." " Be quiet, Blandina," answered a voice deep and hoarse, yet not unkind; and St. Nicholas, looking around to see whence it came, beheld a man, sitting close in the chimney-corner though there was no fire burning, his arms folded close around him, and his head drooping on his bosom. He was clad like one of the children of poverty, and his teeth chattered with cold. St. Nicholas wiped his eyes, for he was a good-hearted saint, and, coming close up to the wretched man, said to him kindly, " How do ye, my good friend ? "

" Friend ?," said the other — " I have no friend but God, and He seems to have deserted me." As he said this, he raised his saddened eyes to the good saint, and, after looking at him a little while as if he was not conscious of his presence, dropped them

* God preserve us !

again, without even asking who he was, or whence he came, or what he wanted. Despair had deadened his faculties, and nothing remained in his mind but the consciousness of suffering.

"*Het is jammer, het is jammer* — it is a pity, it is a pity!" quoth the kind-hearted saint, as he passed his sleeve across his eyes. "But something must be done, and that quickly too." So he shook the poor man somewhat roughly by the shoulder, and cried out, "Ho! ho! what aileth thee, son of my good old friend, honest Johannes Garrebrantze?"

This salutation seemed to rouse the almost lifeless figure, which then unsteadily arose, and, essaying to stand upright, fell into the arms of St. Nicholas, who almost believed it was a lump of ice, so cold and stiff did it seem. Now, be it known that Providence, as a reward for his benevolent disposition, has bestowed on St. Nicholas the privilege of doing good without measure to all who are deserving of his bounty, and this by such means as he thinks proper to the purpose. It is a power he seldom exerts to the uttermost, except on pressing occasions, and this he believed one of them.

Perceiving that the hapless being was wellnigh frozen to death, he called into action the supernatural faculties which had been committed to him, and lo!, in an instant a rousing fire blazed on the hearth, towards which the meagre wretch, instinctively as it were, edged his chair, and stretched out one of his bony hands, that was as stiff as an icicle. The light flashed so brightly in the face of the little ones and their mother, that they awoke; and, seeing the cheerful blaze, arose in their miserable clothing, which they had worn to aid in keeping them warm, and hied as fast as they could to bask in its blessed cheer. So eager were they, that for a while they were unconscious of the presence of a stranger, although St. Nicholas had now assumed his proper person, that he might not be taken for some one of those diabolical wizards who, being always in mischief, are ashamed to show their faces among honest people.

At length the poor man, who was called, after his father, Johannes Garrebrantze, being somewhat revived by the genial warmth of the fire, looked around, and became aware of the presence of the stranger. This inspired him with a secret awe, for which he could not account; insomuch that his voice trembled, though now he was not cold, when, after some hesitation, he said:—

"Stranger, thou art welcome to this naked house. I would I were better able to offer thee the hospitalities of the season, but I will wish thee a happy New-year, and that is all I can bestow." The good *yffrouw*, his wife, repeated the wish, and straightway began to apologize for the untidy state of her apartment.

"Make no apologies," replied the excellent saint; "I come to give, not to receive. To-night I treat, to-morrow you may return the kindness to others."

"I?" said Johannes Garrebrantze; "I have nothing to bestow but good wishes, and nothing to receive but the scorn and neglect of the world. If I had anything to give thee to eat or drink, thou shouldst have it with all my heart. But the new year, which brings jollity to the hearts of others, brings nothing but hunger and despair to me and mine."

"Thou hast seen better days, I warrant thee," answered the saint; "for thou speakest like a scholar of Leyden. Tell me thy story, Johannes, my son, and we shall see whether in good time thou wilt not hold up thy head as high as a church-steeple."

"Alas! to what purpose, since man assuredly has, and Heaven seems to have, forsaken me?"

"Hush!" cried St. Nicholas; "Heaven never forsakes the broken spirit, or turns a deaf ear to the cries of innocent children. It is for the wicked never to hope, the virtuous never to despair. I predict thou shalt live to see better days."

"I must see them soon then, for I, my wife, and my children, have been without food since twenty-four hours past."

"What! God be with us! is there such lack of charity in the burghers of the *Colonie*, that they will suffer a neighbour to starve under their very noses? *Onbegrypelyk!* — I'll not believe it."

"They know not my necessities."

"No? What! — hast thou no tongue to speak them?"

"I am too proud to beg."

"And too lazy to work," cried St. Nicholas, in a severe tone.

"Look you," answered the other, holding up his right arm with his left, and showing that the sinews were stiffened by rheumatism.

"Is it so, my friend? Well, but thou mightest still have bent thy spirit to ask charity for thy starving wife and children, though, in truth, begging is the last thing an honest man ought to stoop to. But, *Goeden Hemel!*, here am I talking, while thou and thine are perishing with hunger."

Saying which, St. Nicholas straightway bade the good *yffrouw* to bring forth the little pine table, which she did, making sundry excuses for the absence of a table-cloth; and, when she had done so, he incontinently spread out upon it such store of good things from his little cart, as made the hungry children's mouths to water, and smote the hearts of their parents with joyful thanksgivings. "Eat, drink, and be merry," said St. Nicholas, "for to-morrow thou shalt not die, but live."

The heart of the good saint expanded, like as the morning-glory does to the first rays of the sun, while he sat rubbing his hands at seeing them eat with such a zest as made him almost think it was worth while to be hungry, in order to enjoy such triumphant satisfaction. When they had done, and returned their pious thanks to Heaven and the charitable stranger, St. Nicholas willed the honest man to expound the causes which had brought him to his present deplorable condition. "My own folly," said he. And the other sagely replied, — "I thought as much. Beshrew me, friend, if in all my experience, (and I have lived long, and seen much), I ever encountered distress and poverty that could not be traced to its source in folly or vice. Heaven is too bountiful to entail misery on its creatures, save through their own transgressions. But, I pray thee, go on with thy story."

The good man then went on to relate that his father, old Johannes Garrebrantze —

"Ah!", quoth St. Nicholas, "I knew him well. He was an honest man, and that, in these times of all sorts of improvements, except in mind and morals, is little less than miraculous. But I interrupt thee, friend — proceed with thy story, once more."

The son of Johannes again resumed his narration, and related how his father had left him a competent estate in the *Colonie*, on which he lived in good credit, and in the enjoyment of a reasonable competency, with his wife and children, until within a few years past, when, seeing a vast number of three-story houses with folding doors and marble mantel-pieces rising up all around him, he began to be ashamed of his little one-story house with the gable end to the street, and —

"Ah! Johannes," interrupted the pale wife, "do not spare me. It was I that in the vanity of my heart put such notions in thy head. It was I that tempted thee."

"It was the *duyvel*," muttered St. Nicholas, "in the shape of a pretty wife."

Johannes gave his helpmate a look of affectionate forgiveness, and went on to tell St. Nicholas how, egged on by the evil example of his neighbours, he had at last committed sacrilege against his household gods, and pulled down the home of his fathers, commencing a new one on its ruins.

"Donderdag!" quoth the saint to himself; "and the bricks came from *faderland*, too!"

When Johannes had about half finished his new house, he discovered one day, to his great astonishment and dismay, that all his money, which he had been saving for his children, was gone. His strong box was empty, and his house but half-finished, although, after estimating the cost, he had allowed one third more in order to be sure in the business.

Johannes was now at a dead stand. The idea of

borrowing money and running in debt never entered his head before, nor would have entered now, had it not been suggested to him by a neighbour, a great speculator, who had lately built a whole street of houses, not a single brick of which belonged to him in reality. He had borrowed the money, mortgaged the property, and expected to grow rich by a sudden rise. Poor Johannes may be excused for listening to the seductions of this losel varlet, seeing he had a house half-finished on his hands; he *did* listen, and was betrayed into borrowing money of a bank just then established in the *Colonie* on a capital paid in according to law — that is, not paid at all — the directors of which were very anxious to exchange their rags for lands and houses.

Johannes finished his house in glorious style, and, having opened this new mine of wealth, furnished it still more gloriously. Moreover, as it would have been sheer nonsense not to live gloriously in such a glorious establishment, he spent thrice his income in order to keep up his respectability. He was going on swimmingly, when what is called a reaction took place; which means, as far as I can understand, that the bank directors, having been pleased to make money plenty to increase their dividends, are pleased thereafter to make it scarce for the same purpose. Instead of lending it in the name of the bank, it is credibly reported they do it through certain brokers, who charge lawful interest and unlawful commission, and thus cheat the law with a clear conscience. But I thank Heaven devoutly that I know nothing of their wicked mysteries, and therefore will say no more about them.

Be this as it may, Johannes was called upon all of a sudden to pay his notes to the bank, for the reaction had commenced, and there were no more renewals. The directors wanted all the money, to lend out at three per cent. a month. It became necessary to raise the wind, as they say in Wall street, and Johannes, by the advice of his good friend the speculative genius, went with him to a certain money-lender of his acquaintance, who was reckoned a good Christian, because he always charged most usury where there was the greatest necessity for a loan. To a rich man he would lend at something like a reasonable interest, but to a man in great distress for money he showed about as much mercy as a weazel does to a chicken. He sucked their blood till there was not a drop left in their bodies. This he did six days in the week, and on the seventh went three times to church, to enable him to begin on Monday in a Christian spirit. Out on such varlets, I say; they bring religion itself into disrepute, and add the sin of hypocrisy to men to that of insult to Heaven.

Suffice it to say that poor Johannes Garrebrantze the younger went down hill faster than he ever went up in his life; and, inasmuch as I scorn these details of petty roguery as unworthy of my cloth and calling, I shall content myself with merely premising that, through a process very common nowadays, the poor man speedily dissipated all the patrimony left him by his worthy father in paying commission to the money-lender. He finally became bankrupt; and, as he was absolutely uninitiated in the odd science of getting rich by such a manœuvre, was left without a shilling in the world. He retired from his fine house, which was forthwith occupied by his good friend the money-lender, whose nose had been tweaked by St. Nicholas, as heretofore recorded, and sought shelter in the wretched building where he was found by that benevolent worthy. Destitute of resources, and entirely unacquainted with the art of living by his wits or his labour, though he tried hard both ways, poor Johannes became gradually steeped in poverty to the very lips; and, being totally disabled by rheumatism, might, peradventure, with all his family, have perished that very night, had not Providence mercifully sent the good St. Nicholas to their relief.

"*Wat donderdag!*", exclaimed the saint, when he had done — "*wat donderdag!* — was that your house down yonder, with the fine bedroom, the wardrobes, the looking-glass as big as the moon, and the bedstead with a cocked-hat and feathers?"

"Even so," replied the other, hanging down his head.

"*Is het mogelyk!*" And, after considering a little while, the good saint, slapping his hand on the table, broke forth again — "By *donderdag*, but I'll soon settle this business."

He then began to hum an old Dutch hymn, which by its soothing and wholesome monotony so operated upon Johannes and his family, that one and all fell fast asleep in their chairs.

The good St. Nicholas then lighted his pipe, and seating himself by the fire, revolved in his mind the best mode of proceeding on this occasion. At first he determined to divest the rich money-lender of all his ill-gotten gains, and bestow them on poor Johannes and his family. But when he considered that the losel caitiff was already sufficiently punished in being condemned to the sordid toils of money-making, and in the privation of all those social and benevolent feel ings which, while they contribute to our own happiness, administer to that of others; that he was for ever beset with the consuming cares of avarice, the hope of gain, and the fear of losses; and that, rich as he was, he suffered all the gnawing pangs of an insatiable desire for more; — when he considered all this, St. Nicholas decided to leave him to the certain punishment of wealth wrongfully acquired, and the chances of losing it by the inordinate appetite for its increase, which sooner or later produces all the consequences of reckless imprudence.

"Let the splutterkin alone," thought St. Nicholas, "and he will become the instrument of his own punishment."

Then he went on to think what he should do for poor Johannes and his little children. Though he had been severely punished for his folly, yet did the good saint, who in his nightly holiday peregrinations had seen more of human life and human passions than the sun ever shone upon, very well know that sudden wealth, or sudden poverty, is a sore trial of the heart of man, in like manner as the sudden transition from light to darkness, or darkness to light, produces a temporary blindness. It was true that Johannes had received a severe lesson, but the great mass of mankind are prone to forget the chastening rod of experience, as they do the pangs of sickness when they are past. He therefore settled in his mind, that the return of Johannes to competence and prosperity should be by the salutary process of his own exertions, and that he should learn their value by the pains it cost to attain them. "*Het is goed visschen in troebel water*," quoth he, "for then a man knows the value of what he catches."

It was broad daylight before he had finished his pipe and his cogitations, when, placing his old polished delft pipe carefully in his button-hole, the good saint sallied forth, leaving Johannes and his family still fast asleep in their chairs. Directly opposite the miserable abode of Johannes there dwelt a little fat Dutchman, with money-bags to match, who had all his life manfully stemmed the torrent of modern innovation. He eschewed all sorts of paper-money, as an invention of people without property to get hold of those that had it; abhorred the practice of widening streets; and despised in his heart all public improvements except canals, a sneaking notion for which he inherited from old *faderland*. He was honest as the light of the blessed sun; and though he opened his best parlour but twice a year, to have it cleaned and put to rights, yet this I will say of him, that the poor man who wanted a dinner was never turned away from his table. The worthy burgher was standing at the street-door, which opened in the middle, and leaning over the lower half, so that the smoke of his pipe ascended in the clear frosty morning in a little white column far into the sky before it was dissipated.

St. Nicholas stopped his wagon right before his door, and cried out in a clear, hearty voice,

"Good-morning, good-morning, mynheer; and a happy New-year to you!"

"Good-morning," cried the hale old burgher, "and many happy New-years to *you*. Hast got any good fat hen-turkeys to sell?"—for he took him for a countryman coming in to market. St. Nicholas answered and said that he had been on a different errand that morning; and the other cordially invited him to alight, come in, and take a glass of hot spiced rum, with the which it was his custom to regale all comers at the jolly New-year. The invitation was frankly accepted, for the worthy St. Nicholas, though no toper, was never a member of the temperance society. He chose to be keeper of his own conscience, and was of opinion that a man who is obliged to sign an obligation not to drink will be very likely to break it the first convenient opportunity.

As they sat cosily together, by a rousing fire of wholesome and enlivening hickory, the little plump Dutchman occasionally inveighing stoutly against paper-money, railroads, improving streets, and the like, the compassionate saint took occasion to utter a wish that the poor man over the way and his starving family had some of the good things that were so rife on New-year's day, for he had occasion to know that they were suffering all the evils of the most abject poverty.

"The splutterkin!," exclaimed the little fat burgher—"he is as proud as Lucifer himself. I had a suspicion of this, and sought divers occasions to get acquainted with him, that I might have some excuse for prying into his necessities, and take the privilege of an old neighbour to relieve them. But, *vuur en vlammen!* would you believe it—he avoided me just as if he owed me money, and couldn't pay."

St. Nicholas observed, that if it was ever excusable for a man to be proud, it was when he fell into a state where every one, high and low, worthless and honourable, looked down upon him with contempt. Then he related to him the story of poor Johannes, and, taking from his pocket a heavy purse, he offered it to the worthy old burgher, who swore he would be *dondered* if he wanted any of his money.

"But hearken to me," said the saint; "yon foolish lad is the son of an old friend of mine, who did me many a kindness in his day, for which I am willing to requite his posterity. Thou shalt take this purse and bestow a small portion of it, as from thyself, as a loan from time to time, as thou seest he deserves it by his exertions. It may happen, as I hope it will, that in good time he will acquire again the competency he hath lost by his own folly and inexperience; and, as he began the world a worthy, respectable citizen, I beseech thee to do this — to be his friend, and to watch over him and his little ones, in the name of St. Nicholas."

The portly burgher promised that he would, and they parted with marvellous civility, St. Nicholas having promised to visit him again should his life be spared. He then mounted his wagon, and the unsuspicious Dutchman having turned his head for an instant, when he looked again could see nothing of the saint or his equipage. "*Is het mogelyk!*", exclaimed he, and his mind misgave him that there was something unaccountable in the matter.

My story is already too long, peradventure, else would I describe the astonishment of Johannes and his wife, when they awoke and found that the benevolent stranger had departed without bidding them farewell. They would have thought all that had passed but a dream, had not the fragments of the good things on which they regaled during the night borne testimony to its reality. Neither will I detail how, step by step, aided by the advice and countenance of the worthy little Dutchman, and the judicious manner of his dispensing the bounty of St. Nicholas, Johannes Garrebrantze, by a course of industry, economy, and integrity, at length attained once again the station he had lost by his follies and extravagance. Suffice it to say, that though he practised a rational self-denial in all his expenditures, he neither became a miser, nor did he value money, except as the means of obtaining the comforts of life, and administering to the happiness of others.

In the mean time, the money-lender, not being content with the wealth he had obtained by taking undue advantage of the distresses of others, and becoming every day more greedy, launched out into mighty speculations. He founded a score of towns without any houses in them; dealt by hundreds of thousands in fancy stocks; and finally became the victim of one of his own speculations, by in time coming to believe in the very deceptions he had practised upon others. It is an old saying, that the greatest rogue in the world, sooner or later, meets with his match; and so it happened with the money-lender. He was seduced into the purchase of a town without any houses in it, at an expense of millions; was met by one of those reactions that play the mischief with honest labourers, and thus finally perished in a bottomless pit of his own digging. Finding himself sinking, he resorted to forgeries, and had by this means raised money to such an amount, that his villany almost approached to the sublime. His property, as the phrase is, came under the hammer, and Johannes purchased his own house at half the price it cost him in building.

The good St. Nicholas trembled at the new ordeal to which Johannes had subjected himself; but, finding, when he visited him, as he did regularly every New-year's eve, that he was cured of his foolish vanities, and that his wife was one of the best house-keepers in all Fort Orange, he discarded his apprehensions, and rejoiced in the prosperity that was borne so meekly and wisely. The little fat Dutchman lived a long time in expectation that the stranger in the one-horse wagon would come for the payment of his purse of money; but, finding that year after year rolled away without his appearing, often said to himself, as he sat on his stoop with a pipe in his mouth,

"I'll be *dondered* if I don't believe it was the good St. Nicholas."

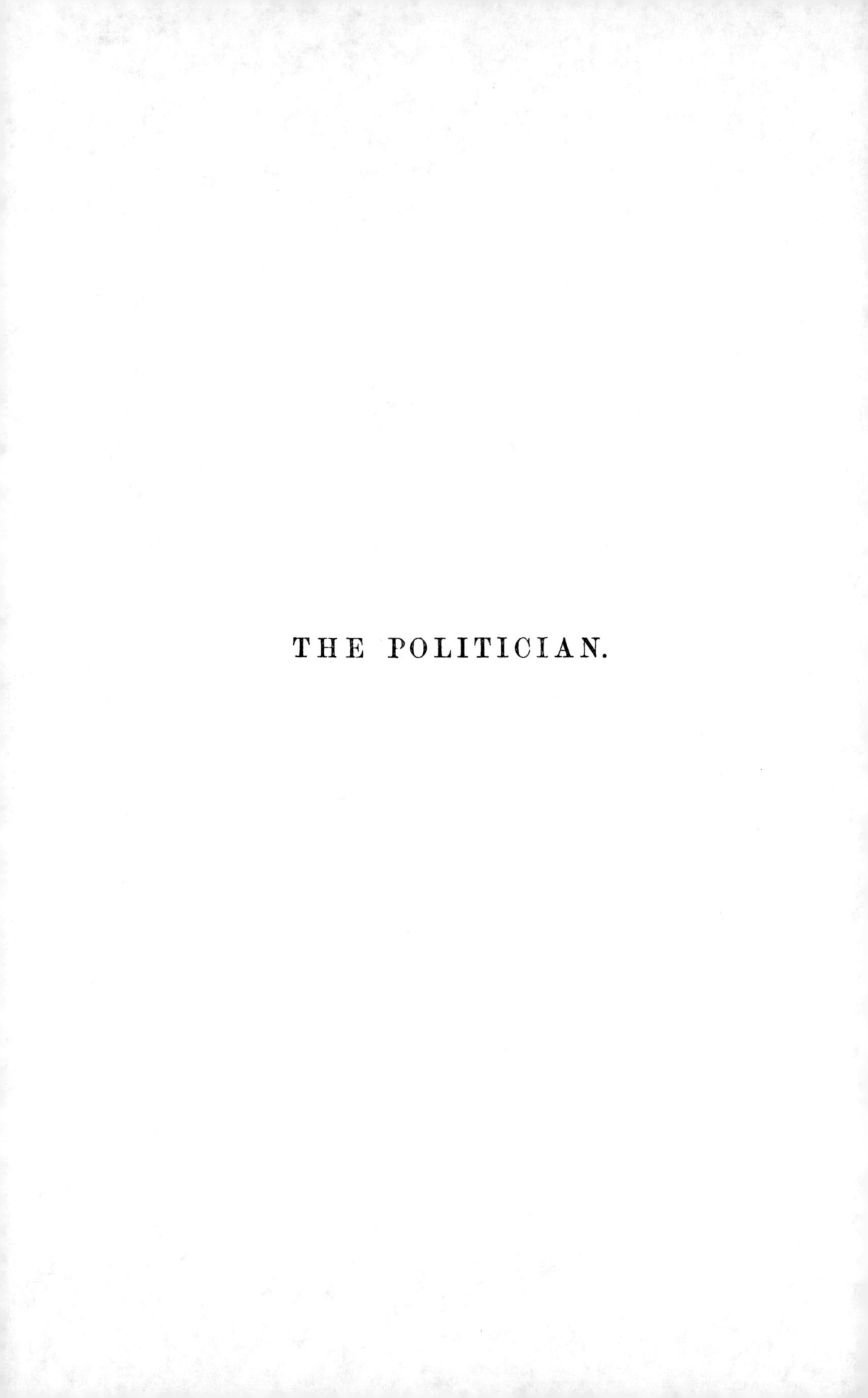

THE POLITICIAN.

THE POLITICIAN.

"———— Toys called honours
Make men on whom they are bestowed no better
Than glorious slaves, the servants of the vulgar.
Men sweat at helm as well as at the oar.
Here is a glass within shall show you, sir,
The vanity of these silkworms that do think
They toil not, 'cause they spin their thread so fine."

RANDOLPH.

ONE of the most dangerous characters in the world is a man who habitually sacrifices the eternal, immutable, obligations of truth and justice, and the charities of social life, at the shrine of an abstract principle, about which one half of mankind differs from the other half. Whether this abstract principle is connected with religion, or politics, is of little consequence; since, after all, morals constitute the essence of religion, and social duties the foundation of government. Whatever is essential to the conduct of our lives, to the performance of our duties to our families our neighbours and our country, is easy of comprehension; and it requires neither argument nor metaphysics to teach us what is right or what is wrong. These are great fundamental principles, modified indeed by the state of society and the habits of different nations; but their nature and obligations are every where the same, inflexible and universal in their application. A close examination of the history of the world in every age will go far to convince us, that a vast portion of the crimes and miseries and oppressions of mankind has originated in a difference, not in morals, but in abstract ideas; not in fundamental principles, but in vague and flimsy theories, incomprehensible to the great mass, and having not the remotest connection with our moral and social duties. When men come to assume these contested principles, these metaphysical refinements, as indispensable to the salvation of the soul or the preservation of the state, and to substitute them in the place of the everlasting pillars of truth and justice, they cast themselves loose from their moorings, to drift at random in the stream, the sport of every eddy, the dupes of every bubble, the victims of every shoal and quicksand. Instead of sailing by the bright star of mariners, which sparkles for ever in the same pure sphere, they shape their course by the fleeting vapour which is never the same; which rises in the morning, a fog; ascends, a fantastic cloud; and vanishes in the splendours of the noontide sun.

The following sketch of my own history will serve to illustrate the preceding observations, by showing how near an adherence to certain vague, contested, abstract principles in politics, brought me to a breach of all the cardinal virtues.

I am a politician by inheritance. My guardian, for I was early left an orphan, was the great man of a little state that had more banks and great men than any state of its inches in the universe. The state was too small to accommodate more than one great man at a time; and the consequence was an incessant struggle to keep one another's heads under water. Like the buckets of a well, as one rose the other sunk; and the filling of one was the emptying of the other. These struggles for the helm of the little vessel of state kept up a perpetual excitement. The puddle of our politics was ever in a mighty storm, and, like Pope's sylph, our illustrious great men were continually in danger of perishing in the foam of a cup of hot chocolate. Then, our political barque was so small that the veriest zephyr was enough to upset her, and Gulliver's frog would have shipwrecked us outright.

From my earliest years, I heard nothing but politics. Our family circle were all politicians; men, women, and children. The wife of my guardian made it a point of faith never to believe any thing good of the females of the opposite party; and though she was too conscientious to invent scandals herself, she religiously believed the slanders of others. Her candour never went beyond acknowledging that she believed ignorance, and not wickedness, was at the bottom of their want of political principle. The only daughter, naturally an amiable girl, publicly gave out she would never marry any one who did not believe her father to be a greater man than the Honourable Dibble Dibblee, innkeeper at Dibbleesville, his most formidable rival. Love however proved at last too potent for politics, and she relented in favour of a handsome and rich Dibbleeite.

For my part, I was nurtured at the breast of politics, and imbibed a nutriment gloriously concocted of a hundred absurd, ridiculous, unneighbourly, and unchristian prejudices and antipathies. With me the world was divided, not into the good and the bad, the wise and the foolish, but into the adherents of the Honourable Dibble Dibblee, innkeeper at Dibbleesville, and those of the Honourable Peleg Peashell, cash-store-keeper at Peashellville. At school I signalized my devotion to principle, by refusing to share my good-will or my gingerbread with boys of the opposite party; and many are the battles I fought in vindication of the wisdom, purity, and consistency of the Honourable Peleg, my worthy guardian, who, I verily believe even to this day, was an honest politician till the age of forty. After that, I will not answer for any man, not even my own guardian. The prime object of my antipathy was a lad of the name of Redfield, a gay, careless, sprightly, mercurial genius, who always professed to belong to no party, and whom I for that reason considered utterly destitute of all principle. Several times I attempted to beat principle into him; but he had the obstinacy of a Puritan and the boldness of a lion. I always got worsted; but my consolation was that I was the champion of principle, and must not be discouraged.

At the time I am speaking of, parties were at the height of contention, and the demons of discord, in the disguise of two editors of party newspapers, flapped their sooty wings over the little state. There was a great contest of principle, on the decision of which depended the very existence of the liberties, not only of our little state, but of the whole Union. I never could find out what this principle was, exactly; but it turned on the question, whether a certain bridge about to be built should be a free bridge or a toll-bridge. The whole state divided on this great question of principle. The Honourable Peleg Peashell was at the head of the free bridge, on which was based the great arch of our political union; and the Honourable Dibble Dibblee, whose principles were always exactly opposite, forthwith took the field as leader of the toll-bridge party. The Honourable Peleg declared it was against his principles to pay toll; and the Honourable Dibble Dibblee found it equally against his principles to apply any part of his money to building a bridge which was to bring him nothing in return. Both sides accused the other of being governed by interested motives. Such is the injustice of party feelings! There was a *tertium quid* party, growling in an undertone, which was opposed to having any bridge at all, upon the principle, that as it would be no advantage to them, and at the same time cost them money, it was their interest to oppose the whole affair. The leader of this party was the Honourable Tobias Dob, a ruling elder of the principal church in Dobsboroughvilleton.

The fate of a pending election rested on this bridge, and the fate of the bridge rested on the election. The principle to be decided was one on which the liberties of the whole confederation depended. Is it therefore to be wondered at, that the good people of our patriotic state should consider the destinies of the world and the future welfare of all mankind as mainly depending on the decision of this great question? or can we be surprised, if, in a contest for such momentous principles, affecting not only the present age but all posterity, the passions of men should be excited, and all the charities of life forgotten, in this vital struggle for the human race, present and to come? Heavens! how our political puddle did foam, and swell, and lash its sides, and blow up bubbles, and disturb the sleepy serenity of the worms inhabiting its precincts!

On the day of election each party took the field, under its own appropriate banner. The party of the Honourable Peleg Peashell had for its motto, "Principle, not Interest;" that of the Honourable Dibble Dibblee, "Interest, not Principle;" and the Honourable Tobias Dob paraded his *tertium quids* under that of, "Principle, and Interest." Here was room enough, and reason enough too, in all conscience, for the goddess of contention to act a most splendid part; and, accordingly, had the ancestors of the different parties been fighting from the creation of the world, their posterity could not have hated each other as did my worthy fellow-citizens — for the time being. They abused one another by word of mouth; they published handbills and caricatures; and such was the disruption of the social principle, that the adherents of the Honourable Peleg Peashell passed an unanimous resolution to abstain from visiting the tavern of the Honourable Dibble Dibblee from that time forward. The friends of the Honourable Dibble retorted upon those of the Honourable Peleg, by passing an unanimous resolution not to buy any thing at his cash-store; and the *tertium quids* also passed a resolution, that, "Whereas all men are born free and equal, and whereas the liberty of speech and action is the inalienable right of all, therefore, resolved unanimously, that the Honourable Peleg Peashell is a fool; the Honourable Dibble Dibblee, a rogue; and the

Honourable Tobias Dob, a man to whom the age has produced few equals and no superior."

(*Signed*) "Upright Primm, *Moderator*."

The Honourable Peleg had unfortunately broken the bridge of his nose in early life, and the breach had never been properly repaired. His adversary took advantage of him, by publishing a caricature of a man in that unlucky predicament, crying out, "No bridge — down with the bridges!" Whereupon the other party retorted, by a figure standing under an old fashioned sign-post, (which every body knows marvellously resembles a gallows), with a label bearing the following posy: "Hang all republicans! I'm for the publican party — huzza! give us a sling." The Honourable Tobias would also have inflicted a caricature upon his adversaries, but, as ill luck would have it, the election fund gave out just at the crisis. This incident brought on a negotiation, in which the Honourable Dibble Dibblee intimated an offer to treat the *tertium quids* during the remainder of the election, gratis, provided they would promise to drink moderately, and vote for him. Thereupon the Honourable Tobias found his principles inclining a little to one side; but the Honourable Peleg, having got notice of this intrigue, took measures to bolster him up again, by proposing a coalition. He offered to make the Honourable Tobias a judge of the Superior Court, with a salary of sixty dollars, if he would bring over his *tertium quids*. Tobias — I beg pardon — the Honourable Tobias Dob, balanced for a moment between the vital principle of benefiting his friends, and the vital principle of benefiting himself. After a sore struggle the latter prevailed, and the Honourable

Peleg Peashell was elected governor. His friends pronounced it the greatest triumph of principle that had ever been achieved upon earth; but, truth obliges me to say, the friends of the Honourable Dibble Dibblee slandered their opponents with the opprobrium of a corrupt coalition. To be even with them, the friends of the Honourable Peleg denounced the others as a corrupt combination. Thenceforward the question of toll and no toll was swallowed up in the great principle involved in the question of coalition and combination. The *tertium quids*, who still kept together for the purpose of selling themselves again to the highest bidder, insisted there was no difference between a coalition and a combination, and therefore they would join neither. "You are mistaken," said my old school-mate and antagonist, Redfield, — "you are mistaken; there is all the difference in the world. A coalition is a combination of honest men, to get into office; and a combination is a coalition of honest men, to get them out. They are no more alike than a salamander and a bull-frog; they inhabit the opposite elements."

It was in this contest that I first brought into practical operation the principles I had imbibed from the conversation and example of my worthy guardian. Young and inexperienced as I was, I most firmly believed that the Honourable Peleg Peashell was the most honest as well as capable man in the state; that it depended in a great measure on his election, whether freedom or slavery should predominate in the world; and, consequently, that those who opposed him must be devoid of principle as well as patriotism. It was one of the maxims of the Honourable Peleg, that all minor principles ought to yield to one great principle, by which the life of every great man should be governed. Once convinced that the safety or welfare of a nation or a community depended on the success of a party struggle, it was not only justifiable, but an inflexible duty, to sacrifice all other duties and obligations to the attainment of the great object. If it happened that our individual interest or advancement was connected with, or dependent on, the triumph of the great principle, so much the better; we could kill two birds with one stone, and not only save our country, but provide for our families at the same time. The Honourable Peleg was a great man, and my guardian; his opinions and example could therefore hardly fail of having a vast influence on mine.

When this vital struggle about toll or no toll, which was to settle the great principle on which depended the liberties of ourselves and our posterity, commenced, my guardian hinted to me that now was the time to gain immortal glory, by assisting in the salvation of my country. I begged to be put in the way of achieving this great service.

" There is my neighbour Brookfield, whose influence is considerable. He supports my enemies and the enemies of the great principle on which the salvation of the country depends. I want to destroy that influence."

" Very well, sir. Shall I attack his opinions in the public papers ? "

" Attack his opinions! Attack a fiddlestick, Oakford. You may as well fight with a shadow. No, no; attack him personally, cut up his moral character; that is the way, boy. Even people that have no morals themselves are very tenacious of the morals of others."

"But, sir, I know nothing of the morals of Mr. Brookfield, but what is greatly to his credit. I can't in conscience publish or utter any thing against his character. His opinions"——

"Pish! opinions! — opinions are nothing, unless they grow into actions. You must make him out to be a great rogue, or I shall lose my election."

"I can't, sir; it goes against my conscience."

"Conscience! — what has conscience to do with principle? You would sacrifice the liberties of your country and the happiness of unborn millions to a scruple of conscience. Ah! George, you will never make a politician."

"But, sir, Mr. Brookfield is my friend; I have visited at his house almost every day for the last two years, and he and his family have treated me like one of themselves. It would be ungrateful."

"And so," said the Honourable Peleg, with a sneer, "and so you would place your own private, and personal, and, let me say, selfish feelings, in opposition to a great principle on which the salvation of your country depends."

"But, sir, by attacking the moral character of Mr. Brookfield, I should not only injure his own feelings, but perhaps destroy the happiness of his wife and daughter, who are innocent of all offence against you."

"Ah! George, I see how it is; you are smitten with Miss Deliverance Brookfield, and would sacrifice a great principle to a little interested consideration of your own. I must make a tailor of you; you'll never do for a politician."

The Honourable Peleg left me to consider of the matter. It was a sore struggle, but at last principle triumphed, and I determined most heroically to sacrifice all petty and personal motives to the salvation of my country. My guardian furnished me with certain hints, on which I exercised my genius, in the composition of a most atrocious libel.

"It won't do," said the Honourable Peleg; "it will lay you open to a prosecution for libel."

"Well, what of that, sir? I am willing to encounter any peril for the salvation of my country."

"Yes," said my guardian, after some hesitation, "yes; but there is no occasion to risk your fortune for the purpose. The salvation of the country don't depend on money, but principle. You are about to become a patriot; and a rich patriot has always more influence than a poor one: you must therefore keep your money for the salvation of the country."

My commerce with mankind has since taught me that the capacity of men for worldly affairs is almost entirely founded on experience. Hence it is that so few men go right in the first affair they undertake. It did not occur to me at the time, that, as I was under age, the Honourable Peleg would have been responsible for the libel, had it been published. Be this as it may, I resigned my first literary offspring into the hands of my guardian, who softened it down into hints, innuendoes, and interrogations, and converted it into one of the most mischievous yet legally guiltless instruments of torture ever seen in or out of the Inquisition. The article appeared in the Banner of Truth, our paper; and was followed up, from time to time, with others still more cruelly unintelligible, but at the same time calculated, by their very mystery, to do the more mischief. There was no direct charge; of course there could be no refutation. My conscience goaded me day and night. I had not the face to visit our neighbour any more, after thus wounding his feelings; and this squeamishness, as the Honourable Peleg told me, was another proof that I would never make a great politician. I sometimes ventured to look at the family in church, where the grave depression of Mr. Brookfield, and the paleness of his wife and daughter, went to my heart. But this feeling of compunction hardened at length into one of lofty triumph, that I had sacrificed my early feelings and associations, my selfish considerations, to principle.

One day I met Deliverance Brookfield, by chance, in a spot where we had often played together in childhood, and walked together in youth. She turned her head the other way, and was passing me without notice. The sense of offending guilt overcame for a moment the sublime theory of the Honourable Peleg, and I involuntarily exclaimed, "Miss Brookfield!"

She turned upon me a countenance at once pale and beautiful, but tinged deeply with melancholy reproach, as she looked steadily in my face without speaking.

"Have you forgot me, Miss Brookfield?"

"I believe I have," at length she replied, in a sad kind of languor. "I would never wish to remember one who has repaid the friendship of my father, and the kindness of my mother, by destroying our happiness."

I felt like a scoundrel, but mustered hypocrisy enough to answer in a gay tone,

"My dear Miss Brookfield, nobody thinks any thing of such trifles in politics; nothing but political squibs — forgot in a day — they do no harm to any one."

"None," she replied bitterly; "no harm, except murdering reputations and breaking hearts. My father is dying." And she burst into tears.

"Dying!" cried I, — "Heaven forbid! Of what?"

"Of the wounds you have given him. O George, George!," continued she, "you should come to our house and receive a lesson of what a few slanders can do in destroying the happiness of an innocent family."

She passed on, and I had not courage to stop, or to follow, her. I went to the honourable Peleg, and gave him notice that it was my intention to retract all I had said or insinuated against Mr. Brookfield, in the next day's Banner of Truth.

"And lose me my election — I mean, jeopardize the happiness of millions, and sacrifice a great principle to a little private feeling of compunction?"

"I cannot bear the stings of conscience."

"My dear George, you, and such inexperienced young fellows as yourself, are for ever mistaking the painful efforts which are necessary to the attainment of a high degree of public virtue, for the stings of conscience. If the practice of virtue was not attained by great sacrifices of feeling and inclination, there would be little merit in being virtuous. What if you have destroyed the temporary happiness of two or three people, provided you have ensured the triumph of a great principle, and the salvation of your country? It is the noble, the exalted, the disinterested sacrifice of private inclinations and social feelings to public duty. Did not Brutus condemn his only son?"

"Yes, but he did not calumniate his mother and sisters."

"The greater the sacrifice to public principles, the greater the glory and reward. The election commences to-morrow, and you must strike one more blow."

As it is my design to make my story as useful to the rising generation of politicians as possible, I mean to disclose myself without disguise or reservation. I did let slip another shaft against poor Brookfield, which probably accelerated his progress to the grave, and deprived my kind friend and my pretty playmate of a husband and a father. I would not confess this hateful fact, could I not lay my hand at this moment on my heart, look in the face of Heaven and man, and say, that at the moment of inflicting a death-wound on the happiness of those who had been to me as a mother, a father, and a sister, I had convinced myself I was sacrificing a narrow, selfish feeling, to an enlarged and universal principle of virtuous patriotism. Poor Brookfield died a few days after the election; but the honourable Peleg Peashell gained the victory; and a domestic calamity was not, as he assured me, to be weighed for a moment against the triumph of a great principle, and the salvation of millions of people yet unborn. Brookfield was no more; his family was destitute; his widow heart-broken; his daughter without a protector; and his little son, of about ten years old, left upon the world. But what of that? The great principle had triumphed; the oppression of toll-bridges was prevented; and the honourable Peleg Peashell was governor of a little state containing more banks and more great men than any state of its inches in the universe, with a salary of five hundred dollars a year, and the power to do nothing but consent to the acts of other people.

From this time forward I became the confidential friend and adviser of the great governor of the little state, commander of an army and admiral of a navy that had no existence; who had five hundred dollars a year, with the title of Excellency, and the privilege of doing nothing of his own free will, and of franking letters. The Lord have mercy on a little man who becomes the confidential friend and adviser of a great man. He will be obliged to do for him what he is ashamed to do for himself; to take all the blame of giving bad, and relinquish all the credit of good, counsel; to fetch, and carry, and say, and gainsay, and unsay; to prostitute his soul to unutterable meannesses, and turn the divinity of conscience into a crouching spaniel, obeying every look, wagging his tail in gratitude for kicks, and licking the hand that lugs the ears from his head. I speak from awful experience, for never little man was rode and spurred, over hill, dale, and common, through ditch, swamp, and horse-pond, as I was by that illustrious patriot, the Honourable Peleg Peashell — I beg pardon — his Excellency, the Honourable Peleg Peashell, Esquire.

But I will do his Excellency the justice to say, that he did every thing upon principle, and for the salvation of unborn millions. Life, would he say, is a warfare of conflicting duties and opposing principles; a choice of evils, or a choice of goods. It is the business of a wise man to decide, not between the nearest and the most distant, but between the greater and the lesser, obligation.

"But," said I modestly — for by this time, such is the magic of dependence on great men, I had come to look upon his Excellency as an oracle irrefragable — "But," said I, "suppose one man was holding a red-hot poker to your nose, while another was calling upon you to establish a great principle; would not you attend to the poker before the principle?"

"Certainly I would, sir —" His Excellency never of late called me "sir," but when he was a little out of humour — "Certainly, sir; but it would be only in compliment to the weakness of human nature; for nothing is more certain than that it would be my duty to let the poker burn up my nose, rather than miss the opportunity of benefiting future ages, by the establishment of a great political principle."

"But will your Excellency permit me to ask, how you ascertain to a certainty that a great political principle is right, when perhaps one half of mankind think it wrong?"

"Why, sir, my own reason and experience teach me."

"But another man's reason and experience teach him directly the contrary."

"Then he must be either a great blockhead, or a great knave," replied the Honourable — I mean his Excellency, the Honourable — Peleg Peashell, in a tone that precluded further questioning.

It was many years afterwards that I detected the fallacy of thus raising up an idol, worshipped by one set of men and abhorred by another, and sacrificing to it the eternal and immutable attributes of justice and truth, about which there can be no difference of belief. It was only long experience and reflection that convinced me at last, that the sacrifice of moral and social duties to mere opinions, exalted though these might be to the dignity of great and established principles, must be fatal in the end, not only to the morals of mankind, but to that freedom which is based upon them. I received the responses of his Excellency with profound submission, and continued to act upon them throughout an extended political servitude.

About a year after the great triumph of principle, which resulted in the choice of his Excellency the Honourable Peleg Peashell for Governor of the little state with such a plenty of banks and great men, I came of age, and it was proper for his Excellency to give an account of the administration of my affairs. He put me off from day to day, from month to month, from year to year, until my patience was quite worn out. At length, finding it impossible any longer to satisfy me with excuses, he one day addressed me as follows: —

"My dear young friend, it is not to be supposed that a man whose whole soul is taken up with his public, can pay proper attention to his private, duties. Whenever these come in conflict, it is his pride and glory to sacrifice all for his country, and beggar himself for the salvation of unborn millions. I cannot tell exactly how it happened, but your fortune is gone. Either I have spent it myself, by mistake, in the hurry of my public duties, or some one else has spent it for me. However, this cannot be of much consequence, since the great principle has triumphed, and the salvation of the country is secured beyond all future hazard. Remember how Brutus the elder sacrificed his son, as an example to the Roman militia, and console yourself with the certainty that you have devoted your fortune to the establishment of a great principle."

This reasoning, though it had always proved satisfactory when applied to the affairs of other people, did not exactly relish to my understanding in the present case. It occurred to me, that though a man might honestly sacrifice his own fortune to the establishment of a great principle, he had no right to take the same liberty with that of another, intrusted to his management. I ventured to insinuate something of the sort.

"Pshaw! George," replied his Excellency, "you will never make a great patriot, I'm afraid. Is not the major greater than the minor?"

"Certainly, sir."

"Is not a community greater than an individual?"

"Assuredly, sir."

"Is not the good of the whole, the good of all its parts?"

"Clearly, sir."

"Well, sir!, is not the establishment of a great principle, on which depends the happiness of millions, of far more moment than the temporary inconvenience you will feel from the loss of your fortune?"

"Certainly, sir," said I, very faintly.

"Good — I believe I shall make something of you at last. You are worthy of the confidence of your fellow-citizens. Now listen to me. Another election is coming on, which involves another great principle, on which depends the salvation of the country and the happiness of unborn millions. A great state road is to be laid out by the next legislature, and I have it from excellent authority, that, if we do not exert ourselves, it will be carried over a part of the country so distant from my property, and that of my best friends, as to do us rather an injury than a benefit. Now, though I am interested in this business, that is my misfortune. It is the great principle dependent upon the decision of the question that I am solicitous to vindicate. My intention is to get you into the legislature, provided you will pledge yourself to stand in the breach, and prevent the destruction of our liberties, which mainly depend upon the great principle involved in this road-bill. What say you, — will you pledge yourself to your constituents?"

"Why, sir — if — "

"O, none of your ifs, George — you'll never make a great politician if you stumble before an if."

"But my conscience, sir."

"Your conscience!" — cried his Excellency the Honourable Peleg — "Conscience! Who ever heard of a representative of the people having a conscience? Why, sir, his conscience belongs to his constituents, who think for him and decide for him. One half the time it is his duty to act in the very teeth of his conscience. He is only the whistle on which the people blow any tune they please."

"It appears to me, sir, that this doctrine is rather immoral."

"Immoral!" — cried his Excellency, throwing himself back in his chair, and laughing; — "immoral! What has morality to do with the establishment of a great principle? I ought to have made a tailor of you, I see.

"Lookee, George," continued his Excellency, after he had laughed himself out, "every young man who devotes himself to political life must, in the outset, if he wishes to be successful, surrender his opinions and feelings entirely to the establishment of certain great radical principles. He must have neither morals nor conscience. All he has to do is to inquire whether a thing is necessary to the establishment of these principles, and do it as a matter of course, although abstractedly and in itself it may be in the teeth of law and gospel. For instance, George — why, you are looking at that pretty girl, Silent Parley, instead of listening to me! You will never make a politician."

I begged his Excellency's pardon, and he proceeded: —

"For instance, suppose you were, like myself, in a high official situation, and were solicited by two persons to do two things directly opposite in their nature and consequences; — what would you do?"

"I would inquire into the matter; ascertain, if possible, which was right; and act accordingly."

"You would! Then let me tell you, sir, you would soon be sent to raise cabbages and pumpkins on your farm. No, sir; your duty would be to inquire and ascertain whether the great principle, on which depended your remaining in office, would be best sustained by complying with the wishes of the one or the other of the persons soliciting your interest. Having found this out, there would be no further difficulty in the matter. You would of course decide upon principle."

"Principle, sir! Why really, excuse me, your Excellency, but this is what the country folks call being governed by interest, not principle."

"Pooh, George!, your head is not longer than a pin's; — can you comprehend a syllogism?"

"I believe so, sir, if it has a sufficiency of legs."

"Very well," continued his Excellency — "certain principles are necessary to the salvation of the state and the happiness of unborn millions: I advocate these principles: ergo, it is necessary to the salvation of the state and the happiness of unborn millions that I should be chosen governor, and should repay my champions, as far as it may be in my power. Now, sir, as to my own personal interests: here is the point in which the talents of a great man are most critically tested; I mean, in making his interests and his principles harmonize. If he can do this, he is fit to govern the whole universe; if not, he is fit for nothing but a mechanic. For how can it be supposed that a man who neglects his own interests can take care of those of other people?"

The logic of his Excellency the Honourable Peleg Peashell, Esquire, was conclusive, and I agreed to vote against my conscience, for the good of my country, if necessary; after which I sallied forth, and overtook the pretty Silence Parley. It was a delightful summer afternoon, or rather evening, for the twilight had put on its cloak of gray obscurity, and we walked along the hard white sand of the quiet bay, arm-in-arm, sometimes talking, and sometimes looking at one another in delicious meditation. She was worth a description; but my story is one of principle, and I shall touch on such trifles as love and woman only so far as is necessary to my purpose. After I had sacrificed my kind friend and neighbour, Brookfield, and his family, on the altar of principle, I never could bear to look Deliverance in the face again. Indeed, the mother soon after carried her family to her friends in a distant part of the country, and I saw them no more. Next to Deliverance Brookfield, Miss Silence Parley was the fairest of our maidens, who all were fair, if rosy cheeks, round glowing figures, and sky-clear eyes, could make them so. She was likely to be an heiress, too; and the Honourable Peleg hinted to me one day that it would marvellously conduce to the triumph of a great principle, if I could win and wear her.

"For," said he, "her father is a man of a good deal of political influence, which he does not choose to exert, being one of those selfish blockheads who prefer peace and quiet to the salvation of unborn millions. If you could marry his daughter, I dare say he would come out in favour of the great principle."

This time, for a great wonder I think — (for it is the only time it happened to me in my whole career) — this time, my principles chimed in with my interests, and I determined, if possible, to charm the fair Silence into speaking to the purpose. We were often together alone in the modest, humble, twilight, walking and talking, or sitting and silent. We exchanged looks and little civilities, that spoke expressive meanings; and, in short, it was not long before I saw in the eyes of my pretty Silence the signal of surrender. I had not actually offered myself, but I had determined upon it; when the election approached near at hand, on which the great principle, whether the great state road should pass through the property of the Honourable Dibble Dibblee, innkeeper, of Dibbleeville, or of his Excellency the Honourable Peleg Peashell, Esquire, cash-store-keeper at Peashellville, and (consequently) the salvation of unborn millions, depended.

His Excellency the Honourable Peleg one day took occasion to hint to me, that it might be as well to sound the Honourable Peabody Parley, Esquire, the father of my pretty Silence, as to his using his influence in my behalf in the coming struggle of principle.

"I had better ask his consent to marry his daughter, first," said I.

"No, sir; you had better ask for his support, first," replied his Excellency, peremptorily.

Accordingly I went to the Honourable Peabody Parley — there were as many Honourables in our little state as hidalgos in Spain — I went and asked his support in attaining the high honour of being elected a member of the legislature in the coming contest of principle. The Honourable Peabody told me frankly he would do no such thing, unless I pledged myself to use all my influence in getting the great state road laid out so as to run through a part of his property, where he was going to found a city. This was in direct opposition to the great principle of the Honourable Peleg Peashell, whose property lay in the other extreme of the state. I required time for consideration, and went to consult my guardian. He shook his head, and was angry.

"You must go and pay your addresses to Miss Welcome Hussey Bashaba, daughter to the Honourable Jupiter Ammon Deodatus Bumstead, of Bumsteadvilleton, as soon as possible."

"But, sir, Miss Hussey Bashaba is as ugly as a stone fence with a flounce and fashionable bonnet on it."

"No matter, the safety of the country and the salvation of unborn millions depend on it."

"But, I am all but engaged to Miss Silence Parley; I have committed myself."

"No matter; the triumph of principle will be the greater."

"How so, sir?" replied I, rather perplexed at this mystery.

"How so? Why, the Honourable Mr. Bumstead is the proprietor of a manufactory which can turn out votes enough to carry the election. You must be off at once, for the great contest of principle approaches."

I mounted my horse, after a sore struggle between my heart and the great political principle, and proceeded towards the stately shingle-palace of my prospective father-in-law, to visit my intended, the redoubtable Miss Welcome Hussey Bashaba Bumstead, the daughter, the only daughter, of the Honourable Jupiter Ammon Deodatus Bumstead, of Bumsteadvilleton, the best manufacturing seat in the state, with a great power of water. My horse, being no politician, and withal a most unprincipled quadruped, stopped stock-still at the gate which led to the abode of Miss Silence Parley. She was standing on the piazza, looking like a rosy sylph, expecting me, for she had seen me afar off. My horse was obstinate, and, though I confess I pricked him on violently with my spurs, I held the rein so tight that he could do nothing but rear. This frightened my pretty Silence, who screamed, and ran to open the gate.

She begged me to dismount, and lead my horse in.

"I cannot, just now," said I, in a sneaking, snivelling tone; "I am going on to Bumsteadvilleton."

"To see Miss Hussey Bashaba?", said she, with a mischievous smile of meaning, — for Miss Hussey was the reigning she-dragon of the whole county.

"No," said I, with the face of a robber of a hen-roost; "no, I'm going to buy some cotton shirting."

I could stand it no longer. I clapped spurs to my horse; she waved her lily hand, whiter than snow; and I was out of sight in a minute. It was the greatest triumph of principle I ever achieved.

The Honourable Jupiter Ammon Deodatus received me as he received only his best customers; and Miss Hussey Bashaba smiled upon me like a roaring lion. There is one great comfort in addressing a very ugly woman — she don't require much wooing, provided she is a reasonable creature. Neither are parents very impracticable in cases of this kind. The Honourable Jupiter Ammon promised me his support, and I promised to take his daughter. We were married in a week. The Honourable Jupiter Ammon brought out his two hundred ragamuffins, all men of clear estate, if not freeholders. I was elected by a handsome majority; and again the triumph of principle, on which depended the salvation of unborn millions, was completed, at the trifling expense of the mere sacrifice of a few insignificant moralities, of no consequence but to the owner.

The aggregated wisdom of the state, of which I formed one twentieth part at least, met in good time. His Excellency, the Honourable Peleg Peashell, delivered a speech to both Houses, in which he took a rapid view of the creation of the world — man in a state of nature — the want of principle in the opposition — the profligacy of certain leading politicians; recommended a loan, six canals, nine railroads, and seventeen banks; and concluded with a touch of piety that brought tears into our eyes, as he thanked Heaven for having achieved this last great triumph of principle.

The assembly was divided, as usual, on a great principle, different from that on which the famous toll-bridge rested. The great question on which the great principle was based on which the salvation of unborn millions depended was, whether the great state road was to diverge fifteen degrees thirty seven minutes West, or fifteen degrees thirty seven minutes East-north-east. Such is the influence of propinquity in questions of this sort, that it exercised complete sway on this occasion. In proportion as a member had a propinquity towards the west line or the east, precisely in the same degree did the great fundamental principle which governed his actions incline in that direction; and so intimate was the association between principle and interest, that, had I not actually known to the contrary by my own experience, I should have supposed they were one and the same thing. But there were minor principles, operating in subordination to that of the great state road. One member, for example, was principled against voting for any state road at all, unless the friends of the road would vote for his canal. Another would not so far prostitute his principles as to vote for the canal, unless the friends of the canal would support his application for a bank. In the end, finding the principles of the members to be absolutely incompatible, we hit upon an arrangement which was perfectly satisfactory to the most tender conscience, and came up to the great principle by which every member was governed. The proposition was moved by myself, at the suggestion of his Excellency the Honourable Peleg Peashell, Esquire, Governor and Captain-General of the little state with so many banks and great men. My plan was no other than to jumble together in one bill, roads, canals, and banks, by which the principles of all would be perfectly satisfied, and their scruples quieted for ever. After amending the proposition, at the instance of a philanthropist, by a donation of five hundred dollars to the society for the prevention of tippling, the whole was rolled through triumphantly. Every body's principles were put to rest, and every man had lent a hand to the salvation of unborn millions. Such is the magic of public virtue! There were scarcely half a dozen members agreeing in the first instance, yet so strong was the spirit of friendly compromise, that in the end every member, (with but one exception), voted for the bill, solely on the score of principle — of doing as he would be done unto. The dissentient was a member who so far forgot his duty to his country as actually to be without a project for her benefit. Having nothing to ask, he was unwilling to give any thing away, and voted against my proposition.

It was on this occasion I delivered my maiden speech. Public expectation was on tiptoe; the boys climbed up to the windows of the state house; the ladies of the Honourable Abel Rooney the Honourable Peartree Brombush and the Honourable Roger

Pegg, with their twenty-seven blooming and marriageable daughters, seated themselves in front of the gallery; and the Speaker cried silence, and rattled his hammer so that his tobacco-box bounced off the table. I was penetrated with the justice of my cause, the great principle involved in the question, and the dignity of my auditory. I began : —

" Sir-r-r!

" If I possessed the power to flash conviction, as the lightning does upon the bosom of the thunder-cloud, redundant with fire and brimstone : Sir-r-r, if I could wrest from the sceptre — I mean, if I could wrest the sceptre from reason, and rob the spheres of the music of their voices : Sir-r-r, if I could, by any effort of this feeble hand and tremulous body, pour the tremendous and overwhelming flood of conviction like a wall of adamant over your souls, until they melted in the red-hot embers of conviction : Sir-r-r, if I could freeze your hearts till they offered an icy barrier to the intrusion of all selfish considerations, and reared the massy column of their waters up to the topmost pinnacle of the arching skies : Sir-r-r, if I could swallow up, at a single effort of my imagination, the possibility of believing it possible that the cries of the orphan, the bewailings of reckless and wretched poverty — the exhortations of the halt, the dumb, and the deaf — the mother's groans — the weeping stones — the orphan's moans " —

Here I was interrupted by a burst of hysterical tears from the beautiful blue eyes of the widow of the Honourable Roger Pegg, who was carried home in a state of suppuration. This was the greatest triumph of eloquence ever witnessed in our state. I cannot go through the whole of my speech. It lasted eight hours and three quarters, and I should have made it nine, had not all the candles gone out, and left me and my subject in utter darkness. The reader may judge of its length from the fact, that it was ascertained by an industrious old person who could not bear to be idle, that the word "Sir," occurred three hundred, the monosyllable "I," five hundred, and the word "principle," six hundred and thirty times — the word "interest," not once. Can there be any higher proof of the purity of my motives? The next day the Banner of Truth published my speech, of which I had given a copy beforehand, pronouncing it at the same time superior to the best efforts of the three great orators of antiquity, Marcus, Tullius, and Cicero.

I was now fairly launched upon the billows of immortal glory — so said the Banner of Truth. The little state rung with my exploit, as if it had been a second victory of New Orleans, and people began to talk of me for Congress. The Honourable George Gregory Oakford, (for I too had become Honourable), was the luminary of the age; and, as an evidence of his rising importance, divers worthy persons, (such as men out of employ or who had made a bad bankruptcy for themselves, and young gentlemen too idle for useful employment and too poor to figure without it), paid him their most particular devoirs, and hung to his skirts, like so many cockles. All these were impelled by an instinctive perception, such as animates the canine race to wag their tails and fawn, even upon the beggar who hath a bone to throw away.

But, though a great man myself, there were still greater men than I in "our town." I mean the members of the general committees and of the nominating committees; and, greatest of all, the gentlemen who give the impulse and govern the course of the current by a certain mysterious influence, as inscrutable as that which gives a direction to the winds. Though the study and experience of a whole life have pretty well initiated me into the depths of political alchemy, I confess I could never fathom the obscurity of this part of the science. I could never reach the head of the tide, though I floated on its surface so long; nor have I ever to this day had a clear perception of the means by which certain dull, stupid men, often without a tolerable reputation, and destitute of wealth, contrive to lead the people as they do, and keep the great leaders themselves in most abject subjection. It may be that the majority of mankind are wise enough to know, that those who are most on a par with them and mix the most familiarly in their daily concerns, whose interests are in fact identified with their own, are their best and safest counsellors, and that thus, after all, the popularity of a great man is derived not so much from the splendour of his actions, as from the secret influence of very ordinary men over their friends and neighbours.

As the triumph of a great principle and the salvation of unborn millions depended so materially upon the predominance of the party to which I had become attached, I did not consider myself above courting these masters of the people by every means in my power. I sought them out at their employments, talked politics with them, or rather heard them talk, which is by much the more effectual mode, and agreed with them whenever I could find out what they meant. I brought one of these, an honest shoemaker, nearly to the brink of starvation, by causing him to neglect his business from day to day, in discussing the eternal, invariable principles, which governed toll-bridges and turnpike-roads. I invited these worthy men, (for worthy and well-meaning men a great many of them were), to my house, and hinted to Mrs. Hussey Bashaba Oakford the propriety of drinking tea with their wives, socially, and asking them in return. But Mrs. Hussey Bashaba was one of those unreasonable women that boast themselves — "mistress in my own house." She was, to be sure, no beauty, but she was an heiress, in perspective at least, though as yet her only dowry had been the two hundred votes of the ragamuffin freeholders, a dozen table and tea spoons, and a looking-glass. But she had mighty expectations, and acted accordingly.

My wife treated the committee-men with sour looks from one of the ugliest faces in the state, and contrived so many ingenious ways to make them uneasy, that I was surprised at her talents. If one of the honest gentlemen by accident spilled the ashes from his pipe on the hearth, Mrs. Bashaba would jump up extempore, seize the brush, and exercise it with a most significant and irritable vivacity. If another chanced to bring in a small tribute from mother Earth, upon his independent and sovereign shoes, she would forthwith ask me, with a peculiar emphasis, whether the scraper had been stolen from the door. But woe to the committee-man who dared, by any *lapsus linguæ*, to expectorate on the floor! Mrs. Hussey Bashaba would scream for the help to come with a tub of water and a brush, and set her scrubbing away before the good man's face. As to the wives of the committee, they came once, and once only. Mrs. Bashaba talked all the time about her papa's house, factory, work-people, and all that, and made such a display of importance that they never approached us again. To one she said, "What a pity it is you can't afford to put new panes of glass in your broken windows!" To another, "How sorry I am, my dear Mrs. Artichoke, your husband is not rich enough to build a new house! Are you not afraid that yours will fall, one of these days? For my part, I shouldn't be able to sleep a wink in it." And to a third, "La, my dear Mrs. Birdseye, when did you lose those two front teeth? I declare it makes you look twenty years older." The committee-men and their wives went home, all in a huff with myself and my better half.

"My dear," said I, soothingly, "you have endangered the success of a great principle, and the salvation of unborn millions."

"The salvation of a fiddlestick!" said Mrs. Bashaba: "I can't bear such vulgar people. Why, they eat out of trenchers, and use wooden spoons, like pigs."

"I never heard that pigs used wooden spoons," said I, innocently.

"You never heard! Huh!, of what consequence is it what you have heard? People brought up in a pigsty seldom have an ear for music," said Mrs. Bashaba, as she proceeded to blow the dust off the chairs and tables with her aromatic breath.

My wife was certainly right in valuing herself on her breeding.

The untoward behaviour of Mrs. Bashaba had well-nigh jeopardized the great principle, and destroyed the hopes of posterity. A fortunate accident, or, perhaps, a providential interposition, prevented the woful catastrophe. This was the stoppage of a bank in a remote corner of the state; but which, distant as it was, exercised a vast influence on the affairs of people far and near. This moneyed institution, having no capital, had borrowed the stock of another moneyed institution in the like predicament, and secured the capital thus paid in by a similar loan of its own stock. Both then fell to issuing bills like wildfire, and lending money — paper-money — to any person who could offer them the ghost of a security. My worthy father-in-law, the Honourable Jupiter Ammon Bumstead, was one of those shadows which become substance by the magic operation of modern financiering. He borrowed money, built a manufactory of coarse cottons, and a town which he called Bumsteadvilleton, together with a shingle-palace of infinite dimensions. The twin banks got on very well for a time, by redeeming the bills of one with the bills of the other. The Cow and Grass Company paid the notes of the Wool and Comb Company, like a good sister: and vice versa. Thus they supported each other in the journey of life. At last, however, some malicious and unreasonable person made a demand of three hundred dollars in silver. The Cow and Grass offered the notes of the Wool and Comb, but it would not do; the Cow and Grass fell against the Wool and Comb, the Wool and Comb against the establishment of Bumsteadvilleton, and the Honourable Mr. Bumstead was reduced to his original shadow again. It was the old story of the boy that bought the pig. "The butcher began to kill the ox, the ox began to drink the water, the water to quench the fire, the fire to burn the stick, the stick to lick the pig," and the pig at last went to school; but without being a whit the wiser. The president of the Cow and Grass, who was a member of the legislature, in a paroxysm of indignation, moved that the bills of both these moneyed institutions should be burnt. Another member moved to strike out the word, "bills," and insert the words, "presidents, cashiers, and directors." Among all the members of our honourable body, there was but one man — the mover of the amendment — that was not either president or director of some bank. The amendment was voted down, unanimously; the great principle of banking triumphed; and the salvation of unborn millions was placed upon the eternal basis of paper-money. On this occasion I made another speech, which would have convinced every member present but one, had they not been convinced already. If the reader is a tolerable politician, he will know that there are two kinds of speeches — one for the people within, the other for the people without. The latter are by far the more numerous.

This failure of the Cow and Grass was the luckiest incident of my life. Ninety-nine in a hundred of the people of our state were dependent on the banks in some way or other, either as debtors or stockholders. My speech in favour of the great principle of banking gained all their hearts. The total ruin of my Honourable father-in-law actually, for a time, made a reasonable woman of my wife, and caused her to treat the ladies of the committee-men with vast courtesy. The ladies of the committee-men began to pity poor Mrs. Oakford — and pity is akin to forgiveness — and the result was, that the general committee nominated me as their candidate for Congress by a majority of one: that is to say, not being able to agree, the two parties at length settled the great principle by a throw of the dice. My opponents threw cater, my friends cinque, and the choice was announced as a great triumph of principle over personal feelings and private views.

Being thus triumphantly nominated by the general committee, and endorsed by the sub-committees, it became the duty of the people to vote for me upon principle, though it might happen to be against their conscience, thus magnanimously sacrificing all private feelings and considerations to the public good. In vain did the opposite party exclaim against this attempt to dictate to the people; the people turned out lustily in my favour, and voted me in a member of Congress, against their consciences, for the sake of the great principle. His Excellency the Honourable Peleg Peashell, Esquire, supported me with all his influence, and I him with all mine; not because it was our mutual interest to do so, but because our interests were so dovetailed into the great principle that it was next to impossible to separate them. In the course of this contest, to the best of my belief, I violated my conscience, and forgot the obligations of truth, justice, honour, and sincerity, more than a score of times; but the Honourable Peleg had convinced me it was my duty as a patriot, to sacrifice my duty as a man, on all occasions when they came in conflict with each other. "The first duty of a true patriot is to offer up his conscience on the altar of the public good," said the Honourable Peleg, my mentor. I confess I winced a little, for the idea sometimes came across me, that, as both parties might possibly think themselves equally right in the great principle, and one of them must be in error, a large portion of the people were offering up their consciences in the wrong place. I once propounded this doubt to the Honourable Peleg. "Pooh!" said he, "the opposite party have no conscience; they are wrong in the great principle, and can be right in nothing else. A person radically wrong in political opinions is like a man with a broken back; he can't walk straight for the life of him." I was satisfied.

I departed for the seat of government with six long stall-fed speeches in my portmanteau, for I was determined to convince my constituents, at least, that they had not chosen a dummy to represent them. I wanted to leave Mrs. Hussey Bashaba behind, but she was a little inclined to the green-eyed monster, and determined to share my honours. I represented only some thirty or forty thousand citizens; but my wife represented the whole sex; it was therefore but just that the majority should have its way, and she accompanied me to the scene of my future glories. People who know nothing of the value of a unit, or even a single cipher, when placed in a particular relation, can hardly conceive the importance of a member at the seat of government, where an atmosphere of mutual dependence pervades the whole social system.

There is hardly a hack-driver who is not in some measure the retainer of some great man; and even the poor horses, if they could speak, would undoubtedly proclaim their adherence to certain great fundamental principles. The first time I went with my Bashaba to visit the lady of one of the foreign ministers, the horses stuck in the mud, and refused to proceed. I scolded the hackman. "Plase your Honour," — he was an Irishman, and all Irishmen are patriots — "Plase your Honour, they won't stir, upon principle."

"What do you mean?", said I.

"Plase you, they have just found out that they are going to visit the British minister, and have made up their minds never to pay him that honour till the Catholic question is settled to their satisfaction."

The horses stuck to their principles, and stuck in the mud. There seemed some truth in what the driver said, for the moment he turned their heads the other way they trotted off gallantly towards home. The instinct of animals sometimes nearly approaches to the reason of some men. I was obliged to send for horses of a different party, or more accommodating principles.

The first time we were invited to dinner, my wife was delighted. She was the lady of a member, and happened to take precedence of all the rest. She was led into the dining-room by a foreign minister with a gold-laced coat; and consumed all the next day in writing letters to the ladies of the general committee. The next time she was not quite so well pleased, for there was a senator's lady present, and Mrs. Bashaba fell to the lot of an attaché. What made this the more provoking was, that the senator's lady lived in the same hotel with us, and the propinquity made the slight intolerable. The senator's lady was the delighted one now, and declared that the seat of government was the most charming place in the world. There was a great coolness for several days on the part of Mrs. Welcome Bashaba towards the senator's lady. The third time, matters were still worse. There was a member-of-the-cabinet's lady present, to whom the ambassador was pledged by the rules of etiquette; so that the senator's lady fell to the attaché, and Mrs. Bashaba to the lot of a gentleman with no claim to distinction but talents and character. The senator's lady and the lady of the member came home the best friends in the world. But the latter began to be disgusted with the seat of government, and became quite homesick. It is an ill wind that blows nobody good. Mrs. Bashaba, having been handed into the supper room, at a grand gala given by a foreign minister in honour of his august sovereign's birth-day, by a clerk in the land-office, insisted on going home forthwith. Had it been a clerk in the office of the secretary of state, or even any one of the departments, it might have been borne. But, a clerk in the land-office! — it was impossible to get over the mortification. Fortunately, an old neighbour of mine, nearly fourscore, who had come to the seat of government, (with some two or three hundred more of my constituents), to get an appointment, was going home the very next day. Accordingly I took Mrs. Bashaba in the vein, and sent her off before she had another chance of being handed to dinner by a foreign minister. Previous to her departure, she exacted of me a promise to oppose the administration, and particularly the measures of the secretary whose wife had taken precedence of her at the grand supper, on all occasions. I promised — for I would have promised any thing to get rid of Mrs. Bashaba for the season — and I have the great consolation of knowing that both the honourable senator and myself voted against the administration all the winter, upon the great principle of etiquette, which is in fact the corner-stone of tyranny. Being now my own man, I turned gallant, flirting desperately with the married dames, and still more desperately with the young ladies, who were delighted with the attentions of a member. Let me warn all my readers who are or expect to be members, never to bring their wives to the seat of government. If they are handsome, they will have all the attachés and all the widowers *pro tem.* among the members in their train; and if they are otherwise, unless they happen to be angels outright, their curtain-lectures will be terrible. But it is time to return to my political career.

The first day the House met, and before a Speaker was chosen, being resolved to lose no time in convincing the world I was somebody, I rose to make a motion, and a speech on the subject of reform. "Mister Speaker — Sir-r-r" — "Order!" cried the clerk, rattling his wooden hammer. "Mister Speaker — Sir-r-r, I rise to" — "Sit down — the honourable member is out of order; the house is not yet organized." An old member on my left apprised me that, as there was no Speaker chosen yet, there could be no question debated. When that affair was settled, I rose again to make my great motion on the subject of reform. "Mister Speaker — Sir-r-r-r, the republics of Greece and Rome" — " Mr. Speaker," said an old gray-headed member, " I am sorry to interrupt the honourable member from — from — somewhere — but I beg to make a motion that we proceed to appoint a committee to wait on the President, with information that the House is now organized, and ready to receive any communication from him."

" Mister Speaker, Sir-r-r, I feel myself under an awful responsibility to myself, my constituents, my country, and the world, to oppose that motion;" — for I was a little nettled at this interruption.

" The motion is not debatable," replied the Speaker, mildly.

I sat down, provoked and mortified beyond measure, for I was ready to overflow in a torrent of eloquence. The reading of the message, and other formalities, took up the whole morning; and the house adjourned without hearing my speech. Thus, like Titus, I lost a day; but I made myself all the amends in my power, by speaking it that night in my chamber to two chairs, a three-legged stool, and a chalk bust of Cicero with a broken pedestal, which, at every gesticulation I made, nodded approbation.

My next attempt at a speech on reform was quite unpremeditated. It happened that a party of ladies came into the gallery of the house; and among them was one with whom I was engaged in a fashionable flirtation for the season. I wished above all things to dazzle her with a speech; for, at the seat of government, making a speech is equivalent to gaining a great victory by sea or land.

The moment I saw my belle in the gallery, the fervor of eloquence seized me. Luckily, at that blessed crisis, a member sat down, after a speech of three days, apologizing to the house that exhaustion and fatigue prevented his going deeper into the subject. In my haste, I unfortunately began the one of my six stall-fed speeches least applicable to the question before the house, which related to the Cumberland road,* a road that would be the very best upon earth, if speeches could keep it in repair. My speech, which was the first of my budget I could get at, was on the occupation of the territory of Oregon.

I set out from the seat of government without interruption, every now and then cocking my eye at the divinity who inspired me in the gallery; and was puffing and blowing about half-way up the Rocky Mountains, when a member called me to order.

"The honourable gentleman is not speaking to the question. The Cumberland road does not cross the Rocky Mountains."

"Let the gentleman go on," exclaimed a clear, high-toned voice, in a wicked Cervantesque way, — "let the gentleman alone; he is only making a voyage round the world, and will certainly cross the latitude or longitude of his subject, some time or other."

This sally occasioned a good deal of merriment, and I saw the loadstar of my eloquence showing her ivory teeth on the occasion. I became confused; struck in upon another of my six stall-fed speeches; wandered from that into a third; and finally jumbled them all together into a mass of incongruity, unut-

* The act for laying out a road from Cumberland in Maryland to the State of Ohio, commonly known as "The Cumberland" or "National" road, was passed early in 1806. The subject caused a vast amount of discussion in Congress, for a good many years afterward.

terable and inextricable. Fortunately, the Speaker, not having above thrice the patience of Job, at length called me to order, and I obeyed. Fortunately too for me, the reporter, who had made more great orations than all the orators of ancient or modern times, not being able to take down my speech in short-hand, substituted one of his own, which was read by my constituents with infinite satisfaction and improvement. Shortly after this, I made a motion to exclude the ladies from the gallery; being convinced, from my own experience, that they cause the effusion of more nonsense in the house than nature ever intended men should utter.

I was at first exceedingly discouraged with my excursion to the Rocky Mountains; but, finding it made such a splendid figure in the newspapers, I determined to take the earliest opportunity to get rid of another of my six labours. The next torrent of my eloquence was poured out from the summit-level of a great canal, which, involving as it did a great principle, excited a vast deal of interest in and out of the house. Unfortunately for me, I did not get a chance of speaking until the subject had been exhausted at least a score of times, in a score of speeches. But, for all this, I was resolved not to lose my labours because others had forestalled them. Accordingly, when every other orator had become as exhausted as the summit-levels of some of our canals, I rose in my might, and repeated, not only all that had been said in the House, but all that had been written out of it for the last fifty years. I led the House from the canal of the Red Sea to the canal of the Yellow river; from the canal of Languedoc to the canal of

Caledonia; from the canal of the Duke of Bridgewater to that of Lake Erie: in short, I did what neither Sir Francis Drake, Ferdinand Magellan, Christopher Columbus, nor Captain Cook, ever achieved; I sailed round the world on a canal. Before I had finished one quarter of my tour of inland navigation, more than three fourths of the members were so fully convinced by my arguments, that one after the other left the house, having, as they afterwards assured me, made up their minds on the subject. This time I kept clear of the Rocky Mountains, never quitting my canal for a moment; and, there being no law against repeating the same thing over again a hundred thousand times, I might have spoken till doomsday, had not Mr. Speaker at length waked up, and observed that he believed there was no quorum, and proposed an adjournment.

"Never was there a more complete triumph of argument and eloquence combined," said the Banner of Truth; "the friends of the canal were one and all so convinced, that they did not think it worth while to stay further argument; and its foes fell away before the thunder of his eloquence, as the walls of Jericho crumbled at the blowing of the rams' horns." I was at first a little mortified at the idea of my speech not appearing with an end to it in the report; but the reporter comforted me with the assurance that, so long as a speech had a beginning, it was of little consequence whether it came to any conclusion or not.

I now began to be talked of as a rising politician; for any man who can get on the back of a canal or a railroad is sure of immortality. I became the Neptune of inland seas, a very "Triton of the minnows";

and already began to aspire to an embassy to some one of the new republics * without any government. "He has made the canal," said a great man. "You are mistaken," said the member with the tuneful voice and Cervantesque manner; "the canal has made him." To end my Congressional register:—I got rid of all my speeches, besides offering thirty-six resolutions, calling for information which the several heads of department assured me would require the united labours of six hundred men, six hours in the day for six years, to collect and arrange. In addition to all this, I made about a hundred little extempores; drafted a bill, which was passed after all the sections had been amended so as to mean exactly the contrary of what I intended, and which afterwards became the father of six volumes of commentaries; and wound up triumphantly at the end of the session, by striking out a "but," and inserting an "except," in a bill for the relief of poor Amy Dardin, after a long and animated debate, in which great talents were displayed on both sides.

Towards the close of the last session of my term, a great crisis happened. The whole confederation was divided on a great question which involved a great fundamental principle, and it fell to the lot of Congress to decide by states, each state having a vote. It was now indeed that I felt myself a great man, since a great question, involving a great principle, on which depended the salvation of unborn millions, rested upon my single suffrage. I was the sole representative of my state, and, while others had only the fractional part of a vote, I had a voice potential. The

* In South America.

other states were divided; my state had the casting vote, and I, I alone, became a second Warwick, a king-maker! Had Mrs. Welcome Hussey Bashaba been now at the seat of government, she would not have wanted great men to hand her in to supper. It behooved me to reflect seriously, and to delay my decision to the last moment, although, at this distant period, I feel no hesitation in confessing that I had made up my mind from the first, with a proviso however that I saw no occasion to alter it afterwards. As it was, I kept my opinions as secret as the sources of the Niger. In so doing I acted by the special advice of my master, his Excellency the Honourable Peleg Peashell, Esquire.

"I hold," said he, in one of his letters, marked, private and confidential, — "I hold to a sound maxim in politics as well as morals, that where a man is determined, upon principle, to pursue a certain line of conduct, there is no obligation which ought to restrain him from uniting his interest with his principle, and making the most of the position in which circumstances have placed him. For this purpose, it will be wise and patriotic in you to keep your determination a profound secret, or even affect to lean a little toward the side opposite to that you intend to unite with at last. When a vessel is at anchor, nobody feels much solicitude about her; but a drifting boat always brings a reward for securing it. A word to the wise" — &c.

In pursuance of this advice, I affected to be undecided. I had not made up my mind; I must consult my constituents; I should delay as long as possible, and be governed by circumstances. Both sides beset me with arguments; but, when a man has made up his mind, mere arguments weigh nothing. I preserved my incognito, and talked as mysteriously as an oracle.

One day a confidential friend of one of the great principles — (the reader must not confound princi*ples* with princi*pals*) — came to me, to discuss the subject.

"My dear Mr. Oakford, there can be no comparison between the two principles. You must support our principle."

"My dear sir," said I, "I have not the least hesitation in saying I should support your principle" —— here my friend took my hand warmly, and cried with fervor, "my dear-r-r sir-r-r" —— "But" —— here he dropped my hand suddenly — "But, really, my dear friend, the question depends so little on my single vote or my insignificant influence, that though I mean, if I remain here, to vote on your side, my family affairs are so pressing at home, and my wife is in such a bad state of health, that I rather think I shall ask leave of absence for the rest of the session." A confidential conversation followed, which I cannot disclose, being under the most solemn pledge to the contrary. The result was, that I agreed to remain and support the great principle, being satisfied, by the arguments of my friend, that the salvation of the Union and the welfare of unborn millions depended on my individual vote. The triumph of principle was accordingly achieved by my single arm, and I returned home to await my reward.

In due time, I was invited to preside over a department of the government, in consequence of having so judiciously accommodated my principle to my interest. It was now that I congratulated myself on having sacrificed every thing to principle, and that I expected to reap the reward of my patriotic toils in the cause of unborn millions. I proceeded to the seat of government, and took possession of my honours. But, alas! gentle reader, from that time to the moment when I fell a sacrifice to principle, I never knew a moment's ease. I was a pillar of the state, and Samson with the gates of Gaza on his back was but a type of me. It was not long before I discovered that a statesman exercises power as an ass does, by carrying burdens; and that to be one of the highest of the rulers is only to become one of the lowest of slaves.

The labours and mortifications I underwent in the course of my career of greatness are beyond my power to describe. In the morning, when I came down stairs, I found people waiting to speak with me; I was stopped twenty times on the way to my office, by people having important business; and, on my return to dinner, by other people, who only wanted to say a few words, and kept me till my dinner was cold, and my Bashaba out of all patience. If I dined out, I found a dozen letters to read and answer before I went to bed, all on the most important subjects; that is to say, on subjects very important to others, and of not the least consequence to myself. The good people of my state applied in a body for offices. One was a cousin of my wife; another had written in my favour in the Banner of Truth; a third had his eye put out at the polls, in advocating my cause; a fourth was grandson to a corporal of the revolution; a fifth had once invited me to dinner; and the remaining thirty-odd thousand brought the warmest letters of recommendation from his Excellency the Honourable

Peleg Peashell, Esquire, who was determined I should pay for his guardianship. My whole official life furnished an exemplification of the different lights in which men view themselves and are viewed by others. I scarcely met with a man who was not seeking an office for which he was particularly disqualified, or which his situation ought not to have placed him above soliciting, or accepting when offered. A parson wanted a commission in the army; a soldier, an appointment requiring special knowledge of the civil law; a man who could neither speak nor write his native language, a foreign mission; an independent country-gentleman begged a situation unworthy a broken feather-merchant, thinking, perhaps, with Epaminondas, that he would confer honour on his office, though his office might confer none on him; an honest gentleman from the Emerald Isle, just naturalized, had great claims on a *rale* republican administration, on the score of having fought at Vinegar Hill; another aspired to a seat on the bench, having become exceedingly well versed in criminal jurisprudence, by sustaining several indictments with great gallantry, and coming off with flying colours; and ten thousand at least claimed the gratitude of the executive power, on the ground of having been chairmen or secretaries of ward meetings, and brawling at election polls. There was one fine fellow whose claims were irresistible; he had gained the election for an administration constable, by managing to make one man vote six times at the same poll. There was another fine fellow that quite delighted me; he aspired to a principal clerkship in one of the departments, and his only disqualification was not being able to write. "But then you know, sir, I can make my mark, and the understrappers can do the writing for me."

"Well, but," said I, "what will you be doing, all the while others are performing your duties?"

"Oh, I can give advice to the secretary. I am a capital hand at giving advice."

Another still finer fellow, who had broken three several times, never paid a debt in his life, and borrowed money from every body that would lend, demanded a situation in which millions of the public money would pass through his hands. He brought me recommendations from all his creditors, who saw in his appointment to this office the only chance of ever being paid. I ventured a delicate remonstrance. "My good sir," said he, "you know private character is not necessary in a public character."

I believe I laughed but once, except at the jokes of a greater man than myself, while I remained an object of envy to millions. I was called out of my bed, early one cold winter morning, by a person coming on business of the utmost consequence; and dressed myself in great haste, supposing it might be a summons to a cabinet-council. When I came into my private office, I found a queer, long-sided man, at least six feet high, with a little apple-head, a long queue, and a face, critically round, as rosy as a ripe cherry. He handed me a letter from his Excellency the Honourable Peleg, recommending him particularly to my patronage. I was a little inclined to be rude, but checked myself, remembering that I was the servant of such men as my visitor, and that I might get the reputation of an aristocrat if I made any distinction between man and man.

" Well, my friend, what situation do you wish ? "

" Why-y-y, I'm not very particular ; but some how or other, I think I should like to be a minister. I don't mean of the gospel, but one of them ministers to foreign parts."

" I'm very sorry, very sorry indeed ; there is no vacancy just now. Would not something else suit you ? "

" Why-y-y," answered the apple-headed man, " I wouldn't much care if I took a situation in one of the departments. I wouldn't much mind being a comptroller, or an auditor, or some such thing."

" My dear sir, I'm sorry, very sorry, very sorry indeed, but it happens unfortunately that all these situations are at present filled. Would not you take something else ? "

" My friend stroked his chin, and seemed struggling to bring down the soarings of his high ambition to the existing crisis. At last he answered,

" Why-y-y, ye-s-s ; I don't care if I get a good collectorship, or inspectorship, or surveyorship, or navy-agency, or any thing of that sort."

" Really, my good Mr. Phippenny," said I, " I regret exceedingly, that not only are all these places filled, but that every other place of consequence in the government is at present occupied. Pray think of something else."

He then, after some hesitation, asked for a clerkship, and finally for the place of messenger to one of the public offices. Finding no vacancy here, he seemed in vast perplexity, and looked all around the room, fixing his eye at length on me, and measuring my height from head to foot. Then, putting on one of the drollest looks that ever adorned the face of man, he said,

"Mister, you and I seem to be built pretty much alike, haven't you some old clothes you can spare?"

"Oh, what a falling off was there!" — from a foreign mission to a suit of old clothes, which the reader may be assured I gave him with infinite pleasure, in reward for the only honest laugh I enjoyed for years.

Among others whose names were sent on to me for office, was young Brookfield, son of the worthy man whose hospitalities I had repaid by assisting to lay him in his grave, a victim to the great principle on which the salvation of unborn millions depended. I had now an opportunity to atone for an injury, and repay benefits; but I received at the same time a letter from his Excellency the Honourable Peleg, recommending another person, and warning me against young Brookfield, who belonged to the party in opposition to the great Peleg as well as the great principle. "The great political commandment," said the great Peleg, "is to reward your friends and punish your enemies. There is nothing selfish in this principle, since you do not reward your friends and punish your enemies because they are friends and enemies, but because they are the friends and the enemies of the great principle on which the safety of the Union and the salvation of unborn millions depend." What were the claims of gratitude, or the atonement of injuries, to these sublime considerations? Poor Brookfield was passed over, in favour of an adherent of the great Peleg and the great principle. Brookfield turned his attention to a better object, and in good time rose to respectability and independence; so that, after all, I flatter myself I was the architect of his fortune. I cannot say, however, that he ever evinced much gratitude for my forbearance in his favour.

I speak as if I were acting in these cases without control. But a man living in society cannot do as he pleases at all times; a man in high station, never. He is elbowed and restricted on all sides. He has his equals, his superiors, his very dependents, to influence and thwart his own wishes and resolves; is sometimes the slave of his masters, sometimes of his equals, and sometimes of his slaves. There is but one greater slave than the second man of a nation, and that is the first man of a nation. I was no more master in my office than in my own house, where Mrs. Bashaba managed the home department entirely, and stood in the place of the sovereign people.

My domestic affairs and my domestic enjoyments were, equally with my personal independence, sacrificed to the intense labours and anxieties of my public station. During the session of Congress, I was meted back some of my own measure, by certain watchful and sagacious members, who moved resolution after resolution, calling for information on certain points, from the first organization of the government to the day of call. Some of these resolutions absorbed the time of myself and my clerks for several weeks, and I took pride to myself for the clear and able manner in which I drew up reports, which were received, not read, laid on the table, and forgotten. The object of the honourable member had been gained. He had made a motion; got his name in the newspapers; and acquired among his constituents the reputation of a vigilant guardian of the public interests.

I had various other mortifications, which none can feel or know unless placed in my situation. Sometimes a patriot member would revenge the disappointment of some object, or the refusal of some favour, by attacking my official conduct. At another time the editor of a newspaper, to whom I had perhaps neglected to send an advertisement, would launch a random charge, or a thundering witticism, at my head; and though, as an individual, his good or bad report was of no sort of consequence, still his fiat editorial consecrated the inspirations of ignorance and folly. In short, I sometimes had the pleasure of suspecting that nearly one half my countrymen believed me to be a blockhead or a rogue. To say the truth, had it not been for my perpetual recurrence to the first principles of the great Peleg, I should sometimes have suspected that I deserved the latter distinction; for I confess I often broke my promises, and passed over merit and services, in favour of political influence, which the Honourable Peleg considered synonymous with political principle.

My domestic was still less satisfactory than my public life. The morning was a regular, "never-ending, still-beginning" routine of vexatious toil. I was condemned to listen to applications it was out of my power to comply with; to express regrets which I did not feel; and hold out expectations which I knew would never be realized. I made abundance of enemies, and gained no friends; and I was doomed to meet ingratitude from those on whom I conferred, and enmity from those to whom I refused, benefits.

In short, I was a slave to official duties, that brought neither the rewards of a good conscience, nor remuneration for the reproaches of a wounded one. From my office, where I sat in my chair five or six hours, without any exercise but that of a perplexed and irritated mind, I dragged myself home, to dress for a dinner at six o'clock, to put on silk stockings, sit in a cold room three or four hours, eat enormously, and get the rheumatism or dyspepsy. From thence it was my hard fate to go to a party with Mrs. Bashaba, who entered furiously into the dissipations of the capital, now that the station of her husband ensured her being handed in to supper by a foreign minister, or, in default, by an attaché at least. During the daytime, that good lady was perpetually driving through the solitudes of the streets, paying visits to ladies of distinction, at taverns, or trundling to Georgetown, to ravage the milliners' shops. In one season she disabled three pair of horses, and two coachmen; of whom, one became a cripple with rheumatism, and the other fell into a decline, with a cold caught in driving her to a party five miles off, in a snow-storm.

But this was not the worst. Mrs. Bashaba caught the spirit of the place, and commenced the business of flirtation, with an attaché whose face resembled that of a Newfoundland dog. He was the very personification of whiskers, and was held to be very handsome, for he marvellously favoured Peter the wild boy. It was now that I thanked my stars my wife was not a beauty; for, if she had been, I should have become jealous, and she would have lost her reputation to a certainty. As it was, I considered the devoirs of Peter the wild boy a homage paid to my official dignity, rather than to the attractions of Mrs. Bashaba; and, as nobody envied the attaché, there was no motive for taking away her reputation. The happy result of these happy coincidences was, that I escaped the green-eyed monster, and Mrs. Bashaba scandal.

As I believe none of the writers on natural history have described the race of whiskered animals called Attachés, it may be well to apprize my readers that they constitute the tail of the *corps diplomatique.* They are the shadows of the minister, who is the shadow of his august master, and are, of course, the shadows of a shadow. They must be able to cut up a dish at the ambassador's table; cut a figure among the ladies; and cut a caper at balls. It is their important duty to fill up cards of invitation; answer notes not diplomatic; run about and pick up news; get at every body's secrets, and keep their own; compliment the young ladies; talk scandal with the old ones; trumpet forth every donation of the minister to charitable societies; and put on their embroidered coats on all proper occasions. Above all, they must understand etiquette, and sacrifice the whole decalogue to a point of precedence. Four or five years' practice in these profound mysteries qualifies them for Secretary of Legation.

The unlearned reader must be careful not to confound etiquette with good-breeding, such as is practised among private persons. No two things can be more different, nay, opposite to each other. Among ordinary people, for example, when a stranger, entitled to notice and hospitality, comes into the place, it is considered well-bred to call on him first, and invite him to your house. Etiquette, however, prescribes a different course. The stranger must call on the resident, indirectly solicit his notice, and thrust himself or herself on the hospitalities of the person of distinction. Among well-bred people, if two persons happen to be going into a dining-room together, there will be a little contest of courtesy, not who shall get in first, but who shall give precedence to the other. Among people of etiquette it is exactly the reverse. The point of honour consists in maintaining certain imaginary rights of going first, if it be only at a funeral; and a gentleman or lady whose proper place should be lost would not be able to sleep for a week, without an anodyne. When I was a member of Congress, I came very near occasioning a long and bloody war between the United States and a foreign nation, by insulting the king of the country in taking the hand of a lady who happened to stand next me, to lead her into the supper room. She had been assigned to the minister, who immediately ordered his carriage, went home without his supper, and penned a furious despatch to his government, which he sent off express, by an attaché of three whiskers. The lady never forgave my presumption. Had I been a senator, it might have passed: but, a member of the *lower* House! — it was too bad. Thus it will be perceived that etiquette is the antipodes to good-breeding. The former consists in asserting, the latter in waiving, our pretensions to precedence and superiority on all occasions.

It was curious to see the independent representatives of a free people, making obeisance to the very persons whom they took every occasion to slight in their public speeches, and complying with such docility with the mandates of Monsieur Etiquette. The first thing they did on arriving at the seat of government was to hire a hack and drive furiously round to all the givers of balls and dinners, to leave a card. This entitled them to an invitation to all the balls and dinners, provided they sent in their adhesion in this manner, after every ball and dinner; otherwise they only got an invitation to one ball and dinner, for these things were too good to be had without asking. For my part, while I was a member, I refused this act of homage, which I then considered somewhat degrading, though when I became one of the privileged few I confess I did not find it altogether so unreasonable. The consequence of my refusal was, that I was cut by the whole *corps diplomatique*, attachés and all; dined at home every day by myself, and escaped dyspepsy for that session at least.

At parties, where I saw the same faces and heard the same speeches for a whole session, my great amusement was to observe the various struggles of all classes to obtain that species of distinction which depends, not upon ourselves but on other people. I could always tell where the principal person, the lion of rank, was stationed, by the tide which was tending that way; and, had I not known a single person in the room, I could have pointed him or her out by that infallible indication. Such struggles to get near enough for a speech or smile, a nod, or a shake of the hand! Such looks of triumph when the little ones got side-by-side with the great! and such burstings of self-importance when they had the honour of walking, arm-in-arm, with one above them on the next step of the ladder! Every body seemed to live in the sunshine of reflected honour, and none appeared to found their claims to respect or consideration on the basis of conscious worth or intrinsic merit. I have seen the most insignificant beings on earth, without character or talents, acquire a temporary importance from the mere circumstance of having, by dint of a degrading perseverance, acquired the privilege of being toad-eater to a person of distinction. Nobody could eat supper with an appetite at the lower end of the table; and Mrs. Welcome Bashaba always scolded the servants for a fortnight, when she missed the glory of being gallanted in and out by a qualified hand.

Such was the life I led, year after year. By the time summer came I was completely run down, and it took me all the rest of the year to wind myself up again. If I went to the Springs, I was bored to death by prosing politicians, giving their advice on the conduct of public officers, or slily insinuating claims to honour and place. If I visited a city where there was no such nuisance as a seat of government, for the purpose of relaxing a little in the midst of its gayeties, there too I was beset by wise men and wise women, talking nothing but eternal politics, and reminding me that at such a time they had made application for such a berth, for son, nephew, or second cousin. If I returned to my poor little farm, there it was ten times worse. Every soul, far and near, came to ask for something, for they all had assisted in my elevation; and, like poor Actæon, I was in danger of being torn to pieces by my own hounds. I was obliged to bow and smile, and play the courtier, while my very soul was fretting itself to shreds and tatters;

for it is among the horrors of greatness, in a free country at least, that it must be bought and maintained at the awful, incalculable, price, of being civil to all mankind. Still, such is the fascination of power, I clung to the glorious mischief, though it was gnawing at my vitals and destroying me by inches. I was indeed fast declining, and it is my firm belief that a very few years would have brought me to that great inn where all mankind take up their last night's lodging, had not my life been saved by a lucky change in the great fundamental political principle, on which the salvation of unborn millions depended.

The people have in all ages been charged with gross unsteadiness and ingratitude. But, to do them justice, I believe this instability is only the consequence of their perpetual disappointments. They are promised great things from new rulers, which promises are never realized, and by a natural consequence they change from admiration to indifference, from indifference to contempt or disgust. But, however this may be — *tempora mutantur* — times change, men change, and principles change, if I am to judge from my own experience. Even the great Peleg, my mentor, underwent a metamorphosis. For some time a silent revolution had been preparing and maturing in the public mind, turning on certain great mechanical principles connected with railroads, canals, locks, breakwaters, and cotton machinery. Political principles now seemed fast verging into mechanical principles, and the machinery of state to be almost entirely governed by spinning-jennies, weaver's-beams, and topographical surveys. The revolution of principle, in my native state, was brought about by a great mill-dam;

others turned on improving the navigation of rivers; others on the auction system; others on coarse woollens; and others on prohibiting the importation of vermicelli; — all, fundamental political principles, on which the existence of the Union and the salvation of unborn millions depended. But the most extraordinary change of all was that of a great state — an *imperium in imperio* — whose fundamental principle turned altogether on the question, whether freemasons took their degrees on a red-hot gridiron or not.* This point divided the whole state, and threw the body-politic into convulsions. Committees were appointed; inquisitors authorized to worry and harass whole communities; and constitutional principles set at nought in the discussion of the great fundamental principle of the gridiron. But, (what most strikingly proved the purity of the motives which governed all these revolutionary bodies), in all their arguments, contentions, and struggles, the word "interest" was never once uttered. Nothing but conscience and principle was appealed to, notwithstanding it was the opinion of many honest people, that an appeal to the conscience and principles of the opposite party was like the lady Rosalind swearing by her beard.

Somewhere about this period, the Honourable Peleg, who watched the weathercock of politics as a valetudinarian does the wind, all at once changed his principles, having, as he wrote me, discovered that the great fundamental principle, on which depended the existence of the Union and the salvation of unborn millions, was not what he took it to be. He

* The "Anti-mason" party for some years exerted a powerful influence upon the politics of the State of New York.

brought over the Banner of Truth to his side, by sending the worthy editor a present of the largest pumpkin that ever grew in the state; and the Banner of Truth began forthwith to unsay all that it had been saying for the last ten years. Never man, or woman either, unravelled an old stocking so dexterously and quickly as the editor of the Banner of Truth unravelled and turned inside out all the arguments he had urged in support of the old great fundamental principle. To be prepared for the worst, however, he got a coat made, one half homespun, the other half Regent's-cloth, with a jacket, one side civil, the other military, which he wore as occasion required.

For my part, though I saw the storm coming, I determined to remain firm to my principles, knowing, as I did full well, that it was too late to turn about to any good purpose, for my successor was already designated. The denouement of the great farce now approached; the whole country was convulsed — in the newspapers. I went out, and another came in; one great principle triumphed, on which depended the salvation of unborn millions; and another great principle on which the salvation of unborn millions, in the opinion of millions of living persons, equally depended, went out of fashion, at least for the time being.

Will my readers believe it? I left the seat of government, where I had lost my health, sacrificed my domestic habits, and laboured like a galley-slave at the oar, only to be rewarded with abuse and obloquy from at least one half of my countrymen — I left it with a regret which I can only account for upon the principle that man is born unto trouble, and that it is in his nature to delight to fish in troubled waters. As the City of the Desert passed away from my backward view, I could not help reflecting that I had, peradventure, been all my life fighting shadows, for shadows; and that I was now returning to the starting-place, with nothing saved from the wreck of departed years but a fund of experience which I was now almost too old to turn to advantage. As the great copper kettle turned upsidedown, which deforms one of the finest structures of the age, disappeared behind the forests of the city, I cast a rueful glance at Mrs. Bashaba who sat at my side, and there met the comfortable assurance, that my retirement from the turmoils of public life was not destined to be followed by the calm of domestic repose.

One of the great delights of the seat of government is the necessity a great man labours under, of spending his salary in treating to sumptuous dinners the gentlemen who are every day finding fault with his official conduct. The simplicity of our republican institutions requires that these dinners should be as splendid as possible, and the wines of the most rare and expensive kind. Without these constitutional arguments, it would be almost impossible to carry a measure, or do any thing for the benefit of posterity. Every public functionary is expected to come to the seat of government and depart, as we come into and go out of this world, without bringing any thing with him or taking any thing away. I remember once giving a vast dinner to twenty or thirty members, one of whom was particularly devoted to the wines and viands, and consumed nearly a day's salary. The next day, he made a famous speech on republican simplicity, which he concluded by moving to reduce the enormous salaries of the great public functionaries, whose splendid dinners and silver forks he described with most edifying abhorrence. But, notwithstanding the French wines, the French cookery, and the silver forks, I had saved a few paltry thousands, with which I intended to improve my little box at home, and cultivate a small farm that I had purchased to please one of my constituents who had considerable political influence.

The first time I saw the Honourable Peleg after my return, we had a hot argument on the question whether he or I had deserted the great principle. It ended, like most political discussions, in contention and recrimination. We parted, the worst friends in the world. My farm was now my only resource. At first the perfect ease quiet and independence I enjoyed was intolerable. I became melancholy for want of something to trouble me, and had it not been for Mrs. Bashaba, should have perished for lack of contradiction. But fate seemed determined to persecute me with a life of perfect repose. I lost Mrs. Bashaba a few months after my retirement. The whiskered attaché passed our door without stopping, on his way to Boston, and she never held up her head afterwards. Casting about for something to do, it all at once occurred to me that I would call the Honourable Peleg to a reckoning on the score of his guardianship. I had the cruelty to put him in chancery; but I shared with him the penalty of this unchristian act. I had now enough to occupy my mind, and vex my very soul; and I here record it as my firm opinion, that to be in chancery is worse than to be the head of a department. I several times saw the end of my suit, but it was like a view of those high, snowy, perpendicular summits we behold on approaching the Andes, which the eye sees and the imagination contemplates, but which are inaccessible to mortal tread. When I began the suit, I was possessed of three very good things; I had money, patience, and a great veneration for equity. Before my suit was ended, I had none of the three. But time does wonders; it can even bring a suit in chancery to an end; and at length I got a decision in my favour for a few thousands. But the Honourable Peleg was prepared for me. He had assigned all his property to a bank; the bank had hypotheticated it to an insurance company; the insurance company had failed; the officers and directors had divided the spoil; and I might as well have looked for an honest man among them as for my property. Yet, strange to say, the Honourable Peleg, by sticking close to the great political principle, still managed to preserve the confidence of the people. He had never held a public office where he was intrusted with the public money, without being a defaulter; he had never been charged with the care of another's property, without there being a deficiency in the end; and he had never been president of a bank, that it did not break and defraud the community. Still, his political principles were sound, though his moral principles were rotten; and he was at length selected by the Legislature to prepare a code of criminal jurisprudence for the State, upon the ground, I presume, that you set a thief to catch a thief, and that no man can be better qualified to make laws than he who has been long in the habit of breaking them.

There is a certain homely, unobtrusive philosophy, which makes very little figure in the works of Bolingbroke, Boethius, or any other unfortunate statesman. It may be called philosophy perforce, and is worth all other systems put together. I mean, the capacity of the human mind to accommodate itself to inevitable circumstances, to endure what cannot be cured, and to make the best of a bad bargain. This was now my consolation. I had gradually lost all hope of again coming forward in political life; for the moment one man steps out of the shoes, another stands ready to step into them. If we stop a moment in the great path along which the whole human race is pressing forward, we must be left behind, and can never again overtake the flood that rolls on to success or ruin. By degrees, as this conviction familiarized itself to my thoughts, I turned from the past to the present, and gradually yielded to the philosophy of necessity. I felt that my peace of mind, my health, my subsistence, depended upon exertion; and I began to exert myself. It was at first disagreeable, for a man who had assisted in swaying the destinies of an empire, to second a labourer in planting pumpkins. But I remembered that Dioclesian hoed cabbages; that Joseph the Second was a great maker of red sealing-wax; that Don Carlos of Naples employed his time in shooting rabbits, and Don Ferdinand of Spain his in embroidering satin petticoats — above all, I remembered the course of the great and perfect model of rulers, and that of his virtuous successors, who, one after another, retired from the cares of state, to cultivate their farms, to give an example to the world, and to hear themselves every day blessed from afar off by the voices of millions.

I have now passed almost twenty years in my humble retirement. The world has forgotten me, and I am content to be forgotten. I can now look calmly upon both worlds — that which I am leaving behind, and that to which I am rapidly advancing. The last spark of vanity expired in writing my history, that I might, peradventure, be remembered a little after I am gone. But, to do myself justice, I had other and higher motives.

I have long seen, with fearful and melancholy anticipations, the disproportioned space that politics and party feelings occupy in the lives of my fellow-citizens, to the exclusion of other, and let me add, nobler, pursuits. I have seen the country thrown into a ferment; the charities of life and the bonds of benevolence, the obligations of truth and the ties of justice, all rent as burnt flax, and scattered to the winds as nothing — an offering on the altar of political strife. I have seen the most frivolous objects, and the most contemptible offices, assuming a vast and fallacious magnitude, and exciting the most violent and outrageous struggle for their attainment, as if the parties to the quarrel were contending for the empire of the world. In short, I have seen, as I think, the finger of time pointing to that period, not far distant I fear, when the choice of a chief-magistrate will be considered an object of greater moment than the precepts of morality, the obligations of religion, or the preservation of our liberties. It cannot be disguised, that the spark which lights these political conflagrations is struck out by the violent collision of office-holders and office-seekers; and I am aware that the experience of others weighs little with us in balancing our own conduct and regulating our pursuits. Still, perhaps, a plain narrative of the unsatisfactory results of so many sacrifices of moral principle may serve to mitigate at least the violence of those contests, which end at length in a momentary triumph, followed by a lasting defeat. Men may learn, from my example, how mistaken is the idea, that the possession of power leads to independence, or enables them to indulge their own will. If there is any station in life in which we can do as we please, it will be found much nearer the extreme of the beggar than that of the king.

All the honourable pursuits of life are salutary, provided their rewards are not sought with too great avidity, and at the price of integrity and happiness. It is, moreover, the bounden duty of every citizen to take a strong interest in the conduct of public affairs and the prosperity of his country. But even patriotism, as well as religion, has its limits, beyond which both become fanaticism. He who sacrifices those principles of honour, justice, charity, and truth, which are essential to the happiness of mankind here as well as hereafter, which never change, and in which all agree, to a political principle, which is ever varying, and about which all mankind differ, must in the end become a most mischievous and pernicious citizen.

To conclude, I have chosen to make my drama a farce rather than a tragedy. I pretend not to any authority other than that of experience; but I have seen enough of the world, and of the people of the world, to know that, beautiful as Wisdom is, if she would only sometimes condescend to smile, she would be irresistible.

THE END.

Cambridge: Press of John Wilson & Son.

Charles Scribner & Co.'s New Books.

READY IN OCTOBER (Continued).

LANGUAGE AND THE STUDY OF LANGUAGE. By WILLIAM DWIGHT WHITNEY, Professor of Sanscrit and Instructor in Modern Languages in Yale College. One volume, crown 8vo. Price, . $2 50.

Prof. Whitney's aim in these lectures is to place in a clearly comprehensible form, before the English reader and student, all the principal facts regarding language—its nature and origin, its growth, its classifications, its ethnological bearing, its value to man. Technical and metaphysical phraseology is avoided as much as possible and the progress of the argument is always from that which is well known, or obvious, to that which is more obscure or difficult. It is believed that the work will be widely adopted as a text-book for instruction.

FROUDE (J. A.) SHORT STUDIES ON GREAT SUBJECTS. One vol. crown 8vo. (Uniform with the History of England.) Price, $3.

The essays collected in this volume comprise all Mr. Froude's contributions to current periodical literature during the last few years. They are marked by that great originality and independence of thought, joined with stirring eloquence of expression which have secured him such wide and enduring reputation as an historian.

OLD ROMAN WORLD (The). The Grandeur and Failure of its Civilization. By JOHN LORD, LL.D. One vol. crown 8vo. Price, $3 00.

In this work Dr. Lord describes, in his peculiarly graphic and nervous style, "the greatness and misery of the old Roman world." The volume will be found entertaining instrrctive and profitable in the highest degree, while it will be specially useful as a text-book for higher schools and colleges.

PAULDING'S WORKS. TALES OF THE GOOD WOMAN. One vol. crown 8vo. (Uniform edition.) Price, . . $2 50.

IN NOVEMBER.

IK MARVEL. MY FARM AT EDGEWOOD. With 10 Photographic Illustrations by Rockwood, and a fine Portrait. In one vol. 4to. $10.

EXTEMPORARY PREACHING. By F. BARHAM ZINCKE, Vicar of Wherstead, and Chaplain in Ordinary to the Queen. (*Published by arrangement with the author.*) To be uniform with Bautain's Art of Extemporary Speaking. One vol. 12mo. Price, ... $1 75.

LANGE'S COMMENTARY. "GENESIS." "CORINTHIANS." Each one volume, royal 8vo. Price, per volume, ... $5 00.

PAULDING'S (J. K.) WORKS. A BOOK OF VAGARIES. Containing "The New Mirror for Travellers," "A Satire on the Manners and Costumes of Forty Years Ago," and some miscellaneous papers. By J. K. PAULDING. With an engraved portrait. One vol. crown 8vo. Price, ... $2 50.

IN DECEMBER.

LANGE'S COMMENTARY. "THESSALONIANS." "TIMOTHY." "TITUS." "HEBREWS." One volume, royal 8vo. Price, . $5 00.

PAULDING'S (J. K.) WORKS. DUTCHMAN'S FIRESIDE. One vol. crown 8vo. Price, ... $2 50.

Any of these books will be sent, post-paid, to any address upon receipt of the price.

www.ingramcontent.com/pod-product-compliance
Lightning Source LLC
LaVergne TN
LVHW020114110826
845151LV00001B/157

9781425543099